BURTON THE RED

BURTON THE RED

by

Sandro Dariosto

Per Sempre Anita Edizione
Ferrara Seattle
2013

Printed in the United States of America

per sempre Anita Ediziones
via delle Scienze 17 Ferrara

10 9 8 7 6 5 4 3 2 1

To the happy few

. . . destiny prefers to repeat forms, and what happened once happens often.

--Jorge Luis Borges

Burton with the Thousand
or,
How Il Rosso Lost His Heart Forever

I.

I was returning to my office at the University of M_____ when my brother's telegram arrived. He'd sent it to me there, not knowing if I could be reached in the little one room, basement flat where I lived on a grad student stipend. Rita, the Department secretary, was waiting for me with it, the yellow envelope still in her hand, because she knew it had to be important if it came in a telegram. And of course, it was killing her not to be able to open it.

So I tore it open in front of her, not letting her see, and it read simply this:

"Come quick. Siracusa. Albergo Domus Mariae. I have found him. R."

The wire had been sent from Augusta, Sicily, that very morning. I took it upstairs to the corner of the old Granmora where my desk sat in a room with five other desks that belonged to the five other Teaching Assistants, and I sat down and read it a couple of times over, as if those ten words on the yellow paper might grow into more if I stared at them long enough. But I didn't really need any more, and my brother knew that. He had found him. After fifteen years or more, I added it up in my head. Rob had found him. He didn't even need to say who it was, for I knew: it was Il Rosso.

*   *   *

After a quick trip to the library, I figured out where exactly in the world Augusta was. And then over that night with a lot of prayerful arithmetic and the hope of an advance, as I maxed out my first credit card, I began to find a way. When the morning came, I went out and bought a plane ticket to Catania, both ways, to cover my spring break. Those two weeks of holiday would have to be enough, because I had no more time, and if the truth be told, I didn't have the time or the resources to do even what I did.

I sent Rob a return telegraph that said only: "Siracusa. March 19." Pinching my pennies with every word, I didn't even sign it.

While I'd been in college and then graduate school, my brother had dropped out, done a quick turn in the post-Vietnam Army, and learned to fly a helicopter. He worked now all around the world as a helicopter pilot, but mostly at construction sites in what they call "developing" countries. We kept in touch, but in only intermittent ways.

The last I'd heard from him had been at Christmas time, when he'd shipped me a bottle of Marsala and a three foot tall Sicilian puppet from Gela. He was flying for some corporation with a vague European name I didn't recognize, building offshore oil derricks in the Mediterranean. The puppet, with its pitch black mustache and coffee brown face, all dressed in tin armor with a sword in one hand, was a crusader Rob said. But I think, by the look of that puppet's face, that he hadn't sent me any crusader, whatever Rob thought. He was a Saracen. I wrote him a letter to tell him as much, and sent it with a bottle of Kentucky bourbon to his address in Gela. But I never heard if he received it.

So that was it. We'd not spoken or written since, until the telegram arrived.

*   *   *

My plan was to grade papers on the long flight from Chicago to Milan and then on to Catania, but somehow that didn't happen. Instead my mind wandered through the adventures that Il Rosso had spun about his time in the Anzani Legion, riding and fighting with the Garibaldini across the north of Italy. All the tales he'd told us in his tent, those nights fifteen years ago, how those tales had grown over time in our minds and how he'd enchanted us, my little brother and me. Then there was the way he'd disappeared into the night in his long, red Buick convertible, with its white canvas top, pulling a trailer that was supposed to be filled with Zambutti Sam, the wild mountain gorilla. How he had enchanted us, indeed, and how we still talked about him and searched for him.

You see, Il Rosso was maybe the reason for my brother's wanderlust, for everywhere on the planet that Rob landed, he asked after and searched for traces of that man. And my brother had found work that let him wander the world in search. And whenever we spoke, Rob and I, Il Rosso was always just beneath the surface. Rob would say, "I'm headed to Argentina next spring." He didn't have to say, 'Maybe I'll find some sign of him there.' It was understood.

Now and then, he would write or call to say that he'd run into someone who recognized that name, Jack Burton, or who remembered a guy in a wheelchair and a red shirt, or had been to a little circus with a trained mountain gorilla. And then Jack Burton would come up directly. But Rob never found more than such small hints, and always before his search had led to nowhere.

Until now. And on my Alitalia flight I was restless, because the words on that telegram kept appearing before my eyes. "I have found him," it read. Il Rosso. Found.

And so the long flights passed with a lot of little bottles of red wine and crystal clear grappa, and no papers graded, and too much staring out the window at the tops of gray Atlantic clouds, or black night sky, and at dawn the snowy peaks of the Alps.

As I waited in Milan for the connecting flight to Catania, I tried to read about Siracusa from a guidebook I'd checked out of the library, but nothing would stick in my mind. The words just lay flat on the page and I couldn't connect more than one or two at a time, and always they led straight back to my wandering thoughts of Il Rosso. "I have found him."

It was a short train ride from Catania to Siracusa, and along the way we passed Augusta: just an ugly industrial port, all tanker ships and pipelines. At Siracusa Stazione, I took a cab to the hotel. It rattled through the littered and tired streets of that sad, worn downtown, coated with Sicilian dust and grime. But then we crossed the bridge on Corso Umberto and suddenly everything changed. It was dusk as we wound past the remains of some ancient temple, and then dove into the narrow, shadowy medieval streets of Ortigia. For a moment I thought I was being had, taken on the wild ride of the American tourist. I began to count the little change in my pockets, wondering how much the driver would take me for, cursing my brother and his wild wandering ways, under my breath. For just a moment, I longed for the security of my basement apartment and my stacks of student papers to read. But for only a moment.

Then, before I could mutter anymore, the little Fiat cab jerked out of the dark and crooked street onto a corso that

4

opened out along the Ionian Sea. The driver pulled up in front of a three storey stone building, turned back to me and announced, "Domus Mariae." The face of the old building had a bright white light casting up into the Sicilian dusk off the old stones. I crawled out of the cab, paid the driver a true pittance, took my bag and, with a cough and a sputter, the little Fiat was gone.

At my back, across the tiny street, stood a church, its spires lit indirectly by the bright light of the albergo. I had to buzz to have the wrought iron gate to the hotel opened. Then it was up a narrow stone stairs, well lit, spotlessly clean, to the second floor where, to my surprise, I was greeted in Sicilian by a nun.

"'Sera, Sorella," I said, hesitatingly, and then told her my name.

She took up English immediately, and welcomed me to the Convent of St. Ursula.

"Convent?" I said.

She just smiled, then she went behind her desk and pulled out a big iron key and a square, white envelope.

The Sorella was actually quite young and pretty, I noticed even in her drab black habit. She said, "Follow me; you are already registered." And then she led me up to my room. "Your fratello wanted this room for you," she said, as she opened the door, and led me into the dark.

Instead of turning on the lights, she slipped across the room and threw open two shutters that ran from floor to the high ceiling, and into the dark room charged the soft evening lights of Ortigia glancing off the Ionian Sea below. The gentle roar of the waves spoke in the silence.

It was in that reflected, starry light I saw the twin beds against the opposite wall, and as the pretty Sorella turned to leave, I asked, "Is he here?"

5

"Your fratello will be back tomorrow," she said. "He left you this." And then she handed me the envelope in her hand, along with the big iron key to the room.

"Breakfast begins at 6 in the morning," she said, "If you like, " and then with a "buona sera," she left.

The evening light outside was too delicate; a lamp would destroy it. So I stepped out through the dark wood shutter onto the balcony and opened Rob's envelope in the starlight and the sea shine. There were two pages inside, and the first was Rob's scrawl across a piece of Domus Mariae stationary.

"Back Tuesday," his note read. "The job is done this weekend, then I'm free. So settle in and I'll be there soon. Kaliope is a good trattoria, if you're hungry. A presto, Rob"

Then he added this post script: "Read this and you'll see what I mean."

The other paper inside the envelope was a yellowed sheet, folded in half, brown and brittle at the fold. I opened it gently, trying not to break it. But then a sweet evening breeze drifted up from the sea, and ruffled the papers in my hand. So I stepped back inside the room, sat on one of the beds and resignedly switched on the lamp.

In the yellow light I scanned that old piece of paper and saw first that it was all in Italian. So I didn't try to read it, but my eyes dropped to the bottom of the page and I saw the signature. "Burtoni," it read in a bold black scrawl.

Was this Jack Burton? This bold scribble? This "Burtoni"? How could Rob be so sure? Were we just on some wild pursuit again? Was I spending all my time and every cent I had and more for my little brother's latest pipe dream of finding Il Rosso? "Burtoni" it said in a heavy hand. The name Jack Burton called himself, when he told us his story beside that circus tent, while the sweet strange smoke of his pipe filled the air, more intoxicating than his words.

But I was red-eyed and so jet lagged I couldn't tell you what time of day it was, and I knew that making out the Italian on that old slip of paper was beyond me, just then. Still I knew enough to realize the worst thing I could do was to sleep, and thus stay forever in the jet lagged world of lost time.

So I folded the letter up again carefully, put it in my jacket pocket and unpacked enough to find my dictionary. The pretty little Sorella gave me directions to Kaliope, and I wandered out into the ancient streets of Ortigia, to find something to eat.

Rob was right about the trattoria. Kaliope served me misto fritto of local seafood for antipasto and a breaded cutlet Palermitana for the secondi, all of it washed down by a mezzo of the house wine, served in a short ceramic pitcher. And they played a wonderful brand of old Italian jazz, Gorni Kramer's blues accordion and Renato Selani's piano, that went with the wine and made me feel right at home. Ugo, the owner, who of course knew my brother, brought over a bittersweet liqueur, flavored with almonds, after I was done. "'Berto always has this," he said. Then realizing he was talking to Rob's brother, he pronounced my brother's name with a flat, American accent that rattled from his tongue with difficulty. "Raaab always drinks one of these," and then he added, "We make it ourselves."

And so, warmed by the wine and then by that sweet liqueur, I took out "Burtoni's" letter and began, with my dictionary and some help from Ugo, and a gentleman named Marcello at the table next to me, to translate it. "Mia Rafaela Carissima" it began:

My Dearest Rafaela,

What can I say to you, at this point? How can I make you see? I could say I didn't know, but it is true, I did. The firing squad was my duty. There were orders from the General himself. And you know, it was me he sent because it was me he trusted. Because it was I he knew.

He did not know Lombardo. He knew only of the revolt at Castellnotte, and that these sorts of massacres could not be allowed. Not by our side, not by our partisans. And so the orders came from Colonel Bixio, endorsed by the General himself. Giovanni and I went out to set things in order.

So Rosalino is dead now. And almost all of us who were with him. Only you and I and Giovanni now can tell the true story of that journey across the Nebrodi.

I want only some word from you, that you understand. Forgiveness is too big a word. I do not ask for forgiveness. If you read this, you will see. It is the work of Giovanni Corrao, not mine. I ask you only to understand, and to know that

You will live in my heart forever,
Your Burtoni

After I'd made the letter out, and finished with Ugo's liquor, I wandered the streets of Ortigia, wondering as I strolled how Rob could be so sure that this old undated letter in Italian could be the trace of Jack Burton he was searching for. The spring evening was cool, and in the stone streets a scattering of people strolled hither and thither, in no hurry. Beside the Fontana Archimedea I paused at a café for another bitter to finish the night and tried out my schoolbook Italian on the locals.

We talked about the marzipan in rows of bowls in the café window, little painted tomatoes and cherries and limes and bananas, tiny but so true to life.

"Mia Madre makes them here," the barista told me, "in the back there." He pointed to a closed door.

The hesitant conversation reminded me of how poor my Italian was, and of how both Rob and I had taken it up in school, because of those long ago nights in that circus tent when Jack Burton had salted his yarn with the exclamations and expressions of Risorgimento Italian. Later, when I'd learned a bit of the language, I realized that Burton always spoke with the rhythm and the music of his adopted language, his English was filled with the music of Italian. And this, these sounds, made his words light up and soar in our ears. It was part of the magic of listening to him, part of his enchantment.

The fountain was lit from below, and the shooting spires of water sparkled in the light. It was all so enticing here: the food, the wine, the tumbling waters, the sparkling light. Yet I couldn't help but think that maybe it was all marzipan, just painted sugar, too sweet to eat, but beautiful to look at, though seeming always real and substantial, seeming the fruit of the vineyards and orchards of this hard land. But really it was just a liquor so sweet it made your eyes swim with pleasure, and strong enough to dim your vision for hours at a time.

How could Rob know this old letter had anything at all to do with our old Il Rosso? How did he come upon it? Why was he so certain of what he had?

I wandered back to the Domus Mariae, more than a little drunk, I suppose, more than a little lost, I'm sure, filled with dreams of Il Rosso. But more than filled with doubts.

In the morning the pretty little nun from the night before was gone, replaced by a sallow young man called Ciccio with bad teeth, a smoky voice and no English. I had cappuccino in the café downstairs and pulled out the old letter to read it again without the help of wine and liquor and jet lag. It made no more sense than it did before, and that made me even more uncertain of my brother and his whims. But I looked out on the smooth face of the Ionian Sea, with its long gray oil tankers drifting across the horizon like mirages in the distance, and reminded myself that Aeschylus and Plato had walked these very stone streets. Cicero had loved this very same view. Whatever Rob was up to, this was a place with its beauty worn deep into its stones for thousands of years, and it was a place now, for me, to simply enjoy. The pastry was sweet and fresh, the coffee was too good to believe. The oranges were a deep and godlike red. Soon 'd see my brother, and this would be a spring break with a good story to tell. No matter what it meant.

I went to the morning market by the Ponte Umbertino and bought cheese and fruit and a bottle of wine, and then I found a place by the Fonte Aetusa to sit and eat and gaze at the sea, while the swans and ducks glided across the tiny, soiled pond they called a fountain. When I strolled back to the hotel in the early afternoon, Ciccio was gone and the little Sorella was back, even more pretty than before. When I asked for the key, she smiled brightly and said my brother had it. Upstairs.

I admit it was with a turn and a running step that I bolted up the stairs, and I banged my forehead on the low corner ceiling. But it didn't stop me. When I turned the knob it was unlocked and so I burst in and found my brother, with his back to me, sitting in a straight backed wooden chair, his legs splayed out wide, his feet in boots firmly planted. From behind, his shoulders were broad and flat under a red t-shirt, and I could see where he was balding at the crown of his head. But his head was almost shaved, so it was only the absence of black stubble that showed his early balding.

He looked up from what he was reading, and I saw the same black stubble on his chin, surrounding his grin. He shouted my name out, and then he was on his feet, he set the book on the chair, and we were hugging hard in the center of the room.

It had been three years now since our father died, leaving Rob and me alone in the world it seemed. Mother has been gone a dozen years or more, gone to a throat cancer that spread fast and took her, and left my Father bereft with a loss from which he would never recover. By the time Dad died in a sudden car accident, I guess it seemed a relief, an end to his ongoing grief. Rob and I were both, then, out and on our own, chasing these wildly different lives of ours. But suddenly we were all the family we had. Two brothers, alone in the world and unattached. It made us closer than we might have been, had our parents lived long and well into a happy old age. I suppose it made this strange search for Jack Burton more vivid, too, in its own way. This search for Il Rosso was the only real point of contact we had now, our lives had become so separate. And so I guess we clung to it.

What followed were the 'how the hell are you's' and the 'you're looking old's' that you'd expect. Lots of thumping on shoulders and slapping on knees, and of course there was a wine bottle opened.

Still it didn't take long before I asked him what it was he was reading. It sat there on his chair still, by the balcony, an old leather bound book, worn and frayed at the edges. On the

11

floor beside the chair lay a couple of leather laces, as old as the book. I reached down to pick it up but Rob warned me off.

"Careful," he said. "It's falling apart."

"What is it?"

"It's Jack Burton's journal," Rob said, and then he took a drink from his wine glass. "The diary of Il Rosso, when he rode with the Thousand across this island. With Garibaldi and the Thousand."

I cracked it open. "Are you sure?" I said and saw the same bold scrawl running across the pages, unnumbered and loose now from their old binding.

"I think so," Rob nodded thoughtfully. Then he reached over and took it from me, closing it carefully and then picking the laces off the floor, he gently bound the old leather volume back together. "I think it is," he repeated, as if to convince himself.

"Where did it come from?" I asked.

Rob didn't answer me, he just tucked the volume carefully in his pack.

"And the letter?" I said, pulling it out of my coat pocket. "Where did you find this?" I said.

Rob reached for it, but with a grin I pulled it away and tucked it carefully in my pocket again. He laughed. "Let's get something to eat," he said. "I'm too hungry. Then I'll tell you all about it, over dinner."

"With the thousand!" I said, as we headed off across the Corso Matteotti, just coming to life for the evening passeggiata. "I Mille. But that's better than a hundred and twenty years ago."

"You're the history major," Rob said, striding ahead of me on the Corso.

"But that means he was over 100 back when we knew him, at home," I said.

"That's old news," Rob said, as he stepped in the door of a café on the edge of Piazza Archimedea. "You've already said that. Many times, Will. Too many times."

Then he ordered us both espresso and ignored me while he spoke easy Italian with the barista. I found myself eyeing the marzipan again. "Show off," I said.

"When in Siracusa," he said in Italian, "speak with the Siragusans." And I noticed then he pronounced the "c" in the city's name with the clipped and guttural "g" of the Sicilians.

After an hour of strolling around, Rob still had not answered any of my questions. He bought us each a cannolo at a café for later, and found a little tourist store where he bought a jar of red marmalade, and handled a little crusader puppet like the one he'd sent me for Christmas. Before long the doors of the restaurants were opening, and he led us around near the Piazza del Duomo to the side street where Trattoria Kaliope lay.

Ugo greeted us with excitement and he sat us at a table next to the kitchen so he could linger and chat, when the business permitted. We never ordered. The food that Ugo chose for us just came in waves. Over a full pitcher of the house wine, Rob told us his story.

"Just like I always do, when I landed at the terminal in Augusta, I started asking around. Taormina and the touristy spots north didn't seem like the kind of places worth looking in. Catania seemed too big, too easy to get lost in, so I headed south on the trains. I'd just get off at one town or another, find a local hang out, ask around if anybody had seen or heard of Jack Burton. Or of Il Rosso, or Gianni Burtoni."

"Who knows what he was calling himself, but I knew that if he'd been around, he'd be remembered. So it was like always. The train station in Lentini, an evening in Belvedere at a café, a bar in Grammiche. I tried little towns, and into the interior, but no trace. Catania was still there waiting, but it seemed impossible to grab a hold of, and maybe not where Jack Burton would spend much time anyway.

"Still, everywhere I went I struck out. Not a sign of him. But you know, I'm used to that. It's the way it always goes. And it's sort of my little entertainment. A way to get out and meet people, you know. Hang with the locals. I was going to be here in Augusta for six to nine months. There was plenty of time to wander about.

"So one weekend, about a month ago, I wandered in here because a guy in a café down by the Ponte said the fish was good.

"After a glass of wine and a little swordfish involtini, I started asking around, and Ugo here, he started to laugh.

"See, he remembered an old Americano, when he was a boy, who came into his father's restaurant, spoke great Italian, and was looking for anybody named Crisianna. Ugo remembered him, because he was in a wheelchair."

"It's true," Ugo interrupted us, speaking in Italian. "He was named Burtoni, and he said he'd lived around here once, long, long ago. But all this happened when I was just a little ragazzo, and we didn't see many Americans then. And even if we did, he was different. So I remembered him."

"Crisianna," I said. "Who was that?"

"You'll see, you'll see," Rob held up his hand. But then someone came in the door of Kaliope, and Ugo was gone to seat them, and another waiter arrived with two pork cutlets, breaded in the Sicilian way.

"So how do we know this Burtoni of Ugo's was our Jack Burton?" I said.

But Rob was deep into the pleasure of his plate, he held up a piece of cutlet on his fork and said, "You like it?" and then set into chewing it.

When Ugo sauntered back, a few moments later, keeping an eye on the door and the kitchen, both, the story went on.

"Signor Burtoni could maneuver around in that wheelchair like he was driving a Ferrari, my friends. That's what really impressed me, the way he could handle that thing. Made me want one of my own. A wheelchair! Mio Dio! But my Papa told him, 'Yes, little Sister Crisianna, she is at the convent.'"

"Who is this 'Crisianna'?" I said.

"That's just what your brother kept saying," Ugo laughed.

"But then Ugo tells me this nun was still here," Rob said, his hand holding the fork and gesturing now at the air. "She's running a hotel for the order."

"The Domus Mariae," I said.

Rob nodded, "Suor Crisianna," he said.

"Not that cute little sorella at the desk?"

Ugo laughed at that.

"No, of course not," Rob said. Then he grinned at me, "So you noticed her too."

Ugo liked that even better, but he put on a phony wooden face and crossed himself "Sister Crisianna is as old and tough as the stones of Siracusa," he said in Italian.

"So, to make a long story short, I go off and find this nun who runs the albergo and Ugo is right. She's a tough one. Not a smile or a blink when I ask her about Il Rosso. Nothing."

"He tells her that I sent him," Ugo said, placing a palm on his chest. Then he let the hand course through the air like he was chasing off a butterfly. He rolled his eyes back dramatically, "that didn't help," he said.

Rob chuckled and went on, "I stayed at the albergo, so I could go back three times to see her. The first time to ask her about him, and that time I described Il Rosso. Nothing. The second time I told the sister about you and me, two kids, and how we found him with the circus, way off in America. How we fell in love with him. How we wanted to run away with him. Still, nothing. Not a word about him. About anything, really."

Ugo wiped his palm straight down over his face. "La Suor di Pietra," he said, "the Sister of Stone."

"So I gave up, but one last time as I was checking out of the Domus, I asked after her. She was back in the office, hidden away, scowling at the books. I pressed my way in anyway and I thanked her for the pleasant stay, and for all her time, for listening to me.

"That was when she pulled this out," he patted the bag beside him on the floor where he had the notebook tucked away. "She had it under her desk and suddenly she handed it over to me. And she handled it like it was a holy missal or something.

"'This may be what you're looking for,' she said. If I hadn't come back that last time, really the fourth time I'd bothered her, she'd never have given it to me.

"I didn't ask her what it was. She didn't say anything to me about bringing it back. She knew once I'd read it, she would see me again. I just took it, whatever it was, and rode the train back up to Augusta. At night after work I'd read it, and after a couple of days, I wired you."

"What makes you think it is his," I said.

Ugo leaned over and chuckled right at me. "You're no romantic, Signore, like your brother," he said. But then someone else appeared in the doorway of the trattoria and Ugo had to go back to work.

"You read it over, tonight. Then you can tell me you don't think it's him," Rob answered.

16

"Is it in Italian? Like the letter? Because, brother, I'm too tired to try to read it in Italian tonight." What I meant was the wine had been too good at dinner for me to attempt to read anything in Italian.

Rob just shook his head no. "It's English. But the letter, in Italian, it was stuck in the back of the book. I'm not sure what to make of that."

"What do you mean?"

"You'll see," was all he'd say.

As we strolled slowly back to the hotel, Rob stopped at the café where he'd bought our cannoli, and he ordered me a double shot of coffee. He had another glass of wine and he broke out our desert at a table in the square. Then he handed me the old notebook across a little café table, and said, "Read it, brother. Read enough of it to convince yourself."

So Rob sipped at his wine and made occasional small talk with passers by, and with the barista, when he went back inside for more wine. The Piazza Archimedea was busy that time of night, even though only this little bar and another café were still open. Still the people of Ortigia we're strolling and talking away as the night air grew slowly cooler.

The leather on the notebook was old and frayed, and the binding was broken so some pages were loose and floating free. Inside the front cover, embossed in the leather, was the name of the

binder. 'Liguria Libri,' it said. And then underneath, 'Genova.' There was no mention of Italia, since at the time this book was bound, Italia was only a wild-eyed dream, a seditious idea burning in a few rebellious minds.

Nowhere could I find any place where the writer who had filled this book with words had written his name. The book was inscribed nowhere and to no one. But the handwriting I recognized immediately. It belonged to the same "Burtoni" who had written the letter I had in my pocket. I was full of good food and wine, but the jolt of coffee and then the yarn told in the old pages kept me awake. Here follows a fair copy of what I could make out in the journal of Jack Burton, called herein Burtoni, but known by us all as Il Rosso.

1.

27 March 1860

We are two days out at sea as I finally start to write this down. I meant to begin right from the moment it all commenced, to keep a true record of this adventure for all of time just as it happened, for if we succeed, as I trust we will, we will change the course of history for the rest of the ages. So was my intention, but our departure at night from the port of Genova in secret was greeted first by pursuit from the old blue navy of Savoy, and then by the rush of hard weather that nearly swamped us. These are not good omens for the future of our voyage, but we know, all of us, that omens can be damned. It is the time. It has come. We must press on.

As Count Pilo has said, many times in the last 48 hours, "This time, comrades, we will make Italy or we will die." We are only three, and I will tell you about each of us, from what I know, later on, when there is time. But tonight as the half moon rests on the quiet sea at last, let me say that we are all of us patriots, republicans deep in our hearts. And all of us have fought beside the General, or been sent into exile with Mazzini. And we go now together to begin the revolution.

*   *   *

Two nights ago, after midnight, we embarked without a light aboard. But no more had we slipped away from the peaceful Genova harbor in our little twelve foot paranza, rowing quietly out to sea, when the Savoy patrol saw us.

"We've been spotted," Corrao whispered out from the starboard where he held his oar.

"Pull hard, men," cried Pilo. "For Italia."

And so, as Corrao and I worked the oars in unison, our commander Rosalino Pilo left the tiller and lifted the two sails to the breeze.

I saw a series of lanterns blink and flash across the black water and I knew that the shore patrol was signaling to someone between us and the open sea. In the cloudy night, the ocean breeze blew in toward land, and it took Pilo a good long while to get our lateen sails up and the paranza turned right to feel the wind. And in that time, from behind me, a long schooner drifted into sight, its rows of lights brighter than the scattered lights of midnight Genova. Suddenly she was in pursuit of us.

"Pull harder, boys," Pilo cried out, because we were not secret anymore.

The black schooner was bearing down on us, having the advantage of the wind behind her. The lanterns shone out on the dark water, and the schooner cut closer to us and we could hear clearly their calls for us to pull up and to identify ourselves.

I'm sure that many aboard that royal schooner would be on our side, if they knew where we were sailing. I'm certain that on her decks stood seamen who would choose to join us in our cause. But we all knew, Pilo, Corrao and I, that if they stopped us, all would be lost. For officially, the governments of the North are sworn to treaties and truces, and the raising of

19

rebellions is not in their plans. Not in their open and public plans, at any rate. Whatever the sailors on that black schooner believed, her Captain would arrest us, he would seize our little boat and its meager cargo, and then he would turn us all over to the military police in Genova. We will be hung or sent back into exile. They can not do otherwise. We knew this rebellion will end before it even starts, if we are stopped.

The schooner fired a warning shot, to halt us, a single cannon fired over our bow to announce their firm command of the situation. The shot plunged out into the sea ahead of us, and rocked our little boat.

"Pull, boys," cried the Count through his clenched teeth, as he fought with the tiller to bring our ship around and use the wind to make a run close along the coast. In the dark, and close in, there was a chance for us to make our escape, where the schooner could not follow.

In our shallow hold we have only a couple week's food and a few dozen old muskets, with enough ammunition and some fine bayonets to make them presentable, and one crate of grenades. Not much to start a revolution, but all we had. And the Captain of that schooner doesn't know that this is all we carry. He is in pursuit of smugglers, running contraband tobacco and brandy. We are thieves running in the darkest of the night. For him, it is just a evening patrol, the routine, he has no dreams of any future but a warm cup of tea in the morning, and a little lazy sleep.

No one knows our cause, tonight. Only the three of us, and back in England, Mazzini, I am told. There were two strangers who provided us this boat just a few days ago, but they were paid off, without knowing we were running anything more than the common contraband.

The Captain of that schooner doesn't know any of the dreams that pull these oars beneath his guns.

Suddenly the schooner fired a second shot, as Pilo steered us in toward the shore where the bigger ship could not follow. And that second blast came from a pair of cannon, and this time it was no warning, no announcement. This time they meant to put us on the bottom.

They saw us turn this old fishing boat around and run, so all the warning shots were done. I heard the fierce scream of one shot go over my head, missing our mast by only a few feet. The second shot dropped in the sea just to our fore, and the boat rocked over to the port and then we took on water from both sides, before this true little ship righted herself and held to, though low now in the sea.

I felt the thump of the cannon shot right beneath my feet, and what with the water running on our decks, I was sure she had hit us, and we were taking on the sea. For a moment I was frozen.

"Ahead, lad!" I heard Corrao beller, and it shook me out of my fears. Even in the dark, his bearded face seemed black and square and furious. I was sitting, oar in the water, staring at the waves sloshing across our decks and out at the black sea. "She's bearing for us!" Corrao yelled, and pulled hard on his oar.

I looked up, and there stood the bow of that black schooner, not fifty feet to our port, standing above us like a giant tree, but she was cutting through the water, her sails bellied full, like she was under steam. And she was coming directly at us amidships. By God, they meant to cut us in two, to send our contraband cargo to the bottom, and then fish us out of the seas later, or hunt us down with dogs on the shore. And that would make a night of it for them. And with the way she was bearing at us, there could be no escape.

"Pull harder," Corrao bellered again, and I heard Count Pilo climbing around behind me at the tiller and I put my head down, and drew full on the oar, and I prepared myself for a cold, black swim to nowhere. Nowhere but the black bottom of the sea.

2.

28 March 1860
Ligurian Sea, no sight of land.

Yesterday the light grew too dim for me to continue to write, and it's agreed among us that, with the secrecy of our voyage, we don't burn lanterns or candles at night. Rather than scribble in the dark, I always know that while our weather stays fair, I will have time to write.

How did it arrive that we escaped the black prow of that nameless schooner? I'm not sure I can say. Not being a man of God, I'm not prone to dreams of Providence. But I must confess, it does now seem that some proud fate played into our hands that night, lest we be sunk at the bottom of the harbor now, and never even escape Genova, or even escape a cold and certain death.

As that schooner drove toward us, while Corrao and I leaned into our oars with more than all our strength, the little paranza handled slowly for all the sea we'd taken on.

The Count, I think, pulled hard on the tiller and somehow turned our little boat to the side, the black prow of the schooner slipped past in front of us, catching the tip of our bowsprit and turning us hard in the water, the way old Corrao and I couldn't turn her.

We banged amidships against the schooner, and it took all that I had to hang on to the oar in my hands. I heard the high-pitched whine of seasoned old wood grinding against wood, but not the sound of any cracking or breaking. And far above, the sailors of that patrolling schooner could have shot straight down at us where we sat. But the big ship just sped past. We were so full of water, I guess, we were low and stable while the great schooner was fleet. It swept past and turned us like a little top all the way around in the water. We spun slowly around until the wake of that speeding schooner began to break against our starboard prow.

"Heave to, boys," shouted the Count, as he lifted the tiller high to let the paranza spin. "Heave to, lad," Corrao echoed Pilo.

"Look," Pilo almost whispered in awe, as he set the tiller back in the water, and the breeze gently filled our sails. "Lads, we have come through," the Count shouted then, almost in disbelief, but with great heart.

Off to our port, the schooner sped away from us, her sails bellied full. And we pulled up to cut an angle through her wake, and our paranza headed straight out to sea. "Pull, men, pull," cried the Count. "Pull as you've never pulled before."

I laid into my oar, but I wondered how the Count planned to escape. We were turned now toward the open sea, where surely that quick schooner could hunt us down. Pilo had us headed out away from the shadowy shoreline, and what I thought was our best chance to slip away from them.

I was watching off to our port side as the long schooner began a wide arc to turn around, and I pulled my oar in a heavy rhythm with Corrao. The schooner was moving fast, but maneuvering to catch us slowed her down, and this gave us our main chance. Yet I still didn't see how Pilo thought we could outrun her, once she was righted and on course for us.

I heard Corrao's loud belly of a laugh, and Pilo yelled, "Pull those oars, lads, " as he set the tiller and then he ran past us toward the mainmast right at my back. Corrao was grunting happily with every pull. And this little fishing boat danced over the wake. Above my head I saw what Pilo was about. He was gathering in the sails. It would make us less visible, I realized. We would, without those broad white sails, become a little black shadow moving into the dark of night..

"Don't let up now," Pilo shouted, his arms pulling in the sail cloth. "We're almost through."

I felt a cool gust of wind at my back, and it was filled with a light salty spray, that seemed to mop my sweating brow like a caring hand. I pulled at the oar in my hands until I nearly fell over backwards, but then I lifted her and kept to the rhythm with Corrao beside me.

The schooner, in her wide arc, was parallel to us now in the distance. But she was turned in headed for the shoreline, at that moment going away from us toward the lights of Genova. But I knew once she'd righted herself, she'd be bearing down on us again, but this time with the wind behind her. Count Pilo had made sure of that. I saw that, if my arms and back held out, maybe we could outrun her, even with our paranza taking on all that water.

Count Pilo rose up behind us then. Our two sails were down now, and Corrao and I were the only way the little boat moved in the water. The young Count slapped me on the back, and then he slapped Corrao too, and he laughed a rebellious laugh. "The Gods are on our side tonight, lads," he roared up at the sky. "Pull hard, boys. For Liberta'."

We were moving lithe as a swordfish through the sea, it seemed, the splash of waves on our back, the cool wind drying the sweat on our necks. The strength in my arms seemed then to pull the little boat through the rising seas with a sure ease.

Pilo stepped past us then and took up the tiller again, and he began to guide us straight out into the wind, and out to sea. Slowly, with every stroke of the oar, that turning schooner with all its lights began to grow dim. First it became just a black shadow, with lights casting about, and in just a moment or two I looked up from my hands working the oar to realize the harbor lights of Genova had disappeared in the night.

All around us, with the sea rising and tossing our prow, we had sliced into a mist. A strange blue fog, on the head of some storm, was rolling into shore, into the harbor. And as it enveloped us, I understood what the Count was cheering about. We had escaped into the fog.

With our backs to the ocean, pulling at those long oars, I never saw the bank of fog Pilo was steering for, but I understood as Genova disappeared from sight, this was how he knew we could escape. This was why he'd called out to thank the Gods driving our fate. With the fog growing thicker, and the seas rolling heavy and heavier, we had indeed slipped away into the night, off free and bearing south for the Tyrrhenian Sea.

We will never know how long that schooner searched for us. Perhaps for the whole damned night. Perhaps for just a few moments more. But I don't think she came after us for long. Luck was on our side, and as far as she was concerned, we were just a fortunate band of smugglers. In rough seas and dark fog, that schooner lay close to port, I'm sure, searching for easier prey, prey without so much fickle fortune to bear, prey without some proud Fate pulling the oars along on her side.

I suppose it was the better part of an hour, pulling hard in a rhythm against the waves, my lungs feeling good and strong at the exertion, before my pal Corrao nudged me with the water bottle. "Burtoni, boy, take yourself a drink, by god," Corrao said, pushing my shoulder with the bottom of a black wine jug. "We've done it, lad," he said, with sure finality, "We've done it."

You must understand, Giovanni Corrao is a dark, black man, his head and chin covered with a stark black hair, wavy more than curly. His nose is like a hawk's curled beak under the shadow of a thick squared brow. Out of that darkness, his brown eyes were always lit from behind by a smiling light.

I sat up straight and lifted my oar out of the water, and then I took the bottle from Corrao.

"We gave them the slip," Corrao laughed. "We did!" His head nodded with the swagger of pride.

The bottle was filled with cold fresh water, and while it felt good going down, the water surprised me. I was ready for the fat taste of victory wine in that bottle.

"Hey," I said, "Where's the wine?"

Corrao just laughed some more at that.

"Later, piu piccolo," said the Count from the tiller. "We're not loose of them yet. Not for sure."

So I took another deep swallow of the cool water, and handed the bottle back to Corrao, who was still chuckling as he set it down on the deck between his feet.

I took a deep breath and relaxed a moment, still holding my oar high in the air. That was when I noticed how low in the water the old paranza lay. We were rocking in the rising seas, and when the boat leaned into a wave instead of cutting it sharp, water lapped in and rolled over our feet on the decks, and then seeped into the heart of the little ship. Pilo needed to keep the paranza headed straight into the rolling waves just to keep us afloat.

But though he was only ten feet away, or less, I could barely see the Count in the thickening fog. Even Corrao, alongside me across the deck, faded into the mist a little. The sharp outline of his thick black hair had disappeared into the dark night and the fog.

All around us, as the boat rose and fell in the sea, there was nothing but black water and fog. Since we had not a single light on board, we were essentially invisible. We had vanished into the dim dark sea.

"Rubio," said Corrao. This is the name we call Count Rosalino Pilo now, one of the count's many secret names. "What should we do now, Rubio?" said Corrao.

"Where are we?" I asked, looking all around me at the encroaching mist. I suppose I sounded frightened, forlorn and young.

From the vague shadows that made up the end of our little barque, as it rocked up and down, Rosalino Pilo answered us. "I'll keep her headed into the wind. That wind is blowing in from the sea. You lads row to your heart's contentment, and in the morning we'll come out of this. Then we'll find our way."

Corrao looked over at me, and the light of his eyes told me that I was as vague to him as he was to me. "Ready," he shouted, since it was harder and harder to see. "One and pull," he said, to get us in to the rhythm of our work together.

I set my oar down in the water and leaned back into it, as the boat rolled a bit to the port, and took on more water. Lifting the oar and leaning forward, I noticed a hard, warm wind at my back, and I heard the crash and creak of our prow as it pushed on through the sea.

After a few strokes of the oar, the noise of the water slapping against our ship grew regular and loud. As if to urge us on, out of the fog at our stern, I heard the Count's voice. He began recite the lines of a poem, or perhaps I should say he was chanting them, as if we'd begun some great religious ritual and not some adventure to start a revolution. He sang out these words, out of the dark mist where he'd become a nearly invisible shadow to us.

"Felice te che il regno ampio de venti,
Ippolito, a tuoi verdi anni corrrevi!" he sang.

His voice was high and light, and it drifted out of the darkness, and after just a line or two, Corrao joined him, reciting these ines about heroes of old, lines they both knew by heart, songs of Achilles and his shield and of Odysseus on his wandering ship, and even of the glorious tombs of Dante and Galileo. Then they paused, but we didn't stop the slow beating of oars and the wind swept across the empty mainmast above. Alone, Pilo continued the song, but it was turned now to a lament.

> "E me che I tempi ed il desio d'onore
> fan per diversa gente ir fuggitivo,
> me ad evocar gli eroi chiamin le Muse
> del mortale pensiero animatrici."

And then Pilo repeated this line, now singing it over and over as if it was a refrain:

> "Chiamin le Muse! Chiamin le Muse!" sang out. "Me ad evocar gli eroi chiamin le Muse!"*

But then Corrao broke back in, singing out to the green years of youth, and to the realms filled with kind winds, and as he sang, Rosalino Pilo joined in again, and slowly the fog around us seemed to lift.

I saw him clearly then, his arm was wrapped around the tiller to hold it steady. He is a small man, Rosalino Pilo, without the heft and size of Corrao. But he clung tightly to that tiller, hugging it to him, and he sang loudly along with dark Corrao.

---

*It was later that year, once I had returned home to the U of M_____ that my history degree became handy. With a bit of library research and some help from Professor Gianluca Matteo in the Italian Department, I learned that these lines come from "Dei Sepolcri" by the poet Ugo Foscolo (1778-1827). Addressed to Foscolo's fellow poet Ippolitio Pindemonte, the poem sings of the power of tombs to inspire the heroes of the nation. The lines which Burton included in Italian in his text I have roughly translated as follows: "O happy in your green years you roam, Ippolito,/ this kingdom filled with gentle winds. . . . But for me, the times and my hunger for honor/ make me a fugitive in different lands,/ crying out to the Muses for help, calling out to the Muses for heroes!" This, indeed, is what Pilo and Carrao have turned into a refrain: "Call to the Muses! Call to the Muses! Call out to the Muse for heroes!"

The mist seemed to move then, away from us, floating away toward the shore, I think. It was like a low night animal, a crouching wolf slipping away into the dark, moving with a suddenness that caught me by surprise.

Still, even with the fog leaching away, and the wind at my back rising, the night was darker than ever. I glanced up as I was pulling back on the oar, and I saw not even one star twinkle in the thick black sky.

"Hold to, my heroes," cried out the Count, trying to warm us, but the end of his words disappeared into the cold crash of a wave topping over us. The water threw me from my seat, and I lost my hold of the oar. For a moment, I couldn't tell what was up or down, for everything was water, and the deck was only something that struck me once on my back and then once on my shoulder. The shock of that second blow made me gasp, and then all I did was swallow long, deep lungs full of sea water. I was sure I was overboard, and I heard the Count's lament for heroes clearly in my head, though I could not find air to breathe, and all my ears could hear was the dizzying rush of water all around. Lost and overboard, I was sure.

3.

29 march 1860
Somewhere in the Ligurian Sea

As I gaze now out at the still sea around me, with our sails slack above us, it is so hard to believe, it seems impossible these are the same waters that nearly swallowed us just a few nights ago. But as we sit here becalmed, I have time again to write it all down.

It was good, fearless Giovanni Corrao, with those thick forearms and heavy shoulders, who saved me. If not for my shady friend, I would have been tossed overboard, lost and drowned by those fearsome waters, lying now at the bottom of this too, too placid sea.

For what seems to me now like an age, like an era, I was topsy-turvy, unable to say even what was up or down in this world, not even knowing what way I should swim to fight for air. But then, suddenly, the flat wooden deck rose up in front of me like a wall emerging out of fog, and it struck me full on in the face. For a brief moment, I felt I could somehow strain to stand up, to find air. If only I could crawl up onto my hands and knees on that deck, I would breathe again. But then the water rose once more, lifting me into the air, or down into the bowels of the ocean, I couldn't tell which. But I felt the deck slide away from me, out of my helpless grasp. I was lost, and I was lost now for good, at last. I could surrender, I could just relax and let this Ligurian Sea carry me away.

But right at that most hopeless of moments, the grasp of a firm hand seized me by my wrist, and out of the swirling confusion, Corrao pulled me toward him. Up, down, sideways, I don't know. But toward him. Soon, somehow, he had an arm swung over one of my shoulders, across my chest and then under the other arm. He hugged me to him, and slowly, as the old fishing boat tossed in those crashing seas, I began to right myself. I caught my wind, first, and then I began to understand up from down, the heavens from the belly of the sea.

Gradually, between the swirls of the waves across the lurching deck, I saw where I was. Giovanni Corrao had lashed himself along with his oar to the railing on the starboard. And from there he'd grasped me out of the waters, and held me with his one free arm against him. He was speaking to me, but it took a long while for his words to make any sense.

When I felt stronger, I tried to squirm free of Corrao's grasp, but he wouldn't let go. He kept speaking to me, and until I answered him clearly, until I spoke, and made some kind of sense, I was deep in his clutches. He would not let me go.

I looked from stern to bow of our little ship, but through the crashing waves I saw not one sign of Rosalino Pilo. These were not clear thoughts, you must know, O Historians and Thinkers of a distant age, they were just a physical realization, as I understood somehow that the Count had been washed away by the sea, just as I would have been, were it not for that grasp of Giovanni Corrao. The paranza bucked through the waters like a tired, worn horse at the end of its longest run. Pitching up at the bow, then plunging down into the sea, with her stern kicked high, trying to throw us off, but only halfheartedly. Mostly she wanted to take on water, and then haul us all to the bottom, toward some watery home.

I can't remember much else, for I lost consciousness somewhere then, a consciousness that deep down in my heart I wearily believed was lost for good.

When I came to, hours later, the ship was dead still on this flat endless sea. Her decks remained wet under the high sun, though slowly I realized the very boards I lay on were dry as sand. It was only the decks to the starboard and the stern that still shone wet in the bright sunlight. And I heard the slosh of water being thrown, in a rhythm steady and strong.

The boat was listing heavily, you see, staying afloat only because of the calm seas, and her old spirit. She'd brought home many a fisherman feared lost and gone in her time. She was trying to do it again.

"Are you sleeping it off?" shouted Corrao's voice.

I lifted myself up, weakly, and turned to look over my shoulder. The oar was beside me, and it was lashed with a rope to the railing, along with my right arm. Corrao had tied me down so I could not roll off into the sea.

I heard his deep laugh at me, "Didn't know what was more important," he said, "you, Burtoni, or that last damn oar." He stopped to laugh again, and I saw him bend at the waist and then stand up again with a bucket in his hand, and toss the water inside it overboard. "So I tied you both down," he said, bending again for another bucket of water.

"Are you well enough to help, lad?"

It was the Count's voice, followed by the slosh of a bucket of water. The sound of it made me crawl up onto my hands and knees, until I could see him. I suppose my mouth was hanging open. Probably I looked like a thirsty dog.

"I thought you were . . ." I said.

But Pilo stood there, at the stern where the sea was trying calmly to lap up over our decks. "If we can bail our little bark out, and let her right herself, we can be back on our way, lad. Trusty little ship, she is."

"Before some other god damned thing blows in on us," Corrao blustered, without stopping his bailing for a moment. "Another damn storm like that last one would send us all straight to the bottom right now."

"Don't worry about that," said the Count, ignoring Corrao. "The skies are clear."

"Yes, and there's not even the breath of a wind for our sails," whined Corrao.

"But are you up to helping us yet, lad?"

I got to my feet on the slanted deck. As I started, then, to untie myself from the railing and the oar, Corrao began to laugh. "Blasted, lazy bones, threw our other oar away." He seemed to increase the speed of his bailing with every word. "Can't be trusted to row, boy, but you sure as hell could lend us a hand bailing her out."

Then, just as I stood up straight, he hit me with a bucketful of sea water.

"Giovanni!" barked the Count. "Overboard. And leave the lad get his feet."

But I had, instead, to try to grab at that last remaining oar, for in untying myself, I'd untied it. And Corrao's bucket of water and insults sent it drifting across the slanted decks, and then off into the Ligurian Sea.

"Damnation," I yelled, as it slipped from my hands and away.

But Corrao just laughed some more, and kept bailing away. "One's not much good, without the other, boy."

The way he calls me boy is a taunt. But he doesn't know my real age, and all that I've seen. He doesn't even know why the Count has me aboard.

When the time comes, I will try to tell him.

So the three of us worked, and that old boat was sound. She was not taking on any water. With every bucket we tossed, she rose up a little in the sea and began to right herself. And slowly the stern lifted and she put her bow back down in the water, and we began to feel stronger and better, singing and whistling and joking on the becalmed seas.

Finally, at one point I was below decks, lifting my bucket up to Corrao, as he tossed the empty down to me, and then threw the new water overboard, when Rosalino strode over to the tiller and gazed down her lines at the bowsprit pointing to the south. Then he stepped over and took a bucket full of seawater from me, as I tried to hand it up to Corrao. "Watch," he said to us both.

I stuck my head up from below, and saw the Count walk gamely over to the ship's prow. She was nearly righted now, and the Count looked back at us. His brown, determined eyes peered straight into my heart. Then he gently poured that bucket of water over the prow, like it was sacramental wine.

"I christen thee," he announced, stentorianly, "La Speranza. The hope of the nation."

Of course he knew what Giovanni Corrao did not, when he named our ship. La Speranza.

And he only knew La Speranza by name because I told him. When the Count found me, hanging around the Genovese port, looking for work, someone had pointed me out to him. I still don't know who, but it could have been anyone. You see, it costs nothing at all, not even half a penny to talk, especially in a harbor town, and everyone has some sort of yarn to tell. Some of them are lies, and some are the truth. But each and every story is bigger and braver than the one just told. Mine, you can be sure, just like you can trust what I put down here in this journal, my tale is all true. All of it.

At any rate, it was early in February, just a few months ago; I met Rosalino Pilo in a tavern by the docks. He called himself Giuseppe Fioratti then, another of his many secret names, and there was no hint that he was a Count from Sicily. He was short and lithe, and he wore his hair long like a revolutionary. He just poured me a glass of wine from the bottle he carried, sat down across the table from me, and said, "People tell me you were in the Anzani Brigade."

I didn't answer. Not even to correct him about the Legion. The way the police are, you don't answer a question like that to just anyone who walks up to you, even with long hair and a free glass of wine. Especially when he's offering a free glass of wine. In parts of this peninsula that are still in the control of the Austrians, just answering that question would make you a criminal.

"Giuseppe Fioratti," Pilo said, to introduce himself.

And so we chatted for a while, about the sea and ships, and then he came around to Switzerland. He lowered his voice, and glanced quickly around the room. "I spent a few years in Geneva, in exile, if you know what I mean. After Rome fell in '49."

I still didn't trust him, since he might have been a spy. And so I thanked him for the wine, and I got up and left.

"I lived in the Republic of Rome, Burtoni." He raised his glass to me, and whispered just loud enough so I could hear, "To the heroes of '49."

But he was strange, and there was a light burning in his eyes that reminded me of my dear old Ciccio Anzani, dead now these ten long years. It was the fire of dreams that I saw in this stranger who called himself Fioratti. And it reminded me of my lost days in Montevideo and of the Generalissimo and our long voyage to Niza, when I learned to read and write. So that I can now put this history down on paper.

So I asked around cautiously and found a few old salts in the harbor taverns, men I knew I could trust, and asked them just who this stranger was that he could know enough to ask me abut the Anzani Legion. One by one, they all grew quiet and cautious. Even though they knew me well, and knew they could talk with me of these things, they were careful and slow. And all they ever told me was that Giuseppe Fioratti was not his real name.

Did that make him a spy or a patriot? In the end, there was no way for me to tell. No one seemed to know who he really was. Or no one felt safe enough to say openly.

That was when I stumbled on Corrao. One night at a stinking hole called Il Gufo sulla Luna he was feeling good and deep into the bottom of his cups, this thick dark man covered with hair, singing loudly in a baritone voice that was as rich as it was flat. He noticed me come in, and before long he had an arm around my shoulders, trying to lead me outside, singing and laughing as we went. But I'd been around enough to know trouble when I saw it, to know the stink of a spy, even if it was singing and offering decent brandy.

So I pulled free of his grip, and tried to walk away. He cursed at me, and then put his paw back on my shoulder, tried to pull me back. I just dusted him off, and you could see the happy drinkers in the tavern squaring up around us, sensing a good tumble in sight. Entertainment for the night, it was. And shaping up nicely, it was, too.

But this drunken fool wouldn't back off. "Burtoni?" he grinned. "It's you? Right? Burtoni?"

I didn't know who the hell he was, or how he got my name, but he put a hand on my shoulder again.

I'm afraid I was tired, and I'd had it with him. I'd already dusted him off once, and I'm a lot older and wiser than I look. I know how to lose a drunk. So I wheeled around, put a fist into his bearded chin, not much, but just enough to knock him down. He did surprise me, how stable he was on his feet though. He seemed drunk, but it took more than I thought it would to set him down.

As I stepped past him and out of Il Gufo into the street, I heard him laughing, as if we'd shared a joke or some such thing. It was only a moment, and I heard his laughter again following me out the door. "Wait, Burtoni," he called out from inside, so I picked up my step.

He caught me a few blocks away, along the docks, breathless and grinning. "Wait, Burtoni, we need you!" he said.

I was about to paste him again, when he held his hands up in the air, and he said, "Il Generale needs you."

I stopped, but I didn't lower my fists.

"Who the hell are you?" I said.

His big grin came back and he stuck out one of those paws, offering to shake my hand, the hand that had just now knocked him on his arse. "Giovanni Corrao," he said, with those same crazy, burning eyes I'd seen in Fioratti. "You sailed with him, from Montevideo, didn't you?"

And that was how this all began.

4.

30 March 1860

We've been stuck drifting for two days now. Our little Speranza is all straight and right, ship shape in the water, but the sea is so still and so glassy smooth after that storm, we simply sit here and drift aimlessly. We, who have such great purposes before us, we drift aimlessly along on the glassy sea. Still this lifeless water gives me plenty of time now to write it all down here. Everything. But it's not getting us any closer to Sicily, with these guns and grenades in our hold. All this sitting and drifting along is beginning to drive me crazy, especially since Corrao has now taken up his singing again. What a sin it all seems.

5.

31 March

Last night, under the clear half moon, a northern breeze drifted in and lifted our sails, and we were by dawn in sight of Corsica. The seas are still and swift, and at last we are making time. By midday we should be through the straights and past Isola d'Elba and on into the Tyrrehenian Sea. Now we are all singing, together, and the seas are flowing with us.

We've not seen another ship since we slipped out of Genova. But that is probably more because of the storm, and the heavy calm that followed it than for any other reason. It will be good to set our course out and away from Sardinia and Toscana, sail into the deepest stretches of the sea and away from the other fishing boats with tongues that wag and too many stories to tell.

Today Pilo and I, under his command, will spend the better part of the daylight checking the muskets. With all the water we took on at the start, they will be in tough shape. And while we were becalmed, none of us had the spirit to care. Dead water deadens the soul, you know, and it is lethal to the dreams of the heart.

But now, today, the fine seas remind us that we may be needing these arms soon, so the Count and I will work, oiling and cleaning, while Corrao guides the paranza through the waters.

6.

1 April
Tyrrhenian Sea
Bound for Messina

The sunset came to end this fine day, and in its last light I saw a distant island. Pilo was at the tiller again, and I wondered aloud to him, "Why are you putting us in so close to shore?"

Count Pilo's eyes gazed past me at the distant shore, and he didn't answer me.

I glanced over at Corrao, leaning forward at the bow again, but he was gazing off to the west as well. "What island is that?" I said.

I knew we were days away from Sicily still. But they didn't answer me, neither one. Their steady gazes told me only that I should know what was out there.

"Sardinia," I said, trying not to sound confused.

"In the distance, yes," Corrao said wistfully. "Beyond," he said.

"Well then, what is this, and why are we cutting in so close to shore? Why do we take the chance?"

As we rounded its shoreline, we sailed up suddenly on a thin line of smoke rising straight up from the dark trees. "There," Pilo whispered, without any gesture other than his direct gaze.

"What is it?"

I thought maybe we were going to put in to pick up more arms, or food, or volunteers, perhaps. But then Corrao looked knowingly back at me and said only one word, "Caprera," and I understood.

No more did he say that name than Pilo cut our little paranza seaward, and I understood we'd had our look. It was straight on now to Sicilia, to Italia.

The time has come this evening for me, at last, to put down here in words the high and true purpose of our voyage. It will be written here, on paper, so that come what may after we land, or between this day and that day when we come ashore, history will have a clear record of us. For it is, indeed, my friends, history we intend to make.

That island of Caprera, with the sun setting over that little cabin, Isola Caprera was our real goal, my friends. You who come after us and read these words must understand.

After the failures of '48, when I ran with him north to Lugano, to escape the Austrian noose. After the Republic of Rome fell in '49, and again the peasants in the countryside failed to rise. And after he left his dearest Anita in a quick and sudden grave in the swamps south of Commachio, by a farmhouse near Mandriole. And then, when the war last year failed, and France and Austria divided up the north between themselves, and Count Cavour made a deal with the French to give away Niza, the General's own home, where his Anita's bones now lay. After all this, the Generalissimo went home to his little Isola Caprera. He said he would have no more of any of our wars, because enough was enough, and it was clear to him that the common little man, still a slave to the priests and the nuns, would not yet rise up to make a free Italy. And so he was done with it. Until the time was right, until the people were ready, if ever that grave day might come, he was done with it.

"There can be no Italia without him," Pilo said, as our Speranza cut away from Caprera toward the open sea. "Not in our lifetimes," he said. Not even in mine, I wondered, but I didn't speak. "Without him to lead us," Pilo said, hiding all his emotions, "all is lost."

But that, my friend, my fellow patriots, that is why we sail our little hopes across these seas to Messina. There is trouble stirring there on the island of Sicily, trouble for all my years.

"Here is the thing," Pilo had whispered to me, with Corrao looking on, as we three sat with another stranger in a corner of Il Gufo sulla Luna in Genova. "If we can reach Sicilia, with a few guns, and with my friends there . . . "

The stranger had nodded his head as Pilo spoke, and he whispered, "We have friends there."

"If we land there," said the Count, "and bring these guns as a sign, and we tell them that the General is coming, then they will rise up all over the island, in the little villages and in the mountains inland. I know they will, men. They have heart, the Sicilians. They must."

The stranger laughed, and then Giovanni Corrao spoke, leaning forward toward us and nodding his head to the emphasis of his words. "When the General hears that the peasants have revolted, then the General will rise up."

"Yes, he'll leave his little Caprera homestead and he'll lead us," Pilo said, with real fervor.

"And lead the volunteers I'm gathering here in Quarto," the stranger said.

"So, to Sicilia," Pilo finished it. Then the little Count's eyes darted from me to Corrao and back again. He took a sip of wine and he said, "We are the springs in the clock, my friends, and if we are brave and true to our dream, we can set off the alarm, we can rouse up the sleeping giant of Caprera, and then awaken the hearts of all Italia." His fist was closed tight as a seaman's knot, but he dared not pound the table nor raise it in the air. Not yet, and not here.

The stranger, who's name I still have not been told, leaned across the rough table too and he filled all our glasses from the bottle he'd bought, and then he raised his glass to us all. "To Sicilia," he whispered.

"To Italia," answered the Count, pushing his fingers through his long brown hair, and that night we drank to the bottom of that bottle together.

So now, I sit on this deck of the Speranza, knowing that I was chosen by Pilo to be here because of the way the General had adopted me, back in '48. I didn't really know him, it was Anzani who was my friend. We both loved Anzani, and in truth that was why the General loved me.

But it is why I am here. I might just be one more call to awaken the giant, when the General hears that it is I, the one he named Il Rosso at the foot of the Alps, who is fighting for him now in the Madonie and all the way to the Conco d'Oro.

Corrao is singing again, "Felice te che," and Pilo sits quietly at the helm, steering our course, silent as the moon and stars, and our sails are full with the happy winds of our green years. It is only days and we shall see the island, and then know our fates, and with our fate runs the fate of our homeland.

7.

9 April
Straits of Messina

This morning Speranza came within sight of Sicily, and then Rosalino kept us far out to sea. It is afternoon now, and we have dropped our sails and are at anchor, drifting a little in the Tyrrhenian Sea. We must stay alert now. Bourbon ships may be on patrol, and we've had no word now for nearly two weeks. We don't know what is happening on the shore.

We have come to stir up trouble, for we have a little hold full of weapons and we must be wary. There is no way for us to know if we have been discovered.

Pilo, in these last busy days, has told us a little, but in case we are arrested, Corrao and I know only what we must, only this:

There is a man, we know him only as Sole, who is waiting for us in Messina. Sole and his people will lead us into the interior. Sole knows only that a man named Robiolo is coming at night, and perhaps other things we don't know. Once we are organized, I believe, we will begin the revolt, moving along through the villages in the high country. Whether or goal is Messina or on the other end of the island, at the capital Palermo, I can't say. These are things Corrao and I will learn when the proper time comes. When it is necessary, we will learn it, and not before.

I suspect Giovanni many know more than I do about all of this, but he won't speak. And I know there is no point in asking him either. We just press forward with the tasks at hand.

Tonight, we wait for darkness, and then we will slip silently through the Straits and land somewhere to the south on the shores of Sicilia, and we will begin our work to rouse the sleeping giant of Caprera. God speed to us all. Quick departure to all our foes.

For Italia.

II.

There is a break in Jack Burton's journal here. Two blank pages, and a few pages, it is hard to say how many, have been torn out of the leather binding as well.

Rob noticed me pause at those empty pages, flipping them back and forth, touching the torn edges of the missing pages. "So what do you think?" he said. "Am I right?"

I shrugged, and he groaned and laughed at the same time.

"I'm right," he said. "I know I am."

"I don't know," I hedged. "It could be anybody."

"Oh, the hell it could," Rob shook his head in disgust. "Come with me for a walk and I'll tell you all the ways we know it was his."

I understood that Rob was right, but somehow, waiting to believe that this thing was true, that also seemed right. "It's been a long time," was all I said.

"You're damn right it's been a long time," Rob said. "I've been looking for something like this since we were just kids." Rob paused and grinned. "Since he snuck off and left us under the Big Top. Don't you remember?"

"I remember," I said. But I didn't say what I thought then: I'm not as hungry for this as you are, little brother.

The stone streets of Ortigia led us past a few well-lit cafes, and a few shops. Rob navigated like a native, and in moments we were strolling Via Minerva and the Duomo soared above us. Buried in the stone walls, but still visible even in the dusk light, stood tall columns, three stories high, framing the structure of the cathedral. But they were old, older than the Christian church that had swallowed them, they were probably Roman, maybe even Greek, and despite their great age, they seemed stronger and more certain than the masonry of Christianity that had surmounted them. It was as if time, though we put it to use in our lives and our beliefs, in our own history, our personal stories, still the old circular big top of seasonal time stood not just at the root, but even at the fundament and the frame of all our poor but beautiful structures. Our buildings. Our civilizations. Our beliefs.

Though the cathedral was centuries old, and as we rounded the corner and walked into the Piazza del Duomo, those old pagan columns stood to remind us of how temporary we are, even in our greatest ages and our grandest dreams. They were eight, ten, twelve centuries old, we are only standing in the shadow of the temples of the past, and our grandness becomes mere grandiosity.

From the Piazza, we could see the beautiful baroque facade that Andrea Palma had built, with its fine run of stairs, and its swift arches and saintly statues gazing down benevolently at us. But coming at it as we did, those old temple columns, now hidden away, stood firm and upright in my mind.

It made me wonder again about Jack Burton. Nothing about him added up. This strong, burly man in the wheelchair we met one day, fifteen years ago, beside a carnival tent. Nothing about him added up. Telling us stories about his adventures in the Italian Alps a hundred years before, and smoking his funny little pipe. And not this journal, in my hands, tucked under my arm as my brother and I strolled across a Sicilian piazza, telling another yarn, and again a hundred years old. None of it added up. It was all impossible, and I should have laughed at it and ignored it. But I didn't. I didn't do any of that.

"I know it's him," Rob said, and he led us over to a table outside a café, just across the piazza from the façade of the Duomo. "First of all, it fits," he said. "Everything in that book fits with the story he told us back when we were kids. Don't you remember?"

I didn't answer, for obviously my very presence there with him told us both that I remembered.

But Rob took my silence, rightly, for reservations. "And it sounds just like him. Just like the way he talked." He pointed at the notebook that I'd laid now on the table between us. "I swear, I can hear his voice speaking to us when I read that."

"I think you're smelling that funky smoke of his, too." I said.

Rob frowned, and just then a waiter approached, and Rob ordered a liter of red wine.

"That's too much," I said.

"We've got time," he said, and waved an open hand at the old leather book. "You've got to finish the rest of that, 'cause obviously you don't get it."

"Get it?"

"When you finish that, you'll know what I mean. We've got some traveling to do, big brother."

The wine came, with glasses and a little plate of cheeses and salumi, and Rob poured as he said, "Go on, read the rest of it. There's not much more after the break. Besides, you're right at the place where it starts to get really interesting."

As I picked up the old journal again, I conceded, "There is all that stuff about Anzani."

"That's right," Rob settled back in his chair to watch the passeggiatta in the square, and took a sip of the wine. "'Dear Old Ciccio,' remember? That was how he used to say it."

I nodded my head and opened the notebook to where I'd left off. "'Caro Cicio,'" I said, hearing Jack Burton's voice in my head. "But it's impossible," I muttered.

"It's all impossible," Rob agreed, and then held up his glass to admire the dark red of the wine in the evening light. "But it's why we're both here tonight, isn't it?"

What could I do but laugh at that, at the raw truth of it. With my thumb, I felt the nubs of the pages which had been cut out of the old loose binding.

"Go on, read some more," he said. "We've got work to do when you're done, and once you stop doubting everything." He was disgusted.

As my eyes rested on the page, I heard him mutter again, "Impossible." But I couldn't tell whether he was mocking me, or himself.

8.

10 April
Sicilia

Everything has changed now. My lord, I can barely write these words. For everything has changed utterly, the world whole and entire, and all because she was there on the shore. Yes. Rafaella was there on the shore. But wait. I must back up and start from the beginning, from the whole, glorious revolutionary start. So all of History will dare to understand.

*　　　　*　　　　*

47

Last night after the moon had set, we raised our sails and, without a light on board, without even Giovanni's old pipe, we slipped through the Straits in the dark. To the starboard twinkled the lights of Messina, and off to our port lay the dark shadows of Calabria.

The breeze was light and favorable, so we cut through the quiet water gently, not one of us speaking even one word. It seemed the current of the Straits was with us, forcing us along into the future, pushing ahead, ahead, ever ahead. We saw the grand merchant ships anchored in the harbor of Messina, their lanterns casting lovely shadows on the rippled sea. Once we'd rounded the city at a distance, and made it through the narrows, Corrao headed her back in toward the shores of the island. Pilo stood next to him, and whispered in his ear our bearings, and then the Count would stride up to the bow of the Speranza, pushing a hand back through his long hair, and silently scan the coastline.

It was not long before, in the dark hills to the south, two lanterns shone out brightly for a moment, waived to the right and then to the left in unison, and then went out. Pilo only turned to look back at Corrao at the tiller, and Giovanni nodded. Without a word passing between them, Corrao headed the paranza for that point on the coast.

Pilo waved me over, and then lit our two lanterns, handing me one in silence. I understood. Together, without a sound, we waved our lanterns in imitation of the lights we'd seen on shore. Then the Count gestured with a flat palm across his chest, and I snuffed the flame, as he did the same.

In a moment or two, we saw again the two lights shining from the shore. How many nights, and how many times each night, had they waited for us there, signaling out to the dark sea, hoping against hope that we had made our way? I had no way of knowing. But now at long last, after weeks of sailing, we had come in. It lifted all our hearts on board the ship. As it must have lifted hers too.

That was when, from out of the east behind us, a great battleship appeared. Tall on the sea, and lit with lanterns in rows, she seemed to come roiling out of nowhere. But I'm sure, in the dark, and in our concentration on our dreams of a Sicilian shore, and our search for the signals on the coast, we didn't see her right behind us. But once Pilo and I had lit those two lanterns, we had suddenly appeared out of the dark to the sailors on that war ship.

If she were Bourbon, we were surely done for. We were so close in to her, she could sink us in the night seas. And if not, we surely could not dare to put in to meet our signals now. At the first sound of her cannon fire, everyone ashore would vanish into the mountains, and we would have to make a run back out into the Ionian Sea, to try to slip away into the night before morning light. I don't know that we had enough speed to outrun that great warship and her guns, but we would try. We would sure as hell try.

At that moment, I admit it, I felt tears welling up in my eyes. O, to have come this far, to have slipped away from the Piedmontese in a Genovese fog, to have survived the high seas and then the deadly calm for days, to have found our way here, and seen the shore, to have spotted the clear signal lights, and then only to have our Speranza sent to the bottom by the Bourbon bastards of Naples: It was more than even my old heart could bear.

"Ahoy!" came the call across the waters of the Strait. And then in a moment, the shout followed, "Who goes there?" We were close enough we could see the men on her decks, and she was pulling abreast to put us under her guns. "What vessel are you? Show your flag or prepare yourself for our guns," the voice in the megaphone said.

Pilo looked over at me, and he started to laugh loudly. "Inglese," he said. And I heard Corrao back at the wheel, laughing too.

"Siamo Speranza!" the Count shouted out to the great black warship. Then he turned to me and said, "Tell the Inglese who we are, Burtoni."

I leaned up against the railing and called out, "We are the Speranza!"

"What is your cargo?" the megaphone answered us.

"We are bearing freedom and liberty to Sicily!" I sang out.

There was silence from the English ship. And then the voice in the megaphone asked, "What flag are you flying, Speranza?"

"The tricolore," I shouted back.

"Italia!" shouted Pilo. And then together with Corrao, again, "Italia!"

The English ship sat in the water behind us for a long moment, and then we began to see her turn away, as she showed us her great square helm, like a fine tall building on the water. She sailed away from us then, moving swiftly, but before she'd gone far, a different voice from her decks cried out, without the megaphone to help. "God speed to you, Speranza!" the shout came. And then one great "Huzzah!" rose up from her crew.

God speed, Speranza, indeed.

Near to shore, those lanterns going on and off, led us into a break between two large rocks, and with a hard run we beached our dear Speranza on the white sands. I leapt out into the sea knee deep and held her firm, Pilo was on the other side, then someone from the shore appeared out of the dark and the three of us pulled the Speranza up and firmly onto the beach, as Corrao scurried about, lowering our sails.

Our helper from the shore looked at me, and I saw her grey-blue eyes that seemed bright in the dark. That's right, it was she, dressed in pants and boots, her black hair tied back with a bandanna, knee deep in the water with us. "Rubiolo?" she said to me. Her voice is light and musical. I have sung and even cooed to many a lass, and had my head turned. Never. But this night, standing in the seawater, gazing back into her big eyes, I couldn't speak.

"Sole?" Pilo said to her, from the other side of the Speranza's bow.

She turned away from me to the Count and answered him, "Sole is not here tonight. But I will take you to him." There is a different music to her Italian, there is a curve and a gentleness to it, and it lands too easily on my ear. I was already in danger.

"Va bene," said Pilo to her.

She turned back toward the dark shadows of the volcanic rocks on the shore, and sang out, "Salvatore."

I must stop here. I admit that all of this has nothing to do with the history I am trying to write now. This is not a real and significant part of the record. And yet, I write it down, anyway. You see, with all my years, with the ladies of Montevideo and Nizza and even Genova in my past, with all that, she is different.

There is something about the Sicilian lilt to her words. I hear it too, at times, in Rosalino Pilo, when he is most off guard and at ease. And Corrao, too, had his own gruff twist to his words. But hers is different still. Rafaella, that is her name. You see, from the very first words she spoke, I somehow wanted to hear her say my name with that same sweet Sicilian twist. And something in me was broken, like a shattered oar, when right from the start tonight she turned and spoke to the Count. Right from the start, I wanted to hear her voice. I want to hear it now, and I want to hear her say my name.

This is dangerous.

Rafaella led us up off the beach tonight, with all our cargo in this Salvatore's cart. But I'm still a little confused now, and tired, and as I write this down, so I'm not sure it's making much sense anymore.

Salvatore called her Rafaella. That's how I come to know her name. But I'm not making any sense here. I will try again tomorrow, when I'm not so tired. Maybe it is just I am so tired.

Still I need to write this all down, now, before I forget it. As we followed the cart up into the black volcanic hills, and away from the sea, I looked back down on the lonely shore. And in the not far distance, standing guard over our old fishing boat, and over us I guess, I saw that British ship, at rest and all alight. If there had been time, we might have signaled to them. But there was no time.

So I touched Rafaella on her shoulder, and when she turned those eyes on me again, I just pointed out to sea. She looked from me to the British, and then gave me a nod. We rounded a knob on the hill, and the sea and our true old Speranza were gone, out of sight. She has disappeared into history. La Speranza.

I can write no more.

9.

11 April
From a mountain outside of Messina

This girl, this lovely Rafaella, she brought us here with a two-wheeled cart and a mule. And Salvatore is a little old man, even shorter than she is, and he led the cart out onto the beach, with its big red wheels five feet tall. From there, with few words spoken, we unloaded the paranza and put the muskets and the grenades we have smuggled here into their cart.

And then she brought us here, to where I sit now writing. We are inside a little stone house, and it is morning now. Rafaella is gone, somewhere, and it is time for us to rest, I suppose this is what they mean for us to do. Yet tired as I am, I can't sleep for more than a few moments. The excitement in me makes my heart beat in my very ears. Pounding for he future we have dreamed of, for so many years, it is here. I can feel it, in the air I breathe, in the earth I stand upon. In my heart. It is here.

At first light, I slipped outside to look around, and I can see we are hiding in the hills above the city. The great port of Messina stretches out beneath us, and from here we can look out on the Straits. In the distance, past the ships sailing calmly through toward the Mediterranean, lie the shores of Calabria, clearly in sight.

Corrao and Pilo are asleep, and Salvatore's wife, she calls herself Ada (I don't know who is using a true name and who a false), is moving about the little cottage. When she sees me writing here in the morning sun, she brings me coffee and a chunk of crisp and simple bread, like a cracker, and a chunk of some pungent, salty white cheese.

Moments ago I asked her where Salvatore was, but I am in trouble. I was really just trying to discover when lovely Rafaella will return. I can still see her now, in my mind's eye. I wonder, is this her true name? Rafaella.

Last night, when we all arrived here, she did not come inside straight away. Salvatore introduced us to Ada, and Ada showed us where to bed down. But Rafaella disappeared with the two-wheeled cart full of weapons and ammunition off somewhere back into the hills behind the house. So we were seated inside around a rough table, Pilo and Corrao and I, with Ada dishing out a plain hot soup for us, when Rafaella slipped silently back into the warm room. I almost didn't notice. Almost.

"Hidden?" asked Pilo.

She nodded yes. And then, in that light of the kitchen fire, I truly saw her for the first time. She looked around at all of us, one at a time, sizing us up I suppose at that rough table.

Her nose is little and round, with a tiny little upturned point, and her mouth beneath it is full and wide. Her lower lip is plump and lovely. It is her eyes that make me catch my breath though, for they are a shining gray, in almost any light, and they are wide and intense. They are not like any other woman's eyes I have ever seen. And she looks at you straight in the eyes, too, unlike most of the rough girls I've known. I'm afraid, this one, she seems to see straight into me then, with those deep gray eyes, and somehow I can't bear it and I can't look away. I have not been shy and tongue-tied like this around a woman in years, many years.

I am in trouble.

Ada handed her a glass of dark wine, and Rafaella drank it down in one long draught. And then came the truly remarkable thing. At least beyond her dancing eyes. You see, she took the sky blue scarf from around her brow, and with one shake of her head, turbulent curls of long black hair fell loose and all around her oval face. Her hair is like a beautiful dark cloud around the moonlight of her face. And clouds seems to move and develop around her, so black they are almost blue in the soft warm light of the kitchen.

There is news, and I must get back to this history. You see, Rafaella returned late this morning, or rather this Sole finally came to meet us, and she was with him. And this comrade called Sole was bringing news.

I must write it down here, for the record, lest I fall off the trail of my history. Let me start over: It was late when they arrived, and Pilo and Corrao were up now and rested. But we are all three of us restless. We have not come this far to hide out in a peasant's house and watch the Neapolitan ships drift by below on the Straits. We have come to act upon the world and to make a change.

And what Sole told us then only made our restlessness more unbearable.

"The revolt has started," he said. He's a short man, this Sole, but lean and hard and he sports a startling shock of grey hair from his head, thick and fierce, even though it is close cropped. His beard in straight white, cut short as the hair on his head, and all the hair frames his dark tanned face. But he is not dark from hours of hard work in the sun on land or sea, like Salvatore is dark, like Giovanni and I are dark. His skin is smooth and supple, plump and rosy as a girl's. But it is dark, and his gray eyes sparkle inside this frame of silvery white hair. Perhaps it is that silver hair that makes his face seem so shaded.

Pilo sits up straight at the word of this revolt, and Corrao is immediately on his feet. The time has come. It is now, we think. The Sicilians are at the ready. We are ready.

But Sole raised his hand, like a priest, and said, "My friends, it is not going well." Then with a grand gesture, Sole sat us all back down around the table.

I sat on the bench seat then, to be next to Rafaella, and I was a little startled to sense how small she was. Suddenly she seemed frail and vulnerable, not the way she seemed before. Last night she was short and intent, filled with power and confidence. Today she is just tiny and frail. Her hair was bound up again, this time in a blood red scarf, and she folded her hands as if in prayer, and set them on the table while we listened to Pilo and Sole talk. This is the first time I have seen her clearly in daylight. Now her lovely eyes are not so startling, but the shape of her face, the beautiful cut of her high cheekbones and the pale freckles across her cheeks, they still leave me speechless. Her gaze is completely locked on this Sole, though. She seems indeed to dote on his every word, and I don't know yet what to make of that. Is it patriotism I sense in her eyes and the fold of her little hands, or is it something else? He, on the other hand, seems to ignore her, to take her for granted.

"They rose up on the fourth," Sole said. "But their plan was discovered. Somehow. Francesco Riso, a stone mason from Palermo, he is a brave man, I have known for many yers. And my friends Riso has led the peasants and the citizens of the city, but somehow their plans were discovered."

"How?" asked Pilo, frowning.

"No one knows, Rubiolo. Or at least none of us knows." Sole said, "But I do know this, my comrade. We must be careful and we must not trust anyone, because someone gave up Francesco Riso and his men. I do know this, that spies and turncoats are everywhere."

"What happened?" Corrao asked.

"The plan was to gather just before nightfall at the Gancia. The Gancia is an old monastery in the city," Sole said, looking over at me. He understood that Pilo and Corrao know Palermo well. "They had arms and ammunition hidden there, at the Gancia, and Riso the mason was to meet there with twenty or thirty men. At dark they would take to the streets and begin the revolt. The city would rise up; the Palermitani would revolt and drive out the Bourbons. Palermo would declare herself free, just as she did back in the days of the Vespers. And again that would be the beginning of a free Sicilia."

Sole stopped there, for a moment he lowered his head and he placed his dark forehead in his hands and stared at the tabletop. Rafaella unfolded her hands and she put one on Sole's shoulder, to comfort him. It was a gesture that meant they were close, they were familiar. Perhaps they were even more than that. This I'm afraid was hard news for me, and my heart was sinking, and sinking, simply at the touch of her hand on another's shoulder. I told myself that it was the failed revolt that worried me, but I was lying to myself.

"Lombardo," Salvatore whispered, trying to comfort him. I think he was using this Sole's real name, a mistake, but one that was safe with us, I knew.

"What happened?" Pilo asked again. "Sole?" he repeated, when this secretive man didn't answer.

I noticed it was Ada who spoke first. "Lombardo and Riso are old friends in the society," she said to the three of us. "They are like fratelli. They are men of honor."

"Riso is tough, Lombardo," Salvatore whispered to him. "He will be all right."

Rafaella stroked this Lombardo's shoulders, and he slowly raised his head up from his hands, looked at her and then he went on proudly. "The soldiers arrived at Gancia before dark, and they knew who and what they were looking for. They seized the monastery, they tied up the monks in two's and three's, and then they ransacked the building."

"And Riso?" Corrao said.

Lombardo looked over at him. "He is in their prison, I fear, my comrade." The man we called Sole paused, and it had a dramatic effect, his silence falling on all of us. "I am sure he is being tortured by them, as we speak right now. But Ciccio Riso is brave, he bears a true heart within his breast. He is a man of honor. He will not give up any names. You can be sure."

Pilo slid over to one side in his chair, as if he were about to rise up. "And the revolt?" he said, impatient to return to the point.

Lombardo turned slowly, looked him directly in the eyes, and he said one word, "Crushed." But he seemed defiant when he said it, not defeated. There was something vicious and cornered in his eyes. I understood he could be dangerous, not one you could safely cross, and my heart sank even lower then. I was already, I'm afraid, planning to cross him.

"It can't be over," Pilo met his straight gaze with the same hunger and defiance.

"Oh, there are some squadre left, contadini from the hills, who creep down into the city at night, take a few shots and then disappear." Then Sole gazed over at Pilo. "But they won't last. There's no organization, Rubiolo. The revolt is broken. And when the crops start to come in, then these men, these contadini will be needed at home, back in the mountains, and then the squadre will just vanish. They'll disappear without a trace. And with them goes our revolt, Signor Rubiolo. That's the end of it. I'm afraid, my friends, you have traveled far through many dangers, only to arrive too late. It is what always happens here, on our cursed island. It is over, Rubiolo. Over, I say."

Then a dark shadow covered his lowered eyes, and Rafaella put an arm around him, moving her body toward him and away from me where I sat, dumbly listening to all this black talk. The blackness of heart filled the morning light.

I thought Salvatore might curse at these words of Sole's, but before anyone else could respond, Count Rosalino Pilo sat back in his stiff wooden chair, threw back his head, tossed his long hair like a mane, and laughed out loud. All of us were frowning at him then. The Count paused, he looked quickly at Giovanni Corrao and then over at me, to keep us silent, to make us complicit in the lie he was about to tell.

"No, my dear Sole," he said. "All is not lost. We will, indeed, make Italia this time."

Lombardo lifted his head in disbelief, and he was about to object. "Rubiolo," he muttered, but Pilo cut him off with this simple statement.

"He is coming, Sole." There was a moment of profound silence while everyone in the room digested Pilo's lie. He let his glance briefly land on Corrao and on me again, to be certain we would stay quiet. "That is why we are here, Sole. To prepare the way for him, and to pass the word, so that everyone is ready. All these peasant squadre in the hills, and the laborers in the city streets. Everyone. Because he is coming, with thousands of volunteers from the north, and with ships filled with supplies. Do you understand? He is coming."

I ventured a glance over at Corrao, and I found he was looking back at me, his face like a stone, but our eyes were big with the deceit when they met.

"The General will come?" said Salvatore, in disbelief.

Pilo is a great liar. He didn't even crack a smile as he said, "We've come to pass on this word, Sole? We've come to prepare his way." I noticed that Count Rosalino, while he stretched an arm out to indicate the three of us together, the "General's advance guard," he was careful not to look either Corrao or me in the eye.

But this Lombardo, who calls himself Sole for the cause, he is cagey. Before he would show any excitement or even any interest, he wanted to know the facts, "When?" He leaned forward just a little over the tabletop, toward Pilo, and Rafaella's arm dropped away from him, hesitantly. I can't help it, I felt my heart lift. Probably, it showed in my face, and it made our lie about the General seem more true than the truth. "Where is he landing?" Lombardo asked, his eyes seeming hungry again.

She brought her tiny hand back to the table, but she didn't fold them together like before. It was just an impulse. Without thinking, I reached over with my big paw and I held both of hers in my hand, and gently squeezed them. Our eyes truly met for the first time. Hers spoke simply, 'Is it true?' I'm not sure at all what mine were meant to say. They made me forget Lombardo's strange intensity. I'm afraid they made me forget everything. I am already deeply in trouble.

Rosalino Pilo was clever, though, and his answer to Lombardo was direct. "There are spies, everywhere, Sole. You said so yourself."

Lombardo nodded yes, knowingly. Rafaella squeezed my hand back and then drew away, but her gaze lingered on mine for a moment or two longer, and like a child my heart beat harder then. But I am an old man, despite the way I look. I am not an innocent child.

"What do we need to do?" Lombardo said.

Pilo gave out a list of orders then, and most of it, though I was looking straight at him and trying to listen closely, I don't remember. As my heart beat in my chest as if I was running a race, these men laid out the plans. Most of the guns would stay hidden, with Salvatore and Sole, until they were needed. Pilo and Corrao and I would travel overland, through the villages along the way to Palermo. We would spread the word, we would plant the seeds of revolt and prepare the way for the General's arrival. And there were many other plans laid out across that table today, but they have all disappeared from my memory because I heard just one thing: Rafaella is to be our guide.

Ada said something to Rafaella then. I don't know what it was. But she got up from her place at the table and went outside with Ada. Pilo and Lombardo just continued to talk, and Salvatore and Corrao were joining in, but as I sit here and write this down now, I can only say there were some disagreements about how we should travel across the island. What was the best and safest route for us to take? Which villages would be most ripe to hear our message? But to me it was all only a list of names, one town after another, and none that meant anything to me. I've never been here before, so to me one town sounds like another.

So after awhile, I got up and I followed the two women outside. I found them sitting down the hillside in the afternoon sun, on a bench with a basket of oranges between them, talking and peeling away the rinds slowly. As I approached them, they fell silent, and suddenly Ada stood up. I don't know why. She made a few weak excuses, grinning broadly at Rafaella, and then she left.

Rafaella handed me a little round orange, and gestured for me to sit on the bench beside her, with the basket of sweet fruit between us. Her fingers were stained pink with the juice of the orange. She pulled a section loose and handed it to me, and its flesh was a deep red. "Have you tasted these before?" she said.

Sweet, but with a cutting bitterness buried beneath the sugar, that orange was the best I have ever tasted. I told her so.

"Salvatore and Ada grow them, down there," she pointed down into the walls of the valley below us, away from the sea.

I can't tell you now what I said. O, I can hear her voice in my mind, singing, and I think we talked a lot about how brave it was of her, to lead us across the mountains. I know she said that I was very brave to come this far, across the ocean, to help free an island I'd never even seen before. I answered with just one word: the General's name.

It surprises me now, when I think of it, but Rafaella didn't ask me anything about the General. In the past, whenever his name crossed my lips in conversation, it had always led to "Do you know him?" and then to a string of questions about him that make me just disappear into the thinnest air. And there is not one question among them all that I don't take great pride in answering. It is a great and even boastful joy to be able to say you know him.

But not Rafaella. And not this afternoon. She seemed to take it all in stride, unshaken by the General's great fame, or my closeness to him. With her, this is all so refreshing, like the red orange flesh in my hands. Instead of talk about the General, she told me about a place we would go to soon. It was her favorite place in the world, a little village high up in the mountains, with a view of Mount Etna, and a sharp cliff that drops to the sea, and groves of almond trees and grape vineyards on the steep slopes, and an old stone villa high on a rock overlooking it all.

"When I was a little girl," she told me with her grey eyes shining, "I would spend the summers up there in my father's little house. I'll take you up there. When we reach that place, someday soon."

"What's it called?" I asked, mainly just to keep gazing at her and listening to her voice.

"I used to help when we harvested the grapes and then we'd make the wine and put it away in barrels. And my Nonna would make her almond cake, and in the long summer evenings, we'd have a glass of wine and a big slice of her sweet cake, drizzled with honey from the bees on the mountainside."

"Where is this place?" I asked.

"There is an English family there now," she said, probably because she could hear the accent in my speech. "They own the villa now, or it seems they do, and they live up in the castle on the rock. The Duke and Duchess of Brumonte."

"I'm not English," I told her.

"They're really very nice, Burtoni," she said my name, and the sound of it echoed around in my chest, almost making it hard for me to breathe. How can I be so lost so soon, like a little boy with his first love. "I think you will like them. especially the Duke. The Duchess is a little, oh, you know. She knows he is a Duchess."

I took her hand again, this time it had a red orange in it, and her fingers were sticky with the juice. I wanted to kiss them clean. "Please," I said. "I want you to call me by my name. Call me Jack."

"Jack," she said, though in her mouth it came out like "Jaaqquo," and that made me laugh.

"Rafaella," I said.

"I like Burtoni better," she said.

"Burtoni is fine."

But then she took another try at "Jack," and laughed at herself. Her laugh tinkled like the magic of little church bells at early morning mass.

"Burtoni is fine," I said.

"Rafaella," we heard a deep voice call out, and when we looked up we saw Lombardo and Pilo, two short men striding vigorously down the hill, their arms working like pumps, their chins held up, stiff and strong in the air. But Lombardo seemed to be in a hurry, even more in a hurry than Count Rosalino.

"Cara Rafaella," Lombardo ordered. "Take this and post it with the English in the harbor, dear." He handed her a sealed letter, and his name for her lingered in my ear. I could see the letter was written in Rosalino's hand, but I couldn't make out to whom it was addressed, yet Lombardo seemed to place great importance on it, and on its swift delivery. So clearly he was leaving it in the hands of someone he could trust.

"Hurry back here tonight, cara mia, and be careful," he turned from her to Pilo. "She can lead you out of here, after dark."

"We'll be ready," I said, and the two men seemed a little startled that I was speaking. But I was looking again into Rafaella's eyes, and I didn't care what they thought. Lombardo took her in his arms again, and she looked away from me. With a gentle embrace, he whispered something in her ear, then he kissed her cheek and held her at arm's length. "Be careful, but hurry back," he said. "Come to me, when you return, all right, my dearest?"

From that moment on, I could not catch her gaze. She would not look back at me.

After she was gone down to Messina, Lombardo spoke something in Sicilian to Salvatore, being careful that neither Count Pilo nor Corrao heard it. He made a point though of letting me hear, since he knew I couldn't understand. He needed to remind me, for some reason, that I was just another foreigner. Then he left in a rush, away in a different direction from where he had sent Rafaella.

Ada led us to a small bedroom, and showed us where we could rest until dark. Corrao stretched out on the one bed, but my heart was still beating and my eyes were wide as open windows on a summer night, trying to let the coolness of rest in. But even if I tried, my eyes would not stay closed.

"Who was that letter for?" I asked, as soon as the three of us were alone.

Corrao, on the bed, let out a hardy guffaw and then rolled over on his side with his back to us, in order to try to sleep. "While you were off with the lovely signorina," he muttered, "Rosalino put on quite a show."

"Watch your tongue, Giovanni," Pilo snapped. "We don't know who might be listening to us."

Corrao guffawed again, "Ol' Rubiolo, indeed," he said, and then snorted himself into a more comfortable position as he settled on the bed.

"Who?" I asked again. I was stretched out on the floor with a straw pillow under my arm, leaning over toward where Pilo sat on the floor beside me.

Pilo said, with a face of absolute stone, "I wrote to il Generale to tell him the revolt has begun."

"But?" I said, and Pilo slid closer on the floor next to me, with his eyes on the door out into the little kitchen where we'd just eaten.

"He's playing the great game, Burtoni," muttered Corrao, with his back to us. And he spoke ever so softly, beneath his breath.

Then Pilo whispered quietly to me, " The General wants to know that the people have risen up in revolution before he will once again commit himself to the fight, correct?" His glance rested on the open door a moment, and then Pilo spoke even more softly. "The Sicilians are afraid to rise up without Il Generale to lead them on into the fight. So, you see, we will just give them both the little push they want. Tutte a due."

"We'll do what?"

"I wrote to tell the General the revolution has begun. So now he will come. And for the next few weeks, Burtoni, it is our job to tell the people of this island that the General is on

65

his way, whether he is or not. You see, this is what I plan. We'll stir up this revolt, the three of us, everywhere we go all across the island, so it makes enough noise to bring on Il Generalissimo himself. He won't be able to stay away."

Corrao couldn't help but chuckle, even if he was trying to ignore us and sleep. "Brilliant," Corrao muttered, sounding content in a way. He is enjoying the trick in it all, he is. Giovanni Corrao, you see, he loves to be on the inside of any little game we might play.

"But you told me in Genova . . . "

Pilo broke it off, just to silence me. With a shush, he went on, "I told you just what I told Il Generale. And now, my friend Burtoni, it is up to you and brother Carrao and me to make it all come true. Every story I've told. We'll make them all true. "

"But what if . . ."

"There are no 'what if's' now, Comrade Burtoni. It is up to the three of us to make my little words become the God's truth. And then," Pilo sat back against the bed, and took out paper and ink, "then together we will all make Italia." He held up just one finger in the air. "Italia will be one. But the beginning rests with the three of us."

I started to speak, but he showed me an empty hand, then, and said, "Now, I need to write a few more letters, and you, my friend, you need to get some rest. Little Rafaella's pretty eyes, or not."

I glanced over at him sharply, but he just grinned at me like an elf. "Get some rest, lad" he said. "You will need it, soon enough."

And yet I couldn't sleep, and so instead I have written all this down. And soon Rafaella will return. Pilo tells me now to put this away, to get some sleep before nightfall. It is an order now. I'm not a sailor or even a rebel anymore, he says to me. I'm soldier.

But waiting for her, how can I sleep?

10.

14 April
Randazzo

O these Sicilian hills are a hard, hard country, filled with scrabble and dust even in the spring, and especially when we travel at night. The horses, not fine ones by any means, are slow and the roads at their best are just wagon ruts in the dirt, peppered with stones. So the horses step along slowly and precariously. There is only the four of us. Most of the time, Rafaella leads the way, because she is the one among us who knows the way.

When daylight came, on our first morning, the 12th, we were still miles from anywhere. But it was not Rafaella's fault, or the fault of these old horses we ride. It was our narrow escape from Salvatore's house that put us behind.

That first night here in Sicilia I had finally fallen asleep, when suddenly Ada was shaking me, but she had her hand covering my mouth. ""Shh!" she whispered, into my face. The room was black with night, and she led us quickly crawling out the one window in the room. Salvatore was right outside, and carrying our few things with us, we scurried across the dirt farmyard following him to a long, ramshackle shed, and inside it were these four old horses, the same horses we are riding now.

Without a word, Salvatore led us in beneath those horses in the narrow stall that was really built for just two animals. And then with his hands he covered us with straw. I was still disoriented, not really awake enough to know what was happening, and the night air was cold. Behind me, I could sense Pilo and Corrao, but we made not a sound. None of us. And the smell of the manure was ripe and fresh, because we were lying in it.

That was when I felt her hand reach over and take hold of mine, just the way I had held hers at the table. She whispered almost soundlessly, like a breath, and I felt it on my cheek more than I heard it. "Soldati," was all she said.

We lay still for the longest while, and I wondered how we would know when it was clear. They must have found the Speranza. Surely the British would not have turned us in. But I heard Lombardo's and Pilo's words echoing in my mind. 'The spies are everywhere.' And I knew, just as Pilo and Corrao did, that if we were captured, it would be a quick firing squad for us, and the end of Sicily's dreams of the General's arrival. So now, even to breathe seemed a chance.

There was a clatter of horses and the sounds of several men running outside. Then I heard Lombardo's voice. "What do you think you are doing?" A few men called in the distance, and I heard Ada cry, "Stay out of there."

That led to a lot of crashing around in the distance, and the boot stomps and called orders moved past us in the night. It may have been my sleepyheadedness, but all of these alarms came and went quickly, swooping back and forth outside, roving through the night. Then there was quiet for a while, and it went on for a long, long moment. I grew restless, and the stench of that crowded stall was growing old. I started to move my legs, but immediately Rafaella's hand tightened around mine, and just her touch told me to lie still, that Salvatore or Ada would tell us when it was safe to move, when we might escape.

Suddenly, out of the night, I heard a sharp voice threaten, "Where are they?" Then there was a loud slap, and the sound of feet scuffling in the dirt. "Where are they?" the man's voice shouted shrilly now, and I heard Ada crying.

"Keep your filthy hands off of her," Salvatore threatened right back. And then, just outside the shed, there were the scuffling sounds of men wrestling.

"That's enough," Lombardo's voice said calmly.

"What's in here?" the shrill officer said, speaking now, but without much breath.

"Go on in and see for yourself," spat out Salvatore. "Spaniard," he added with scorn.

But Lombardo spoke calmly again, maybe too calmly. "It is just their stable, Bosco. Go Ahead. Take a look for yourself. See what you can find."

"I will," this Bosco said, crisply now.

The door creaked open on its rusted iron hinges, and Lombardo said from outside, "Just a few old horses in there, Commander Bosco. What are you looking for?"

"You know who I'm looking for."

"Really? And who might that be, Signor Bosco?" The vivid strain of insult in Lombardo's voice told me how well he knew this Bourbon Commander. He knew him well enough to understand exactly how to get under his skin.

I lay still, not even breathing at that point. I felt isolated then, trying to sense Pilo and Corrao behind me, and despite Rafaella's hand curled in mine, I felt alone.

"Why so many horses?" Bosco asked, and some soldiers, three or four of them, stomped in. The bayonets were set on their rifles, I knew without seeing.

69

"Salvatore keeps some of mine in his pasture," Lombardo lied easily. "The bay and the black mare are mine, Commander, sir?"

This Bosco laughed, and tried to sound as insulting as Lombardo did. "Nice horses, Signor Avvocato." Then the Commander jerked a hand at his soldiers, "Go ahead."

"That old mare there, I've had her a long time," Lombardo kept lying, and now he acted defensive about his animals. "Don't make fun of her, she's a good horse, Signor Bosco."

The soldiers began to fork through the straw and manure with their bayonets. I wanted to scream at them, then. I wanted to hurl myself over Rafaella to protect her. But what I wanted wasn't what I should do, and I knew it. The smart thing was to be still, and I did the smart thing.

The soldiers, pushing around in the manure, stirred up the horses, and they began nervously clomping around in the tight stall. Behind me the big brown bay stumbled, its back feet losing their grip, so he reared up a little. He had stepped on Corrao's shin, but I didn't know that until later. All four horses bumped against one another, and they snorted and reared back their heads. Their restlessness slowed the three soldiers down to a pause. That's when the big black mare lifted her tail, and she spouted out a stream of soft, grassy shit, followed by the long fluting song of gas. The clumpy shit landed right on my shoulder, and it was loose enough to slide down through the straw and onto my arm. Her gas was acrid and bitter, and it filled that little shed so everyone in it could taste the inside of her stomach in the back of their mouths.

"That mare is sick," one of the soldiers moaned, his accent bore a hint of Spanish.

"We better separate her out, Salvatore," Lombardo said from the doorway, "or the others might get ill too."

The mare, as if she'd been trained, let fly with another hissing vent of gas, and then she snorted.

"Let's get out of here," Bosco said. And his soldiers happily complied, as the bunch of them backed out of that little doorway.

We all lay completely still for the longest time, waiting for Bosco and his Bourbon soldiers to be truly gone, wary of some trick, some quick return of the bayonets we'd so narrowly escaped.

Rafaella's hand slipped away from mine, and I felt even more alone. I suppose I must have sighed or grunted or something, without knowing it. But that was what started it, for I heard Giovanni Carrao start to laugh, and then stifle himself. But that only started Count Pilo, and then Corrao couldn't help himself.

"That sweet old horse sure got us out of a pile of shit," Corrao whispered.

"Maybe you," Pilo answered, and at that, even Rafaella began to laugh at me.

So I sat up out of the straw, looked around me in the dark stall at these mounds of hay, jiggling with laughter, and I said, "It's not funny."

But then Rafaella pushed the straw away from her face, and I realized that she had taken her hand away to escape the horseshit that was drooling its way down my arm. I saw her grin, and I saw the trembling of her shoulder in laughter. The grassy clumps of shit had run now from my neck down my arm and into my lap, and the relief of our narrow escape showered over me then, and I too began to laugh, louder than all the rest of them.

"What's this horse's name?" I asked, and patted our savior on her sour, stinking ass.

"She's Joan of Arc," answered Rafaella.

I started to laugh again at that noble name, when Pilo grabbed my arm—the one that was soaked in Joan of Arc's shit—and he pulled me back to the ground. A flurry of straw covered me again, and I heard Corrao utter a quick, "Shh!"

Outside there were footsteps running quickly toward the shed. We didn't hear the rattle of any boots or guns, but in the distance there was the rattle of scattered gunfire, and strange, almost human screams. It was followed by a string of curses the like of which I'd never heard before on any ship, in any battle, even from those veterans of the bloody wars of Argentina. What's more, it was a woman hurling out that language.

There came a long silence after the gunfire, followed by the sound again of struggle just outside the shed. "Leave it be," Salvatore said. But Ada answered him with another jolting stream of profanity, but in Sicilian now, so I know it was profanity only because of the way that she spoke it.

We all breathed easier when we recognized those voices. The iron hinges creaked again, and Salvatore and Ada stepped inside, closing the door quickly behind then.

"Let's go!" Salvatore said, whispering loudly. "Presto! Before they come back."

Without another word, we all rose up and in a few moments those four horses were saddled and all our things were packed on them. "Take the road through the mountains to Novara," Salvatore told Rafaella. I heard her whispering back and forth with Ada in Sicilian, but there was no time then to ask what was happening.

In moments we slipped off down into the trees at the edge of the house, on those four old horses. Rafaella was at the head, leading us without a light visible. I am on Joan of Arc, as seems fitting. And I brought up our rear, more to keep me downwind than anything else. None of us were smelling too fresh though, after hiding in that stall and bearing up under Joan of Arc's heroic waste. I heard nothing, saw nothing of the Bourbon troops, and both Ada and Salvatore disappeared back toward the little house without another word, not even a farewell.

It was only later, this morning by the stream, that I clearly understood what had happened. Lombardo had led Bosco and his troops off to the next peasant's house in these hills with reports that we'd been seen there, and we had slipped away in the opposite direction, hoping not to be noticed until we'd vanished into the rugged mountains.

"How did they know we were here?" Pilo asked.

Rafaella shrugged.

"Someone talked about us," Corrao said bitterly, " in the wrong places."

No one answered him, or said anymore about it. We could have been seen by dozens of locals, and we all knew it. But we also knew the truth that spies were everywhere, and it was impossible to know for certain whose side anyone was on. Except for the three of us, and Rafaella. She too was one of us now.

"What was all that gunfire?" I asked, "and those screams?"

"Commander Bosco, when he couldn't find us, he had his men shoot all of Salvatore's pigs," Rafaella said.

The sound of those screaming animals will stay with us all forever, I believe. "There'll be some butchering to do today," said Pilo, trying to show a stone cold humor.

There was silence, and no one wanted to laugh.

"And in the future, too," Corrao muttered, hate spilling from him out into the night.

"We'll have none of that, Giovanni Corrao," Pilo said, sounding off orders now. "We're not here to butcher anyone. We've come with freedom in our dreams. There's no place for revenge in our revolution, Brother Corrao. No place. No place at all."

Corrao was silent through Pilo's little speech, but when the Count was finished, just a beat too late, he said, "Yes sir, Rubiolo."

Night approaches now, and soon we will be off again after dark toward a village called Novara di Sicilia, I have been told. It is a town, according to Pilo, where the seeds of revolution are ready to sprout. How we know this, I am not sure, but still it is the direction where Rafaella leads us. As I write this down, Pilo is again working on something of his own, though I don't know what it is. Tomorrow we truly begin, he says, so he tells us over and over to rest, but to remain watchful. This is how each of our days will go now, at least until the revolution itself begins. We will sleep the afternoons away, in almond groves like this one in the high country, and tonight we will make our way on to Novara. But at this moment Rafaella sleeps peacefully beside a large stone fence, with the common, gray-green cactus scattered all around her. When her eyes are closed, she seems helpless and a child. But we have all seen her move through the dangerous night with great courage and with a true heart. She is far, far from helpless. She is no child, however she seems in her sleep. I want to protect her from every danger, I know. But it is a protection she doesn't need.

What does she need?

I must stop now. I must try to sleep.

11.

15 April
In the Peloritani above Novara di Sicilia

Yesterday, once we had stopped in the daylight, Rafaella washed our clothes. She had been sleeping amongst the flowering cactus, and Pilo was writing still. I put this journal down and was trying to sleep when she suddenly walked up, knelt down with one knee next to me, and with a hand on my shoulder, she said "Burtoni, give me your clothes."

I thought for a moment I was dreaming, my chance had come, but then she handed me her blanket, the one she'd been sleeping in moments before, and she walked over to where Corrao was sleeping near the horses.

I climbed out of my filthy shirt and pants, still decorated by old Joan of Arc, and I wrapped Rafaella's blanket around me. Pilo was still writing away, but she took his shirt from him, and she collected Corrao's clothes too, where he was sleeping soundly near the horses.

She carried away our clothes down into a narrow, carved gully, and out of our sight. In the warm spring sun, lying under her blanket without my clothes, the smell of the damp earth mixing with the warm scent of Rafaella in the blanket, I fell soundly, soundly asleep.

It was late in the afternoon when I awoke, feeling a little chill. Pilo was sleeping now finally, and Corrao was deeply asleep, his head resting on his saddle. Rafaella was nowhere to be seen.

So I got up and with her blanket wrapped around my shoulders, naked as a baby except for my boots, I tromped down into the gully where she had disappeared with our clothes.

The old ground was rocky, but rich and black with volcanic soil, and all around spread a strange mix of grass with cactus and brush on the hillsides. There was a trail, yet it was not easy walking. But as I wound down through that notch, it opened out into a fine mountain stream, clattering along over mossy rocks beneath the cactus dotted hills. I heard Rafaella humming and singing in Sicilian before I saw her. She was sitting in the sun, her bare feet beside the stream, with her toes dangling in the water.

My clothes, and Pilo's and Corrao's, were spread out across the grey green brush, drying in the hot sun on the hillside above her. She had her sleeves rolled up above her elbows, and her long hair was bound up in a knot made of itself on top of her head. She was so lost in the sun and her song, she didn't hear me approaching.

I said her name, a magic charm it was, and she looked up, not startled, but not expecting me either. For immediately her hands went up and untied that knot of hair, letting it fall across her shoulders. Then her hands brushed her sleeves down on her arms, and dusted off her blouse.

"Thank you," I said to her, and waved my hand at my clothes drying in the Sicilian sun.

She just laughed, and then said, "It was better than riding along with you smelling like Joan d'Arc." I went over and sat next to her in the sunlight, with her blanket wrapped around me, "We go down into Novara at nightfall," she said.

Then she rested her head on my shoulder and a lock of her long hair draped across my chest.

"What was the name of that village where you grew up?"

"I didn't grow up there," she said, and pushed the hair back out of her face, without lifting her head from my shoulder. "I spent the summers there, some years, when my father was too busy in the courts."

"But what is it called?"

"Castellnotte."

"Will you take me there?"

She sat up, drawing her legs up and wrapping her arms around them in a hug. With a toss of her head, the long hair fell down past the middle of her back. "Soon," she said. "Next, after Novara, then Tortorici, Randazzo. Then we'll come there."

"Will your father still be there? I would like to meet him."

She sat up straight, her head erect on her long neck, a frown of disbelief on her face. There was a long silence, while we both began to figure many things out. "You already know him," she said.

"I do?"

"My father is the man you call Sole. Lombardo Crisianna."

"Sole?" I said.

She nodded.

"The Sole who sent you off with Pilo's letter?"

"Rubiolo's letter," she corrected me, and reminding me that we needed to use their underground names, even though she had just revealed her father's name to me.

"But you were sitting by him at . . ." I stopped there, in order not to embarrass myself any further.

Rafaella was quiet for a moment, and then she began to laugh. "You mean you thought Father was my . . ." This time

77

she could say no more, and she just laughed and laughed at me to fill out the rest of the words. I saw, then, that those sparkling gray eyes of hers were the same as the stark eyes in Lombardo's sharp gaze.

After a moment, I said simply, "I am happy."

Rafaella put her arms around me, her forehead on the point of my shoulder, and as she laughed her long black hair draped around me, and she hugged me tight.

"Time to go, miei ragazzi," Pilo's voice came drifting down the gully, and Rafaella and I looked up. The sound of the rushing water covered his every step. He was standing up above us in the brush, gathering up all the sun-dried clothes.

Pilo said no more than that, but in seconds Rafaella had slipped on her shoes, stood and climbed back up to the horses and to Corrao. She never looked back at me but it was not that she was embarrassed. She was simply back to the great work that lies ahead of us. I will have to wait. We will have to wait. History waits for no one.

As Pilo and I were climbing back up the hillside into the trees, he said, " I miss my Rosetta, Burtoni."

"Who is Rosetta, Count?"

"La donna mia," he said, and his steps seemed to slow and wander a bit in the volcanic gravel. "Mia carissima, Burtoni. She is back in Genova, and someday I hope to join her there, when all of this is over. When it is all accomplished, I will join her in Italia. Not in Savoia or Piedmonte or Liguria, or hiding in Switzerland again. I will join her in Italia."

Not once, in all the many weeks we've spent together now, have I ever heard Rosalino Pilo speak of anyone, let alone of anyone special, any Rosetta. So what he said now was a complete surprise. And it drew us closer together too, as comrades, as brothers.

"Someday," he said, hugging the bundle of dry and clean clothes warmed by the sun. "My Rosetta and I, we will live together, in a free land. And then maybe, my friend," he looked over at me with a warmth that was new. "Maybe you will come to visit us, Burtoni, from your Sicilian village. From your free Sicilia. With your carissima, no?" And he grinned at me with a wink. "She is a beautiful girl, Burtoni," he said, "and she has a great heart. You have chosen well."

I said something, I don't even remember now what I said exactly. I tried to laugh it off, I guess. But all the while I was remembering the hug of Rafaella's arms around my shoulders, and I dreamed of mountaintop villages above the sea. Of this place called Castellnotte, of which she speaks.

I dream and I remember it all now.

12.

16 April
Novara di Sicilia

We rode down into town last night in the dark, and we spent the few hours just before dawn posting our handwritten signs on all the walls. They are written in Sicilian by Rosalino, so I can't make most of it out. But I can make out the broad print at the top, proclaiming that the General is on his way. The General and his army.

In a little piazza below the village church, with a rise of ten stairs up to the wooden doors of this little duomo, Count Rosalino Pilo lined us up. He stood at the top of the stairs and Corrao and I stood a few steps lower, at attention. Two steps lower still, between us, we stacked five of the muskets, their bayonets fixed, and we rested them up like a haystack, the points of those new bayonets reaching for the blue Sicilian sky. And then, to finish the effect, one step beneath the muskets Pilo had us scatter a few handfuls of shot, and an open crate of grenades, to make it seem we had ammunition to waste.

Pilo was wearing his saber in its scabbard, his long hair swept back on his shoulders, and with the façade of the church behind us, and all of these weapons at his feet, with Corrao and me at stern attention, he did look tall and fierce. Even if he was short and slight and pale, he stood like a prince up there looking down at the little square.

It was Rafaella's job to gather up the Novarani as they slowly awoke to their day. She wandered around the square, and into some of the side streets, and she knocked on doors and windows. She pointed at the hand-lettered bills we'd posted in the dark. There may have been some scowls and grumbling at first, but I must admit, one look into Rafaella's sweet face, and all the grumbling stopped. It is partly her beauty, but it is also the intensity and the truth in her eyes. I know that I will follow her where ever she leads. But this magic of hers seems to hold many others under its spell.

Once there were a dozen or so people gathered before the steps, Pilo began to speak. He used Sicilian, and for these people this means everything. Their guttural, clipped language with its softening 'oo's' to rhyme the words reaches deep into their hearts in ways I can only guess at, and it means I can only guess at exactly what Count Pilo was saying. But I could hear enough to know that he was promising them the General. Il

Generale is coming, with an army of thousands, and if they stand forth now, their land will be free. They will be free.

While Pilo was speaking, a thin short priest poked his head out of the church. The look on his face said simply, 'Who is stirring up trouble, here on the church steps, when my people should be coming to mass.' But then he seemed to listen, and I saw real fear in his eyes, and he just as quietly disappeared back inside his church. If Rosalino Pilo even saw him, he never let on.

The crowd was silent though. They listened carefully, and never even spoke among themselves. After about half an hour, Pilo said to Corrao and me, "Collect the muskets, boys. Let's go."

It seemed to me we had failed. Pilo walked down into his little congregation, and there was then a lot of whispered and urgent conversation. Some of the Novarani wandered up the stairs past us and went into the church, though mostly they were the women. Giovanni and I gathered up the arms and the open crate, and then carefully collected the artfully strewn ammunition, every priceless piece of it, and carried it all off to the horses we'd ridden in on. Rafaella had disappeared somewhere.

When we came back, the piazza was nearly empty, along with all my hopes, and I noticed, glancing around the square, that every one of our handbills was gone. They had vanished into someone's hands. Completely stripped away, like some hidden shame. 'And this is where we came to begin the revolution,' I thought.

After that, Rafaella led us down one of the streets, I won't record here which one and I won't now write down any names. It is too dangerous, I realize now, in a town like this, if this journal should fall into the wrong hands, into the hands of someone we can't trust. Spies are everywhere. I must always remind myself of this.

So we walked down the narrow street and Rafaella led us to some friends of hers who quietly fed us and showed us to a few beds where we could rest in the warm afternoon. There was only one strange thing, and this I will put down. The priest came later, and he ate with us and he blessed our food. I don't know what this means, or whose side he is on, but I am suspicious. To many of these men wearing collars can't be trusted. And he may be one of them.

So it has been a long journey, and a long ride to get here, only to find this failure. Only to hide in some stranger's house, and eat with the town priest. The Novarani, with their fear and their paralysis, their lack of will and courage. It all makes me think of the General on his island, and I understand now why he wants to stay there. Why he waits.

But as we try to sleep out of the afternoon sun, Rosalino Pilo is writing letters again, to leave here to be posted. One of them, I see, is long and written to his Rosetta. But the other, it is very brief. It just tells lies to the General, I'm sure. Lies that will lead him into war. Our war. Our imagined war.

If it weren't that I found Rafaella here, I fear all would be lost. Today, everything is a waste. Except there is now for me Rafaella.

13.

17 April
near Tortorici

Our ride was long, all through the night on rugged mountain trails, then in the morning we entered the next village, Tortorici, it was called. Rafaella leads us to the towns we need to reach, the towns ready to head our call. And today there are ten of us.

You see, yesterday I was wrong. Because there was no shouting, no marching in the streets, no taking up arms and waving them in the air, because the Novarani were so quiet and calm as they listened to Count Pilo speak, so I thought all was lost. But Rafaella Crisiana was right, after all.

We got up late after night had fallen, ate a heavy pasta soaked in oil with a plain red wine, took the bread and olives and fruit they gave us, and the four of us rode out of town. At the edge of the village seven men met us. Six of them were on horseback, and the little priest was there on foot. Four of the Novarani brought muskets with them, the fifth hand an old cutlass, and the sixth one called Gaetano was carrying just a hatchet in his hands. But they all to a man came armed.

Then the priest blessed us, for whatever that is worth. But I still don't trust him, or his kind. I've seen too many of them now, to trust any of them from the first, though they seem different down here in the South, in Sicily.

And yet, now we are ten, and we are gazing down in the first morning light on the next little town Rafaella has found for us. She seems to know just where we should go. And

Count Pilo, he's not really grinning, but he sits astride that horse like a proud general, now, his hair streaming back in the breeze like a lion, because he is making his lies come true.

14.

20 April
Randazzo

Too busy now to write. We have ridden hard these last days, and the Nebrodi are hard, rugged mountains to cross, and harder still to cross in the dark. There are so many streams with torrents running fast and full of the late spring waters, and it would be easy with a slip or a fall to lose a horse along here. Rafaella directs us, but she no longer leads the way. It is too dangerous in the dark. One of the local men always leads the way now, sometimes on foot, and they wind us through the oak and maple groves and around the streams where we would most certainly be lost without them. We stop each morning at a different town, and as it was with the Novarani, each evening we leave with more men. Alcara Li Fosi. Cesaro. Today Randazzo.

We are now twenty-five strong. So when this morning we lined up in front of the little duomo, there are few weapons to stack up on the stairs. Instead now there are columns of men, rag tag but fierce, and now there are shouts and cheers when Pilo speaks. No more the worried silences. No more the furrowed brows and closed mouths. No more the furtive glances around the piazza. Our numbers have loosed our tongues.

I understand too how it all works. Each morning, as we arrive in a village, Rafaella moves about in the soft dawn light and posts our broadsides on the walls of the main piazza. This is so that the awakening contadini understand, when they see us armed and arranged before their church. Those who can read pass the word quickly. We are not a band of brigands, though this must certainly be what we look like. And we are not the hated Neapolitans, not the Bourbon horde. We have not come to take or to demand or to steal. We have come to ask for their help, for help on the pathways to their own freedom.

So then Count Pilo makes his speech, with his growing squadron at his feet, and at the end we brandish our arms, and we all shout, "Viva Sicilia!" and "Liberta!"

And yes, we are now a squadron, and soon perhaps we will even be a brigade. We grow and grow with each passing day.

After the last shout of "Liberta!" the men break up to be fed and to sleep, for still we travel only at night. But now we don't need to demand or even ask for supplies, for at every village the people take us in. We are fed, simply but well, and our animals are cared for.

And while we are resting, Rafaella walks back to the piazza and carefully takes down each one of those posted sheets, rolls them up and packs them away. Remember, they are handwritten, by Count Rosalino himself. It was Rafaella and Rosalino made them together, back in the hills above Messina before we set out. Written in proper Sicilian, they aren't being torn down or hidden, as I thought they were. No, they are too valuable to be wasted. So she gathers them all back up, and tucks them safely away until the next village is in oursight.

*   *   *

Tomorrow, I believe, we reach Castellnotte. It is Rafaella's old home. And it is half the way to Palermo, or close to that.

Again Rosalino Pilo writes a letter, to be left and posted to the General, as we make our way on toward the capitol. Corrao often laughs at him, making fun of Pilo's little tre colore lies. But that is just Corrao's way. In truth, he likes a lie, especially when it works.

15.

23 April
near Mistrette

The squadron has grown to over fifty now. It is becoming hard to keep track of us all, and harder still to feed us when we descend upon the next little village. It takes all their resources, and more. Still we never need to ask for food or for places to sleep. But everyone who joins us now must bring his own weapon, and this has begun to be a problem. The people here are poor, too poor to give up the one gun they have in a household that needs it to hunt for their sustenance. It is too great a sacrifice, too precious a tool, to irreplaceable to lose. But still they keep joining us. Even if they are

86

barehanded, they come.   They swear, some of them, they will fight with bare fists. They follow us, more and more of them, each night. More.

16.

24 April

The little village of Castellnotte sits on a high hillside and gazes down from those heights to the sea. If you walk out from the Chiesa Santa Lucia and its little piazza you come to a short stone wall, perhaps 2 feet high, and from there descends a staircase about ten feet wide, switching back and forth down the rock face, it leads down the steep rock walls to the shore.

When everything was quiet, in the sleepy afternoon, Rafaella took my hand and said, "I want you to see something, my Burtoni." And so she led me down those stairs in the white sea light, all the way down to the rocky shoreline, a hundred long steps or more, back and forth on the switches.   And all along the way down, she kept pointing at islands far out in the sea. "Watch how they disappear, how the horizon rises as we come down," she said, and she kept a firm hold on my hand.

I thought that the turquoise blue water and creamy white peaks of its waves on the rose gray stones of the shoreline were what she wanted to show me, or maybe it was something about those disappearing islands out on the ocean that was her point, for we nearly ran down the stairs, and all the way she kept her tight grip on my hand. But I was wrong, for the very moment we reached the waterline, she wrapped her arms around me and turned me back toward the village above, and in that shining light I saw what she wanted me to see.

You see, every single one of those hundred and more steps was trimmed around its entire edge with small ceramic tiles. As I gazed up from the rocky beach, I saw a pathway that ascended from the seashore up to the face of the church, and each and every step glistened with the blue of the Mediterranean and the yellow of the lemons and a especially with a startlingly pure white of their hearts. Here and there you see splashes and hints of the red a royal cardinal wears. But all of it is surrounded in their pure shining white.

"It's beautiful, isn't it?" Rafaella said.

She still held me tight, and my arms were wrapped in the strength of her hug, so that I couldn't hold her the way I wanted to embrace her. The stairs led my eyes up with all their colors until they reached to the graceful arch of the portico of Santa Lucia, and from this distance it was as blue as the clear Sicilian sky, and glowing white with touches of orange and red. It, too, is one great ceramic tile, all of them painted by hand by the artists of Castellnotte. High above the church, framing it all, stood the gray stone fortification of La Rocca. There lay the castle where the English duke and his family lived. And all of this, together, is beautiful Castellnotte.

Suddenly Rafaella kissed me on the cheek and let me go. Then she took my hand and began leading me back up the stairs, but now we stopped for a moment at almost every step to admire the paintings on the tiles. I could see that each step took a different subject, and every little six-inch square of majolica was carefully painted. There was a step of tulips in red and yellows and oranges, with lime green stems. There was a step of blue green fish, and the next above a step of decorated fishing boats, all of them in a rainbow of shades. There was a step of red purple grapes, and one of lemons, and one of little tangerines and blood red oranges like Rafaella had eaten the night we met.

"This is one of my favorites," she said, and sat down on the stair with her legs curled up alongside her so I could see. "These are the fishermen, see all their brown faces."

It is surprising how, as I gazed down the stairway, they seem just plain and normal stones from above. All of the majolica is hidden from your eyes when you look down except for an occasional hint of color, like a tiny wildflower in a crack. But once you turn and look up, toward the village, toward the church of Santa Lucia, it all becomes a riot of crazy hues framed in sharp, stark white.

Behind Rafaella, on the step above the fishermen, the row of tiles were all tiny women's faces, with bright smiling red lips and almond eyes feathered with black lashes like waves. I sat down on the step next to her, and a horrible awkward silence fell over both of us. I took her hands in mine and I gazed in her eyes, as sweet and almond-shaped as the faces surrounding her on the tiles. But then I glanced away, and my heart was pounding again, and my mind was empty of words, as dry as my mouth. Here I was, having chased the women of Montevideo and Nizza and Genova around and around, and with at least a bit of success. But now I was as dumb and speechless as a boy.

"What is it?" she said, with her red smiling lips and her dark black eyes. And she said, "What do you want to say? Burtoni?"

I stared out at the sea to try to find some of the words that were singing in my heart, filled with confusion and fears, not just the blood and passion of my years, but then she simply whispered the words that I was searching for. "Burtoni," Rafaella said. "I am yours."

She gazed fearlessly into me, with the same courage that has led this whole squadron here to Castellnotte. "You know that, don't you?" she said.

I nodded yes, but still I was mute and stupid. She smiled at me, and then she laughed and tossed her head so her long hair furled back and her lips parted, and she was more beautiful than all the tiny painted beauties surrounding her on the stair. Then she said, "Burtoni? Don't you have something to say to me?"

My face grew hot and my stupid tongue was still parched and dead. Then somehow, I blurted out, "My heart is yours alone, Rafaella." Then without thinking, I added, "Forever."

How can I tell her what that means? How do I explain to her my strange affliction? Why? Why did I say that word? For me, "Forever" is so very long a time. I can't even say how long a time, for I don't know. How dare I speak that word, ever? How dare I? I am a freak. I have no right to speak to her in such a way. Forever? The damnation of Forever.

But Rafaella does not notice my turmoil, or she takes it to be just bashfulness. So she leaned forward, and she took my silly face in her two hands and kissed me on the lips. And then, before I could really respond, she leapt up and scurried ahead of me up the stairs. Two at a time she leapt over them, the sunflowers and the sailing ships, the olive trees and the shepherdesses, the angels and the mariners, and so many more above us on our path.

She never stopped running until she reached the piazza above. She didn't pause to gaze down at another stair, until I caught her finally, both of us laughing, right at the door of the church. I wrapped my arms around her then, and held her tight, and she seemed so tiny in my embrace. "Someday," I said to her, "When all this is over . . . "

But Rafaella's gaze drew my eyes up to the large majolica in the façade crowning the church door. It held a pale sky blue, ten feet across, and the dark haired figure of the Saint stood there alone, with wafts of brown and green Sicilian landscape behind her. It was the image of that Saint that made me quiet.

She was beautiful, dressed in billowing rose and white, her hair black and flowing around the almond of her face, with startlingly blue eyes gazing gently down at us, all sinners at her feet. Her hands were folded peacefully in prayer, and like this little village, she seemed quiet and distant from every trouble, and lovely almost beyond compare.

But there in the crease of her neck, beneath her placid, restful face, beneath her benevolent gaze, a dagger was thrust into the martyr's neck, and from it a medallion of ruby red blood dripped down onto her breast, frightening in that bare brilliant red surrounded by a world that seemed made of peaceful rose and heaven blue and purest white. This image was so startling that my words, right as I spoke, drifted off into meaninglessness. I couldn't finish this thought of 'someday.' Someday. We both fell silent, though I realized then that Rafaella had brought me here to see just that, to see this troubling Saint. "Who is she?" I said, after a moment.

"Santa Lucia," she said. And then, "Isn't she beautiful?"

Before I could answer in any way, Rafaella grabbed my hands again and, like a child, she cried, "Come on! I want you to meet the Duke." And so we began to run again up out of the piazza toward La Rocca, the barren castle standing above is. "Oh, and the Duchess too," she said, a laughing afterthought.

Rosalino Pilo has paused here in the mountains near Mistrette, because our force of men needs to get organized. There are so many of us now, he has divided our squadron into two. He leads one, and Captain Corrao the other. So yes, he is Captain Giovanni Corrao now.

Perhaps Rosalino could have made us into three squadrons, and given me a lead. But I think that my apparent youth deceives him. He thinks I'm just a boy, a wild lad, which means he hasn't stopped to count all the years that led him to me. He is not thinking about Anzani, or the flight from Morrazone. If he did, he would know that my looks betray me. I am no boy. And if he can count, he would know that. But Rosalino Pilo in the end, I guess, doesn't care. My looks deceive him. And two squadrons we are.

But then, I did disappear yesterday with Rafaella, for the whole afternoon and we did not report back to Captain Pilo until this morning. So perhaps that is it. Rosalino only smiled at me, when I reported back in the morning. He gave me that look, just like he did when he was talking about his Rosetta back in the hills above Novara.

And maybe he is right. Maybe I am too in love, too head over heels, to be trusted to lead a squadron into war. Recklessness in love does not lead to wisdom in battle. He knows this, as do I. "Burtoni, you take care of the horses for me, lad, and then just be sure your musket is clean," he ordered. And then he said, "Corrao and I will be drilling these new recruits all afternoon. We've got to make some real soldiers out of them, before we reach Palermo. And before the General arrives."

Before I could ask, 'Have you heard? Is he coming?' Count Pilo grinned and ordered, "After you are done, take the afternoon off. Go find your girl, lad. Go on. Time is short."

But my Rafaella is busy doing something for the Duchess. And that is why I have time now to write this all down here, in all this great detail. I have time to think alone now, and to prepare for the battle ahead. If I choose.

Lord Burmonte, the Duke of Castellnotte, opened the door himself. He is a tall, lean man with a military bearing, clean-shaven and with his steely grey hair close cropped. He seemed a bit distracted, preoccupied with some worrisome business, until his gaze passed over me and lighted on Rafaella Crisiana. Then his mouth dropped open before it spread into a broad, winning smile.

"My girl," he said in amazement, and Rafaella nearly leapt into his open armed embrace. Then he held her by the shoulders and gazed at her at arm's length, smiling and shaking his head now in disbelief. He didn't know what to say, but he seemed to know enough not to ask questions about what brought her here. "And who is this?" he asked her, smiling now at me, and offering a firm handshake. His Italian was awkward and formal, but accurate.

"Jack Burton," Rafaella said my name, in that way of hers that makes it sound so foreign. Then she said, grinning widely at me before she spoke, "Mio fidanzato."

"Ahh!" said the old Duke, his eyebrows arching up. "Welcome to Castellnotte, Jack Burton," he said all in flat, plain English.

I was still taken a little by surprise at Rafaella's announcement, but I shook the Duke's hand and managed to say, in Italian, "Here they call me Burtoni, sir."

"Burtoni," the Duke said. "Burtoni it is. Come in, my boy. Come in." Rafaella was already through the doorway.

"I must call Lady Eleanor," the Duke said. "She will be so surprised to see you, dear Rafaella, and to hear your news. Gaetano?" he called out.

A Sicilian boy, in his early teens, scurried out from inside wearing an outrageously stiff and ill-fitting suit. "Gaetano, tell the Duchess we have some surprise guests." The Duke wheeled around to look at us again, as Gaetano disappeared somewhere back into the rooms of the castle. "Mia carina," he said smiling, his head dropping a little to lean toward her. "And her caro fidanzato. You have grown up so quickly, carina!"

Lady Eleanor Burmonte, the Duchess of Castellnotte, met us in a grand room, with frescoed ceilings twelve feet high and an eight-foot fireplace with a decorated mantle that reached nearly to that ceiling. She is shorter and rounder that the Duke, but just as gray. Like the Duke, there is an orderliness about her and she stands straight and stiff, which didn't keep the room from dwarfing her. She seemed both more surprised and less delighted to see us than the Duke. "Why, little Rafaella Crisiana, what brings you back to Castellnotte? How is your dear father Lombardo? What is he up to these days?"

We were still very careful to keep our secrets, so we didn't answer any of her questions. The Duke leapt however straight into the opening our silence left without a second thought. "And this, Eleanor," he said with an arm out toward me, speaking in English again, "is Jack Burton."

"Really," said the Duchess.

I stepped forward, awkwardly, and stuck out my hand to shake hers. But the Duchess just moved her hand toward me, hanging from a limp wrist, and too high in the air to shake. Rafaella started to giggle at this awkward moment, me with my paw stuck out frankly toward her and Lady Eleanor with her dangling hand in my face, and then at long last I realized I was supposed to kiss her hand. Since I've always spent most of my time around the docks or in the army, this is something I've never done before, and trust me, it was tough for me not to chuckle at myself when I heard Rafaella's giggles.

But the Duke, he is a clever old dog, and perceptive as a ship's cat. He swooped over in one move and had one arm around my shoulder and the other around the Duchess. "Signor Burtoni, Eleanor, is our Rafaella's intended."

"Really," said the Duchess again. And as her arm dropped to her side, she took a new look at me, as if to appraise the property more carefully. Then she looked over again at Rafaella and smiled. Remember, we have been living on horseback in these same clothes for better than a week since Rafaella washed out the remains of Jean d'Arc from them. And Rafaella is in trousers nearly the same as mine, and nothing even near to a dress, certainly no dress like the Duchess was wearing, with lace edging that brushes against the spotless marble floors. But I guess from the way she reacted, the Duchess like the Duke had seen Rafaella in pants before.

"Congratulations, Rafaella," the Duchess said. "And you too, Mister Burton."

"Burtoni is fine, ma'am," I said at the same time as the Duke said, "Signor Burtoni, Eleanor."

And so we all laughed, and it lightened the air in general, at least as much as I can ever expect from this Duchess of Castellnotte, I suspect.

Then the Duchess nodded her head curtly at me, and said, in Italian finally, "Signor Burtoni, can you and your fidanzata stay to dinner?"

I was still getting used to hearing that word, and I had to stop myself from asking like a fool, 'Who?' And it was all so confusing, and in too many languages. I fell back into my American English, of a sort. "Yup," I said, sounding like a peasant to these British ears.

That made us all laugh again.

It may have been a poor countryside, but you'd never know it by that table the Duke and Duchess placed before us. The evening started with platters of olives and crusty bread from a wood-fired oven, along with a white buttery cheese coated with fennel seeds and covered with the pale green olive oil from the estate of Castellnotte. We drank fruity white wine along with this, and the Duchess busily directed "the staff" from her end of the long table, while the Duke proudly described the olives and the oil and what parts of his estate they came from.

I thought this would be the whole meal, so I dug in heartily. I really couldn't conceive of what was to come. Not after weeks of sea voyaging and horseback travel through backcountry, I couldn't.

Gaetano led the way, but there must have been a dozen or more young ladies and lads who waited on us, bringing in the food in shifts and then sweeping away our dirty plates, and always filling our wine glasses. Next they brought out small plates with tagliatelle in the same oil, coated like a snowfall with some white salty cheese. Then came a glass of a hardy simple red wine, and that was still only for starters. For the main meal, at last, slices of duck breast arrived in a sauce of sweet orange and vinegar. And remember, this was all unplanned. Rafaella had just dropped in out of the heavens on them.

While we were eating the tagliatelle, the Duchess called Gaetano over to her place at the table, and whispered but one word to him. "Spada," she said quietly, so neither the Duke nor Rafaella heard, as they were talking. And so then out came another small side plate, with grilled slices of eggplant, and on each plate there was a thin slice of swordfish, rolled with eggplant and ham and grilled through, the whole of it drizzled in the rich oil flecked with green bits of olive.

Rafaella squealed with delight and laughed out loud when she saw the swordfish arrive. "Involtini!" she squealed. And that made the Duchess laugh too, smiling fondly at her.

"This was our little Rafaella's favorite," the Duke explained to me. "When she lived here at Castellnotte."

The wine was going a bit to my head by now, I have to admit. I have never in all my years eaten like this, and we were far from done. The children brought out tumblers of cool spring water then and little platters with thinly sliced fennel sprinkled with raisins and drizzled again with that rich oil. As we nibbled on it with our fingers, I realized it was meant to clear away the heavy taste of the duck and the richness of the buttery swordfish. For at the end, out came little cakes seasoned with fennel seeds and orange and accompanied with a tiny stemmed glass of a brown, bittersweet liquor scented with almonds.

By this point, I was as full as I've ever been, and my head was spinning with all the wine and liquor. A grand sense of contentment billowed up from deep in my heart, and I understood at the end of this magical day what it is about

Castellnotte that makes it all so enchanting to Rafaella. Castellnotte is not part of our everyday world. No, it is alone, and separate, and it is magic, indeed. It is a land of dreams.

Almost all of our talk at the table was about the food, and the Duke in particular revelled in describing the delicacies of each course. But Rafaella too kept telling me about where this wine or that eggplant and these sweet fennel bulbs came from all around Castellnotte. During that long, wondrous meal, there was only once a sour moment. While we were eating the rich duck breast, Rafaella held up her glass of red wine and said, "My father planted these grapes before I was born."

"Long before you were born, my dear one," the Duke of Brumonte said, with a warm smile. "It was Lombardo and your Grandfather Rafaello who put them in the ground, back when Lombardo was just a wee little lad. Long before Eleanor and I came to Castellnotte. But here we sit, enjoying the fruits of old Rafaello's artistry and his labor, with you my carina Rafaella, his granddaughter. "

"And our granddaughter too," the Duchess added, along with her own sweet smile.

"Grandfather loved these grapes," Rafaella said.

Then the Duchess spoke from her end of the table, and a sudden frigidness that was peculiar came over her. "And how is Lombardo?" she asked one more time. " We haven't heard from him for a long, long while now."

There was an awkward moment of silence, and the Duke glanced at me as the Duchess's and Rafaella's eyes met across the loaded table. "He is well," Rafaella answered, not saying much at all.

"And his law practice there," The Duke leapt in to ward off anymore of the awkward silences, "it is doing well too?"

"Well" said the Duchess, ignoring her husband's question, "we do miss Lombardo here. This place was never so well run as when he ran it."

"That was years ago," Rafaella said, sounding as cool now as the Duchess.

"Nearly twenty years ago," the Duchess added precisely.

"He was most remarkable at managing this estate, I must say," the Duke nodded along. "We took it over, you know, Signor Burtoni, not long after his father died. And the two of them, Rafaello and Lombardo, they had built up Castellnotte to what we are enjoying tonight. Without Lombardo and his father Rafaello this place would be just a run down mess. But they made it into an estate."

"And what is he doing now in Messina?" the Duchess interrupted.

Rafaella glanced at me as if to remind me to keep still, but I didn't need to be reminded, and she saw that immediately. "He has his law practice," she answered the Duchess vaguely, but stared at me the whole while.

"And is he still mixed up with these country ruffians and their revolutions?" the Duchess asked.

That was when the real, heavy silence fell across the table. Rafaella turned an iron gaze on the Duchess, and didn't answer. I sat there awkwardly for a moment, and I felt my temper rising. These English nobles with their high ways were not about to insult my Rafaella. So it was going to be difficult for me to keep my mouth shut.

The Duke, whose glance flitted back and forth among the three of us, appraising each one of us, calmly changed the subject. "So, have you chosen a day for the wedding, carina?"

At that, Rafaella let a smile drift slowly onto her lips, a miracle it was, and she followed the Duke's lead. Grinning, she looked over at me across the table and said, "Sort of. But not exactly."

"And what does that mean?" the Duke of Brumonte laughed.

Both Rafaella and I were remembering my pledge on the majolica stairs: 'Someday, when all of this is over . . .'

"It means we know when," I said as I smiled back at her, at my fidanzata, "so we don't really have a date yet."

I said those words without fear or worry, with only a great lightness in my heart. Maybe it was easy because there was no date to be set. And maybe I had no date to be set. And maybe I had no fears because there is so much to be afraid of between now and that someday. It is easier to imagine myself winding up hanging from some Bourbon gallows, or lingering away on some desert island prison built of the hardest stone, than it is to imagine that 'someday' we spoke of, no, that 'someday 'we both dream of.

Yet I don't think that is it. You see, a deep commitment has lodged down in my heart and I have found a partner for my soul in this tangled, ugly world. With her I will fly always, but never away. She is too filled with courage. And so these words are easy and fearless for me. They arise in my heart gently and with boundless joy.

The iciness of that moment passed quickly, and we did not speak again of Lombardo or of rebellions. The Duke and the Duchess never asked how we had come there or where we were headed. As if in silent agreement, those questions never arose, and Rafaella and I never spoke of them before Lord Brumonte and Lady Eleanor.

Suddenly, the Duchess sat up straight and over that strong almond liquor, she suddenly proposed, "Would you like to have the wedding here, child?"

The Duke sprang to life at those words as well. "What a wonderful idea!" he exclaimed. "It would be such a celebration, and Eleanor and I would just love to help get you two launched properly. The way you deserve, mia carina."

I could see that Rafaella like the idea, her gray eyes brightened to a soft sea green, but she looked over at me and paused. At that moment, I assumed she was looking at me for approval, and how could I turn her down. Especially with my head full of wine, capped off by that sneaky sweet liquor.

"I think this is a fine idea," I spouted up, letting all the grapes talk.

But the moment I spoke out, my Rafaella looked down at the table, and she surprised me again. "I suppose we could," she said, without looking up at any of us.

"Oh, it would be wonderful, " the Duke slapped his hands together, and then rubbed them happily as if he were ready to get to work.

And the Duchess, I thought for a moment she was going to jump up and call to the servants and commence with the decorating right then and there. "You know, Rafaella, the giardino d'arancia in the courtyard would be perfect, especially in the spring when the fruit is so full. But next fall too, when they begin to blossom. Then it would be perfect for a wedding."

Rafaella raised her head at the mention of this garden. "The orange grove," she whispered toward me, and then gazing in my eyes, she said, "I suppose we could, if it is what you want."

"If it is what you want," I said, and reached across the corner of the table to take her hand.

"If it is what you both would like," said the Duke. And then he added, "Wonderful."

And he made us all laugh at that.

I spent that night sleeping in a billowy soft feather bed, softer than any bed I've ever known. The Duke winked at me, and then he and the Duchess swept Rafaella away safely, deep within the complicated, stone hallways of La Rocca. It took a long while for me to fall asleep that night, my excitement was jumbled and confused by all I have seen and heard and learned on this amazing day, this miraculous day that has changed the whole of my life. An old jaded cuss like me, swept away by the drink and by the twinkle in a young girl's eye. But in the end the wine and the twinkle did their trick, and my head drifted away without any protest down into the deep, fluffy pillows.

Still it was early, before first light, when I awoke, still a bit groggy and not really rested, but now unable to sleep. The effects of all the alcohol had worn away and left me tired but awake and sleepless. I listened as the birds awakened and began to sing. And then I realized it was time for us to leave this dreamy, easy existence. Count Rosalino Pilo and his two squadrons were awaiting us, waiting to press on toward Palermo. And they would need Rafaella and me to arouse the sleeping giant of Caprera. So it was time to leave the lantern lights and the long full tables and the shining majolica colors of Castellnotte.

She arrived at my door as the early light poured in the windows. Rafaella was dressed again for the road, just as I was. The dust of the Nebrodi foothills was on our boots. The call of our duty has returned, like the worn off wine, and we made ready to depart. It was clear to me, though I'm not sure why, that Rafaella wanted to slip away before the Duke and Duchess awoke.

She led me silently down a back hallway and downstairs through the servants' quarters. Already the children who work in the castle were up and moving about, quietly working in the depths of La Rocca.

Rafaella put one finger to her lips to keep me silent, and then she opened a dark green wooden shutter so I could look out onto the courtyard. She didn't need to explain what it was that she was showing me, or why she wanted me to see it. Slabs of pink streaked marble cut into a octagons and then fit into a pattern that radiated out like sunlight from the center and stretched under the arches around the little courtyard. Each stone was edged with a lively green border of something as old and mossy as the castle. Dead center in the courtyard stood a short ancient tree, surrounded with a stone hexagonal bench that echoed the shapes of the flooring stones. And all around the periphery of the courtyard were similar old dwarf trees, maybe at most ten feet high. Eight of them, like the eight sides to the cut pieces of marble. And they were all filled with round bright oranges, and here and there the fruit had ripened and fallen onto the marble stones. Tiny birds were flitting about and just beginning to sing in the early light. This, I know in my heart in a moment, is the giardino d'arancia.

I smiled and nodded my head to show her that I understood and approved. This little orchard will be a wonderful place to be married, to be joined forever. And I didn't allow myself to think about what forever meant.

That was when Gaetano appeared, and he led us down more stairs and out into the stables, where two fresh horses awaited us. Not the Jean d'Arc and the old nag we had ridden to Castellnotte. Gaetano took my hand, and he held my shoulder in his other hand and said in a whisper, "I would join you. But I must feed my mother and my two little sisters. So for now, my friends, only my heart goes out from here with you. Take my courage at your side, sir."

Then he gave Rafaella a hard long hug, the embrace of a deep old familial love. I understood from that embrace that they had worked together here, when Gaetano must have been just a child. I noticed then that a younger boy and two girls stood back in the shadows of the stable. We mounted up on these fine fresh horses, and then Gaetano said, "When the time comes, we will be with you." And he gave my horse a gentle slap. The other young servants opened a gate for us and out we rode into the gentle morning light.

Rafaella led us down out of the village and then up into the high hills where the squadrons of Pilo were waiting. When we were out of sight of the castle, I called out to her and for a moment we slowed our horses to a walk.

"It is beautiful," I said to her, "Castellnotte."

She just smiled and nodded in agreement.

"But, Rafaella, why did you hesitate? Isn't that orange grove where we should be married?"

She looked away at the woods, the same way she had looked down at the table last night, when the Duchess proposed the garden. A sudden shadow passed over us, and then she said without ever looking back at me, "Yes,

Castellnotte is where we should be married." She paused and then looked at me again. "That garden would be wonderful."

I rode on a few more steps at a canter. Then I pulled my horse up to a stop. "What's wrong, Rafaella. What's bothering you, that you won't say?"

She let her horse step loosely over some stones, and she said then looking directly at me, "I don't know, Jack Burton, if my father will ever return here." At that, she gave the spur to her horse and I followed her off across the hillsides at a gallop, searching for the fires of the squadrons of the Count.

Giovanni Corrao met me with a scowl and a long silence when we returned. He looked Rafaella and me both over slowly, and then said only, "Fine horses." He turned and walked away.

Rosalino though, he was different. When I reported to him, hurrying to his side while Rafaella took care of the horses, Pilo was sitting on a large stone, pen in hand, writing another missive to the General, or another announcement that the General had arrived, I'm not sure which. He looked up at me, and a broad grin spread across his face. I expected him to say my name, from the way he looked up, and then follow that with a happy halloo. And then I was prepared to get on with it, to ask for my orders, under whose command I would serve. These were the words I prepared in my head, and I was ready to stand and serve them up. But Pilo stunned me with what he said.

He let out a little chuckle to accompany that broad smile of his, and then he said, nodding his head sagely, "That Rafaella, lad, she must be some kind of woman!"

17.

6 May
Piani dei Greci

We have reached the hills above the Conca d'Oro, and at night we look down now on the lights of Palermo. I have not written for days, for there are now more than 150 of us. Men are coming from the countryside and from the villages we've never even been near, for the word is out now. Everyone who arrives has heard, the General is coming. The revolt is not over, it has only just begun. "Piddu," they call him in their dialect here. Piddu will be landing soon, they say, bringing thousands of men from the north.

So now, you see, it is taking all our time, Pilo and Corrao and I, to try to keep some sort of order here. Some of these men, like the dozen picciotti from Corleone who arrived three days ago, they are already in gangs, already organized with leaders of their own, and these boys take even more watching. For they could get an idea in mind, and one of these gangs might run off and start some attack too soon, before we are ready. Wild as these hills they live in, they are.

It is easy to see why the revolts here have failed so many times in the past. There is a deep disorder here, and a fundamental distrust of everyone but your blood family. And even there, the disruption seems to be lurking just under the surface. But at the same time, there are generations and generations of rebellion and dissent here, and their hunger to throw off the oppressor is true and deep and firm. Amongst themselves at night by the fires they speak of the Normans, not these Bourbons who rule from Napoli. And they sing songs about the revolt of "I Vesperi" some 600 years ago. I can see it too in their stone faces, in the way they look at me as a stranger and wonder silently why I am here. Rebellion is deep down in their bones. As deep as their distrust.

But "Piddu" they trust. I don't know why, but their "Piddu" they trust, even though he comes from the north. Even though they've never seen him before, and wouldn't know him now if he strolled into our camps right now. But Piddu they trust.

18.

12 May
Piani die Greci

It has come true. Pilo's plan has worked.

We now count ourselves in the hundreds, and every day more picciotti pour into this camp that has become a village almost overnight. They come in gangs now, and they are loosely organized and everyone is armed with something, some hunting musket or an old pistol. I can tell that Corrao is excited by them, their billowing spirit charges him like horse under hard rein.

This morning just after dawn a rider arrived from the west coast. His winded horse came into the camp, he fell from the saddle and asked for Rubiolo. Because he had one of Pilo's many secret names on his lips, we brought him straight away to the Count.

I was awakened by the cheers and shouts rolling through the camp. "Piddu," they called and some other things in their language I couldn't understand. Rafaella was lying beside me, when they brought this boy into Rosalino. The men around him were practically holding him up.

"Rubiolo?" the boy said to Count Pilo, who was standing now in the tent. Pilo just nodded a curt and regal yes. At moments of quiet command like this, the nobility of his roots showed in his every move.

Then the boy spoke, the words of his dialect spilling out quickly, and all around him men began to shout and wave their guns in the air.

"He has landed in Marsala, and taken the city," Rafaella whispered in my ear. I held her tightly, but none of us made a sound. We waited for Pilo's reaction, while the shouts of "Piddu" and "Marsala" echoed through the camps. The guns began to be fired in the air, foolishly wasting the precious little ammunition we had.

Rosalino Pilo was calm, without even a smile crossing his lips. He looked over for just a moment at me, and I expected him to wink. But he was too controlled for even that. He just nodded his head at me. His plan had worked, by God. The sleeping giant of Caprera was awake now, and he was on the march.

Then Pilo looked at one of the picciotti waving his handgun around in the air, and ordered him sharply, "Put that away. Get this boy some wine, and something to eat."

Then he turned to Corrao and said, "Giovanni, get out there and remind these men that they are soldiers and not boys. They should be saving their bullets for the King of Naples."

With a nod, Corrao disappeared outside quickly and before long we all heard his deep voice shouting orders, drawing these Sicilians into their squadrons. Soon the night was silent again, broken by random cheers for "Piddu" rising spontaneously from out of the earth itself and only then, so it seemed, from the men.

While the boy ate, Pilo sat with him drinking a glass of wine and asking him calmly question after question. For most of Rosalino's queries the lad seemed to have no answer, or at best only vague information. In the end Pilo turned from the table and said to Rafaella, "Find me a rider who knows the way to Marsala. And one who knows all the back roads and byways, Crisiana. Not just the main route."

She left my side and began asking questions in Sicilian outside. In ten or fifteen minutes, she returned with one of the picciotti, a man in his twenties, dark and short. "He knows the way," she said to Pilo.

"What is your name?" Pilo asked, speaking in Sicilian.

"Michele."

"You speak Italian, boy?" he spoke in Italian, using the familiar "tu."

"Yes," the lad said.

"So please tell me, then, where are you from, Michele," Pilo barked, still speaking in Italian, but switching now to the formal 'you.'

"Calatafimi," the boy answered.

Pilo nodded, then he sat down and dashed off a quick letter to the General, and signed his name large and florid. When he was finished, he spoke again in his most formal Tuscan. "Take this missive from us to the General," Pilo said. Handing Michele the folded paper. "When you speak to him, tell him where we are and that we await his orders, and tell him we are more than 300 ready men."

"To Piddu?" the boy's eyes glowed with his excitement.

"Yes, to il Generale himself," Rosalino went on in his Tuscan. "And to no one else. Use the back ways that you know, Michele." As he stepped away, and the lad was still standing big eyed and not moving, Pilo turned back around and speaking in Sicilian again, ordered Him. "At once, to Piddu!"

"Avanti!" the lad shouted, to show off his Italian. "Presto! Avanti!" And then he was gone at a run.

19.

16 May
Piana die Greci

Until yesterday, we heard nothing but rumors. Rosalino kept us drilling in the fields, and he had us all cleaning and oiling our weapons. The General was coming, Piddu was near, and we were all anxious. Now was the time to be truly ready. The truth is at hand.

"It will be good to see him again," I said to Rafaella one night by the fire. And not without a little pride.

"He will remember you?" she said.

"He gave me my name!" I answered, showing off to her. "Burtoni?"

"No," I objected. "Il Rosso," I announced.

She can see through me, so easily. Rafaella just laughed at me, and called me, "John Burton," in a stiff English accent.

"Il Rosso," I said in reply. Then we both laughed.

But yesterday Michele returned with the grand news. He had ridden with Piddu up from Marsala into the interior of the island. On a rise outside his hometown the General and his thousand men had met the Bourbon army, and they had fought all day long, under the Sicilian sun. And in the end, as the darkness fell, the Bourbons had retreated from the fields of Calatafimi, back to Palermo. Piddu and the thousand had won the day. The Bourbon horde had marched out to meet them, thousands and thousands of them in the hills outside Michele's home, on the plain near Calatafimi. But the thousand in their red shirts had stood their ground, and repulsed the horde.

So now the revolution has surely begun, and with its first battles won.

Along with that news, Michele brought us orders from the General. The first we have followed already, we started immediately, tonight. The Red Shirts are coming to take Palermo, to drive the next horde of Bourbons out of the capitol. So our first task is to let the city know we are coming.

Corrao was the man who took charge, proudly. But the Count seemed to sit back and observe his friend with a smile. Corrao is the voice that speaks in Sicilian to the squadrons, but Rosalino Pilo is the leader, and the orders Corrao now speaks are coming through Pilo and from the General, from "Piddu."

Giovanni quickly gathered us into groups of 10 or 15, each little band with someone from a different local village, someone who knows the immediate area. We slipped off at dusk onto the various hillsides and then, as soon as it was dark, each band built a bonfire on a mountain promontory above the city and fanned it until it burned bright and tall.

"We will let Palermo know that the Red Shirts are coming," sang out Corrao. He raised both his arms in the air and shook his fists at the heavens. "Let them know we are here. Piddu has come!"

So it was that thirty or forty fires burned all across the mountainsides above the city. Maybe there were more, for I believe that some of the women and boys in the villages slipped off to the hills and lit signal fires too. But the mountains above Palermo tonight were speckled with light.

Corrao's orders said we should just light our fire and keep it burning until any police or guards drew near, and then we were to withdraw quickly back to the Piani. We were not to waste a shot.

Rafaella and I went out with a band led by a lad from Corleone, I'll call him Giulio after Caesar, though that is not his real name. He led us to a barren rocky bluff that gazed out over the Conca d'Oro, and we gathered wood and lit our fire. It took all ten of us to feed that blazing fire because it burned high and it burned bright all night long. And no one ever came. As sunlight broke over the edges of the sea, we abandoned the blaze to let it die down and we retreated to Piani dei Greci, following our orders.

When we returned, everyone was tired, because we'd all had the same experience. No sign of troops. No polizia. Our only fight was to keep the hungry fires burning bright the whole night long.

Tomorrow night we will return, Giulio and Rafaella and we all, we will keep the fires burning until Il Generale arrives.

20.

17 May
Piani dei Greci

Tonight there were fires down in the fringes of the city. I know that these were not our squadrons. These were the fires of the Palermitani, telling us they understand.

But one thing is different now. Those fires of the Palermitani do not last. They flare up here, and they flare up there. And always, before long, they disappear. I think the Bourbon patrols are busy dousing fires in the nighttime. And this is good, because it means that when we come, when Piddu arrives at last, they will be just as tired as we are. But more afraid.

I must write these things down. They have little or nothing to do with the great events growing all around us, I suppose, yet it was strange. I want to put down the odd talk and the funny behavior of my friend Giovanni Corrao in these hours as we wait to make history or to die. And maybe that is the explanation. Maybe Giovanni, like all of us, understands that he, that we, that none of us, may come out of the other side of this revolution alive. And so, sometimes the talk we make is strange, perhaps more important than it seems.

Yesterday morning, my Rafaella had fallen asleep while I as still awake. I find it hard sometimes, even when I am tired as the old paranza that brought us here, I can't sleep in the daylight. And so I left her sleeping and found a quiet spot under a tree and sat down to write in this journal about the lighting of the bonfires, and the fine news of the Battle of Calatafimi.

Most everyone is resting or asleep, and the field below me is scattered with men under their blankets napping or eating. From behind me somewhere, from somewhere in the rocky foothills, my friend Corrao crept up beside me. Maybe he was just trying to let everyone sleep, but he was so quiet he startled me as he sat down alongside me, and I finished the sentence I was writing and closed this book.

"Writing it all down again?" he said.

And I nodded.

"Like always," he chuckled. "Who is it for, Burtoni?"

I shrugged. "I don't know. I guess it is for whoever finds it, if . . . "

There was a moment of silence between us, broken then by Corrao's deep laugh, "If we don't make it, eh?"

"Yes, I guess that's . . ." I said.

Again there was a moment of quiet and we were looking out at the men sleeping on the warm grass below.

"Are you putting me in there, Burtoni?"

"Yes, Corrao. You are in it."

"And Rosalino?"

I nodded yes.

"Good," Corrao said. Then he reached into a little pack at his side and pulled something out. As he handed it to me, with a "here," I realized it was my red shirt, the one I'd worn in '49 when I rode with the General. The shirt Il Generale gave me, when he gave me my name.

"Where did you get that?" I said.

"From out of your stuff," he answered, and as I started to object, he raised his hand to quiet me, and said, "Burtoni, it's time for you to wear it. This is no time to be hiding it in a

114

little bag. It will remind us to be ready, that he is coming soon." He took his hands off of the shirt and left it in my hands. "Now is the time to wear it, little Il Rosso!"

I nodded again, because he was right, and I remembered telling him during those long, still days on the quiet sea aboard The Speranza about this shirt, and my name Il Rosso, and how I came by both of them. He'd laughed at me back then, and just said, "I know at least a hundred sailors who claim that they came here with the General, and everyone of them has a red shirt to prove it. And some of those shirts even have bullet holes in them for proof. But none of them has a name to go with it. Il Rosso," he laughed. Yet he never has called me by that name. He has always called me Burtoni, and that's it.

But today, after he appeared with my shirt, filched from my pack, he seemed for the first time to believe me. To believe I'd earned that name, that it came from him, Il Generale.

"What is he like, Burtoni?" Corrao asked me, seeming weaker and more fearful than I'd ever noticed before. This was not the man with the barrel-chested laugh and the thick forearms who'd kept me from drifting overboard into the stormy sea. This was a simple man, preparing himself for coming battle, readying himself to face death and wanting to know if everything he'd heard about Il Generale was as true as he hoped. He didn't repeat the question, he just sat waiting for any answer. It took me a little while to digest what he needed to hear from me, and for the first time I believe he understood that my years and all my experience through them were older and longer than the way my young face appeared.

And so I was in no hurry. I took care to respond. "He is fair haired, and not tall, but his shoulders are broad and his strength is surprising. He is square like you, Giovanni, and plain spoken, like you too. But when he sits atop a horse, all his years in the wars on the Pampas show forth. In a saddle he is the warrior of Montevideo. And no one stands aboard a ship like he does, Corrao. No one. Giovanni, my friend, the General's sea legs are round and strong and solid. So he is always on the level, no matter how his ship is tossed."

Corrao nodded and it seemed to mean that all this he already knew. "But why do we follow him, Burtoni?" he asked. "He's lost now twice, and he's spent more time in exile than even Mazzini. Why do we keep following him?"

A grin spread across my face, I think, because I was recalling how it was to ride with him across the alps to Lugano. And I was remembering sailing the South Atlantic with him to Spain and then into Nice. "Because, Giovanni Corrao, he lifts your heart. When you are standing beside him, you know that the cause is great and that you must rise to it bravely, rise above yourself. Because, Giovanni Corrao, in his eyes we are all equal and on the road to our great freedom. And nothing will ever hold us back. Beside him, you know that is true. You don't just believe it, Giovanni, you know it."

Corrao listened quietly, soaking it all in, and then he added his own thoughts. "No, Burtoni, that's not it. Or maybe it is, but it's not all of it. I have never seen him, yet I know this much about him. He is one of us, Burtoni. He may be braver and more true of heart. He may be greater than we are. But he is one of us, still." He paused and then asked, "Isn't that true?"

While he spoke, I was pulling off my rugged shirt and then I slipped the red tunic over my head and shoulders. When I was done, I hitched my belt around my waist. "When you meet him, soon, Giovanni Corrao, you will see," I said. "Like me, you will want to follow him anywhere, because you know he is the truth."

Across the plain below us I saw Rosalino Pilo striding toward us, perhaps with some news, but perhaps not, because he seemed relaxed and happy. The Count seemed at peace, here on the verge of certain battle.

116

"See, Burtoni, the General is our General because," and at that moment he lowered his voice, "because he is not like that one. No, my lad," as he seemed to be fooled again by my face and forget my years, "the Generalissimo is one of us, Burtoni. Just a man. A sailor. A working merchant mariner, Burtoni. With calluses on his hands and shoulders broad from toting the rich man's freight. Unlike that one." He nodded his head toward Count Pilo, and Rosalino took it as a salutation. So he waved back at us, a big grand wave of the arm and with a lift in his step.

"Some of us, Burtoni, are not just common men," Corrao whispered. "No matter what they say. Some of us are 'Nobility.' Some of us come from a higher birth, with fine skin and soft hands, Burtoni, and so we can only trust them so far. We have to watch them and be careful that, when the moment comes," Corrao raised his arm and waved broadly back at the Count, "They don't just take over for themselves. I'm afraid many of these poor contadini would follow them right along, and just replace one king with a new one."

I was stunned by this talk and at first it made me laugh out loud. "Not our Rosalino, you don't mean. Corrao, Pilo's heart is brave. He has suffered with us, for us, for years. Why, it's because of him, his little lies, that the General is even here."

Corrao smiled and his face brightened and he said, "Of course, not Count Pilo of Grigenti. I'm not speaking of the Count," he said loudly and assuredly, "and his lies."

I gave him a puzzled look. But he just rose to his feet and saluted Rosalino.

"Giovanni, we have great news," Count Pilo shouted over as he drew closer. Then he looked down at me, "Burtoni, we have our orders to move!"

"The Bourbons are holding Monreale now," Pilo told us, once he strode up to us and then hunkered down on his haunches, near where I sat on the ground. "We have our orders. We are to maneuver up into the hills above them."

"San Martino," Corrao said, the Palermo street kid who knows the landscape now and understands the lay of it almost instinctively. He looked out over the surrounding hills.

Pilo grinned and nodded to him, "That's right, Captain Corrao. We are to take up the high ground near that monastery, with both of our squadrons on Castellacio. Then we just hold the King's troops down there, while the General and his brigade will march around them. He will enter the city from the south and the east, instead of where they're expecting him to come from the southwest, from Calatafimi."

"So our job is just to keep the enemy busy," I said, "to the southeast."

Corrao finished the thought, "While il Generale flanks them and takes Palermo from behind."

"The Bourbons will be trapped between us," I said. "It's brilliant, sir."

"But we are the key, comrades," Count Pilo said, his head nodding. "If we can hold them in Monreale, then Palermo is ours, and the Bourbon troops will be ours too."

Corrao laughed at that, and sat back down against a tree. "We're the bait in the General's trap," he said, with a smile on his face. .

That was when a short Sicilian man came running up the hillside toward us. "Dottore, Dottore," he was calling out as he ran.

I glanced around to see who this man might be calling out for, but there was no one beyond us on the hillside. Still the fellow kept running towards us, and now he was waving in our direction. "Dottore, Dottore," he called out.

A big grin spread out across Count Pilo's face. "Must be a lad from the Vucciria, eh, Giovanni?" And then Pilo started to laugh.

Giovanni Corrao squirmed a little where he was seated on the ground, but then he stood up again. To my surprise, the young fellow rushed straight up to Corrao, and grabbed him by the forearms. "Dottore, it's my brother, Dottore. He's cut his arm open with a bayonet. You must come now. He's bleeding all over, Dottore Calogero." I thought the young man had gone mad, or something.

But Pilo stifled his grin as much as he could, and then he said, "Dr. Calogero, do you need any help, sir?"

Again, I was glancing back over my shoulder to see whom I had missed, who else was present. But Pilo was staring wryly at our man, Giovanni Corrao.

"No, your lordship," Corrao said with a little ice in his voice. "I believe I can handle this."

"Dottore, we must hurry," the young fellow said.

"Yes," Corrao said, "Fine. Where is he?" And off they both went at a quick jog down into the encampment on the field below.

"Dr. Calogero?" I said, and looked over at Pilo.

That made the Count laugh in a happy way I'd not heard from him before. "Calogero?" I repeated.

"Oh, my Burtoni, there is a lot you don't know about our dear friend, Signor Corrao."

"But," I said, "Dr. Calogero?" And so I laughed too.

Pilo chuckled and shook his head a little, as he slid down from his haunches and sat just exactly where Corrao had been sitting moments before. He reached out, as he settled in, and touched the red shirt on my back. "It's good that you are wearing it, Burtoni. It will bring some dreams and some bravery into the hearts of these little contadini and picciotti, now, as we head into this war for real."

"It was Giovanni's idea," I said. "He brought it out to me." Pilo smiled thoughtfully and muttered Corrao's name a little wistfully.

"Who is this Dr. Calogero?" I said.

"Giovanni Corrao, my friend, has been many things." Pilo's smile was affectionate as he spoke. "You see, Burtoni, he was born in the Vucciria." He paused there, as if that would explain everything, and then he remembered I was not a Sicilian, had never before been to this island, much less to its capital city.

"The Vucciria is a neighborhood in Palermo, Burtoni. It's rough. It's always been rough. During the daylight hours, it is one of the greatest bazaars in the world; everywhere tables and tents, and you can buy or sell almost anything you want." Then he raised his eyebrows and repeated, "Anything, Burtoni. Almost anything you might want."

I nodded that I understood.

"But at night, the market disappears and another world comes to life in the shadows of the alleys and the narrow streets. Everything, Burtoni, is still for sale in the Vucciria. But the customers and the merchants have changed, and the tables are gone, and the dealing happens in the corners, away from the lights. And our friend Giovanni grew up there. In the Vucciria. His mother, well, she didn't know who his father was. Or which one, if you understand me. So he has only his mother's name."

From the way Count Pilo spoke I remembered what Corrao had said. I remembered his warnings. The Count is different than we are, Corrao had said. Our little Rosalino has an old and revered name, tied deeply to the Sicilian south. He is of 'higher birth' than we are, Giovanni Corrao and I. He is a Pilo di Grigento.

"But, Rosalino, this is what we are fighting for, isn't it? So that names don't mean anything?" I said, speaking not just to him.

Count Pilo smiles and nods his head yes, thoughtfully. "It is true."

"We are fighting so that every man can make his own name."

"Or perhaps," Pilo added, "in Giovanni's case, several names." Then he laughed again at something and went on. "This is why Signor Corrao is so useful to us, my friend. This is why we need him so. He is invisible, because he has been visible in so many ways. I don't even know, Burtoni, if Giovanni Corrao is his true name. Since I have known him, here in Sicily over the last 20 years or so, he has been Corrado, Corrani, Cerini, Ceriani, and probably a few more."

"And now," I asked, "he's a Doctor?"

"When I came back to Sicily, from Switzerland, from my first exile—it was ten years ago, I guess—the people in Lugano, well, we won't use their names in case we need them again. But when I came back here, dressed as a peasant, I heard this name. Go to Palermo, get down in the Vucciria, and ask for Dottore Calogero. He will set you up. This is what our people in Lugano told me." I noticed Rosalino Pilo was staring out at the men in the field as he spoke. He seemed to relax and nestle into his memory. "So when I got to Palermo I asked around the market, and every time, before anyone would show me the way, they always glanced all around to see who might be with me, who might be trying to listen. Then they would tell me the name of a street. It always turned out to be just a side alley, with nothing there. So I thought, this Dottore must be a big man. Everyone is afraid to tell me who he is.

"Finally, after I came back to the market for the third day in a row and asked the same questions to the same fishmonger, once again he looked carefully all around before he spoke. He had a long blade in his hand, and he was slicing a thick steak from the side of a swordfish. He looked away from me and up at the fish's head with its long snout on display above us, and then he muttered quietly the name of a café."

I couldn't help but notice that Pilo never mentioned the name of this café or any of the names of the fishmonger or anybody else. Not even to me, who'd ridden this far with him and who was preparing to fight and maybe die at his side. Not even to me would he, after ten years, speak those names out loud.

That was when I realized that for Corrao, or Calogero, or whoever he was, and for Rosalino too, what he was telling me now had nothing to do with the General or this revolution. What he was telling me now had to do with this island of Sicily, with Palermo.

"Burtoni, I didn't say thanks, I didn't even nod in acknowledgement. The fishmonger, he just glanced at my eyes once, for just an instant. I didn't even think of repeating the name of the place he'd mentioned. I just gave him a little money and, loudly, he handed me a piece of swordfish, saying 'Grazie, Signore!' And then he began calling out his wares to the market again, as if nothing had passed between us but a piece of fish. I didn't look back as I strolled away slowly into the market.

"And so I wandered around in the Vucciria, through the alleys and side streets, and I shopped a little and bought some fruit. I gave the piece of swordfish away to an old woman on the street. And I looked and looked for this café. But it was nowhere to be found. And I knew better than to ask about it. The very mention of its name might make it disappear, or make me disappear.

"After dark, the Vucciria changes though. All the little shops and wide spread stalls roll up their wares and go away, and the streets fill up with people strolling the passeggiata. I wandered around, and I began to ask people where there was a café. Not any particular café, lest I be sent off with another wild misdirection. I just asked for a good café. Good local places for a coffee, maybe a sweet, a glass of wine. And so I was led off into some dark corners and a few blind alleys, and after about three hours of wandering around in and through the neighborhood, I came upon a narrow lane, not even wide enough for two people to pass one another with ease. A pale light shone out onto the stones of the alley, but it came from out of my view. I noticed people entering and leaving silently and quickly from there. They didn't seem to be wanting coffee, or a drink of wine. I walked down toward the light and found a sign bearing the name of the café. I know I had walked past two or three times during that day, and no café existed on that spot in the daylight. But now, in the shadows and the dark, it was there."

It was clear to me once again that the Count was carefully leaving all the names unmentioned, even to me, and even after ten years had passed.

"Inside there was a small crowd from the bazaar, and I ordered a coffee and drank it standing at the bar. It was odd, but no one spoke to me, though I tried to make small talk. So finally, I just asked plainly to see the Doctor.

"Suddenly everyone in the room stopped to look at me, and examine me up and down, but only for an instant. Then all at once the chatter began in earnest, about everything except the Doctor I'd asked for. How was the fishing? They said to one another. When would the olives be ready? How was the crop going to be? Who was trying to marry a signorina named Anita? It was as if I'd never spoken of any doctor, or even spoken at all.

"I finished my coffee, and thought to leave, but I knew from the way the people responded that I was in the right place. This was where the fishmonger had sent me. So I didn't order anything else, I just stood and took up space at the bar. Someone even offered to buy me a bitter; I turned it down and just stood and waited some more. After a while, a short dark man in the rugged clothes of a sailor approached the bar and muttered, 'Come with me, your lordship.'

"He took me through a back door to the office behind the little café, where another man sat on a chair in the corner, and two men with long knives stood beside him. He asked who I was, and what I wanted. I realized that if I didn't tell them something they wanted to hear, I would not walk out of that room alive. But I told him only that I came from Switzerland and I was looking for Dr. Calogero. I didn't say my name. Perhaps by that time they already knew it.

"He listened to me, and then he listened to my silence for a while, and then he said to the long knives, 'Okay.'

"They took me from there out into a back alley, where we all knew they could easily have sliced me and left me to bleed to death, a place where no one would dare to answer my cries for help. Then we entered through another door and went up some stairs and finally we reached a room where an old, white-haired man sat reading from a newspaper. 'You are looking for Dottore Calogero,' he said flatly, but in a thick Sicilian that was hard for me, who grew up here on this island, to understand. His statement was not a question; it was recognition of a stated fact. I nodded yes anyway. He wanted only to know who sent me. I took a chance, and I said the names I knew, the aliases of two men in Lugano who'd sent me to Palermo. The old man nodded at each name, and then in Sicilian again, he ordered, 'Take him," to the two long knives.

"It went on like this for a while, Burtoni," Pilo said. "There were more doors and empty rooms, stairways and alleys. At one point we even crossed over some red tiled roofs and climbed from one building to another on a rickety ladder. And then we picked up two more toughs, these were carrying straight razors and they liked to test their sharpness with their thumbs whenever they were still. I answered more of their questions with the same few, bare facts. I never told them anymore than I already had, but it always was enough to move me on to the next set of stairs and through another doorway to more back alleys.

"Finally we entered a large room packed with people. A salon really, filled with furniture that was old and probably stolen. There were children with their mothers, old workmen with only a few teeth left, a young and pretty girl ready to give birth. They were all waiting to see the Dottore, this Calogero, beyond a closed door at the far end of the busy, silent room.

"'Wait here,' one of the razors said, and then they went inside leaving me with the two long knives amidst the sick and poor in the salon. At first I figured it would likely be a long wait, but in just a moment or two, the door opened and out popped one of the razors. He looked me directly in the eye, and that look led me inside.

"'What did I find inside there, Burtoni?" Pilo began to laugh loudly. "First there was a little child, with his shirt off, and his mama tearfully touching him and standing at his side. The boy was sitting up on a table to be examined by the Dottore. And who do you think he was?" Count Pilo stopped and shook his head and muttered something I couldn't hear about a thief under his breath.

"Dottore Calogero?" I said, incredulous.

"Yes, Burtoni," Pilo said. "It was our lad Giovanni. Signor Corrao, Corrado, Coriano, all in one. Dottore Calogero."

"But," I asked, "is he really a doctor?"

"Well, let's put it this way, lad," Pilo raised his eyebrows and cocked his head. "I don't think our boy Giovanni has any papers from the University of Padova. Unless, of course, he bought them in the fish market, wrapped around a piece of tuna." Then Rosalino Pilo shrugged and said, "But those patients of his, they did believe in him, Burtoni. There must have been a few of them got better, after they saw . . ."

" . . . Dottore Calogero," I repeated, and then we both laughed.

"Get some rest, Burtoni," the Count told me after that. "Tonight after dark we move past Monreale to the Monastery, and then, lad, the real fight will begin. You'll need your rest soon."

Later, before we left the plain at dark that night, I told Rafaella this story that Count Pilo told me, about our Dottore. But she seemed more interested in the convoluted search it took to find Giovanni, than she was in his medical practice. "You're right," I said to her. "Why would it be so hard to find the doctor? Was he hiding his practice from the Police?"

"No," she told me, and then explained it to me from out of her own Sicilian roots. "This doctoring, that's just a skill he has, a talent. He's a healer. The police would leave him alone for that. But that's not all he is. He is a man of honor. The Count may have some royal blood in his veins, but I think our Corrao, he belongs to a different kind of blood. It's not his family name. But from his skills and his honor, and the way he is protected, our friend Corrao belongs to one of the 'families' who run this island. The Bourbons and their police, they think they rule here in Sicilia, but this land belongs to the families who really make all the decisions. And the way Signor Corrao is protected, trust me, my love, Giovanni Corrao is a much bigger man around here than he appears. Much bigger than Rosalino can even imagine."

"Corrao," I said.

"If that is even his name," Rafaella whispered.

21.

18 May
Monastero di San Martino, above Monreale

We arrived here two nights ago in the mountains that stand over the village of Monreale. The whole three hundred of us are arrayed now across the hillside looking down at the road below. As yet the troops of the Bourbons have not advanced out of Palermo toward us, so everything remains quiet. But if those troops don't find us soon, we will have to challenge them in some way, or our decoy will not work.

This morning Rosalino caught Rafaella and I returning from the village of Monreale at dawn. He had a big grin on his face as he watched us walk into the main encampment, hand in hand. I guess the change in me, in us, was obvious, at least to Rosalino. Our world is entirely different now; it has grown to a proportion I don't quite understand yet, and the Count can see this in us right away, even from a distance.

Rosalino pulled me aside, almost immediately, and I thought it was to brief me on the plans for the battle ahead. But instead he clapped me on the shoulder and then he held me tight and he told me how beautiful my Rafaella was with her hand in mine in the morning light. How could he know? I wondered. Then he surprised me.

"Burtoni, I don't think I'll ever see my Rosetta again." His eyes welled up with tears quickly. "When I see the two of you together, I know how much I have lost. I have lost her. Burtoni, this is very special, what you two have. You love her with all your heart, lad. With all your heart. Once this war begins, there is not any one of us who knows who he will ever see again."

"But Rosalino," I said, "You will walk with her through the free streets of Roma. I know you will."

"That's right, Burtoni," but his eyes were welling up again. "We'll all meet at Castel Sant'Angelo with the General, and we'll stroll to the Pantheon arm in arm, singing songs of the old Roman Republic reborn. All of us. Rosetta and I, Rafaella and you. Together, and free, in peace at last."

But then, without wiping his eyes in his pride, a tear began to slip down his cheek. "Take care of her, Burtoni. She is precious. Never let her down. Remember, nothing is worth losing her. Nothing." Then he shook his head no, and wiped the tear away, in order to silence himself.

He quickly walked away, and I saw Corrao watching the two of us, as we parted. We had come so far together, like brothers. I know we will never part. We will be free together. After this dark time, we will be free. After.

We must.

Last night, once the dark had fallen on the monastery, Rafaella came to me and, just as she did in Castellnotte, she took my hand and whispered, "I want you to see something." But this time there was an urgency that was new in her voice. "Before the battle begins, you must see this."

And so I followed her down a narrow foot path from the mountainside and at one point, when I could hardly see her in the darkness, I whispered out desperately, "Where are we going, Rafaella?"

She stopped and turned back. "I want you to see the most beautiful place in the world, my love. You must see the sunrise over the Cloisters, before all this war begins." At that, she turned and pressed on down the footpath through the pinewoods toward the village that slowly emerged below. There was not a single light anywhere, but under the waning moon, she led me down through the old stone streets.

We slipped silently around the piazza, with the tall grey shadow of the Cathedral above it. She knew her way, and led me over to a stone wall. We climbed on a wooden ladder over that wall, then crept over the tiles of the roof, until silently we landed on our feet, with a leap, inside an enclosed garden.

Rafaella took my hand then, and with her other hand she held a finger up to her lips to keep me silent. She led me over to a fountain that tinkled softly under the starry sky, reflecting the pale quarter moon in its water. There we sat on the damp, warm grass and slowly the garden emerged around me, as my eyes grew comfortable with the light.

We were stretched out in the corner of a perfect square, and within that square were four perfectly square little gardens. The old fountain where we lay was the only thing asymmetrical, though it was a perfect square too.

Slowly I saw that all around me, the garden was surrounded by a colonnade, made of pointed arches above paired columns. With time I began to see that, while every arch was perfect, and every pair of colonettes matched the form of all the others, they were all different too. Some were decorated with mosaics, muted by the moonlight. Others were carved with geometric patterns in the stone. And then I saw that some others had lost their mosaics, or part of the colored stones and glass, and had left behind the ghost-like shadows of their lost brilliance, swirling around and around up the pillars.

With time I began to see that these arches, some of them, had themes. One was decorated with horses at the capitols, another had lions, another little cupids, and some other bore saints with folded hands and mitered heads. And there were still others that simply showed an angular or a curving design. But all of these details were subtle, and disappeared into a grand unity that celebrated the whole of the garden as one perfection united.

Rafaella held me and we lay there together, keeping one another warm until the sun began to rise, and the shadows of the colonnade slowly grew sharper.

Then, before it was entirely light, Rafaella led me through a door and back inside, into the cathedral, dark and empty, with only the flickering lights of votive candles to show the way. She knelt down on the empty stone floor, and began to silently pray. The whole place, in the darkness, made me uneasy, but I stood next to her. After the way we'd been so close in the garden, I did not want us to be apart, though there were no prayers in my heart. Slowly, as it grew light outside, the light began to filter through the stained glass, and the church began to reveal itself to me, with its sweeping arches and grand heights. The ceiling began to sparkle with the gold, and mosaics came together out of the shadows, dark bearded faces with olive eyes like Corrao's, and women with black flowing hair like Rafaella's.

As I looked around above me at the miracle of the ceiling, I saw what Rafaella knelt before. It was a huge mosaic of the Christ figure, with his arms stretched out around the dome, the creator of all, embracing us all. There was a peaceful liquidity to his gaze, as if He was a well we could, all of us, everyone of us, fall into for sustenance and refuge. And the grand circle of his arms spread out and curled around, and centered the whole church, no, it centered the whole world in the reach of His embrace, and He held us all to His heart, in safety and love and in sparkling, golden light.

Then, into the warm vastness of that sacred, silent space, broke the sharp detail of a lone footstep. Just a scuffed foot on the old stones. But it shattered everything in its wake, and it echoed like a canon beneath the Pantocreator.

Captured, seized, stopped before the battles ever begin. Traitors, betrayers of the cause. All these thoughts rushed through my mind. We had, in our indulgence, in our love, we let it all get away from us, and now we were caught.

Rafaella heard it too, and she silently pulled me down on my knees, and I understood. We were pilgrims. Penitents prostrate before God. She did not need to say a word.

But I understood what she had forgotten, or ignored. I was wearing the red shirt. Whoever it was who had stepped into the vastness of that room, if they were Bourbon or Royalist, they would know the meaning of that shirt. It seemed so ironic now to be caught with it, this gift from the General himself, handed over to me by Corrao and urged on me by Count Pilo, all to inspire the hearts of the squadrons of Monreale. And now it was only a blazon on my chest to send me to an island prison, or maybe even to a firing squad.

He came forward out of the shadows, dressed entirely in black. His footsteps now tapped across the marble stones. Rafaella and I both kept our heads down in apparent piety. "Bless you, my children," he said, in a Sicilian tinged Latin.

"Good morning, Father," Rafaella said, looking up at the priest. So I followed her eyes. He was short, so short and swarthy that clearly he was a local. His hair was the same hard silver gray as Rafaella's father, and his face was deeply creased with worry. He said something in Sicilian, and I understood enough to know he was telling us when the Mass would begin. Rafaella answered him, saying we had to go. My silence told the priest what he wanted to know, if my looks had not already. I did not come from this island.

The father then looked me up and down, and then he spoke in flawless, unaccented Italian. "That is a bright color you wear, young man. Be careful. It may shine down here too brightly, if you know what I mean."

"I understand," I said, as Rafaella and I both got up on our feet.

He nodded yes, and then he raised one hand and made a cross over us, blessing us in gesture as well as word. After that, without saying more, the old priest turned and walked loudly back to the sacristy.

"Come," Rafaella said, making the sign of the cross. "He's telling us to get out of here," she said.

Silently, but very quickly, we left the cathedral by a side door and came out below the building. In the early light, she led me around under the walls of the chevet, ornate and beautifully patterned above us, and then we were soon at the upper edge of the village.

"Will he?" I asked.

"I don't know," Rafaella said. "I can't tell whose side he is on. But he did not want any trouble in his church."

We scurried up deeper into the pinewoods, and out of the morning light. Once we were hidden in the shadows of the trees, I stopped her so we could look down at the still sleeping village of Monreale. From this height, the cathedral and the cloister attached to it were truly a miracle, and I wanted to say this to Rafaella. I wanted to thank her for this beauty, and for the night we shared, but once we stopped and looked back, we both saw that not everyone in the village was sound asleep.

Down below that piazza, on the steep road that wound up into town from Palermo, there was a pair of soldiers, in blue Bourbon uniforms, smoking on guard duty. Rafaella and I both knew that if there were guards out, then a regiment or two could not be far behind. The movement of men had come up from Palermo. The Bourbons have taken our bait.

"We must get back up to the monastery," I said. "Pilo needs to know that the troops are coming. It has started." I turned to head back up into the pinewood, but Rafaella stopped me, for just an instant.

"No matter what happens now," she said and stared deeply into my eyes, "We are husband and wife now. Always." For a moment, I lost my way. I swear I did not know where I was. I moved toward her, to kiss her. But then she said, "Pilo needs us. We must hurry."

It was this that Rosalino saw in us, as we climbed hurriedly back to San Martino. The grin on his face tells me he knows it all.

22.

21 May
San Martino

O What torture just a few hours can bring. How the world can change, in a moment. From the heights of my joy, to this. In just the flash of a gun barrel.

They came at us in thousands. And we, we are only a few hundred boys. Clearly they took the bait, and they were hungry, for the thousands came at us with a fury, believing they had the General in their grasp. And we held them. We did.

But O Rosalino. Can he make it?

No more.

Rosalino Pilo, Count of Grigento. O fine Rubiolo. Farewell.

23.

26 May
Gibilrossa Pass

At dawn tomorrow we will enter Palermo, at the first light of a Sunday morning. The word has spread through the countryside, but the enemy seems still not to know where we will come from. We are in sight of the city below us, and all of us are united now with the General. Captain Corrao leads the squadrons, but now he is under the General's command.

Rafaella has turned and headed back for Messina, to send word to her father of our success, and so I am alone now. I am under Giovanni Corrao's command.

And Rosalino, he is gone.

His sudden death has taught me, taught us all, how quickly we can be gone, any one of us. No matter how great a soul we might be. No matter how brave we are. No matter how much we have done, nor how essential we are to the success of our great cause. No matter at all. I don't know if I will survive what comes tomorrow, in the great battle for Palermo. And so now, by firelight, in the near dark long before dawn, I must again put this down so all who wish to know can know the truth. For I was there, he was by my side. And even now, the wild accusations are flying all around us. Corrao. Some of the picciotti of Corleone, and a few others who will dare to talk openly, they say it was Giovanni Corrao. It was his bullet, they say. But I was there. So I must put it all down, even if it takes me the rest of this night.

*   *   *

The first charge of the Bourbons was ferocious. They came at us in thousands and thousands with guns blazing, rushing up the hill and everything was furious for a time. We had positioned ourselves in the stones and shallow hollows just below the monastery, and our lines held, because Pilo had placed us in this superior position. We are only 300, and they are ten times our number, but they fell under our fire, and it was clear that we could hold them as long as our ammunition lasted. And that would be enough time for the General to march round his way and to prepare to enter the capitol from behind them, with surprise at his side.

Pilo was wise, though, and told us to hold our fire, as soon as the Bourbon troops began to fall back. He led us fearlessly, roving from every placement to each position in the stones. Wherever the Bourbon charge came hardest, Pilo was there and he always stood firm.

After the first attack had been repulsed, we had only two wounded, and Corrao, or Dottore Calogero I suppose I should call him, was busy bandaging their wounds. A proud huzzah rose up from the picciotti. "Good work, comrades," Pilo shouted to us all, and shifted from placement to placement to watch for the Bourbon movements below us.

In a short while, the troops charged at us again, from a different side of the hill. They were fools, or led by fools. We were weaker there under the steep embankment, because they were more exposed across a shelf of shale. Pilo just rolled his rifles over to back up the men on the embankment, and the poor Bourbon troops fell below us under our careful fire. We did not rain fire on them, we drizzled. But it was a deadly mist of fire. Not one of them even reached the rocks where we were perched in defense. They died at our feet without a purpose, and this time we took no casualties. Not one.

But we had still spent valuable ammunition, and all of us knew it. If they kept coming, the ugly time of bayonets would soon arrive. And we would have to hold the line with our lives.

After those two costly charges up the hills, all was quiet for a long while. But we knew it was not over. We had held the monastery, at almost no cost beyond the ammunition we'd spent. They could not know we were in short supply, after only those two assaults. So we held our fire and hoped they would keep taking the bait, and that fear of our superior position would limit their approach.

If it all fell into a slow siege, it would be the best. For the General and his thousand could round on them and take Palermo while we fended off the Bourbon attacks here at San Martino. But if they kept on bravely, we would soon be in danger of being overrun, and all would be lost. For us surely. Perhaps for the thousand. And then, for our dreams and our country.

But we had to put our brave faces on, for if the Bourbons grew weary of our defenses, and repaired to the edge of the Capitol, the surprise of the coming assault behind them would be lost. Pilo knew it was a delicate task put before him by the General. We had to appear vulnerable, but at the same time we had to hold our position. Either a rousing victory that sent the Bourbon's fleeing, or a hasty retreat from our monastery, either might expose our Legions to a full attack of the Bourbon forces, just when the General was in his weakest position, with the Red Shirts sprawled across the mountains reaching for their advantage.

Pilo understood this, but he never spoke any of it. He was ready to die for it, with the rest of us. Perhaps he knew.

Sometime after that second assault, the disagreement broke out between Pilo and Corrao. Some of the talk now has made too much of this, I think, for it was not like they say. It was simpler than that.

Corrao announced to the Count that he was taking three men up the mountainside of Castellaccio. "They may be sending sharpshooters up there above us," he said.

"We need you here, at the line. The next attack won't be long in coming, Giovanni. I need you on the front line," Pilo answered.

"But, Rubiolo," Corrao said, using the old code-name he knew Pilo by in Genova on purpose. "If they get to a position above us, with even a few men, our advantage is lost. They'll pick us off slowly, until we flee."

Pilo paused and looked up at the two mountainsides above the monastery, Castellaccio and Giardinello. "I see," he muttered. In his head he knew, I think, that such an attack would be a good thing, for it would take a long while for the Bourbons to 'pick us off' from the heights. A long enough time for the General to arrive at the Quattro Canti in the heart of Palermo. He turned away then, and simply ordered Corrao, "Send five men up there to keep watch. But I need you here, Giovanni."

"But, Rubiolo," Corrao said, using that old name again, "it won't help us to know. Surely they are thinking of this, they can see Giardinello just as we can. We need to be prepared to stop then, if they try for it."

But Count Pilo just rounded on him, looking tired in his eyes, but he spoke slowly and distinctly, "Captain Corrao, I said send five good men to keep watch. And you will return to your squadron."

Giovanni Corrao glared at his friend, but failed to say "yes, Sir." He just wheeled on one boot heel and strode away, chin in the air.

This, you must know, is what the wagging tongues all saw. This is the moment they point to for their proof. Because Giovanni followed these orders from Count Pilo, but only up to a point. Not truly as Rosalino Pilo wished. Corrao took just four of his best men from his squadron, the best marksmen, the bravest hearts. He sent them out of the Abbey yard and up the steep side of Castellaccio above us. But the fifth man, the one who was not following his commander's orders, the one who led the other four marksmen up the mountainside, he called himself Comrade Calogero, the mysterious Dottore of the Vucciria.

It was later, after Corrao and his men were long gone, climbing up the side of Castellaccio, they say that Rosalino began writing to the General. He was asking il Generale to send help, and the letter he started with just his first word on the paper, was meant to warn the General of our dire situation, just 300 men before the stubborn onslaught of 3000. Send reinforcements to relieve us, to help us hold them off. Send the ammunition that even the Thousand were short of. Send them all soon, before the bayonets are unfurled. This is what they say he meant to write. This is what would be on that paper Rosalino never finished.

But I know differently. The one word he did write, it was not 'Generalissimo.' It was not 'Generale.' It was not even 'Piddu.' No.

The one word he wrote was: "Carissima."

*   *   *

Rosalino took me over to a scattering of broken stones at the edge of the old monastery. Two large rocks stand there, you can see them and the stains on them if you want. As we walked silently, he took pen and paper from an inner pocket of this coat. He sat himself down between the large stones, and smoothed the paper out on the flattest part of the stone he could find.

I was standing next to him, staring at the scene around me. I was standing right beside him, when he said his last words on this rugged earth. "Burtoni," he said, without ever looking up, with the pen in his hand and the inkbottle sitting on the stone. "I want you to take this, and get it to Rosetta, if something happens to . . . " His voice trailed off there, as if he knew what was coming somehow. And as if he had finally realized something about me, about my deceptive age, and about how I seemed always to emerge from great danger and survive.

But the stone he was trying to write on was too rough. Rosalino smoothed the paper this way and then smoothed it that way. If he'd only been writing a message to the General, that roughened stone would have been flat enough. His scrawl, as long as it was readable, would have done for the necessary job.

But he was not writing a plea to il Generale. And so, Rosalino wanted that letter to look right. He stood up then and moved to the side, and then placed the paper on the flat of my shoulder blade. I bent forward a little to level the surface of the paper out for him, and he rested a hand on my back. If I had not bent over ever so slightly, perhaps I would have taken the bullet, and perhaps only in my shoulder or in an arm. Perhaps.

140

Then Rosalino wrote that one word on the paper, and said his last words to me. "If I don't make it out of here, Burtoni, take this to my Rosetta."

Corrao was right, you see. The Bourbon officers, whoever they are, they could see the futility of charging and charging and charging again up the hill into our fire and our bayonets. Some one of them could also see the advantage of Giardinello and Castellaccio, of pinching us off and trapping us beneath them, caught between the full army below us and an armed squad above us on the heights. But it was not just a few sharpshooters to heckle us. No. You see, during that quiet respite the Bourbons had moved a whole column of troops up from Monreale into the steep heights of Castellaccio, and quietly amassed their forces up there while we waited and watched for them to come at us again from below.

We first heard a scattering of shots from up in those steep hillsides, and then two of Corrao's men came running into our position around the Monastery walls, and they began to shout out a warning. "Above us! Look out! They have made the hillside! Up there!" Or something like that they shouted. I don't remember, because all of this happened in an instant. At once. It happened all at once, and in confusion. The hail of Bourbon fire followed hard on their cries. It poured down on us and chased the words of Corrao's men away from our ears.

*　　　*　　　*

Pilo looked up at the sound of their cries from his paper and his eyes passed mine as I glanced over my shoulder at him. But he was just turning back to see where all the shouting came from. There was nothing extraordinary in his eyes, no fear, no surprise, no fire, and no confusion. Nothing but a simple glance up, interrupting his words for a moment, as if someone had walked into a closed room. And then he was struck.

His face disappeared before my eyes. The bullet, or bullets, struck him straight on and turned his whole countenance into a sudden mass of red blood. He did not speak or even utter a cry. It all just fell onto him, like a bolt charging at him from some demonic curse.

His body became rigid for a moment, and he threw up one of his arms before his head uselessly. And then he went limp, and I caught him and held him up and eased his still struggling body down onto the ground. I think that I was screaming for help, but this I don't recall now for sure. I don't really know.

Later, after he was gone, I found the letter, the piece of paper with just that one word 'Carissima' written carefully on it, I found it stuffed in my pocket. Not folded. Just a crumpled ball of paper stuck in the pocket of my pants. Without even a speck of his blood on it.

I do not remember it falling to the ground. I don't remember picking it up, though I must have. I don't even remember thinking of it. I don't know how or when I came by it. But it was there in the morning. "Carissima." In my pocket. His last word.

The pen and the ink have disappeared.

Corrao was beside us almost immediately. Some of the picciotti say he was there too soon. It was almost as if he knew that the Count had been struck, they say. But together he and I picked Pilo up. The assault from below us rose then, and the Bourbon bullets rained down on us from the mountainside above. Someone, somewhere, yelled, "retreat," and that started it. The squadrons, with their leader fallen, were done and in disarray, and the men began to flee before the Bourbon charge and the battle, from the moment on, belonged to our enemies.

The Abbot of San Martino, a good man called Friar Ubaldo, came running bravely out onto that field of fire, when he saw that Pilo had fallen. There were two monks behind him carrying a litter. And so we hurriedly lay Rosalino on it, without a word between us, and then we fled, as fast as we could carry him, out of San Martino della Scalla.

On the backside of the hill lay a little village, just a few cottages grouped around a well was all. And as our squadrons vanished into the hills, disappearing, abandoning their arms, turning back into the local peasants as they ran, Corrao and I carried Rosalino inside a little hovel in that village called Niviera. The contadini there took us in and hid us far from the Bourbon troops ranging the hillsides behind us, hunting for the 'rebels.'

Rosalino was breathing steadily, and he lay still, resting easily. Corrao cleaned the wound and only then could we see how hurt he was. He could not speak or see, and he did not respond when we spoke to him. His face was gone, all the detail of it, the patrician nose, the piercing brown eyes, the curling lips that loved to smile, all gone. "Rosalino," Corrao spoke to him with great tenderness, as he held Pilo's hand. I placed my hand over the other one, but there was no response. "Rosalino," Corrao said. But the Count did not flinch or even move in answer. "Rosalino."   And yet his great and brave heart kept beating, and he was alive still, lying quietly as sleep, breathing through the red wound that had replaced his face.

There are those today who say it was a bullet from Giovanni Corrao that did him in, that Giovanni wanted the Count gone, wanted his place in the General's eyes. But I am here to tell you they are liars. It was in that cowardly hail of Bourbon bullets raining in their thousands down all the way from Napoli to here in tiny San Martino that Rosalino Pilo fell.

You have never seen a dying man, lost to us already, comforted more gently that Rosalino was. Giovanni Corrao sat with him, I swear to you, and spoke to him quietly. He cleaned that wound that was once the Count's face so gently that Rosalino never stirred with discomfort. And Giovanni, he refused to leave Rosalino's side.

But as nightfall came, and the world began to grow quiet, Rosalino began to stir. His legs moved and kicked, as sweat of a fever began to wrack him, until suddenly he began to shiver violently. Corrao wrapped him in his jacket and in mine, but the poor people of Niviera had nothing to put around him and not even much to put in the fire to warm the dark room. Though truthfully, it was not cold, and I doubt we could have warmed the room enough to comfort poor Rosalino.

The Abbot Ubaldo, praying quietly for the Count in the damp corner of the cottage all that afternoon, said finally, "It is safe now. We must move him back up to the Abbey where we can keep his Excellency, Count di Grigento, comfortable."

"But he's too weak. He won't survive the move," I protested, tucking my tunic in again around Rosalino's bare squirming feet.

"Yes he will," Corrao interrupted my whining. "Rosalino Pilo is tough, and he is not easily departing from this war. He has started it, by God's own arse, he has. Now he wants to fight some more, Burtoni. Don't you see that."

So we wrapped him in everything we could and we carried him up on the litter to the warm stone rooms inside the monastery. I know that Ubaldo wanted the Count di Grigento to die in a sacred place, with the benefits of his church, and the Friar was doing his part to save the Count's soul. And I almost don't dare to say this here, because so many little tongues are wagging against Corrao, but Giovanni may have just hoped to ease his friend off quickly into the next world by carrying him up through the cool of the night.

"Dottore?" the Abbot said to Corrao, and then he led us out of the low door and into the early mountain cold.

Ubaldo brought us to a small cell just off the monastery chapel and there we laid Rosalino on a bed the brothers had carried in. They kept him under wool blankets and on crisp clean sheets, and they kept a great fire roaring in a fireplace in the corner. And right outside the closed door, in the chapel, the brothers chanted their prayers in a constant soft hymn for Rosalino's soul. They were treating him as if he was a dieing brother, a member of the order.

I remembered him, drinking heartily and laughing in the old Il Gufo sulla Luna, Rubiolo telling jokes to this Doctor Calogero and many others. I remembered the way he laughed at me when I saved us all by coating myself with Joan d'Arc's shit. And at one point, Corrao and I began to sing to him his own song about the heroes of old, the one he sang to cheer us on, when we were all sailing aboard the Speranza for Sicilia. And I was surprised when Ubaldo, getting a sense of the tune, knew the words and joined in with a smile. "Foscolo," he said, though I am still not sure what he meant.

It is hard to believe that Rosalino has come to this, lying senseless in a chapel surrounded by chanting monks, when just yesterday he was ordering the squadrons around and singing the praises of Liberta', and Italia, waiting for word from il Generalissimo.

Corrao said to me, "Burtoni, you go and get some sleep. I will stay with him. Tomorrow we will need our strength, and the next day, to ride with the General into Palermo. Just as Rosalino dreamed we would."

I protested again, but the Abbot stood up and took me by the arm and led me out into the chapel. "He's right, my son," Friar Ubaldo said. "There's no more you can do here. And after you've rested, you can return and let your friend get some rest too."

He treated me, as everyone does, as if I'm a boy. No one ever recognizes the length of my experience, the time that I have spent in life, the long run of history that I have seen. No, they see only the false youth in my face.

Everything I said to Friar Ubaldo made no difference. He led me out and closed the door, and we left Corrao alone with Rosalino in that small, warm room. So I went off to a huge dormitory, lined with rows of beds, and lay down to sleep. Yet before I could really close my eyes, Corrao was there beside the bed.

"Burtoni," he whispered to me, "our friend is gone."

I sat up in bed and moved to get up, but he held me gently in place with just one hand. Then the tears broke loose in my eyes.

"Burtoni, it is better this way. He did not need to suffer anymore." Corrao said, "Get your rest. There is no more for us to do for him now. But we will need you tomorrow in the streets of Palermo. This is what Rosalino Pilo dreamed, when he was with us. We must both be prepared."

I pushed that hand aside, and ran across the chapel and into that little room. The Abbot was there, kneeling at the bedside, praying. The oils and instruments of the Last Rites were beside him on a table, but he was already done, and putting them away. Two brothers were already cleaning the body for burial.

Friar Ubaldo looked up at me, nodded yes. Then he stood and took my hands in his. For a long moment, he said nothing, respecting the loss in my eyes. Then he quietly said, "We will take care of this, my son."

It haunts me, even if it was right, that only Giovanni was with him in that room, behind that closed door, when Rosalino Pilo died. If what I think happened, if it did happen in that room, then I should have been there to help. Giovanni could have trusted me, then and there. He should have trusted me to help. But he did not.

And I won't to write down here what has occurred, even though Giovanni Corrao and I, Jack Burton, will always deny it. I won't write it down here. There are already too many tongues wagging with lies and suspicions.

Now the dawn approaches, and I am rested and ready at first light to enter the city with Comrade Corrao at our lead. And Il Generale above us all.

Today we will make him the Emperor of Sicily. Today the dreams of Rosalino Pilo will come true, or Giovanni Corrao and I, Jack Burton called Il Rosso, will die trying to make it so.

For Rosalino. And for his dream.

III

The loosed pages of Jack Burton's notebook end there. I leafed back through them, hoping to find more somehow, But that was the end of what the old nun had given us.

"It's not possible," I said again, looking up at Rob.

"No, it isn't possible," he said, smiling and sipping from his wine glass.

"But it is him, isn't it," I said, not really asking any questions. I had not one doubt this journal was written by Jack Burton.

Rob didn't answer me. He simply stood up from the table and led me slowly back toward the Domus Mariae, through the ancient stones of Ortigia.

Back in our room, I opened the tall wooden doors to let in the sea air, and on the silvery horizon past the rocking fishing boats docked below us, the lights of oil tankers glided across the horizon toward a distant shore. The world seemed a different place, gazing out of that old convent window on the ancient sea.

"Is this all there is to it?" I said to Rob, and he understood what I meant. On one level, I was just asking: Do we know if there is more to Jack Burton's journal? Is this all that he wrote? Did he stop there at the mountainside of Monreale, on the verge of taking Palermo with Garibaldi? But Rob also understood the broader feeling of my question too, the slow frustrations of always chasing after Burton, but never really drawing any closer. He felt those frustrations too, perhaps more pointedly than I did.

"You know what happened next, Mr. History Professor Man , don't you?"

I didn't need to answer him, but I looked from the shining Ionian Sea to the ancient stone fortifications abutting the island of Ortigia, and I said, "Garibaldi and his Red Shirts invaded Palermo, and then swept across the north of Sicily, stopping for a big fight at Milazzo, and gathering more volunteer forces as they went. Then they crossed the straits of Messina and marched slowly north until they took Naples, with hardly a fight."

"Where they met up with the King, Vittorio Emmanuel, and . . . "

" . . . and Italy was united. Sort of . . . " I interrupted him and looked over at Rob. "You know that's not what I'm talking about."

Rob laughed, and then he walked over and stretched out on his bed, kicking off his boots. "What you've read is all I've been able to get so far, brother." He put both hands behind his head, and rested against the bed frame.

"But I want to know what happened to those torn out pages? Not just at the end, but in the middle. Did somebody steal those pages? What was on them? Did Giovanni Corrao use them for a napkin? Was it Rosalino Pilo's grocery list? Or did it have the names of the squadron leaders listed? What's missing from there? And why?"

Rob just laughed at me again and I understood this is why he'd wired me to come. This is why I was here. "Take a look at the letter again," he said to me. "If you put those pages into that book, you'll see they fit perfectly, right at the end. He tore them out of the back of that journal, to write his letter to Rafaella."

"So you don't think there is anymore? This is it, this is all there is? "

Rob shrugged, "Remember, there are those missing pages from the middle. Where ever they might be."

"Whatever they are?"

Rob nodded his head. "Somebody who didn't want them in there, removed them."

"And what is that letter talking about, Roberto? If you're right, and those pages come from the end of this notebook, then he wrote that letter after he finished this journal."

Rob nodded yes. "And what is it talking about?" He grinned again, "That's why you are here, big brother. You are the history man. And together we're going to see what we can find out. Now that you know, just like I said you would, that this journal was truly written by our man Jack Burton, now we can really begin."

"I never said I knew that this was by Burton."

"You did. You said it just now."

"I did not. It can't be. Do you know how to add?"

"I do. And it can't. But it is."

I didn't answer.

"And you, Will, you know it's true."

There was a long moment's pause, a silence filled with anticipation, and then we both broke into happy, raucous laughter. At long last, after 15 years of poking around, we'd located a real true trace of the man. He was no longer just a fragment of childish circus dreams. We'd found him again, Jack Burton of the Red Shirt. Lost to us since the days of our youth, we'd found him. In a way.

"Tomorrow morning, we find the old Nun and we start digging around to see what more she knows about our boy, Jack Burton," Rob said, "Burtoni, of the Red Shirt."

What neither of us spoke out loud then was the real goal of our search: to find Burton again, or to find out what happened to him. Perhaps he was at last dead and gone, freed from his impossible life, resting finally in his own haunted peace. Just a little slice of the great circus of history. But neither Rob nor I believed that. Could he really be gone?

Completely gone? Somewhere, out there, old as the wind, he lived still. And Odd as it seems, that is what we believed. Burton lives, by God. Viva Burtoni!

In the morning, the spring sun shone into our room and woke me up. Rob was already up, studying that two-page letter in Italian. "Let's get some coffee," he said as I came to, hoping to hurry me up.

It was the pretty little nun who made cappuccini for us in the breakfast room. Her brown eyes sparkled behind a smile that would make either of us want to stay forever in Sicily. "What a shame," Rob said, and I just nodded my head and slurped the light foam from the lip of my cup.

"We need to see the Sister," Rob told the little sorrella.

"Sister Teresa?" she asked.

"Yes, we need to give her something back," Rob said.

"Oh, that old book she gave you," the little sorrella smiled her bewitching smile again.

"Oh, you know about it," I said, not asking a question, just stating a fact.

"Yes," she said, drawing the word out with hesitation. "But Sister Teresa is gone," the little sorrella said brightly. "She said you can leave that old journal with me. I will bring it safely back to her. But, you are not leaving now, are you?"

When she asked like that, who could dream of leaving Ortigia? But Rob stuck to his plan, "We need to talk to Sister Teresa, before we leave. You see, Sister, . . . "

"Oh, that will be a long while. Sister Teresa is gone on her retreat. She won't be back for weeks, and there is no talking to anyone but her confessor until then." The stern, serious frown on the little nun's face told us there could be no exceptions to the rule. "But you're not leaving?" she repeated.

Rob glanced over at me, and his eyes said, 'Okay, brother, you try.'

"Sister?" I said, "What is your name, Sister?"

The little nun smiled again sweetly at me. "Chiara," she said, looking over at Rob, too.

"Sister Claire!" I exclaimed with a grin, translating her name into flat Midwestern English.

"You know Santa Chiara."

After that weak exchange, I just pleaded with her in my most dulcet tones, "Sister Chiara, my brother and I really need to speak with Sister Teresa. I have to return to the university in another few days or so. Rob has to go back to work. We can't wait for her, Sister." She nodded her head at me, gazing at us with those big dark eyes of hers, and she began to pick up the empty cups and plates from our table.

"Can we send her a note, at least?" I said, now desperately. Could we really get this close, only to reach a dead end?

Sister Chiara shook her head no. "The Sister is on retreat. Only an emergency of the highest importance can disturb her prayers and reflections." But the little sorrella was now wearing a tiny smirk on her face; she knew something she wasn't sharing

Rob interrupted us, "So what do we do, Sister Chiara?" Both of his hands were in the air, palms up and pleading. "Where do we go from here? Do we have to come back? What should we do, Sister?"

That just made the little sorrella laugh out loud. "O Signori, Sister Teresa told us that you would come looking for her, and not just to return the journal. So she left me some instructions for you."

The grin on her pretty face then made me feel foolish. I realized we had been played by the old nun, and by her lovely young accomplice. "Sister Teresa told me that, if you came asking after her, and only if you came asking after her, that I should tell you to go on the bus Wednesday to Castellnotte, and watch for Lombardo to get on, along the way."

"Lombardo," Rob repeated, the name we both recognized from the journal. Was he some kind of aged monster too?

"And what do we do when we find 'Lombardo'?" I asked.

Sister Chiara didn't answer me.

"Does this Lombardo have a last name?" I tried a different tack.

"Sister Teresa said you should tell him who you are looking for. He will know what to do." That was it. That was all Sister Chiara told us, other than where to buy tickets and catch the bus to Castellnotte. Or perhaps it was all she would tell us, at any rate. I suspect that her instructions from old Sister Teresa were very clear and firm. And so, there was no more to tell.

On Wednesday morning at 5 a.m., we were downing espressos with the incoming sailors at a fisherman's café near Piazza delle Poste. Then we climbed on the sky blue AST autobus for a three and a half hour ride to Castellnotte. Rob sat us down near the front of the bus, near to the driver, so that we could find our man.

"Signore, do you know a man named 'Lombardo' from Castellnotte" Rob asked the driver. He looked at the two of us, from one to the other.

"Yes, this bus stops in Castellnotte," he said, his face straight and all business, acting as if he could not make out our Italian. But he was not fooling us, or giving anything up.

"Will you tell us when 'Lombardo' gets on?" Rob asked.

The driver acted as if he hadn't heard.

About twenty minutes late, with the bus only half full, the AST pulled out of the piazza. We lumbered slowly across the already bustling Ponte Umberto and then wound our way through the dirty, 'modern' town of Siracusa. Every now and then, we would pull over at a stop, and a few more workers got on, handing tickets to the driver, and then wandering to the back of the bus. Almost no one got off. No one said much.

The industrial shipyards slowly gave way to the grey green countryside, and then rows of almond trees and citrus trees began to take over the landscape. Driving through the countryside, sometimes an old woman with an empty sack would be standing beside the pavement, at the entrance to a dusty, gray dirt lane. Without a gesture or a word, the bus would lurch down through the gears and pull to a halt, and the old woman would climb on board, without much more than a nod to the uniformed driver.

About an hour and a half later, the AST turned off the highway and climbed up a steep hill to reach the little stone village of Buccheri. We wound through a street so narrow the bus barely fit, but the few Bucherini on the morning streets just twisted to their sides with a practiced ease, letting the big blue bus slide past without a blink or a nod. In the little square, before an old church, we jerked to a stop, and then a dozen or so children piled up into the bus. Even with sleep still in their eyes, and the collars of their uniforms sticking out of light spring jackets like loose feathers, once they were seated they began to chatter in happy Italian like a flock of wild birds. Calling from one end of the bus to the other, squirming in their seats, moving around the bus to tease somebody or flirt with a boy. Then one of the old women from the side of the road would bark out a command, and all would be quiet for a moment that was followed by giggles and stifled laughs, before the squirming and wandering and flirting around the bus began again.

The driver turned the big autobus around inside that tiny square, backing up and pulling forward three times before he could get the AST turned about and then headed out of Buccheri. The whole time, as he deftly maneuvered the bus, the general pandemonium of school kids went on. The driver calmly worked away, undisturbed. We knew he did it all twice a day and nearly every day of the week.

So then it was back down on the steep and narrow road until we reached the highway again. "I see now why it's going to take three hours," Rob muttered in English to me.

There were two more little towns we stopped at along the way. Vizinni was down a steep lane in a valley filled with almonds. Grammicche we watched for a couple of miles sitting up on a high hill above us, until we climbed up to it on another narrow horse cart lane, paved over for buses and cars, but built for mules and goats. In both of these towns we took on another half dozen or so children, and they began to call out to one another as they got on, some of them leaning out of the open windows on the bus, hailing to their friends that there was a seat at the back, all waiting for some new mischief.

Two young girls in their early teens, who got on back in Buccheri, kept looking at Rob and I, and then whispering to one another. At every stop, they moved around in the bus, always finding seats closer to us.

I nudged Rob with an elbow and pointed them out. It was his big smile and a "Buon giorno" that started them to giggling, and then it was clear they wanted to try out their schoolroom English on us.

"Where are you from?" the braver girl said, her eyes darting over at her friend the whole time. The English words sounded foreign and practiced in her mouth.

"Siracusa," Rob answered, emphasizing the Sicilian 'g' sound in his pronunciation.

That made them laugh at us. With our height and our weight, it was pretty clear we weren't from Sicily. "Are you from the United States?" she said, a little too clearly.

Everyone on the bus was now listening, and even all the schoolchildren were quiet, watching to see what might happen.

"Yes," Rob said in English.

"Where are you going?" the dark haired girl said. She was now braver and a little more sure of her English.

"Castellnotte," Rob said. "We are trying to find someone named 'Lombardo' from Castellnotte. Do you know him?"

The two girls glanced at one another, and a round of mysterious giggles trickled through the bus.

"Do you know this 'Lombardo'?" I repeated.

But Rob understood immediately that we had just run into that deep strain of Sicilian reticence, the same as what we got from the bus driver. No one here was going to hand anyone over to a couple of foreigners without first talking to our mysterious Lombardo, and letting him know someone was asking for him.

"Where are you from in the United States?" the fair-haired one said.

"Iowa," said Rob, though this wasn't true for either of us now. "Do you know where Iowa is?" he said.

And so we rode along on the AST across the Sicilian interior, talking with two young school girls about the

American Midwest, both of us trusting that when the moment arrived, we would find our 'Lombardo.'

On the winding road up the hillside to Grammiche, suddenly, as if it was being drawn out of some deep inner pocket, Mount Etna rose like a smoking giant in the blue sky. "Look there," Rob said, pointing past the mountain. A thin line in the distance past the volcano divided the blue sky in two, and I realized it was the edge of the Tyrrhenian Sea at the horizon, just a slightly different shade of blue, edging in mist, where sea met sky past the great gray green mountain.

We wheeled into the main square of Grammiche, and another half dozen kids carrying their backpacks climbed on. And behind them, not wishing to squirm in the door with them came slowly a string of four women, each one carrying an empty shopping sack. Some of them stood in the aisle of the bus, as it was now getting full, and then called out to others, to friends already on the bus. "Marcella, hallo," said one short grey woman in a navy blue dress.

"Anna, how are you?" came the answer from somewhere back in the bus.

"The old man?" someone else said, "Is he better today?"

Marcella just waved her free hand down from her shoulder to her knee in disgust. She didn't say a word, but that made the whole bus laugh.

Then there was some chatter in speedy Sicilian that neither Rob nor I could understand. Rob stood up and I followed him, and we let Marcella and one of her friends sit down. She seemed embarrassed, glancing down at her feet a lot, with the coos and whistles coming from some of the little boys on the bus.

"Marcella," some boy yelled in very clear Italian, "Don't let Marco find out!" And that was followed by uproarious laughter, and Marcella leaned up out of the seat, her jaw set like a rock, and glared down the aisle at all the kids seated on the bus.

Rob nudged me in the rib and pointed out of the front windshield of the bus with a nod of his head. Three old men, all of them darkened by years in the sun, squat and round, not one of them five foot tall, walked slowly arm in arm across the little piazza away from us. When they reached the opposite end, they turned all at once and then locked arms again, and began the slow walk toward the bus, chatting to one another all the while. "They've been walking back and forth like that since we stopped," Rob said with a little grin.

"Since before we stopped," I added.

Rob nodded, still grinning.

"It's market day in Castellnotte," the shyer, fair-haired girl said in English, trying to start our conversation again.

"Oh, I see," Rob said to her.

The driver glanced back at his full and noisy bus, and then he revved up the engine, and it coughed out a little blue smoke. He was watching something out in the piazza then, and he shook his head grumbling. Then he stood up from his seat and hung out the open door of the AST. "'Bardo! Andiamo!" he yelled, and then clambered back up to his seat stiffly, without glancing back. The three little old men kept strolling toward the bus, not even looking up. With an angry "harrumph!" the driver tooted the bus's horn twice.

Eventually the three little old men made it over to the AST, and after a series of hugs and warm two-fisted handshakes, the tallest of the three climbed on board. The driver let out another too loud "harrumph" and shoved the bus's folding door closed with his lever. Then, with a blind nod at the old man, he began to turn the bus around so we could work our way out of the piazza.

The short brown man clambered up out of the stairwell onto the main aisle at the front of the bus, and then he leaned down to wave his farewell to his friends in the square. But they had already begun their arm in arm stroll back across the piazza. The old man shrugged his shoulders and turned again to where Rob and I were still standing in the aisle in front of him.

"Marcella, buon giorno," he said, and she nodded hello while she kept her eyes on the floor of the bus.

The old man seemed a bit confused, and he looked down the rows of filled seats to the back of the bus, at all the schoolchildren who were suddenly so quiet. He threw out an open palm, with his other hand he held a seat back for balance. "Miei raggazzi, come andati?"

That started a wave of chuckling and giggling through the autobus, and a few of the children piped up, "Buon giorno. Nonno!" But oddly, no one said the old man's name, the way they had called out to Marcella and Anna and to the others.

I looked at Rob, and he whispered, "This is our boy." And then Rob glanced down at our two friends, the girls with their schoolbook English, but they refused to look back at us, their faces stone still, gazing firmly out of the bus window to the piazza outside. Robbed nodded to me.

"Lombardo," he said flatly, without any hint of a question in his voice. The bus, if possible, grew even more quiet.

The little brown man, square and short with piercing brown eyes, didn't answer but a quizzical smirk wrinkled his mouth. The bus driver's head twisted just a touch as he listened in over the working engines of the bus. He, like everyone else on that bus, was waiting to see if Lombardo would answer, or if they would need to continue keeping him a secret. But Lombardo answered, "Yes." Then he paused and waited for Rob and I to identify ourselves.

"This is my brother," Rob said my name after he had named himself.

"Buon giorno," Lombardo said, the smirk gone. But his eyes were even more intense. After a moment, he said, "How do I know you?" meaning really how did we know him. Marcella glanced up, but not at us in the aisle. The driver leaned a bit farther over in his seat, and cut the engine noticeably.

"We come from Siracusa," Rob said, sticking out a hand toward him. But Lombardo didn't take it just yet.

"We were staying at the Domus Mariae," Rob went on. "Sister Teresa sent us here to look for you. She gave us your name, and said you would be here on this bus."

"Sister Teresa," he said, looking at us now as he leaned toward us, but he still didn't take Rob's outstretched hand. "What did she want?" he muttered.

I thought maybe this was the wrong way to go at it, so I butted in. "Actually, Signor Lombardo, it was the little Sister Chiara who sent us. She gave us your name."

Lombardo stepped back as if the bus had jolted over a rock, and his head leaned back as he looked past my brother at me in the aisle. Marcella almost turned around in her seat now to boldly look us over anew. And then a big wide grin spread across Lombardo's face.

The bus then did hit a bump in the road, but it was because we were wandering off the pavement. The driver turned straight back in his seat with another "harrumph" and fought to keep the autobus on the road. And that lead to uproarious laughter from all the schoolboys, followed by a few squeals and nervous giggles from the girls, and the boys, too, who would dare let on they were frightened.

"Sorrella Chiara," Lombardo said. "And what, my new friends, did she say?"

"She said we should take this bus to Castellnotte and ask for you along the way," Rob jumped in.

Lombardo seemed thoughtful for a long moment, and then he looked at me as if I was more trustworthy than my brother.

"How is she?" he asked.

His name was Lombardo Sciascia, he told us, pronounced like it was an old doo-wop song: 'Sha-Sha.' Once he had shaken our hands, the two schoolgirls got up and gave Lombardo their seats. Rob and I scrunched into the seat next to him and rode for the hour or so left to reach Castellnotte, talking all the way.

It was market day there, so the AST made a lot of stops at the roadside along the way, and more and more people climbed on board. The broad chatter in Sicilian that started then and grew louder with every mile was too quick and too strange for even Rob to follow. But we spoke to Lombardo in our best Italian.

The old man quizzed us carefully about Sister Chiara. How did she look? Did she seem happy? Was she healthy? He got a lot of information from us, and we got next to nothing from him. But that was all right. We knew our time would come. Neither of us said a word about Jack Burton.

When the bus pulled into a dusty station at Castellnotte, we climbed out with Signor Sciascia and, before we could offer to buy him lunch, he said, "Are you hungry?" Then he led us in the opposite direction, away from the market piazza where Marcella and her friends were happily headed. Instead we walked along amongst all the school children noisily headed up toward the old part of town. They were heading reluctantly to school. Where Lombardo was leading us, we weren't sure.

We seemed to wander aimlessly through a lot of narrow medieval streets and then Sciascia took us straight through a back door and into the kitchen of a little restaurant. There stood the Nonna, she was cooking, and there was clearly her son in an apron, and his two lovely teenage daughters getting ready to wait on the tables.

"These are my friends," he proudly announced and introduced us by name. "Gaetano here will bring us the best food in town," he said to me, with a wink.

That made the Nonna snort a laugh, since surely she was the one with the recipes. But Lombardo leaned over toward her and said, as if to smooth things over, "They come with words from our little Rosalina."

The Nonna crossed herself and the two girls looked up from their preparations and examined us anew. Rob just smiled. "Sorrella Chiara," he said, making the connection. But both Rob and I had noticed that name. It stood out like a tower deep in the oldest forest: Rosalina. None of these names could be mere coincidence. Not in this country. Not with these traditions.

One of the two girls led us out to a table then in the piazza in front of the restaurant. "Bianco o rosso?" she said, to which Lombardo rattled off a string of instructions in quick Sicilian. We sat in the warm sun, away from the shadow the cathedral cast across the piazza.

As I sipped the cool white wine that the girl brought us, and we ate slices of a hard white cheese and a deep red salami, I pointed up to the violent and beautiful porcelain copula over the door to the church. Rob nodded and said, "Santa Lucia," and we were both remembering the description in Jack Burton's journal.

"Are the stairs still here?" I asked Lombardo, and he grinned and said, "Oh yes, yes," as if the thought of their disappearance was inconceivable. "You have been here before then?" he said.

"No, never," Rob said. "We have just read about it."
He didn't say where.

At that Lombardo Sciascia seemed surprised. "We
don't see many tourists here," he said. "Almost none. We are
pretty far from Taormina and Cefalu." He took a drink of
wine. "From everywhere," he said, a little wistfully perhaps.
"It is quiet here," he sighed, "these days."

Then the food came, slices of swordfish rolled around a
sausage stuffing in a light tomato sauce, married perfectly to
the simple white wine. As we ate, Sciascia pointed up above
the spires of the church to the rock standing over us all, and at
the old castle that stood there. "Castellnotte," he said proudly,
"where we get our name."

"Yes," Rob said, "Castellnotte. Is there still an orange
grove there?" he asked.

Sciascia looked us over carefully, and we got a dose of
his Sicilian reticence. Then, after a long, long moment, he said
carefully, "It is still there. It has not changed much since that
day."

I snuck a quick glance over at Rob, to see if he knew
what day Sciascia was talking about. Our eyes met for just an
instant, and that told me no. But maybe this was why we'd
been sent here. Sciascia, with his native suspiciousness, caught
that little glance between us, I'm sure. He grew
simultaneously more reticent, and more talkative.

"How is it you know my daughter?" he said, and his
eyes were on his plate.

"Your daughter," I said, and stopped eating.

"Rosalina," he said.

Rob was grinning then, as I slowly caught on. "Sister
Chiara," I said.

*   *   *

163

So as we sipped the last of the wine in the warm sun of the piazza, beneath that bright and frightening image of Santa Lucia, my brother explained it all to Sciascia. The way we were trying to find Jack Burton, our old friend from childhood, and how that search had strangely led us here. His daughter Rosalina, the pretty little nun at Domus Mariae, had sent us to Castellnotte to see him, after we'd read the journal the old Sorrella had given us.

Sciascia was quiet through most of it. He interrupted Rob only once. "Sister Teresa?" he said, looking up from under his dark brows, when Rob mentioned the old nun. But that was the only time Rob paused to clear things up. "So that is how we know about the orange grove and the stairs to the sea," he said to finish.

"And does she seem happy?" Sciascia said at the end.

"Sister Teresa?" I said.

He shook his head sharply. He didn't need to know about her. "Rosalina," he said.

I looked over at Rob, and he shrugged one shoulder. "She seems fine," my brother said. "From what we can see. She seems well."

"She's a beautiful girl," I blurted out, forgetting for a moment that I was speaking to her father and that she was a nun.

But Lombardo loved that, a broad proud grin spread across his face and he rocked his chair back on two legs. "Yes." He said. "Rosalina is a beautiful child." But then his face darkened again at some thought, and it seemed better to drop the subject.

"Can we see the Castle?" Rob charged ahead. "Is it open still?"

Lombardo Sciascia stood and rubbed his hand through his short steely hair, and then he stretched a little in the sun. He seemed a bit hesitant to take us there and he said, "It is closed now." But with a jerk of his head, he got us up and led us back out of the piazza. "La Rocca will be open tomorrow. Part of it. Not the gardens, of course, but part of the castello, tomorrow. You see, it is being restored by the government. La Rocca is now a piece of our history, they say. Even if for a long, long time, we were all silent about what happened up there."

He spoke as we strolled through a narrow stone street. "What happened there?" Rob said finally.

This brought Lombardo up short, he turned and looked us over again. "I thought that was why you were here."

"We're here because your daughter sent us here," I said.

He snorted a laugh like the Nonna's in the restaurant.

"We're looking for Jack Burton," my brother said.

Sciascia nodded his head yes and turned back and led us out to a walled ledge. As he sauntered along, he said over his shoulder, "This journal, do you have it with you?"

There was a short stone wall about knee high to a Sicilian that curved around the edge of the square, and we looked from there out at the blue sea to the north. Mount Etna and the Castellnotte stood on the heights behind us.

"I have it right here," Rob pulled it out of his shoulder bag, the leather bound notebook tied up with leather strings. He handed it over to Sciascia who took it and turned it around in his hands. But he didn't open it. He couldn't read it, because it was in English anyway, but clearly he knew what it was. And what it meant too, though we were not yet sure ourselves of that.

"Our La Scala starts from here," he said, pointing with the hand that didn't hold Jack Burton's journal. "This is what Signor Burtoni saw the first time he came here, with Rosalino Pilo and Giovanni Corrado."

"Corrado?" Rob said. "But Burton calls him 'Corrao' in there," and he put a hand on the notebook, while glancing over at me for verification.

Sciascia just grinned, and then said, "It's good that you recognize him under that name. They say around here that the old Dottore was a man of many names, I'm afraid. Here, we call him Corrado. That is his real Sicilian name, you know, though all the history books get it wrong."

I stepped through an opening in the little wall and down a few of the old, uneven steps. When I turned and looked back up, I saw the first few of them. "Rob, you've got to come see this," I called out. Then I scurried down a half dozen more stairs.

They were just as Burton had described them. Every step was pure white and every tile was painted with bold red and blue and yellow figures. Simple, rustic designs, fishes and flowers and boats and human faces. And just as Jack Burton had written, they were hidden from above. You saw nothing but a twisting row of graveled stairs with a few hints of white ceramic edging when you looked down to the seashore. It was as if these artists were afraid to compete with the blue of the beautiful sea. But when you looked back up toward the village, toward their home, it was a true, dancing riot of color.

I admit, they were so beautiful, Rob and I left Sciascia with Burton's journal at the top and we ran all the way down the stairs to the rocky shoreline, so we could see them all, the reach of them all together, and then we slowly worked our way back up every step, admiring each and every one.

From the shoreline, the majolica stairs curled upward slowly and led your eyes directly to the façade of the church, where the ceramic of Santa Lucia was just an accompanying pinnacle of color, its violent martyred subject only a bright abstract design, like the painted stairs. Overshadowing it all, on the rock face above it, stood the vast honeyed walls of the Castle. La Rocca di Castellnotte.

Rob and I stood there on the dock at the bottom looking up wordlessly, both of us remembering Jack Burton and his

Rafaella standing just there, where we were, with all their newborn love, pledging their eternal faith in one another.

But where did it lead them from here?

At the top of La Scala we found Sciascia sitting on a bench waiting for us, in the shade of an old olive tree. He was paging through the journal, though he couldn't read its English, he was gazing down at the handwriting, touching the old letters of Jack Burton's hand. Something in him had changed while we were gone. He seemed softer, gentler, and older too.

Since we couldn't see anything of the Castello until morning, we began to ask about a hotel. He smiled quizzically at us, and led us through the piazza under Santa Lucia's peaceful, upward cast eyes and then out to the edge of the village. "You have a place to stay," he said, in answer to all our questions. "You have a place to stay."

His house was a little three-room building made of stone on the edge of the village, with a clear view of La Rocca above, though his view of the ocean was blocked by a row of painted stone houses on a rise in the ground behind him.

He fed us with simple bread and salami and lots of wine. After the big lunch, it seemed plenty. Then he said, "I will stay in Rosalina's room, and you two will have mine. The bed is bigger. And in the morning, we'll go up to La Rocca, the castello. The three of us will go up, together."

In his room, on the whitewashed wall across from his bed, two pictures hung. One of them we recognized immediately as a photo of the young Rosalina. There was Sister Chiara, smiling and holding a doll, a beautiful young girl about to blossom into womanhood. She must have been twelve or thirteen years old, I'd guess. Nothing about that picture told you this child would grow up to become a nun. I don't know, really, if any photo could show a sign of that future. But if I hadn't known her as Sister Chiara, I would not expect this lovely child to be joining a convent soon.

"Oh, you're just showing your American background, Will," Rob said when I mentioned it to him. "You can't tell that kind of thing from a photograph."

Next to Rosalina's photo hung another photograph, black and white, of a young woman in a simply cut dress with a bouquet of flowers in her hand. She stared deliberately into the camera, and on her lips there was a quizzical smile, not forced but more than a bit confused. There was a shyness evident in her, not clever but genuine, and it drew the viewer in. This woman, standing alone in the village, was the very image of Rosalina Sciascia. The woman in the picture had to be the little Sorrella's mother.

Lombardo strode in, with a quick rap of his knuckles on the doorframe to announce his presence. He found us examining the pair of photos, not matching but alike, on his wall.

"Sister Chiara?" I said, with a nod to the color photo.

"Yes, that's my Rosalina," Lombardo said, "A happy child, she was." He was smiling. Then he stepped over and placed two fingers on the photo, "And this is her mother, my sweet Rosetta. Gone these many years." He made the sign of the cross and muttered silently some prayer.

"Rosalina looks just like her," Rob said boldly.

"She does at that," said Lombardo. "When she was little, after Rosetta was gone, sometimes little Rosalina would frighten me, how much she seemed like her mother. The way she walked. The way she laughed. It would surprise me."

I wanted to ask him what happened to Rosetta Sciascia, but it seemed at that moment prying and we were really strangers still, though it was seeming harder and harder to believe this.

But in the next moment Lombardo changed the subject entirely. He pulled a crisp manila envelope out from under his arm and handed it to me. Rob leaned toward me trying to see what it was. "I think this is what Sister Teresa has sent you here for, though I'm not sure why," Lombardo said.

"What is it?" I said.

Rob pointed at the front of the crisp envelope, where someone had written in a black marker 'G. Corrado.' But he didn't say anything.

"You read Italian?" Lombardo said, and we both nodded yes. "Good," he said. "Inside there is the letter your 'Corrao' wrote to Rafaella Crisiana explaining to her what happened here. This is what I think Sister Teresa wanted you to find here. This is why she sent you to me."

"How do you come by it?" I asked, confused as usual. Rob nudged me in the ribs, trying to say: Be Careful. Doors were opening all around us. Don't spoil it now by shaming them silent with too many questions.

Lombardo just smiled at me. "My Mother, who was named Rosalina too, like my daughter, passed it down to me, as the oldest child in the family. You see, Rafaella Crisiana was my grandmother."

Rob and I stood there, I suppose like gaping idiots, letting all this information settle in. It was hard to put all of it in place right then. It was too much, too fast, suddenly. Sciascia waited only a moment before he added, "You fellows read through this letter, and in the morning we'll go up to the castello. This is what, I guess, Sister Teresa wants us to do. She wants me to take you to La Rocca. I don't know why."

Then he turned slowly away and shut the door behind him as he wished us both a "Buona notte" and added "A domani" too.

*   *   *

A white string bound the manila packet shut. I fumbled around with it to get it open until Rob took it from me impatiently. He pulled it open quickly with a practiced hand, and inside we found a sheaf of loose yellowed pages, covered with a beautiful blue ink, in a hand that carried a great deal of flourish. Though the pages had yellowed, the ink had not faded at all. It was clear this document had been handled carefully, and not often, then stored safely away for at least a hundred years.

"Bingo!" Rob said, as he pulled out the first few pages gently. "This may be what we are looking for."

So we stretched out, side-by-side, both of us sitting with our backs propped at the head of the bed, and we passed the pages gingerly to one another, careful of their fragility and incomprehensible value. If any of the Italian was hard to make out, between the two of us we were able to read it without a dictionary. Most of it was written in a very formal and learned Italian without even a trace of Sicilian, or any other dialect for that matter. Perfect Tuscan, it was. And so it was easier for us to understand than, say, Jack Burton's letter to Rafaella. Or maybe it was just that our Italian was getting better with time. At any rate, we read straight through it to the end, with only a few stops when either Rob or I would say, "Does this mean what I think it does?"

Here follows then a text of what Giovanni Corrao wrote, in my rough translation from his Italian. I have tried to catch the flavor of his formal but passionate voice, though in that attempt I think I have failed. You will notice, I'm sure, his propensity to capitalize words for emphasis. I have left those capitals in place.   There is no date on the document. It begins:

Signorina Crisiana,

I hope that this missive finds you well, or as well as can be expected under these Dire and Darkest circumstances, dearest Rafaella. I have undertaken to write to you at the request of our friend (at least I hope you still think of both him and of me as your friends, for we truly remain so) Sig. Giovanni Burtoni, also known as Jack Burton to some. He felt, as he reported to me, that you might find it more acceptable to hear this explanation from me, than from his pen. I truly don't know why he believes this, but since I too was sent at the head of the operation to Castellnotte, I can certainly report and verify as to the events that occurred there a year ago last August, why they happened and what befell therefore. Some of these things you know, from report or from experience I suppose, but I would like you to have the full and complete facts about these serious events, which have had such dour impact, as they occurred. Without any varnish, I might add.

In order for you to completely understand the actions taken at Castellnotte, as you were at that time resident in Messina, I believe, I must go back to the beginnings a bit, I'm afraid, and describe for you, in the very least, the conditions in which Sig. Burtoni and I found the city upon our arrival.

After our victorious action at Milazzo, we had marched toward Messina with the Thousand, as they are already known. Once again the nearly miraculous tide of battle had turned in our favor, as it had in Palermo, and as it had not so many times before in the past. The Fate of History, my Dearest Rafaella, seemed at last to be running with us, and not biting at our

171

heels. And you were among those of us who had struggled to urge our History forward, to make that History break into a full run. I shall never forget your courage at San Martino when we lost our mutual friend, our dear Comrade in arms, our commander, that great spirit of the Revolution itself, Rosalino. It was you, Rafaella, who roused us then from the fear and stupor of our loss to urge us Onward, Burtoni and me, reminding us of what the Great Pilo himself would want. He would expect us to Press Forward without him, in his very memory, as it were. It was you who brought us back from our despair. And soon we rode with the General into Palermo.

But as we marched on to Messina, which the Bourbons had already abandoned, fleeing on their ships across the straits, we began to receive word of a rising in the mountains. The General had been declared, by acclamation of the Thousand, and by the freed people of Messina, to be the Dictator of Sicily. He was now the full and true ruler of the entire island.

It was his officer, our comrade in the liberation of Sicily, Nino Bixio who at word of these revolts in the interior took young Burtoni and me aside. "We must maintain order now," he told us, frankly. We dared not let Anarchy reign across our new Sicilia, across any part of it even, in the absence of the hated Bourbons For if we did let wild Anarchy rear its head, with its comrade Revenge, all might be lost.

"Take the dozen men at your side, the Heroes of Milazzo, and go out and restore the general order," Bixio commanded us. So it was we were sent to your dear Castellnotte, O Rafaella, with orders to bring these campagnolo revolts under Control and to a Definitive End. But this was not all, I'm afraid. Commander Bixio made our orders very clear, Rafaella. He was explicit in his commands. "You must execute the ringleaders, gentlemen," he said. "They must quickly be made an example, or once again, men, all we have struggled for will be lost."

This "All" that he spoke of, Rafaella, it is our very Country. This is what Commander Bixio meant.

Burtoni and I understood why we were being sent. Because of what we did, with you and with our late, lost Pilo, we were being entrusted with this Crucial if odious task. And I have no doubt, even now, Rafaella, where these hard orders came from: They came from il Generale himself. [At this point, Corrao had underlined the General's title with a forceful line, so I leave it in Italian.]

And so it was we set out on horseback with a dozen of the hardest, truest men at hand. In haste, we traveled with the urgency of the General in our minds, and with the dream of our country in our hearts.

It took us only a day, long and arduous as it was, to cover the hard ground beneath Etna and we reached the outskirts of Castellnotte at barest daylight. At first all seemed orderly. Though the people were lying about the piazza, sleeping off the excess of their celebrations, at dawn everything seemed in Order. The cathedral and the beautiful stairway to the sea, which you know so well from your childhood days, they were clean and shining in the morning light, as if they'd been washed by a purifying rain. All was calm and restful. Yet something was amiss, and it took us only a little time to find its roots.

As we rode into the piazza, some of the sleeping revelers began to stir. "Who is in charge here?" I asked repeatedly, to several of these waking and groggy men. At first they were able to answer with no names, they just looked at one another in a stupor that might have been sleep and might have been drink, and yet might again have been deceit. Certainly, with what I know now, it was all three.

It was Burtoni first who saw the problem. Perhaps it was because he had come to know this village with you at his side. Or at least this is what he told me, on our ride across the Nebrodi. On the step mountainside above us stood the Castle itself, you know it very well. Like a second home you know it, Burtoni claims. From that tall stone edifice, melded out of the rocks of the mountainside, there drifted upward a thin spire of black smoke. "Do you see it?" Burtoni said. And I did indeed. The Castle had been burned down to the stones, enough days before so that only the trace of smoke still wafted upward into the sky. It was, I suppose you would say, still smoldering. So you see, the reports were true, and our Hopes that they had been exaggerated died with that sight, O Rafaella.

We rounded up the men in the piazza and marched them inside the church. They were complacent, like weary sheep. It is dark and ancient inside that little cathedral, as I'm sure you know from many a winter Sunday morning. Light slanted in through narrow stained glass only faintly, though it was a bright summer's morning outside. But inside there were only shafts of colored light in a dusty air filled with old hints of candle smoke and incense. We were met with silence at first, but then I began to question them in Our Sicilian language, translating as I went for Burtoni as I spoke. Everyone else in our force knew this language as their mother tongue. And the sound of our own tongue seemed to loosen theirs.

"Comrade Tre," one of the men said finally. "He's in charge."

"And where is he?" I said, still in Sicilian.

They answered me with a lot of shrugs and glances at one another, until one of them muttered something about the stables. I only needed to nod to Burtoni, and he was gone, for you know, he was familiar with the village at least a little.

After that, it was silent in the cathedral. The villagers refused to speak at all, and I switched back into Italian, which I knew they understood. It is, after all, the language of our country. "So who is Comrade Uno?" I said, but at that they wouldn't even raise their heads.

Burtoni was gone for a long while, perhaps half an hour, and in a little village of that size, that is a long time. I began to ponder sending some of our dozen out to check on him, when finally he strode back into the church.

He was not alone, Signorina Crisiana. He brought back with him someone who I take it you would know well. And Burtoni was visible shaken, his eyes blank and dark with anger, but his shoulders drooped with a strange sadness. Beside him there was a young fair-haired lad of twenty or so. His hands were bound behind his back, and Burtoni shoved him in front of me and snarled at the boy, "On your knees, Gaetano," he said. The boy looked up at me fearfully, and Burtoni said flatly, "This is your 'Comrade Tre.'" But then Burtoni seemed to collapse into a pew seat and he covered his face with a hand.

For a moment, I didn't speak. I waited for these villagers to react or for someone to come forward. The lad just trembled like a puppy, kneeling before me. It was hard to imagine him as the leader of all these men, and not for a moment did I believe that he was.

Burtoni rose to his feet again, glared at all the village men around him in the church, took a deep breath, and then spoke out calm orders to our men, not to let anyone leave the building at any cost. Then he simply looked over at me and said, "You'd better come up with me and see what they have done."

It was as we strode up La Rocca toward the smoldering castle that he explained to me about you, Signorina, and the Duke and Duchess of Castellnotte, how they had raised you after your grandfather died and when your father went off to the university in Messina. You grew up in this tall castle, and the Lord and Lady Burmonte were like a doting aunt and uncle to you.

"And who is this young Gaetano?" I asked Burtoni.

This is when Burtoni told me, O Rafaella dear, of your plans to marry, of your vows on the Scala to one another, and of the way the Duke and Duchess had jumped with a truly parental joy and excitement to plan your celebration. Neither of you ever spoke of this to me, not even as we marched behind the great Pilo, and then with the Generale, across this island, taking first Palermo, and then the fortress of Milazzo and then to Messina. It was obvious, of course, that the two of you were deeply in love, as we might say, with one another. But never from either of you came a word of these plans, of this Marriage.

I know, Signorina, it was wartime, and certain hopes and dreams are better left unstated in times such as ours, when we are all preparing for battle, preparing everyday for the best of all possible worlds or for the worst that anyone can imagine, at the same time. But knowing of this vow or yours, I suppose, is what motivates me to report these sordid events to you as carefully and completely and honestly as I can. I cannot pretend to understand what has fallen between you and good old Burtoni now, but I can try to make clear the circumstances this Good Man struggled under in those days at Castellnotte. And so, I'm afraid, O Dear Rafaella, I will present you with the ugly details. All of them.

"Gaetano was one of Lord Burmonte's servants, a favorite," Burtoni told me. "Gaetano fed us and showed us our rooms the night we stayed here in the castle. Rafaella has known him since he was an infant." This is what good Burtoni told me as we marched together up the mountainside to the castle.

Burtoni stopped as we approached the stone walls at the crest of La Rocca, and spoke without looking at me. He seemed to be steeling himself for what awaited us inside those walls. "Corrao," he said to me, "do you remember the horses we rode, the fresh good horses Rafaella and I rode from here, to catch up with you and Rosalino on the way to Pieni dei

Greci. It was Gaetano. That lad was the one who gave us those horses, all rested and ready, and he said to me then that though he wanted to come, he couldn't come with us to meet the General. But he could give us those fine, fast horses to ride. They were the pick of the Duke's stables. He sent us off with them, because he couldn't join us."

I don't know if this is true, Signorina, but I know that Burtoni believed the boy Gaetano was one of us. And you don't need to be told. You know what the truth is.

Without another word, Burtoni led me up into the Castle grounds. The brassy stone walls still stood tall, and above us I could see that some of the floor work and the furniture was still inside, but the roofing was all gone in the blaze, and the belly of the Castle was charred and exposed to the now harsh morning light.

He led me around through some broken windows and charred doorways into a little square, once a secret interior garden cloister within the Castle. I don't need to describe for you this quiet place, Signorina Crisiana, for you know it well. Our Burtoni told me later that this was The Garden of miniature orange trees hidden away inside the wall, and you had shown him this place yourself in those passed and Better days of your love. This was where you hoped to speak your vows to one another publicly, Burtoni told me, in a lovely, peaceful garden where you had whiled away the summer hours as a child. Let me tell you now what we found there, so perhaps you can understand our dire actions later. Perhaps it will help you to understand.

The walls of the portico around the garden had remained mostly untouched, which told me that the fire in the castle, or most of it, had burned above us. The old citrus trees, which Burtoni described so clearly for me, were all gone, every one of them, though I could see the stumps still resting low in the fitted octagonal stones around them. I could see that the stone floor of the garden had once been designed around them. But now, you see, they had all been cut down and then heaped in the center of the cloister, where the central tree had once stood. Now, there only stood a heap of the charred remains of burnt trees where the bonfire had blazed.

I hesitate to tell you the next part of my report, O Rafaella, for it is distressing yet to me, and I did not know these people event to see them, much less know them as you did, as nigh unto Family. But even for me, it was a horrible sight, Dear Signorina. I am sorry to report it at all, especially to you, but again it may help you to understand our subsequent actions there in Castellnotte. It was not just orders we were following, I am afraid. I must confess to you. We were not just following our orders.

They were burned beyond any recognition, truly just the charred remains of two bodies down there in the still smoking charcoal of the lost orange trees. From the way their remains were still arched, it was clear that they had been bound hands to feet behind their backs. I don't know this for sure, and when we interrogated the townspeople later, no one would say. No one, I tell you. No one. I pause here again before I write it down now. But it seems to my eyes there was no reason to bind these victims in this way unless, I am sorry to say this here, O Rafaella, unless they were still alive when the branches of the orange trees were set ablaze.

"Who are they?" I asked Burtoni.

"I don't know," he answered me, "but I'm afraid I have an idea."

Burtoni stood there for a moment, not a praying man, but we were both searching for some prayer to say, though nothing came to us. "I can't believe Gaetano did this," he whispered after a while.

We walked back down to the church in silence. There was nothing to speak about, really, and we both of us Burtoni and I, we knew what our orders were. We did not have to plan. But this did not make what we were ordered to do any easier to follow, and yet our orders were clear from the start.

We took each of these men then back into the small sacristy, removed from the rest of the guarded villagers, one at a time, and Burtoni and I interrogated them. It was clear before long who those two bodies were, just as Burtoni had feared. They were the Lord and Lady Brumonte. And we heard stories that seemed to mesh about the servants ransacking the Castle. But no one knew who had bound the Duke and Duchess hand to foot and burned them alive. All their stories ended with confusion and doubts and ignorance, and just plain silence.

That is everyone except Gaetano. He alone laid claim to their horrible deaths. "You didn't do it alone," I said to him. "Yes," he answered, "I did." And then he would say no more.

It left us in a delicate position. We now had twenty some sheepish men under arrest, all of them guilty in one way or another, but only Gaetano would lay claim to the murder: 'Comrade Tre' as he called himself. We were here for an execution, though none of these men knew that, or would believe it if they were told. If we followed orders, executing the lot of them, all twenty, we knew we would be gutting the future of this little village. This was the heart of their manhood, half the soul of the town's next generation, indelibly altered forever. These were the fathers and the brothers who would raise the next generation. To take them all to the firing squad—though perhaps they merited it—would leave the women of Castellnotte with the young and the aged to care for, the fields and the herds to work. They would do it, but it would be a cruel and useless act remembered bitterly for generations. And you know, Signorina Rafaella, because you come from this island, are of it as I am, you know how long the Sicilian memory lives. No, Signorina, it was the ringleaders we needed, the one or two who were the true instigators. To execute them, the two or three who led the way, would leave Castellnotte in Order, Strong and Ready to Rebuild. And the message would be sent to everyone, all through the island. This kind of dangerous Anarchy, this Retribution of the common people on the aristocracy would not be tolerated. We need all of us, lords and peasants, ladies and maids, all of us to make new country. Our New Country, O Signorina.

But only Gaetano would lay claim to what had been done there. Everyone else was silent. All twenty or so men were just mute and dumb. Burtoni pulled me aside and we spoke quietly in the sacristy, away from all the other ears, both the villagers' and ours.

"What do we do now?" Burtoni said. I didn't answer, because I wanted to see what he would decide. After a long moment of silence, Burtoni just went on, "Gaetano didn't do this. He's taking the blame to hide someone else."

"Come with me," I said to Burtoni. So I took this young Gaetano by the arm, and with Burtoni following behind us, we marched back into the sacristy behind the altar. It was a little dark room filled with dark wood cabinets that were filled with bright vestments. I sat this Gaetano boy down on the floor and then I spoke into his face, leaning down to glare at him. "All right, Comrade Tre," I said, softly and putting a great little twist on his assumed title. "Do you know who I am?"

And so I talked to him then, talked to him in a way I knew, Sicilian village boy that he was, a way he would understand. You know it too, Signorina, even though you come from way over here and you live in Messina. You know what I mean. I talked to this lad the way we talk where I grew up, in the Albergheria in Palermo. So he would understand that we were Serious. We meant to Act.

I explained to him that we had been sent by the General himself, and that he was now the dictator of the island. His word was the new law. The General was The Big Man, now. [This phrase was written in Sicilian dialect, only later deciphered by Rob and me with the help of Sciascia.] And the General's new law says we are to eliminate those who have caused the problem, and so restore the law and Order of the Dictator to Castellnotte run rampant.

I explained to him that I knew he did not do this alone, if he did it at all. I understood that 'Comrade Tre' was covering up for someone. And while that might seem noble and loyal, what it meant, at bottom, was that he Gaetano was going to Die for whoever these others were. So then I offered the young man my opinion. "When you look at what they've done up there in that castle," I said to the boy, "these other scoundrels you are protecting are not worth your loyalty, and certainly not your nobility."

So then I asked him straight out, "Who is Comrade Uno?"

But the lad was brave. He had a Big Heart, Rafaella. He answered without even a blink or a twitch, with just his courageous, foolish silence.

I told him that. Then I believed I understood something: it must be a woman the boy is so loyal to, I thought. "Or maybe, Gaetano, I should ask you this way: who is Comrade Una?"

181

This got somewhere, for he looked up in my eyes and I could see he wanted to spit at me then. But he was too smart. He said nothing, not a word, and he knew he'd already revealed too much.

"Okay," I said, "we'll have it your way, Comrade. Burtoni?" Together we pulled him up onto his feet and dragged the brave lad out into the church proper. "Bring them all up to the Castle," I ordered, and our men rounded up the twenty or so mute villagers and herded them like the sheep they were up to La Rocca. Burtoni and I led the boy Gaetano along at the head of them. The women and the old men of Castellnotte gradually gathered in a crowd following behind us. It was odd, but there were no children to be found, so I know that some of the women foresaw this trouble to come, and they hid their youngest away from it all.

We then dragged this lad Gaetano into that decimated orange garden and the people of the village followed us in. It is true, I was rough with the boy, I admit it, but you must be certain that I was hoping to get somewhere with them all. So while Sig. Burtoni held both our guns and our men held the twenty in a row so they would have to witness the execution, I tore the shirt off of his back and then I bound the boy's hands behind him, slowly and carefully, and tied a red bandanna around his eyes to blindfold him. All of this, I might add, Signorina, is more than what these cursed villagers did for the Duke and Duchess Burmonte. Then I shoved Gaetano down roughly on his knees so he knelt there bareback beside the burnt remains of the woodpile where the bodies of the duke and duchess lay.

"You and you and you," I picked out three men from among the villagers. "Take off your shirts, and spread them out like this." I took the boy Gaetano's white shirt and laid it like a blanket on the stones. When the three of them had done as I told them, I ordered them to cut the remains of the Duke and Duchess free and to spread their hideous corpscs out onto those cloths before us, so that all could see them clearly. I'm afraid, O Signorina, that the joints in their hips and knees cracked and broke loose from their bodies when these men laid them out, and not one of the villagers who'd gathered to watch fell over fainting and sick, losing the contents of their stomachs, not even one of them, at that sound. Finally one of the now barebacked men collapsed on the stones, and the other two picked him up and helped him back to the row of the twenty.

"So this," I said, waving my arm down at the charred and now broken remains, and I was speaking in the plainest Sicilian I know, Signorina Rafaella, as close to the back and dark alleys of the Alberghia as I could. "This is what your friend young Gaetano here says that he has done, all alone. And for this, Under Orders from the Dictator General of the Kingdom of Sicily, we must execute him." I pulled the revolver out from my belt and pointed it straight at the boy's chest. "No one here knows anything more that might save this boy," I shouted, with my pistol pointed at the lad. "Just this one little boy did it all, set fire to the castle, cut down these trees and burned this old man and this old woman alive here, all by himself."

There was a silence then that echoed loudly around the courtyard, and not even any birds sang, O Signorina. No one in the crowd even moved, much less spoke up in the poor lad's defense. So when I moved my thumb and cocked the hammer back on the pistol, it was loud and crisp in the still smoky air. "All you cowards are willing to let this one brave boy die for you. Or maybe Gaetano is the one and only wicked soul, and he deserves to die alone today."

Still there was nothing from any of them. I glanced over at Sig. Burtoni and he simply nodded his head once. But wait, my dearest Comrade Crisiana, I still had one more move to shake the infernal fruit loose from the tree, Rafaella.

"So be it," I said quietly. Then I announced in my most formal and northern Italian, "By order of the presiding General of the Island of Sicily, in the Kingdom of Italy, you, Gaetano of Castellnotte called 'Comrade Tre,' are sentenced hereby to death by gunfire." As I pulled the trigger, I noticed that your Sig. Burtoni, Rafaella, he closed his eyes. But you see, Signorina Crisiana, at the last moment I jerked the pistol to the side and fired into the ground, instead of into the boy's head. The poor lad collapsed in a faint onto the old stones anyway, and that was what did it, because it looked to all the world and to everyone in that garden as if he had been shot dead in an instant.

That was when, finally, a woman bolted out of the crowd screaming, "It wasn't him. It wasn't him." She ran out of the grasp of several of her neighbors who were trying to hold her back, and then she threw herself beside the boy, lifting up his head. At her touch, Gaetano came around with a start, terrified and confused, blindfolded and bound still, he struggled in the woman's hands and fell over onto his other side. But she was saying his name, cooing at him, and she pulled the blindfold from his eyes, so that his eyes snapped all around, wide and frightened. Slowly she, and then he, realized that he hadn't been shot.

Sig. Burtoni said to her, "Simone?" She was, apparently, another of the servants who waited upon the Duchess in that castle. Someone I believe that you, Rafaella, know well from your time in Castellnotte. Burtoni was truly distressed, Signorina, because he too knew these people, and because he knew very well these were old friends of yours. He knew what this all meant to you, although he could hardly realize what was about to happen to him; O dearest Rafaella, a very earthquake in his soul was bearing down on him. Bearing down like a wraith. And he could not know it was coming. None of us could know.

"Who was it?" I spoke to this Simone. She was, truly, a handsome woman with wild raven hair and dark, deep eyes, someone the men of this village all loved, I am sure. But Burtoni tells me, and I'm certain he has understood this from you, Signorina Crisiana, Simone was someone who was often pursued by young men, but had refused all their proposals. She was someone who dreamed of leaving Castellnotte, of life in Palermo of Napoli, or even in Rome. And her beauty was such that it might have carried her that far, given even part of an opportunity.

"If it wasn't him, Signorina," I said to her, "then tell me, who was it?" But she just ignored me, and doted on Gaetano, struggling to untie his hands. It went on like that for a time, and clearly they were once again refusing to talk, to respond, even to listen. Sig. Burtoni broke in and pulled Simone up onto her feet, and then, with some tears in his eyes (I must point these tears out to you, Rafaella) he bound her hands behind her and pulled Gaetano back up on his feet. But still they refused to answer us, and this lad Gaetano spit on Sig. Burtoni when he was standing again. Burtoni just wiped the boy's spittle off his face, using it as a way to steal away his own tears. Yes, his tears, Rafaella, his Tears.

Still, the twenty stood in silence, and Gaetano with Simone beside him, was now insolent and defiant. I turned to the little crowd of townspeople, and said nothing at first, just pointed at the bodies of the Duke and Duchess, and then I said finally, "Will no one here speak the truth to us?"

The situation, Signorina Rafaella, was in danger of whirling out of our control. This defiance of the two of them, Gaetano and Simone, and the continued silence of the twenty, it could lead to another revolt if we let it continue. We already knew what these people were capable of doing. We might easily have a massacre on our hands. Not at all what Colonel Bixio commanded. Not order, but Pandemonium born of Anarchy.

"Blindfold them both," I ordered, but it was Burtoni who chose to do the work. He understood our orders, and he could see the situation arising. Once they were bound and blindfolded, he stepped alongside me, and drew his pistol out too. With a nod of his head, he let me see that all was ready.

I announced again, this time to both of them, the orders of Execution we served under. It was then that Sig. Burtoni and I together shot them, it was quick and I think painless, for they both lay dead and still on the stones in moments. They did not suffer, Rafaella. I can assure you of that. Our shots were true, and their pain was brief.

I believe I am reporting this all to you because of what happened next. This is why Burtoni asked me to write to you, Rafaella. As hard as it has been thus far on this path, it will be even harder still to report the rest of these dour events to you. But, O Signorina, I swear to you on all that is sacred to me, on my own freedom and on our Country and on my very heartbeat, what I write now (and indeed up to now) is the Certain and Definite Truth. These are the facts of what happened that day. They are not shaded or edited at all, they are the plain facts. I am sorry to report them as they are, but these are the true events of that day, without any addition or any omission.

It seems to me as I write this now that the pistol shots had not yet stopped echoing in our ears when I heard the commotion issuing from somewhere nearby. It was like the jabbering of dogs, and it came ringing up the hillside, cries and yells that were not intelligible even to me, they were I think so deeply in the tongue of Castellnotte. Perhaps they were not even words at all, just the random, ferocious sounds of anger and despair.

There were five of them, short and square to the ground, with wild gray hair curling out of scarves and their faces carved with wrinkles and sun, damp with the sweat of their anger. They carried long pointed sticks and poked and prodded at their man, and herded him toward us like a reluctant old cow. But it wasn't a cow, Signorina. All of us in the garden fell silent, with these now four dead bodies at our feet. But the five old women with their sticks in hand yapped and snarled, and the people of the village parted like sand on a creek bed to let them pass. They herded the man up to us, to Sig. Burtoni and me, and then the five old women pushed him onto the stones beside the still warm and bleeding bodies of Gaetano and Simone. This man was not bound or restrained in any way; he was instead surrounded by these snarling women, with their pointed sticks. He knelt there, afraid and trembling, dearest Rafaella, looking in shock at Simone and then at Gaetano, and not looking up at us.

But there was on Sig. Burtoni's face, you must know this too, O Signorina, a real horror now. We had all seen much on this day, too much to describe accurately, and enough to last us all the rest of our lives. But there was now a shock, a despair in Sig. Burtoni's eyes. His shoulders slumped down and the suffering man nearly dropped the revolver in his hand. He seemed more disturbed than the man kneeling on the ground beside Gaetano and Simone, before the ashes and bones of the Duke and Duchess.

Then two of the old women denounced their prisoner. While they spoke, the other three women continued with their cursing and snarling, and pounded their sticks on the stones. [Corrao now switches again into Sicilian, to report the words of these women. It was Sciascia again who translated the mysterious words for us.] "You have Killed the wrong ones," they said. "You have made a stupid mistake, because of these stupid men in our village. Here is the one they are protecting. We don't know why. You can have him. But kill no one else. Enough is enough. Take this one back to Messina where he came from. He doesn't belong to us anymore. Not after this. Not after what he has done here, out of hate."

I pointed down at the dead bodies of Gaetano and Simone. "Did these two have nothing to do with it?"

All five of the women spat out, not in any unison, but raggedly and one after another, "This is Comrade Uno."

I'm afraid, O Rafaella, that I have no need to tell you who this man was, the man they denounced. You know who it was, and you know what happened next, though you don't know how. You don't know how it happened that your father, Lombardo Crisiana, died.

I am sorry to have to tell you this, Signorina Rafaella, but he had been until then cowering like a lowly cur, driven by old women into our hands. He trembled and refused to look up, and he was nothing like the man who'd met us in the countryside near Messina. There was nothing in him of the courage and determination of Sole who started us out on our patrol with Rosalino Pilo, and with you, O Rafaella. He was broken and weak, and he had at that moment come apart.

I asked the crowd if this was all true, what the old women told us. It was only then that the twenty began to speak, and everything spilled out: the way Lombardo had promised them all their own piece of the land, promised everyone would be free and independent of their debts, and Castellnotte would truly belong to them, to the people who worked the ground, if only they would seize the castle from the Duke. I don't need to tell you this. You know it, in your heart. You know, Rafaella, what he believed and what it led him to do. The twenty spilled it all out then. But what you can't imagine was how weak and ashamed your father seemed, as the people of his home Castellnotte turned on him, and as those old women continued to prod and poke at him with their pointed sticks like he was a cornered, rabid dog.

Again Pandemonium was on the verge of sweeping over us, and the whole crowd was close to losing all Control. I could see this, they were beginning to close in on him like he was a wounded predator. I knew again I had to stop it all at once, before it even started. So I pronounced the sentence on him, almost word for word as it was for Gaetano and Simone. Hearing those words announced—the Order of Execution— seemed to bring a strange calm and courage back to Lombardo.

The old women sensed this change and stopped, and he climbed back up onto his feet. Suddenly he was the Sole we all knew from the beginning days of this revolt. He lifted his head, and shook it so his silver hair fell about his shoulders. And then Sole spoke to the townspeople. "You know, though you turn on me now, you know the truth of what we have done. It was my grandfather who planted these hillsides with grapes and olives. It was he, with the help of your parents and grandparents, who restored those fields until they were full and rich. He passed their fruit down to all of us, and not to a couple of old barren aristocrats, foreign to this land, not even Sicilians. It was he who laid the stones we stand on in this garden. These trees we have cut down and burned, he planted them for us. They were planted for us, for all of us, but in the end they didn't belong to any of us. They were locked away so you could only see them if you worked here. Worked for them.

"All this wealth and all the fruits of our work belonged to only them," Sole didn't need to indicate in anyway the charred bodies lying on the torn cloth before him. "They took it all, because they were born to it, you know. It was given to them by their blood, these two people, who could barely even talk to us. They could barely speak our language, and then only to give us orders. It was all theirs. The fruit of my grandfather's and my father's and of my labor. It was all theirs. And we, We who Worked this ground, Worked these hills, we received only what they handed down to us. Scraps from their grand tables, where our children served them. It was these children here who waited on them," and Sole turned and gazed down at the still remains of Gaetano and Simone.

"O, certainly, they were generous in handing out the fruits of the land to all of us, helping us when we were sick or in trouble. They were kind and gentle, even. And me, they helped to send me off to school while my family, my wife and daughter, worked in their great house. They were kind and forgiving, and they stooped down to help us up.

"But I tell you all, every one of you, none of this was theirs to give. None of it." Sole stopped there, and the people were quiet for a moment longer. "I guess it was not their fault." He went on. "Perhaps we should have returned their kindness, but it was not in my heart to save the old masters. And," the man we called Sole gazed defiantly around at the crowd of villagers. "And it was not in you, either, to forgive them their tiny, brutal arrogance. The arrogance of the entitled, or of those who feel entitled only because of who you are."

190

It was our Sig. Burtoni then, O dearest Rafaella, who interrupted his speech. Sig. Burtoni burst in, with a long angry moan that sounded so tortured it surprised even me. "I knew them, Lombardo," he bellowed out, and your father, Rafaella, he stopped and turned to look at him. There was hatred then in your father's eyes, O Signorina, and as I write this now, I don't understand it. We were all comrades in arms, together, after all. We all fought side by side across Sicilia, to free her. But the hatred in Lombardo's eyes made him—I'm sorry to write this, O Signorina—it made him seem small again. He shrank in my eyes, in all our eyes, at that moment.

Sig. Burtoni went on, in almost a whisper then, and every one of us, the twenty, the villagers, the old women, the red shirts and I, and even Lombardo, we all leaned forward to hear his soft words. "They are not as you say, Sole," he called your father by his old rebel name. "I knew the Duke and the Duchess too, if only briefly. She was hard and proud, but the Duke had a heart as true as this Sicilian sun in spring. And the Duchess, she liked to give orders, but who among us doesn't know a woman with a big heart, a mamma, a nonna, a zia vecchia who likes to give orders. It only means that she cares. We know this, it only means she is worried for us.

"They did not deserve to die this way, Lombardo, and at your hands. If we dream of this island as part of a great country, we cannot go this way, Lombardo, with old hatreds. The old hatreds have to die, along with our old ways. The Counts and Countesses, the Dukes and Duchesses, even the Kings and Queens, they have to be part of us. This is why the General has sent us here," and then Burtoni changed and began to address him with that old red shirt name we knew him by first. "Sole, these are the Orders of the General himself. He is now the Dictator, Sole, the very Law of this Land. Until we all bury these old hatreds, Sole, only then can we be Free."

I hesitate again to tell you this all, Signorina Crisiana. But I fear you must know the whole of it, if I am to do my service to Burtoni, and indeed to you, dear Rafaella. I am sorry to go on, but go on to the end we must.

Rafaella, your father swore then at Burtoni so fiercely he literally spat out these words. "My hatred of them will never be buried, not even in their burned and abandoned graves."

"Then this is the order of the General, Sole, and we must fulfill it," Sig. Burtoni said as he raised his pistol to aim it at Lombardo Crisiana, known in the movement as Sole, your father.

But Burtoni did not execute the order, Signorina. And anyone who was there will attest to this. Jack Burton did not execute your father, O Rafaella, even though he raised a gun to his head, and even though he surely intended to follow his orders. He did not do it, Rafaella. Burtoni did not do it.

It is a hard thing to write this to you, and I suspect you will not believe me. You are likely to think that I am only trying to hide from you what our friend Burtoni did. But Rafaella, O Signorina, that is not true.

This, my dearest Rafaella, is the Truth.

I shot your father. It did it quickly, to spare Burtoni this deed, because I knew well from all our days together, yours Rafaella and mine and his, I knew how he loved you, and how it would burden him to do the task we had been ordered to do.

So I shot Lombardo Crisiana. I will tell you only that he died quickly, if not well.

I report these facts to you fully, Signorina Crisiana. It was I, known to you as Giovanni Corrao, who Executed the Orders of Colonel Nino Bixio on that day, 2 September 1860, in the gardens of Castellnotte, in the newly Free Kingdom of Sicilia. Long Live Italia!

I report this final truth to you, as well. Though our comrade Mr. Jack Burton, who is called by us Gianni Burtoni, though he was present and participated in the police proceedings of that time, he did not Execute Sig. Lombardo Crisiana, your father, our comrade in arms, known by the name of Sole to the Thousand who marched with the General.

I swear to this on the truth of the Thousand Red Shirts, and on all that they have won for Italia.

Signed,

Giovanni Corrao, son of the Albergheria

Post Script: You have, Signorina, I understand, visited their graves. I feel I must also report to you that it was not Burtoni or I who chose the place. It was the people of Castellnotte who buried them high on the mountainside above La Rocca, and it was the People of Castellnotte who insisted that they all, the five of them, be buried together side by side, in order to remember the Tragedy of the whole event.

This ends the complete text, which Rob and I found within that plain manila envelope.

The following morning Lombardo Sciascia took us up the hill to visit the castle grounds, and despite what he'd said the day before, he led us inside into the orange garden. There were young trees, with blood red oranges on them, growing in pots where the stones had carefully been replaced and cleaned. Above us we could hear the sounds of power tools and men talking, as they worked to restore the Castle to its old glory.

Lombardo Sciascia took us over to the very central tree and pointed down to a carved stone plaque with the date and a series of names on it, laid carefully in the stone floor of the garden. It bore that date "2 SEPTEMBRE 1860" on it, and then it read simply, in Italian, "In this garden these heroes lost their lives for the Risorgimento: Gaetano Boldoni – age 17 years; Simone Martelli- age 19 years; William and Elizabeth Shawcross, the Duke and Duchess of Burmonte – ages unknown; Lombardo Crisiana – age 64 years."

"I think this is what Sister Teresa wanted you to see," Sciascia told us. "And I think she wanted you to read that letter, the way Jack Burton didn't." He spoke Burton's name in straight flat English. There was no 'Burtoni' to it, so it sounded out roughly amongst all the Italian.

"Burton?" I said.

"He was here? You met him?" Rob added a little too quickly.

Sciascia laughed and nodded his head. "How do you think he found my sister in Siracusa?"

Rob and I were lost then. Jack Burton's journey was the reverse of ours, it seemed. He must have started out by coming back here, to Castellnotte, where these executions occurred, where surely his love affair with Rafaella Crisiana ended.

Lombardo Sciascia went on to describe the old man. "A couple of years ago, he arrived here on the bus like you two, in his wheelchair, of course. But he was so strong in the arms he almost didn't need help getting out of the bus. It dropped him here in the Piazza San Lucia, just like it did you two. Right away he started to work his way up to La Rocca here in that wheelchair, all on his own, and so some of us started to help him along. It was Cinzia and Lara, I think.

"At any rate, when they realized where he was going, Lara came running to get me. But I was gone to Grammiche to visit friends, just like I was yesterday. So it wasn't until I got off the late bus, and Cinzia sent her two boys Enrico and Andrea to meet me. 'Come down to La Scala,' they said, and took me by the hand, almost dragging me along.

"There at the top of the stairs, where I took you boys yesterday, right there sat this Jack Burton, in his wheel chair. It was the first time I saw him. And Big Andrea, Cinzia's husband, was sitting next to him and they were drinking wine, and Jack Burton was gazing out at the sea, and down at the stairs. He was talking away, spinning yarns about the days of the Thousand, as if he'd been there himself. That's what Andrea told me later.

"So the two lads led me out there, and they explained who I am, you see. That's when old Burton, with his icy blue eyes in that deep rutted brow, his eyes seemed to go blind. He's looking out at the sea, still, but he seemed blind now, from something he sees inside himself. And he wouldn't believe me, at first, you know."

"Wait a minute, Signor Lombardo," Rob said. "What are you talking about?"

Sciascia looked at us as if we were idiots. "I thought that was why Sister Teresa sent you here. You are connected with this Burton fellow, somehow. True?"

"We are," I said.

Rob was quicker that me, he had begun to catch on. "Signor Sciascia, who are you?"

"I thought you lads knew. Why, what the devil is up now." Sciascia threw both hands up in the air with real exasperation, and he muttered to himself, "What the hell are you up to now, Rafaella?"

The sound of that name on his lips pulled us both up short. "Who are you?" I said, quietly, looking down at the plaque full of names written in stone. A ripe blood orange had fallen there beside it, waiting obviously for one of us to pick it up.

"Who are you, Signore?" Rob repeated.

He pointed at the names on the plaque, and then he said, "Lombardo Crisiana was my great-grandfather."

There was silence for a moment as both Rob and I began to piece it together. "My sister Rafaella, though she denies it now by changing her name, she was named after our grandmother."

"And your grandmother is . . .?" Rob said, his eyes as wide as mine.

"Our grandmother was Rafaella Crisiana. That letter from Corrado was addressed to her. This is how I have come to possess it. And it is how my sister Rafaella came to have this journal that she gave to you young lads, I haven't seen that journal for a lot of years, since I was just a boy."

I glanced over to Rob. "That means Sister Teresa at the Domus Mariae is . . . "

"Yes, my sister Rafaella Sciascia."

"But?" I said, still trying to sort it all out.

"And my sister has stolen my dear, my only daughter and lured her off to the convent. My little Rosalina."

Rob began to nod his head up and down slowly. "And your daughter Rosalina, she is named after . . .?"

"She bears our mother's name, Rosalina Sciascia, that is except for now she is a damned nun, Sister Chiara. Because my sister lured her away from us."

Then Lombardo Sciascia stopped, looked at that orange on the ground, and crossed himself, muttering a prayer of forgiveness.

"I got it," Rob said. Then he helped me out. "Rafaella Crisiana had a baby daughter, right Signor Sciascia? And she was named Rosalina."

As Lombardo Sciascia nodded in silent agreement, Rob just looked at me, and said, "Pilo."

"I don't believe it," I said.

"This is just exactly what that Jack Burton said, until I showed him Corrado's letter," said Sciascia.

"And then you told Burton about your daughter in Siracusa, just like you told us, didn't you?" Rob said.

"That's right."

"And that was how Burton found his way to Domus Mariae." Rob pressed on, linking the fragments together that even Lombardo Sciascia hadn't understood.

"Yes, in a damned all to hell hurry, too, with barely a thank you to me," Sciascia said.

"Pilo," I repeated.

The ride back to Siracusa seemed shorter, though it still took all the rest of that day. A large part of it was traveled in silence, though we did see the schoolchildren climb on and ride with us a while, getting off again, going home, to all their little villages along the way. The two girls tried out their English again, a little braver now, quicker to speak. The bus was quieter in general, because it was not market day the way it was the day before, and also because it was the end of the school day. We were all tired.

For most of the ride I just leafed through Burton's old journal, reading around in it randomly. At one point, as the AST maneuvered to turn around in some tiny piazza, I said to Rob, "So it's Rosalino Pilo, isn't it? He is the grandfather of our old Sister Teresa, who was born Rafaella like her grandmother." Rob didn't answer, he just listened. "And Pilo, then, is the great-grandfather of the little sorella, Sister Chiara. That is why her real name is Rosalina. After Pilo, am I right?"

Rob nodded thoughtfully, but he still didn't answer. Something about it all seemed wrong, and it wouldn't go away. And we both sensed it.

It was turning dark by the time the bus returned across Ponte Umbertino. And then Rob said out loud, not expecting any answer, "But why did the old Sister send us off to Castellnotte? I don't understand."

We arrived at Domus Mariae hoping there might be a room, only to find Sister Chiara at the desk, waiting for us, holding our room open without a reservation.

"How did you know we'd be back?" I said.

"I didn't," she answered. "I'm just doing what Sister Teresa told me to do."

So then the little Sister led us upstairs, and warned us not to bump our heads again, and threw open the balcony windows to let in the moonlit sea air, just as she did on my first night there. And she welcomed us back, handing me the key, and to Rob she handed another plump manila envelope, addressed this time to both our names. "How is my father?" she asked. But we had trouble answering, as we stared at that fat package in Rob's hands.

Finally he said, though still distracted, " He misses you. Your father, Rosalina, if I may use that name, he misses you."

She said nothing more, except, " Chiara is my name now, Signori."

Once the little Sister was gone, and while we were still standing in the middle of the room beside our bags, Rob tore open the envelope. From inside it he pulled out a letter, written by the old Sister. There was a small gray key taped to the top of the first page. "Why didn't she give us this before we left for Castellnotte?" Rob asked me, not expecting any answers. "Why did she send us there?"

Then he started to read her letter, and I took the manila envelope out of his hand. Inside it I found what Rob, in his haste, hadn't noticed yet.

"Well, I'll be damned," he whispered, as he was reading.

From out of the envelope I pulled four loose pages written in a hand I recognized well, a hand I'd just spent a bit of time with lately. They were the missing four pages from Jack Burton's journal, the pages cut out so carefully. And now, as you'll see when you read them, we know that it was Burton himself who removed them. He was the one who cut them out so carefully hoping they wouldn't be missed, when Rafaella Crisiana read this history. He believed those pages would never be missed, but once the binding of the journal had broken and fallen apart with age, it revealed the two little slips of cut paper still sewn into the book, where they had been carefully sliced out.

This is what I found that Burton wrote there:

[Please note: unlike all the other entries in this journal, there is no date or location marking the start of this passage. The handwriting simply begins a few lines down on the opening page.]

I don't know now what to do. Somehow he has found me out, probably from the damned slips of my own stupid tongue. I spoke too much, O I shot off my mouth, I went on about meeting the General in Montevideo, and about the Anzani Brigade in '48, about dear old Francesco Anzani himself. This must be how he figured it out, from out of my own braggart's mouth.

And I should have known too, the way he interrogated me. He wanted details, the kind of little details like the names of horses and the height of my Ciccio Anzani and the color of his hair, and even the names of the streets and piazzas in Morazzone. And proudly, stupidly, damnably, I answered them all. As effortlessly as if I'd been there, because of course, I was there. Damn my own flapping, open chattering mouth. What was I thinking?

It was clear he didn't believe me at first. He thought I was lying, you see. And he thought that because he was smart enough to realize I had to be lying, I couldn't have been there; it all happened over ten years ago. Fifteen if you're counting from the days in Argentina, though I really don't go back that far with the General in South America. For most of those years I was on my own in the wanderer's world. So Lombardo thought he had me. He thought I had to be lying, because a boy as young as I am now would have been just a little child, way back then, ten years before.

But no, I couldn't shut myself up. I let my stupid pride overcome my common sense. I suppose I was showing off for him, bragging about my days at sea and in the saddle alongside the great General himself, because after all I was about to ask permission to marry his daughter. I was just working up my courage to ask. And I wanted to seem big and important to him, this little rebel leader from Messina, raised in pretty little Castellnotte by his peasant father. I wanted, standing there in front of him, to be a big man, before I asked for his daughter's hand. So I told him the story of how I got my name from il Generalissimo. O Rafaella.

But old Sole is one sharp individual. He added up the years, once I'd passed this test. When he quietly came to believe that I wasn't lying to him, that I was indeed telling him the truth, then he knew something horrible was wrong with me. I wasn't human, at least not in his eyes.

So being Sole, he confronted me. No messing around for him. He just asked me straight out, "How old are you?"

I wanted to marry his daughter. But Rafaella, I haven't even told her yet about my cursed affliction. She doesn't know my age either. I am still afraid to tell her the truth, because it may frighten her. She might flee, if she understood what I am, for I am a monster. And it all leaves me so alone, so perpetually alone.

But I could not lie to Lombardo. Not anymore. It would not have mattered, even if I had tried to lie to him. He knows something is not right with me. So, I just told him the truth, as far as I know it. What else could I do? It was too late for me to lie to him anymore.

He sat for a long while digesting what I told him, and then asked me feebly a few questions I couldn't answer. "How?" he said. And even worse, "Why?"

I told him, "I wish I knew."

Then suddenly the worst that I can imagine happened. He rose up on his feet from the table where we were sitting over a pitcher of red wine. He said, "I have seen the way my little Rafaella looks at you. And I have seen the way you return her gaze. I am telling you this now, so that it won't become a problem. Stay away from her." He began pointing at me with his finger, in his violent, bossy way. "If I see you even speaking to her, even in the same room with her, I swear to you now, and have not a moment's doubt that I mean this: If I ever even hear your name spoken in her presence, I will come looking for you, and I will slit your monstrous throat myself. And if I can't slit it, someone in my family will do it for me. Do you understand? It will do you no good to get rid of me. If I am gone, the family will take care of it.

"Do you understand?"

I came asking for her hand. But in a moment of foolish pride, I have lost her forever.

Lombardo is right, of course. I am a monster. I have no right to ruin her life. It is as it should be.

Alone. Always.

There, about half way down the page, the writing stopped abruptly. I gazed for a while at the handwriting, pondering what it meant. Then slowly I understood, I think, why Jack Burton had so carefully sliced these few pages out of his journal. It wasn't just to hide his insane secret, for there are plenty of hints all through this notebook surrounding his strange and impossible age. It wasn't just to hide that. He was giving this journal to Rafaella, to win back her heart. It is why he had Giovanni Corrao write the letter to her, urging Corrao to take the blame for her father's death. And really, what difference did it make to Corrao, our slippery Dottore Calogero, who got blamed for an ordered execution. Something about his letter didn't ring all that true. So there it was, in the end, the only reason for Burton to carefully remove these very few pages, before he sent them into the hands of his one, true love.

"You've got to read this," Rob interrupted my thoughts, holding out the letter toward me. "You won't believe this," she said. "I think she's crazy."

I didn't reply, I just handed Rob the four journal pages. He knew, just as I had, what they were. But he didn't know yet what was in them.

"Here is Jack Burton's motive," I said, then I paused and swallowed hard. "There were not just orders to execute Lombardo Crisiana. There was a motive to murder him, too. There's a reason Jack Burton had to see Lombardo Crisiana dead and gone." Rob's eyes seemed to darken at that, but he couldn't object. He just took the papers from my hands.

The new letter was from Sister Teresa, in her neat and careful hand. She wrote to us in a very simple Italian too, I could tell because I could read it all so easily. It was undated, and it bore just our first names at the top, next to the little flat key she'd gently secured with cellophane tape. It read:

These are the missing pages from the journal of Gianni Burtoni, which I gave you to read earlier. You'll see, if you try, that they fit perfectly inside the notebook. The journal, along with the letter my brother showed you, were sent by mail to our grandmother, Rafaella Crisiana, who rode with the Thousand in 1859. These missing pages, she told me, arrived some days later, delivered at night by hand by a masked stranger on horseback from Palermo, who would not use nor leave any name, though he spoke only in Sicilian, and did not seem to understand Italian.

Please do not show even one line of this to young Sister Chiara. And please do not speak to her of these matters. She does not know who she is. And she must not know. Only I know, and now you too. And of course, Burtoni knows as well.

Once you have read them, please return all of these papers to this envelope, and leave them in the top drawer of the desk in this room. The key at the top of this page will lock the drawer and keep all of this safe and secure from curious eyes until I return. Once you have locked this all up, please throw the key away into the sea. I have the only other.

You know now what I am doing. My brother and I are the grandchildren of Jack Burton. [Sister Teresa here, and at several other key places in this letter, reverts to calling Burton by his English name. I am not sure why, but the name always seems to appear at a crucial point when the old nun needs perhaps to distance herself from the evil she calls by that English name.] Our mother, Rosalina Crisiana Sciascia died at a very advanced age, in a violent crash of an automobile, in 1922. However, she always seemed youthful for her age, and everyone remarked on it constantly. My brother and I were raised by our father alone, Gaetano Sciascia, who died some years ago. He of course did not suffer the curse.

Because of the grace and wisdom of God, I entered the convent as a young girl, and so I have never had any children. My brother's wife died young, may God rest Rosetta's soul, and my brother Lombardo has not remarried. You understand, this means that my niece Rosalina Sciascia, you know her as Sister Chiara, she is the last of the line of Jack Burton and Rafaella Crisiana.

It is perhaps too early to tell. I don't know if my brother or I have inherited the curse of Burtoni's blood. We seem, at least to my eyes, to be growing old happily and well, as we should. And my brother suspects nothing. I only came to understand Signor Burtoni's curse when I read over these pages myself, the same one's you have read. And I did not believe them at first. I did not believe a word of this raving until Signor Burtoni appeared on the doorstep of Domus Mariae, asking questions about me and about Sister Chiara. He did not know who I was, and I did not tell him my name. With time, he went away.

I repeat. Sister Chiara knows nothing of any of this. It must remain so, to praise heaven that protects us.

My brother probably complained to you in Castellnotte of the way I "stole" his daughter. I know that he misses her, as she looks so much like her mother, his wife. I know he complained of his loneliness there, without his wife or his only child. But he has never understood what we are involved in. The abomination. It was only the grace of Our Lord and his Holy Mother that led Sister Chiara to me. I prayed long and hard on it, and I have at last come to see that this is the will of God.

Great longevity in life is not a blessing. Though it is often confused for luck, it is not. Only the weak and mistaken dream in their fragile souls of cheating Death, that is all it is. I pray each day, now that Sister Chiara is safe and taken care of in the Order, that if indeed my brother and I have inherited the curse within this bloodline, I pray that we may suffer a sudden and easy death, just as our mother did. I know it is a strange thing to pray for your own death to come soon. But I do. And I pray also that my dear niece, Sister Chiara, will find her end easily, and most importantly, in a goodly time.

I have kept this secret from everyone, even from my family. When Burton appeared here, well, you understand the danger his very existence creates. He is a monster of God, some left over fragment of an Old Testament disorder, unleashed mistakenly on our world.

This is why I have told you these truths here. When you arrived at Domus Mariae looking for him, asking for Jack Burton, describing him, I realized that you two have been sent for him. It is not enough here in Ortigia that I hide these truths from a foolish and depraved world, and that I bring this monstrous line of blood to an end here. You have been sent to me for a reason. Providence is taking care of this curse, in its own way, beyond our understanding. The Lord is providing a way.

Perhaps you have been sent here as angels of Death, to bring this horrible creature to his end. So leave you this information: One year ago we received a letter here at Domus Mariae from him, addressed to Sister Chiara and to me. Fortunately, I saw it before my niece did. I burned it, unopened, destroyed it with fire. Where his soul will end, I believe. His letter is gone, and I know not what was inside it.

May God be with you, in your pursuit of Jack Burton. May you release him at last from his hell. I know only this. The letter came from Jesi.

God bless you in your journey.

Sorella Teresa, once Rafaella Sciascia

At the bottom of the last page she wrote: "Never return here," in English so it could not be misunderstood.

"Does she really think we're out to kill him?" Rob said to me, the moment my eyes rose from the page.

"She's nuts," I repeated.

"And where the hell is Jesi?" Rob said, immediately.

"Oh no. Oh no you don't, Rob. My time is up. I've got classes and students back in the Midwest waiting for me, and a plane ticket out of Catania day after tomorrow. I've got to get back to my life. Enough of God damned Jack Burton."

But Rob was looking past me out the window at the sea. "God damned Jack Burton," he said. Then I swear I heard him mutter under his breath, "Jesi."

The next morning I locked up all the papers in the desk drawer, just the way the Old Nun in her madness wanted them. I was going to toss the key out of the window into the sea just as she wanted, but Rob took it from me, and pocketed it. It's clear he isn't done with old Jack Burton just yet.

In the early afternoon, little Sister Chiara was back at the desk, with her big brown eyes and her smooth olive skin and those slightly plump lips, and I told her I would be checking out in the morning. Her brown eyes seemed disappointed genuinely, and I thought for a moment I would change my mind and stay. But then it occurred to me, somehow, to ask her how old she was. She seemed so very young. I actually opened my mouth to speak, before I told myself to be silent. Perhaps I didn't really want to know that answer.

"Where is Jesi?" Rob asked her, and again she didn't seem surprised.

In fact, she reached down in a fold that hid a pocket in her habit, and pulled out a little map of Italy with a circle on it around the city of Jesi, and she handed it over to Rob. "Jesi is near Ancona," she said. "In Le Marche."

The little Sister was so pretty I wanted to say, let's go there together. But that was just an urge. I have responsibilities, so I didn't speak.

Rob took the map, and said, "Sister Teresa," matter-of-factly.

Sister Chiara nodded her pretty head and smiled yes. Then she pulled out another slip of paper from that same hidden pocket, folded over with my brother's full name written on it. "You have a phone message, too. Someone called early this morning for you, asking for 'Mister Robert,' and they said it was important. It was the company, MacLendon Petrolio, he said. They need to hear from you as soon as possible. But Sister Teresa told me not to disturb your room until both of you gentlemen were finished and checked out of it completely." She pronounced our last name, and the name of the oil company awkwardly, with those pretty plump lips, and again I daydreamed of slipping away with her.

There was just a phone number on that slip of paper. Rob looked worried, and disappointed too, because that number was familiar. You see, his time was up too. "So much for my trip to Jesi," he frowned as he eyed the number.

And he was right. The company wanted him in the Gulf of Mexico, and soon. So he was on a flight from Rome to Dallas, just six or seven hours behind mine. Everyday life was calling him back, too, and so much for Sister Teresa's Angels of Death. So much for Jack Burton, who'd once again given us the slip.

But Rob did leave for Texas behind me by at least half a day. Which gave him plenty of time, a whole morning I'd say, to make some copies before he threw that tiny key away into the deep blue Ionian Sea.

Il Rosso in the North,
or
How Jack Burton Earned His Name

Ho un cuore che troppo senti.
    --Francesco Anzani

1.

"Butto Sam" was blazoned across the side of the cart in red carnival letters a foot tall, with a yellow as a daffodil trim. "Native Upland Gorilla from the African Islands of Darkest Zambutti far off the Cape of Lost Hope," read the print beneath his mighty name.

The gorilla inside that cage came here from the mountainous island of Zambutti, the circus barker had claimed. It was two hundred miles off the coast of South Africa, hauled across the big waters in a crate without bars or windows, with only narrow vents, to sit in the sweltering mid-western American humidity hidden inside a wheeled cart towed behind a big red Buick convertible, to the sound of hurdy-gurdy music and carnival pitches.

What a sweatbox that cart was. How was he fed inside there? I wondered. Did he ever see the light of day? Or the moon and the stars at night?

We understood his suffering, but it only intensified the mystery of that darkness, and of the black beast helpless and caged inside it. I could taste danger at the back of my throat, and for me it was intoxicating.

Our long quest to find Jack Burton began with a simple desire to see what lay down inside the black, barred darkness of a gorilla's cage.

But I was too short, and the little barred window above the t's in Butto Sam's name was too high. There would be no peaking in, not at this black mystery "from the African Islands," not for free anyway. Butto Sam was a paying attraction. So I stood there without even any change in my pocket, gazing up at those bars, hungry for a look.

My little brother stood beside me in short pants, with his back to the cage, staring big eyed at the white circus horses and the one lone elephant chained to the grounds of the schoolyard, all of them grazing together peacefully, like Iowa livestock fattening in the fields. Our little brown dog George sat beside me, with the same glaze of wonderment in his eyes as my kid brother's. "Butto Sam," I whispered, reading the side of the cart.

"Hey, Robbie, " I said. "You want a look at Butto Sam?"

"At who?" Robbie said, and turned the shining bifocals he wore at me.

You see, I realized that there was no way I could climb up high enough to see down through the barred window of that cage. But Robbie could, by golly. If I could boost him up high enough, he could lean on the walls of that cart and maybe he could peer through the thick flat bars and see down into the dark, to the beast below.

"The Upland Gorilla," I barked at him. Didn't he know who Butto Sam was?

Robbie looked up at the high window, and said, "I don't know," sounding more than a little suspicious of what I might be up to.

And I suppose he should have been, since this was hardly the first time I'd come up with an idea that had me safe on the ground while he hung his little behind out over the vast ravine of danger, waving like a flag in the summer breeze. George turned and looked up at me. His scraggly curled tail wagged once, I guess just at the excitement in my voice.

Looming tall above Butto Sam's cart stood our three-storey schoolhouse. High as the clouds and a hundred years old and filled with dust in the empty unused floors, its yellow sandstone walls standing there like they came from the far away desert and the distant beyond, and they framed that gorilla's name in everything that home and school wasn't. Butto Sam, the hidden beast beyond the Cape of All Lost Hopes.

"C'mon, Robbie," I hissed. "I'll boost you up there, and then you tell me what he looks like."

"Who?" my little brother said again.

"What? Are you scared, or something?" I said, my voice rising to a squeak I didn't intend. "Butto Sam!" I pointed at the big red letters on the cart, and at the little window too, I guess. "That's who!" I yelled.

There was no way for Robbie to back down now. "Okay," he said tentatively. He put both his little palms against the wall of Butto Sam's cart, and with my help, as I held his waist, he stepped up on my bended knees.

"Ready?" I said through my clamped teeth.

"Yeah," Robbie sounded a little unsure.

"I'm gonna lift your left foot up on my shoulder," I said.

As I boosted that foot up onto my shoulder, he walked his palms slowly up the wall of that cart, with a teetering thump, thump, thump. Then, we got his other foot up onto my shoulder, and I grunted up at him, "Stand up!" It took another breath, but I managed to add, "Straight!"

I clung to the tire of the cart with both hands to steady myself, hoping to keep my knees from buckling under my little brother's weight. Straining my eyes to see up between his legs, I pulled myself up until I was standing, and Robbie's hands pounded on the walls of the cart some more as he walked them upwards. In a moment or so, we were straight up and teetering in the breeze. We couldn't last that way for long. George was now wending his way around my ankles, his wagging tail lapping at my shins.

"Can you see him?" I blurted out. All I could see was the round bulge of Robbie's tummy under his t-shirt. The strain of trying to speak made me wobble a bit, and for a moment I thought my knees might give out. That sent a tremor up into Robbie's knees, and we nearly crumpled. But I pulled myself steady again on that cart tire, and I heard Robbie's palms slapping on the walls of the cart to get his balance back again.

Then, awakening at the noise, the ape stirred in his cage. I heard a low, soft growl like a grumble from inside, in answer to my grunts and Robbie's slapping palms on the cart. George, standing between my legs, started to growl back at the stirrings of Butto Sam, the Upland Gorilla.

"Can you see him?" I grunted again, because I knew we couldn't last like this for long, a two-tiered tower of wobbly legs and weakening knees. Emboldened by my grunts, George began to growl louder and end each growl with a sharp bark.

Robbie shoved his face up by the bars, and he nearly laid his bifocals against the flat iron. "It's dark in there," he said. "I can't see nothing."

"Look harder," I moaned out now, desperate for him to see something.

"It's too dark, " he said.

But then a pair of black eyes appeared behind the bars. They gazed directly out at Robbie, just inches from his bifocals. I know because Robbie said, "Geez-us!" And then pushed himself back, away from the window.

That sent me wobbling, flat-footed, in some kind of locked to the ground dance trying to keep him up on my shoulders. "Aaah," Robbie wheezed, yet somehow we stayed up and the two of us steadied our shaky tower.

"What d'ya see? " I said.

George growled and then barked fiercely between my legs.

"He's looking right at me," Robbie said, his voice quavering a little. But now my little brother was not moving.

"Whoa!" I said. I strained my head up to look past Robbie, to see what he was seeing. But all I could find between Robbie's outstretched arms were the flat iron bands of the window bars.

"He's looking right at me," Robbie repeated, but sounding calmer.

Oh, I hungered then to see what my little brother saw, standing on my shoulders, gazing deep into those brown black eyes of wildness, seeing down into the wells of light shining up from out of that darkness, from the beast who dwelled on the islands of the African south, from far below the Equator, south past all the horns of Africa, south and south toward the pole on the horizon, staring out at me. In my mind I could see the twinkle of true danger in the untamed eyes of Butto Sam. But I wasn't seeing anything.

All I could really see was inside of Robbie's striped t-shirt, the dimple of his belly button over my head, and above that, if I twisted back my neck until I couldn't breathe, the flat iron bars of Butto Sam's cage.

But then, slowly, four fat, round fingers emerged from the darkness inside the window, followed gradually by a black thick thumb on the other side of the bar. As slowly as a calm lion pacing in its pen, the fingers of Butto Sam wrapped carefully around one of those flat iron bars, and gently held it tight. Underneath that slow, deliberate pace you could sense the pent up power of the great ape.

"Oh, geez," Robbie whispered.

That hand was big enough even I could see those black fingers with their graying knuckles. They were only inches from Robbie's bifocals, but inches long enough that the ape could never reach out and touch him. Still, Robbie started to wobble again, and I strained so hard to hold him up still that I farted. And my squeak was all it took to set George off.

The little mutt dog, fierce and loyal, went from his low, threatening growl into a flurry of crazed barking. George, his hind legs kicking up dust, in his fury, barked so hard that it shot him straight back out behind me, away from between my legs. "Creepers," said Robbie, and wobbled a bit more.

"Stand still," I yelled, desperate not to tumble down under Robbie's wobbling.

That set little George off on another flurry, and finally Butto Sam answered us.

His big hand tightened around the iron band, and he let loose a roaring bellow while he shook the whole cart. George's little barking either stopped or disappeared into the big ape's bellow. Robbie threw one of his hands back to get clear, and he twisted sideways on my shoulders. He had only his one palm touching the cart, and the rest of him was flying free.

And then it came. Inside that white metal box, Butto Sam the Highland Gorilla form the Islands beyond the Cape of Lost Hopes reared back and struck the walls of his cage, whether it was with a foot or his free hand we'll never know. But the force of his blow sent a shiver through the whole cart, through Robbie's one palm on the wall, through my hands clutching the cart tire. And that wooden cart covered with fiberglass and corrugated steel thrummed like a tympani being beaten. And for the first time I wondered how something so frail and jimmied together could hold him.

Out of the corner of my eye, as I held onto the cart wheel and gazed up at the ape's tight fist grasping an iron bar in his cage, I saw Robbie come tumbling backwards off of my shoulders, his bifocals flying off somewhere in the grass. The great black ape pounded the walls, bellowing and barking, so I couldn't believe this little enclosure could possibly hold him now. We had done it. We were in honest to God trouble now. The loss of Robbie's weight on my shoulders, along with the trembling of the cart wheel in my hands, and I suppose if I'm honest, the quaking of my own knees, seemed to lift me right off the ground. Maybe it was just that I jumped in the air. I don't remember. But I know I lost my hold on the cart. I wound up on my ass, tangled up in the squirming legs of my little brother, pushing his kicking shoes away from my face, with George standing on my chest now, barking bravely still up at the roaring Butto Sam.

The little white cart rocked from side to side on its wheels, and the long red Buick it was hitched to bounced on its rear shocks. And Butto Sam bellered and brayed like a mule now, and then like a hound, and finally like every beast in the dark woods I'd ever imagined.

"Calma!" sang out a deep voice from somewhere. "Calma, Sammy." It resonated with the pounding of Butto Sam's steel and fiber glass tympani. Deep and full, it took a third singing out, "Calma, mi' Butto! Silenzio!" before the great ape fell silent.

And that silence, though it lasted for just a moment, it was just a pause really before little George started to growl again. And yet that silence was stunning. The uproar of Butto Sam was gone, though in the moment before it had obtained the world and pummeled it all into low submission, but now it was gone. Gone at the just call of a voice.

"Geez," said Robbie, in the pause.

Little George growled up at the big hand still resting in the window up above us. And then I heard, from behind me, the crinkle of wheels in the dry grass.

I got hold of George by his red collar and pulled myself up out of Robbie's shoes, "It's okay, George, boy. Shhhh," I said to the growling dog. I wish I could say that George went quiet the way the ape had, at the sound of my command. He just growled on and on, ignoring everything but his brave defense of us, two boys stretched out on the dry grass.

But Butto Sam was completely silent. I flopped around in the dust, still holding George's collar in my one hand. All the horses and that elephant had lifted their heads from their grazing, and they all gazed over at us, munching calmly but staring glassy eyed at my brother and me sprawled out in the grass.

I saw his tall, laced boots first, dark and muddy brown they ran all the way up to his knees, with the laces crisscrossing tight from his toe clear up his shin. They were an impressive pair of boots, boots meant to kick around in the corral, to climb the bald rock face, to stride through jungle thickets or wade the shallow everglade swamps. They were polished and sharp, but not new, for they were old and broken in, and the soles had clearly been replaced, and several times at that. . So it was even more startling as I realized those boots rode on the footrests of a wheelchair.

"Are you lads all right?" the deep voice above those boots said.

George turned away from the silent cage of Butto Sam then, broke free of my grip on his collar, and shot barking toward the man in the chair.

"Calma, Butto," his voice said again, before the ape could even respond to the charging little dog.

I rolled over on my side then and managed to get up onto my hands and knees. Robbie was searching though the grass with his hands for his glasses. I watched as little George charged straight over at the man, though the dog's barking turned into low cautious growls as he grew closer to the wheelchair.

"O piu piccolo," the man said, as his voice softened and he reached an open palm out to the little terrier mutt.

The man in the chair wore some kind of brown pants, almost the color of his tall old boots. On his head he had a little brown pork-pie hat, felt but nearly the color as his boots and pants. And all that brown just set off his shirt.

It was a deep, bright red, blousy and full on him. It was untucked and belted at his waist with a thick brown belt. The blousy sleeves were folded back to leave his thick forearms bare.

"Mi' piccolo," he cooed at the little dog with his baritone, and George went quiet, cocked his head and looked up at the man in the red shirt.

His forearms were truly amazing, I'd never seen any so big before, as thick as a low oak branch, and covered with black hair. And his hand, stretched out to the little dog, was broad and rough. "Mi' piccolo," he said again, and now George stepped forward to sniff his fingertips, and then to lick his palm.

Robbie had retrieved his glasses, and was standing up, turning around, but I was still kneeling in the grass.

"So, little ragazzi, everything okay?" The man said. He wore a red neckerchief, a common red farmers' hanky, around his neck, only a little brighter red than that of his shirt.

"Yup, Mister, " said Robbie, dusting off the seat of his pants. I was still speechless. "We're fine," Robbie chirped.

The man in the chair chuckled a little at that, and sat back. "How 'bout you, boy?" he looked down at me. His eyes were green, and dark under the shadow of his brow. He had a gray stubble of a beard, a couple of day's thick growth on his chin, but it was nearly hidden by the great black mustache he wore. I nodded yes, and stood up, hearing Butto Sam relaxing back farther into his cage behind me.

"Speak up, boy, " the man said. "Non parla inglese? Are you all right?"

"Yeah," I said, and my voice sounded weak and squeaky even to me.

"Don't let the fur grow on your tongue, lad. Speak up!"

Robbie started to laugh at that, and his laughter made the man in the chair grin under that big moustache. "Ah, miei ragazzi! Trying to steal a peek at old Butto Sammy for free, were you?"

I just stood there, afraid to answer. Robbie was the one who chimed out, "But we didn't really see nothing, Mister. I only saw a little bit, like his eyes in the dark, and his fingers. And Willie," he pointed over at me, "he didn't see nothing."

"But you were trying, weren't you?' the man said back, his voice booming and his head cocked forward to glare at us. But I noticed his big hand was scruffing at little George's head now. "Weren't you?" he repeated, when neither Robbie nor me spoke up.

I nodded my head yes.

When Robbie saw me confessing, he piped up again. "It was too dark in there to see anything, Mister. We didn't see nothing worth paying for, not Willie nor me. Nothing."

I was looking over at Robbie, standing there like a little rooster, with grass stuck in the hair at the back of his head, and his striped t-shirt twisted around half sideways on him, and with his bifocal glasses all crooked, and I was thinking we were really in for it now, and he should sure enough shut up.

The man in the wheel chair saw me glaring at my little brother, and he listened to Robbie repeat himself, "Nothing worth paying for, Mister." Then the man broke out in a big bellowing laugh, his eyes moving from Robbie to me and to

Robbie again, and then finally they rolled up to the clear summer sky.

"Well, boys, the public has to pay to get a look at Butto Sam, and to see the things that he can do," the man boomed out to the powdery summer clouds above us. "And I'm afraid, O ragazzi, that goes for you Willie, and for you too, my little rooster. What's your name, mi' figlio?"

"Robert," said Robbie, his shoulders pulled back.

"I see," the man said, and he leaned back in his wheelchair. He stopped scruffing at little George's head. With an easy twist of his forearms, he wheeled himself over near Robbie and me. "Willie and Robert," he said, with the air now of a general giving orders softly, because he knew they would be followed.

"Get on home to your mother, you lads, and leave my ape alone. And ask your dear Mama for the coins to come into the Big Top, and then you'll see Butto Sam. But not before, Willie and Robert. Not before, my little ragazzi."

As he spoke, he worked the chair gracefully, herding us away from the cart that held the ape. I skedaddled a good few steps away, past the long red Buick. But not Robbie. He shuffled his shoes in the grass, and moved slowly along, with George beside him, and the man in the chair right behind.

"C'mon, Robbie," I said, "Let's get out of here."

"Robbie, is it?" the man in the wheelchair said. "Bring back some coins tomorrow, little man, and I'll let you shake hands with Butto Sam, Robbie." Then he chuckled that deep laugh in his chest.

Robbie stumbled back a couple of steps, and then said, "So what's your name, Mister. Being that you know mine now." He reached up and pushed his bifocals straight on his nose.

"My friends call me Il Rosso," the man said. "But you can call me Mr. Burton for now, little man. Now go check your mother's purse for some change, Robert the little rooster.

And I'll see you tomorrow, Oh piccolo Robbie." And he laughed and laughed at him, and it made me mad.

"C'mon," I said, and got myself a few more steps away. ""Let's get outta here."

"Mr. Burton?" Robbie said, and stood his ground. "You can call me Robert for now."

Burton laughed big at that. " Senza altro, Mr. Robert," he nodded his head. "Signor Robert, it is."

Finally Robbie skipped over toward me, with little George out in front of him. Robbie was grinning wide now, and he pulled his t-shirt around straight as he came.

"Let's get outta here," I repeated.

As we ran down the hill, past the horses and the elephant, we heard Jack Burton's deep voice, carrying over the grass. "Uno momento, mi' Butto! Aspetti! Aspetti!" But we didn't look back to see what the big man in the chair and the big ape in the box were doing. We just ran, to be free and away. We ran, wondering how we'd ask for the money for tomorrow, for the Big Top. And we dreamed as we went of shaking hands with the great black ape, with Butto Sammy, just the way Mr. Burton said that we could. We ran, hoping against hope and wondering how we could, as we rolled toward home.

The long red Buick was pulled out at the edge of town, in front of the little motel. The joint was just a little strip of five rooms by a gravel parking lot, back from the highway. There was an ancient hotel downtown, but it was filled mostly with several old folks, too frail to take care of themselves. So those five meager rooms of the little motel were it for accommodations in our town. Our house was not far from there. We were neighbors of the Coogans who ran the motel.

But Robbie and I were so focused on the ape in his cage, we never noticed the big Buick over there that evening after dinner, as we headed back to the schoolyard and all its foreign magic.

Butto Sam's cart was still up in the schoolyard, but after dark that night, the cage seemed frighteningly quiet. Robbie and I wandered around it, sitting there unhitched now from the big car, but the ape inside was silent. We decided he was asleep in the cooling dusk, but that didn't mean we had stopped wanting to see him. The elephant was great, and we'd seen a lot of nice horses around here before. But the ape, I think it was mostly that he was hidden from our sight that made him so much more important even that that giant elephant in our school grounds. We ran round the cart for a while, singing softly "Zambooti! Zambooti! Who's afraid-a ole Zambooti?" Still the cart returned only silence to our singsong play, so we slowly sang it louder and louder. But there was nothing.

I stopped when I noticed something sprouting out of the side of the cart. It was a long piece of hose like the one from our mother's vacuum cleaner, and it ran all along the steel bars that made the hitch to pull the cart behind that long smooth Buick. "What is it?" Robbie said.

"How do I know?" I pulled it and Robbie took the end and sang through it in his deepest voice, which wasn't all that deep, "Zamboooooooti Sam!" Still not a sound from the sleeping beast.

Finally I took a stick and scratched at the wall of the cart, and the corrugated steel made a rattling sound. Still, there was no response. So I stuck the tip of that stick through the iron bars of the ape's window. Nothing.

"He's not in there," I decided.

"Then where is he?" Robbie said, not really believing me. He walked up to the walls of the cart and drummed on them with his fists, trying to make it sound like the tympani that Butto Sam had played that afternoon. "Hey! Butto! Come out and play!" Robbie bellered, imitating with his little voice the booming baritone of Mr. Burton. But it was just a little rat-a-tat-tat and the squeaking of a kid, and all it got was the blank gazes of the horses and the elephant pegged around the school grounds.

"He's not in there," I said again.

"Then where is he?" Robbie still couldn't believe that this giant ape might be loose and free in our town.

I shrugged.

"Maybe he's escaped." Robbie started to grin with excitement. "He's out wandering in the wood, down by the river." Then he giggled a little.

"Maybe," I said, as I walked around the cart and touched the latch on the rear door. "But if he's escaped, he was clever enough to lock the door behind himself."

Robbie looked at me for a minute, then he looked at where the long red Buick had sat. "He's with Mr. Burton, " Robbie said.

I nodded yes, and that was the beginning of our search for the red Buick. It wasn't hard, in our little town, for two kids to make the rounds in an evening. So we got little George and we started our quest, and we walked from one end of the town to the other. George scurried out ahead of us, sniffing at the ground, peeing on the bushes and curbs and having a great old time.

It seemed like a long while then, but I suppose in a half hour or so we came upon the car. It was parked right where we had started out from home that night. It was tucked straight and neat, directly in front of the last room in the motel, the room that was farthest away from the motel's office. That was good, because it gave us a way to sneak around the back and not be seen.

First, Robbie and I searched around the red car, long and massive with its smooth, rounded curves and big chrome

226

fenders. "He's keeping Butto Sam in the car," Robbie whispered, "I betcha." We crawled around to the rider's side of it, so we couldn't be seen by anyone down at the office. We crept closer and closer like a pair of thieves, while little George just strolled up and peed on the front tire.

"There's nobody in there," I said.

We peered inside, under the white soft top, at the red leather interior with its white trim. There was a leather jacket in the back seat, and an army green blanket, but other than that the car was empty.

"Look at that shifter," Robbie whispered. There were a pair of hand controls where the shift stick should have been. They were steel and parallel and shot up from the floor of car. The "T" handles on their ends were worn a smooth gray, different than the shine and polish of the other chromed controls in that beautiful automobile.

"That's no shift stick," I said. "This is an automatic on the column, see, Robbie?" I pointed to the white stick on the column by the steering wheel, and the ivory PRNDL written on the dash beneath the curved speedometer.

"Then what are those things?"

"I don't know. I never saw anything like them," I said.

But at the same moment we both spotted the linkage that led down to the Buick's floor pedals. "That one's the gas," Robbie whispered.

"And the other's the brakes."

"Wow," he said a little too loudly. I shushed him, but I didn't need to, for he whispered, "Pretty neat."

We stared at those hand controls for a while, I guess letting the realities of what life is like in a wheelchair sink into our young heads. But then Robbie was the one who got us back on track. "Where you think that big monkey is, Willie?"

I looked over at the screen door to motel room #5. It was a warm summer night, but behind that screen, the metal inside door was closed tight. And now George was over there, sniffing at the corners of the screen.

"He must have taken it in there," I said.

"Let's go see," Robbie slipped away from the rider's side of the car before I could answer, and crept around to the backside of the motel. I followed behind him, staying low to the ground. Little George looked up from the screen door and then scampered along behind me.

There was a window at the back of the motel room, open but with the shades drawn, so all we could see was the light glowing inside. "You think he's in there?" Robbie said, but he didn't need to ask. We both stuck our noses up against the screen, trying to peer through the curtain, praying for a little summer breeze to lift them and let us see inside. But they were prayers without an answer. The heavy curtains hung as limp as if they were wet.

In one lower corner the screen wire had rusted brown. Robbie looked at me, grinned, and then pushed two of his fingers right through the weakened screen. "What are you doing?" I whispered at him. He just grinned and shrugged his shoulders at me.

George began growling low again. We both glanced back at the little dog, to see what was upsetting him. Down at the bottom of the hill below us, I saw Mrs. Coogan, the owner of the motel, strolling along across her yard enjoying the summer evening. "Shhh," I said to Robbie, and pointed down at her, at what I thought George was growling at. And then, while we weren't watching, out of my peripheral vision, I saw the curtains part.

Slowly, it seemed, and silently, the ape's great black face peered out at us through the screen. We froze for a moment, and even George was quiet behind us. Then, at the same moment, Butto Sam reached a paw up to touch Robbie's fingers in the screen, to the accompaniment of George's low growl. It was just an instant in the still summer night, until it all exploded. But I stood, unable to move, watching it all happen.

At the touch of Butto Sam's paw, Robbie screamed and recoiled away from the window, dragging his two fingers out of the screen, falling backward onto the ground. The aluminum window frame thrummed like an autoharp in the quiet night air. George leapt out of the way of Robbie's fall, and then leapt up onto my brother's stomach, from where he began to bark and bark up at the ape in the window. Butto Sam let out a loud startled grunt, not frightened, but quizzical. Down in the yard below, Mrs. Coogan bellowed out, "Hey, you kids!" and shifted up from the stroll to a waddle, racing her way toward us. "What are you kids doing up there?"

Inside the motel room, back past the ape's face, I saw Mr. Burton in his chair. His brown hat was off, and he had bare white feet sitting on the footrests of the wheelchair. But he still wore that bright red shirt. He had a bottle of some hard yellow liquor in his hand, and he was clearly just finishing a swallow. The hair on his head was the same gray and white stubble as what sprouted on his chin, and the whole of that stubble just made the great fur of his moustache seem larger and thicker and blacker.

"Butto," he yells, and pointed at him with the half empty bottle. "Silenzio" George kept up his yapping bark, as Butto Sam silently moved away from the open window and let the curtain fall back into place.

Robbie was on the ground, crying a little but trying to hold it in. His fingers were bleeding from the screen wire, and he was gazing at them, sniffing. But I think his tears were more about his fears than that little blood on his knuckles.

"Let's get out of here, Robbie," I said, bending down and grabbing his arm to pull him up. It didn't do me any good to leave Robbie behind, because I figured if Mrs. Coogan got to one of us, she got us all. In a little town like ours, everybody knew who you were and who you belonged to.

"C'mon," I said, almost lifting Robbie up on his feet by just tugging at his free hand. The other hand he still had stuck in his mouth, to stop the bleeding, or to stop the crying, I'm not sure which.

George turned some of his barking toward Mrs. Coogan then, but he still yapped a few up at the window now and then too, just to make sure the ape knew his place.

Once I had Robbie up and moving, I turned and headed around the backside of the motel. Robbie was only a few steps behind. As we rounded the next corner, leaving Mrs. Coogan far behind us we thought, we sprinted toward the gravel parking lot and the long red Buick. That would be our way out of the neighborhood, I figured. It gave us something to duck under and hide behind, if we needed it, until we could slip away into the dark of falling night.

Little George barked and snarled once more up at the window, before he shot around the corner behind us and then roared past us in a sprint. Up ahead, he disappeared around the corner of the motel where all the doors to the rooms were waiting. We heard him bark once, and then he was quiet. And that was strange enough to slow me down. I could see the tail fins of the Buick out in the lot ahead of us, past the last corner. But I pulled up to a stop at the edge of the corner, and waited, listening to see what was happening, waiting to hear something from noisy little George that would let us know what lay waiting around the corner. But Robbie, a few steps behind me and with those fingers still in his mouth, just ran straight past me and right around the corner, into whatever was there, and I couldn't yell at him to stop, we were to close to whatever was waiting with George on the other side. So I pressed up flat against the white slate siding of the motel, and waited to see what happened next.

"Hi," I heard Robbie say meekly, sounding startled.

And then there was more quiet.

There should have been a bark or something out of George, and surely somebody should have answered Robbie. But there was nothing for the longest moment. I tried to imagine what had happened to the little dog and my baby brother. If they'd fallen in a hole, or into a policeman's grasp, or even into the jaws of an enraged Butto Sammy, there should at least have been a little yelp before they disappeared. But there was nothing. And that was really frightening.

So after a moment of listening and waiting, I cautiously leaned over and tried to peek around the corner to see what had happened. But the sight of just the top of my head was greeted by a deep baritone laugh, and so I pulled back against the corner hideaway, having seen nothing. That laugh though could only belong to the big man in the wheelchair.

"Come out, Willie," Robbie yelled far too loudly. "It's okay." Then George gave out a happy little yip. It vanished into the deep rolling laughter.

So I stepped slowly out around the corner to find Mr. Burton sitting in front of the closed door to his room, with George resting happily up in his lap getting scruffed around his collar, and with my little brother standing beside them both, grinning with his two fingers stuck back in his mouth again.

But over Mr. Burton's shoulder, not too far past this happy and contented little scene, I could see the top of the stairs that led up to the motel. Before I could digest what I saw, before I could mutter a weak hello to the laughing man, Mrs. Coogan at full throttle crested the top of the stairs, arms pumping and head bobbing from her exertion.

"William and Robert," she bellowed, and barked out last names out too. "You boys stay right there!" We must have looked to her like were ready to bolt.

Mr. Burton's laughter died away, and with one hand he wheeled himself around so his back was to the closed door of his room.

"Stay right where you are," she yelled in a whisper, remembering now she was running outside the doors to all those guest rooms of her motel. George let out a low growl in her direction, but Burton scratched the dog's chest, and muttered, "Easy, mi' cane, easy," and George was quiet. There was not one sound from behind the door at Mr. Burton's back, where all of us but Mrs. Coogan knew a great African gorilla from the darkest Zambutti lurked waiting. Mrs. Coogan could not know what danger she was in, and I wondered if I should rightly warn her. But that night Butto Sammy was a wonderfully silent great African gorilla.

Mrs. Coogan came to a stop just a few steps away from us. "Good evening, Mr. Burton," she said, sounding obsequious. "I hope these boys haven't disturbed you."

Burton didn't answer right away. He looked over at me, looked deep in my eyes, and then he sent the same calm gaze toward Robbie. Neither of us spoke up. We had him, by the gorilla, so to speak, and everybody there except Mrs. Coogan knew it. But neither Robbie nor I said a word.

"These boys?" Burton said, and turned his mock surprise at the motel keeper. "My two little friends here?" His big hand reached over and rested on Robbie's shoulder.

"I saw them," Mrs. Coogan reared her head back on her shoulders and looked down her plump button nose at all of us. "They were out behind your room, Mr. Burton." And she leaned forward to point at me, ignoring Robbie and our dog beside the man in the wheelchair. "Where they should not have been. And where they're old enough to know better than to be sneaking around." That last part was punctuated with a couple of thrusts of her index finger straight at my heart.

"Oh, these are my friends, Ma'am," Burton smiled up at her from under his great moustache. "Mi' amici piccoli!" he sang in his baritone. "They weren't disturbing me, Ma'am, they were just up for a visit with the circus man. Right? Boys?"

Robbie nodded silently, and I guess I did too.

Mrs. Coogan just made a loud "Harrumph!" through that little nose she was gazing down at us from, and then she looked up at the roof of her motel for a moment, hoping to find some answer there, I guess.

George growled a little again, as it seemed the dog was growling at the motel keeper, but I think he heard something from inside that room, some low movement from the great ape lurking inside, something too soft and animal for our ears to hear.   I realized again Mrs. Coogan was in some danger she didn't recognize. Little did she know that the beast of the jungle was waiting as quietly as a predator for her to make the wrong move, to become the hopeless, trapped prey, just the other side of that cheap motel door.   Again I felt in some way compelled to warn her, but at the some time I didn't want to give Burton up. I think now that moment held the first great decision of my life: to save the official and obsequious or to protect the unknown and the wild.

I knew of course what I was supposed to do. I knew the right thing to do. I needed to save the small town and the local from the great threat of the outside. It was my duty to get that strange danger and ferocity safely under lock and key, and to control the wild and rescue the order of the everyday.

But at that moment the everyday was squat and wide and wearing a polka dot summer dress, and what's more, it looked down its nose at us.

That very moment, I think, was the real beginning of my life long search for Jack Burton, Il Rosso, the lost and long forgotten Red Shirt. Once I decided to leave Mrs. Coogan hanging there, with her nose in the air, just some unknowing bait before the great beast, the direction of all the rest of my years was sealed and delivered. And my search to find Jack Burton, the real Jack Burton, had begun. But of course, I didn't know any of this then.   I was just keeping a secret. Dangerous, yes, but still just a secret.

Burton gently placed that large hand of his on George's head, encircling it with his fingers. "Calma, calma," he whispered as he pulled the dog's ears down softly with just his left hand. George's tongue hung out in a smiling pant and he turned his head and looked up at Mr. Burton lovingly. "Piu piccolo, calma," Burton whispered to him again. I knew somehow he was whispering to the beast behind the door as well.

Mrs. Coogan drew in a great, exasperated breath, and then she began with her orders. "William. Robert. You boys head on home now." Her glare moved from me to Robbie and then back again. The weight of her sentence landed on that final word, "Now." Robbie nodded yes at her, but he didn't move away from Mr. Burton's arm still resting on his shoulders. "I'll be calling to talk with your mother about this. You know you are supposed to say away from . . . " Mrs. Coogan paused, not out of some second thought, but in order to make her point to Burton, sitting there with his arm still around the child. " . . . these circus people," she finished, now glaring at the man in the wheel chair.

She pulled Robbie from Burton's grasp them, and herded us away from him. We scuffled a few steps into the gravel parking lot, never looking away from the man in the red shirt sitting in the wheelchair.

"Come to the circus tomorrow, O ragazzi," Burton called out to us, smiling. "I think we can get you inside." Then he winked at both of us.

That wink made us partners of his. Robbie looked over at me and grinned, because he understood that too, and then he looked back at the man in the wheelchair. We were all together, Burton and Robbie and I, accomplices now together, concealing that great ape hidden just behind the door, we knew, just out of reach of the everyday, lurking just out of the quotidian sight.

Mrs. Coogan reached over and pulled little George out of Burton's lap and set the dog on the ground. His tail twitched and the little black dog looked back up at the man in the chair. "Go on," Mrs. Coogan shooed at George with the back of her hand. "Scoot," she said. George skittered back a step or two in the rocks and weeds toward where Robbie and I were standing in the gravel, but he was still facing Burton, and his tail still twitched in anticipation of something.

But Mrs. Coogan was done with us. As far as she was concerned, we knew what we were supposed to be doing, we'd been given our orders and put back on the safe and narrow path, the direction home. There was nothing more to deal with us. Even though we all three still stood in the gravel next to the red Buick watching, we were already gone home in her eyes. If she'd turned around and looked at the three of us, I think she'd been surprised to see us still there.

Instead, she put her fists on her polka dot hips and turned toward the wheelchair. "Now, Mr. Burton, sir, we've got some things to talk about," she said.

"See you tomorrow, mi' boys," Burton said with a wave of his hand that freed us to leave somehow, forced us to go really. "A domani," he yelled, "ragazzi!" And so we scurried away and left him in the clutches of that polka dot dress.

That night, in our twin beds in the dark, Robbie said to me, "Are you sleeping, Willie?" I was wide awake, my eyes wired open with excitement, my heart still beating fast at the prospect of going to the circus tomorrow. Of really seeing Butto Sam, not through some window or curtain or brace of bars. But just there, the whole of him, in all his wildness and power. But I knew if I answered, we would both be up all night, squirming and whispering at one another. And it would become a long, long night. It would take until forever for the sun to rise and the day of the circus to dawn. So I didn't answer my brother. It was the only way to make tomorrow come sooner. And though it took a long while, I heard Robbie sleeping eventually, and I never let on I was awake. Somehow, in a dark that I can't remember, I slept too.

The next day, the circus day, was hard with disappointment. There had been a phone call from Mrs. Coogan, of course, and then there was a lot of explaining that needed to be done, and that we couldn't do. And that, shortly, was the end of all hope. The world of Zambutti and the African Islands and their darkest reaches, of elephants and plumed white horses, was suddenly only a distant dream.

Little George never came around and the edges of our lawn were trimmed and squared, and every little dandelion was dug out, root and all. And not just the flowering ones, but every one, every leaf we could find, and some besides that were pointed out to us. And then there was a garage to sweep and hedges to trim, and then a set of twin beds changed and turned and dusted and vacuumed.

And so it grew dark, and all the circuses were miles away, forever and unjustly traveling away from us. And Butto Sam was just a name written in red on some remembered wall, nothing better than an illusion, a word in a dusty library book no one reads anymore.

At the end of it all, of that horrid, long day, we were confined to our room. Sent to the prison with twin beds we'd been forced to dust and clean all day while our friends and mates went to the magic world of the Circus of Butto Sammy, seeing all the marvels we would hear about again and again in the days to come, but never see. But never know.

The world was a cruel place on that day of the traveling circus.

Still, while our dreams may have been imprisoned, our spirits indeed ran free.

In the darkest of dark of night, I slipped out of my bed. I saw Robbie buried in the tumble of covers and pillows in the bed across from mine. Silently, I pulled on my heavy corduroy trousers and with my shoes and with a cap on my head, I slipped over to the window. Even I was amazed at my own silent stealth, because Robbie never once even rustled around.

The screen was so easy to shift out of place that it popped loose and clattered down into the soft grass outside the window. At the noise of the screen I froze, and only slowly turned back to look at Robbie's still form lying in the bed. I expected to see him sitting up, rubbing his eyes and looking at me vaguely in the dark, trying to see without his glasses. And then I would have to take him along, we'd have to run away together and all of my escape would be slower, and with bifocals, and probably impossible. And all because of a window screen flopping down into the summer grass.

I heard a soft, "Shhhh!" behind me.

Remember, I was turned back, looking over at Robbie's little form stretched out on his bed, waiting for him to sit up. The window to freedom was at my back. And that "shhh!" behind me came from outside.

It made me jump, and I twisted back away from the open window, and fell on my bum on the hardwood floor with a thump. Out the window I saw nothing but the stars and the swash of the Milky Way in the sky.

Then Robbie's head popped up inside the window. "Will," he whispered so quietly I barely understood him, "you're going to get us caught." Then his head disappeared into the dark outside again.

I sat there for a moment, my butt on the floor, resting back on the palms of my hands behind me, staring at my black Converse tennis shoes out in front of me, and listening to my heart beat in my ears.

Then Robbie's head, in his Cub's cap, floated up into the window from the dark outside again. "Will! Are you coming?" Robbie said. "Or are you staying home?"

I glanced back over my shoulder at the lifeless clump of bedding in Robbie's bed, still half expecting it to sit up and speak some sense to me.

"But you're not getting us caught," Robbie's disembodied head outside in the dark said at me. It paused a moment, then a little disembodied hand rose up and pushed the bifocals up on his nose.

"C'mon," Robbie whispered. And then disappeared.

I clambered back up onto my feet, and then realized if I wasn't silent I would wake up the whole house, and the great escape would be over. So with a new resolve to be quiet, I crawled out the open window and hopped down into the grass next to the screen.

Robbie emerged out of the shadows of an elm tree, out near the highway. He lifted up an arm and waved me onward and over to him, and then like some resistance fighter in the night, he disappeared back into the dark of the elm.

I scurried over to the tree, and found him there waiting. "Let's go," he whispered. He reached down and hefted up a little olive green rucksack, tossed it over one shoulder and straightened his cap.

His clothing was all dark and he wore the dirt brown jacket to his snowsuit, even in the warmth of the summer night. He slipped away across the highway and headed toward the other end of town, moving from tree to tree quickly.

It took only a moment to catch up with him, because I was wearing my most heavy cords and a sweatshirt, with my fastest Connie's on my feet. And I wasn't lurking at every tree, looking both ways, and then darting to the next tree. I just upped my heels and licked it, running full bore across the highway and then down the sidewalk. Speed was my key, not deceit.

I caught up with him by an old elm, three houses down the street. "Hey," I said, "where are we going?" I looked down at his feet and noticed he was wearing his Sunday church shoes, the brown ones with wingtipped toes. But you couldn't see the wingtips, because they were covered with his hand-me-down rubbers, the brown ones I used to "forget" at the schoolhouse so I didn't have to wear them, even though they had Hop-a-long Cassidy buttons on the side. Since I wouldn't wear them, and he grew into them, so Robbie inherited those rubbers from me.

"I'm going to join up with Mr. Burton," Robbie said. "Ill-a-Rose-o!" he whispered, imitating the deep sound of Burton's voice, as he followed my eyes down to the rubbers on his feet. "How about you?" Robbie asked, as he scuffed his heel in the grass to show off how well he was prepared. "Are you coming too?" He hefted one of the straps on his backpack up higher on his shoulder. "You didn't bring your stuff, Will."

I looked down at his face and saw that the edges of his hair were damp with sweat. "I don't know about that," I said.

Robbie nodded his head at me, as if he knew that I wouldn't have the guts to go through with it. I just wanted to see the circus, that was all I was good for. This is what his eyes said to me.

"Why don't you let me carry that," I said, putting my hand on that little khaki sack.

He stared at me, getting ready to object.

"Ill-a-Rose-o!" I whispered, making my voice into the deepest baritone I could.

Robbie gazed at me for a long moment, then with a nod of his head, he slipped the rucksack off his shoulders and handed it to me. Maybe he was hoping I would join in the adventure, maybe he didn't want to risk it all alone. Maybe he just trusted me to join in, or maybe it was just that he was tired and hot from running in a winter coat through the summer night. But he handed me his bag and then he wiped his damp brow on the sleeve of his coat.

"I think I'll just carry this," he said, and slipped the heavy coat off.

His rucksack was heavy and hard as metal, and when I slipped it onto my shoulder it dug into my lower back with some sharp edges inside. But I didn't say anything about it, or I knew he'd take it back. "Ill-a-rose-o!" I said louder, and Robbie grinned at me, holding his coat in his arms. He had a wool sweater on under the coat, and beneath that I saw my old boy scout shirt, the one I always used for camping out.

"Ill-a-rose-o!" Robbie said.

And then we were off at a sprint to the edge of town. We came around the back way, by the alleys, to the rear of the motel, and there we found a light on in Mr. Burton's window. We'd made it this far by staying away from the main drag all through town, so we never even thought of going around to the front of the motel, under the lights of the gravel lot, and knocking on the man's door. That was no way for two young adventurers to approach the doorway to our destiny.

No, we crept quietly up to that lit rear window, watching always and everywhere for Mrs. Coogan to be lurking about. But the night was dark and moonless, with great broken clouds now moving over the stars and across the Milky Way. Mr. Burton's window was open and the night breezes had parted the curtains. This was the way to begin the story of our adventures.

I put my finger up to my lips, and Robbie nodded. Then I pulled his heavy rucksack off my back, and carried the lunk of it under my arms. Together we slunk up to the window, staying low and out of sight.

We both remembered Butto Sammy greeting us in that window, startling us onto our backsides, so we were careful and quiet this time. Robbie stayed crouched on the ground beneath the window. While I slowly stuck my head up to look inside, Robbie kept the cautious watch for Mother Coogan, who might still be roaming around.

Slowly I peeked up through the screen, and I couldn't believe what I saw inside. At first I just sensed someone moving around in the room, under the yellow lights of the ceiling bulb. Then a little brush of wind slipped past my ear and lifted the curtains up away from the window. They fluttered just a touch, before they drooped back down, but in that instant I saw them.

And I'd never seen anything like them before. What I expected, of course, was the man in his chair and that great ape of his, the one I'd still not gotten a straight look at for all my trying, lumbering around the room somewhere. Instead, I saw them.

The taller one was wearing only her panties, and her back was toward me, as she ran both her hands up through her long tussle of bright red hair. Her friend was sitting on the edge of the bed, wearing a little baby blue robe that hung open and draped down around her onto the bed. She had a cigarette in one hand and she turned her head, drew in a long draught of tobacco. Then slowly she tilted her head back and blew the smoke out through her ruby painted lips. The tilt of her head and the movement of her arm away with the cigarette opened up that thin robe and showed me the nothing beneath it, and especially it showed me the triangle of black hair in her lap.

It might be the air I sucked in, but whatever it was, the breeze died and the curtains fell back down in place. I dropped down on the ground, with my back against the motel wall and sat by my brother.

"What is it?" he whispered.

But I couldn't speak. I just sat still and tried to keep my eyes from bugging out, because they felt at that moment like I might never shut them again.

"Ill-a-rose-o?" Robbie whispered.

I swallowed. I shook my head no. Then I turned around again and stuck my head up there for another look.

They were talking softly to one another, and I could see only that the red-haired one was walking around while the one in the amazing blue robe sat and smoked. But I couldn't see in, because those curtains hung thick and dense and still, heavy as stones in a doorway. And in the summer air there was not now even a hint of a breeze.

But it was summer, and I knew the breeze would come suddenly, and at some time, at some moment, the one with the red hair would turn around. I shifted side to side a little, trying to peek through any curve in the curtains, all to no avail.

They spoke back and forth to one another something I couldn't hear, and then the redhead sang a little bit of some song. Robbie, on the ground beside me, whispered, "Will, who is it?"

I just shushed him and gestured with my hand for him to stay down and keep a look out. But I didn't move from my place, waiting for that sweet summer breeze to shake open my world again.

I wasn't paying much attention to Robbie. I was focused on my next glimpse through the screen. So I didn't notice him slowly standing up, like a commando, with his back to the window, still the good lookout. When he was up straight, and standing on the opposite side of the window, he threw a quick glance over his shoulder at the window.

Inside the two women were laughing now, and Robbie looked over at me with big eyes of his own. With two short waves of my hand, I gestured him to get down but he wasn't paying any attention. I realized then that, unlike me, there was deep disappointment in his face. He'd come here planning to run away on an adventure with the deep voiced man in the chair and his great ape companion. It was the beginning for Robbie of his great escape. Instead he found his hero tangled up with a couple of "girls."

But me, one peep through those curtains at the black dream down in her lap, and I'd completely forgotten about Burton and his monkey. I was having trouble breathing and holding my breath in anticipation at the same time.

But not Robbie. With his back against the motel wall, he pushed up his bifocals on his nose and then scanned the horizon like a trooper preparing to move. Then he cast his head to the side and called out over his shoulder, into the screen and the open window and through the dead, drooping curtains.

"Mr. Burton, are you in there?"

I guess he was going to save the hero from damnation, and get us all rolling on our real journey. There was no time for this dallying around with women.

I know I winced, and sunk down into the ground, and there was a soft scream from one of the women inside. Robbie just stood with his back flat against the wall, hidden from view by anyone who might look out through the window.

"Mr. Burton, sir?" he called out again.

I heard scurrying footsteps inside the room and then saw a stream of smoke shoot through the screen above me. It had to be the one in little blue robe at the window. "Who's out there?" she said, and the light behind her in the room switched off so there was only a strong but indirect light coming from the bathroom inside.

I didn't say anything; I was just frozen in place beneath the window. I heard her suck in another toke on the cigarette, and then behind her the other woman, the red head, whispered, "Who is it, Shirley?"

Another stream of smoke flowed out through the screen, as Shirley said, "Billy, is that you? If that's you I'm gonna kill you."

Right then all the stories I'd been told about the wild wandering lives of circus people welled up in me, like a flooded basement of fears under my feet. The thievery, the pick pocketing, the conning you out of your hard earned money, the money you worked for at honest jobs, not flim-flam work like theirs. The knife fights and the gambling, and the dancing dangerous music under dark lights in unspeakable clothes. And yes, the stealing of children.

All those stories, gathered up in just a few years of living from generations and generations of hate and distrust, they were there beneath me, like rising water in a cloud burst. So I hung low to the ground, out of the sight of that window, just as I thought Robbie would. And I began to think quickly of where and how to bolt off into the dark, searching for ways of escape.

But right then Robbie, with a determined look in his eyes, stepped out from the wall and faced the window, stepped into the pale, indirect light it cast out onto him. Shirley in the blue robe gasped at his deliberate move in the dark. She was startled, but she didn't drop the curtain.

"We're looking for Mr. Burton, ma'am," Robbie said.

"Jack?" Shirley said, incredulous.

"Who is it, Shirley?" the red head's voice came from deeper inside the room. "Is it that boyfriend of yours?"

"You're looking for Jack?" Shirley of the robe said.

"Could you get Mr. Burton for us, please?" Robbie said.

"Is it Billy?" I heard the pad of the red head's bare feet coming toward the window across the linoleum floor.

"It's just some little kid," Shirley said. "What's your name, kid?"

"Never mind that, ma'am," said Robbie. "We need to talk to Mr. Burton."

"We?" said the redhead from behind Shirley.

"Who's we?" said Shirley.

I saw the redhead's face poke out into the light from the screen, so I plastered myself up against the wall even closer, if that was possible.

"Billy, are you out there?" said Shirley of the robe. "If you put some pint assed kid up to this, I'll hang your hide on these walls in here." She drew in a long, hot tug on her cigarette, so I hard a toke I could hear the little cigarette pop in her hand as she drew in.

"There's no Billy here," said Robbie, defiant. "It's just me and my brother Will, and we're here to talk to Mr. Burton." He added, "Ma'am," a bit too late.

There was a long silent pause then, followed by the cackling laughter of both women. They both said "Jack" once or twice in the midst of their chuckles.

"Come around to the front door, little man," Shirley of the robe said. "And bring your brother, so we can see you two big boys in the light." Then they cackled a little more, muttering "Jack" back and forth between them.

Robbie looked down at me, the determination solid in the set of his jaw. He didn't nod his head, he didn't say a word, he just shoved the glasses up on his nose one more time and then turned and strutted off around the motel, like a proud warrior headed toward battle formation.

I sat for a moment, feeling my plans and hopes of escape drifting away. The curtain had fallen back down over the window and the lights had come back on inside the room and while I thought about bolting away, I knew I couldn't leave Robbie alone in the clutches of those women, kidnapped by the gypsy caravan. So I stood up and looked inside one more time, because I couldn't resist one last peek. But there was nothing to see. The door across the room was open onto the parking lot, but I knew this only because the curtains were pinned hard against the screen from the breeze flowing across the room now. I couldn't even see their shadows inside, much less any of my dreams.

So I followed Robbie around the motel one more time. He was fearlessly out in front of me again, all his caution thrown by the way. First I noticed what wasn't there. Out in the gravel lot there was no Buick, not a red one or any other kind. Where Burton's great car had sat there was only a Kaiser, pea green where it wasn't rusted out. But there was not even a tire track left behind by the long red Buick convertible, with its silver trimmed wings and its pearl white soft top.

I began to understand, then, that we had not stumbled on some kind of tryst. This was not Mr. Burton entertaining. These two women were certainly the "exotic" dancers from the carnival show, but they had taken Burton's room somehow. They were not guests in the fun I could only then begin to imagine, the magnetic but still mysterious body of joy I could only guess at. There was no scent of anything male in the vicinity, other than my kid brother and me.

The redhead was waiting in the open door to the motel room, wearing now a long flannel shirt, red and brown like her hair. She had her hand on her hip and as Robbie walked boldly over to her, I hung back a ways. It was a mixture of fear and fascination, for that redhead had the fullest lips I'd ever seen, and even under that flannel, shirt I could see the loose shape of her large breasts hanging free.

"Where's Mr. Burton?" demanded Robbie.

"Come on in here, little man," said Shirley's voice from inside the room. "And where's that big brother of yours?"

"He's out here," said the redhead. Then she waved me toward her, "Come on," she said and smiled with those full lips of hers, redder than even Jack Burton's Buick. "We won't bite," she chuckled again.

My feet led me over to the door, while the rest of me was in complete turmoil. As I approached the light in the doorway, with my head down, she put an arm around my shoulder and I saw that her toenails were painted the color of her lips, the color of her shirt, the color of the missing Buick car.

"He's a cutie too," Red said, as we stepped into the room together. I looked up and my eyes were met with two shocks at once. First, Robbie was sitting happily on Shirley's miraculous lap, and she had both her arms wrapped around him. And second Shirley, despite that dark black vision I'd seen down inside her little blue robe, was a bright yellow blonde.

I knew then that we were lost. Both Robbie and I, we were about to disappear into the carnival world, never to return. The dancing girls would whirl us away into some wandering life of elephants and show horses and little skimpy clothes covered with plastic sequins and painted lips. We would live now lost in a world of deep dyed hair and painted moustaches, showing fine under the hard hot lights inside the dark tents. We were lost.

"What do you boys want?" Red said, and her arm dropped from my shoulders. I felt the warmth of her around me fade away, and the room suddenly seemed a cool refrigerator, and me with a fever. She left the motel room door open behind us, the light from the floor lamps cast out onto the rusty Kaiser and the loose gravel.

"We're looking for Mr. Burton," Robbie said from Shirley's lap. "Ill-rose-O!" he said, as if that explained it all.

"This was his room," I muttered, and I saw both Shirley and Red lean forward toward me, trying to hear my shy explanation. "Last night," I added, trying to speak louder.

"Jack?" said Red incredulously.

Shirley sat back and hugged Robbie to her, and then she fluffed at his light brown hair around his ear, and straightened the ball cap on his head. "What do you two little lads want with Jack Burton?" she said.

Robbie struggled a bit against her hug with his shoulders, and I looked down from her long exposed thigh to her knee and then along the line of her calf to see that her toenails were painted flamingo pink.

"We're going to be part of his troupe and train all the gorillas in Zambutti," Robbie explained as if it were soon to be a news flash, just a back page story it was so obvious. But where he'd come up with this whole plan of his was news to me. "He lives with a gorilla, you know, " he said.

That made the two women laugh again, and I saw when Red opened her mouth how crooked and yellowed her teeth were behind those rich, painted lips.

"He invited us to come to the circus today," I said, trying to make some sense for them of this garbled dream of my brother's, though I'm not entirely sure why. I guess the part of me still fascinated by their polished and waxed veneer did not want to seem silly and little like a kid. " But we couldn't get there," I said, leaving out the way we'd been grounded by Mrs. Coogan's report. "So we thought we'd come over here tonight," I said. "He was here, last night."

"He invited you to come to the show?" said Shirley, still not believing us, still toying with the hair under my brother's cap. There was a little line of sweat now cutting down from the dark roots of her blonde hair, and etching a route through the smooth powdery make up on her temple and cheek. I saw the hard wrinkles around her eyes, covered by the powder and with the black lines of her eye makeup. "Why would Jack do that?" Shirley said to Red.

"Because we didn't tell on him," Robbie announced, and then he wriggled out of Shirley's grasp. He stood square in front of her and he straightened his scout shirt and pushed his glasses up as he said, "Mrs. Coogan caught us up here, but we didn't tell on him, that he had a gorilla in his room."

This led to another good laugh from the painted dancing girls, and Shirley uncrossed her long legs enough for me to glimpse down in the secret places again. My eyes had not deceived me through the screen; her blonde hair was as phony as the smooth pink blush on her cheeks and the fat red curl of her lips. But still, the long lines of her legs, like angles of terrifying light under that thin robe, were enchantment itself.

"So you boys are the reason he got tossed out of here," said Shirley as she laughed, and wrapped that blue robe around her lap cavalierly, showing off more than she hid. I know now how practiced that flurry of the robes was, but I couldn't recognize it then. I was too young, and I was soon to be lost.

Both Robbie and I were quiet, because even Robbie didn't know what to say.

"He pulled that cripple thing with the motel lady two days ago, you know," Red said, "and he beat us out of the last room left in this little backwater. She sent us all the way to the city to get a room, because she thought we weren't up to 'her standards.'" That's when Red strolled a step or two over, and closed the motel room door. "You could see it in the old lady's eyes, couldn't you, Shirley?" Red said. "We weren't up to 'her standards,' you know." She slipped over next to me then, and her arm wrapped around me, warm and filled with some strange incredible promise.

"But then here she called us up this morning, at the hotel she sent us to," Shirley leaned over and took Robbie's hands in hers, showing off a lot more of her chest under that little robe. I'm sure I was bug eyed, I know my mouth was dry. "Long distance and everything," Shirley drew Robbie to her lap again, as if they were in a dance.

"'I've got a room for you girls now,' the old lady said on the phone," Red took up the story, imitating Mrs. Coogan's pius. singsong voice pretty well, and now I felt fingertips at the base of my neck, touching me like little live wires.   Shirley gave Robbie a hug, and the tie of that robe fell loose showing us a whole lot more of herself.

"We didn't know 'till later it was Jack's room she had for us. The old lady tossed him out because he was going to be a 'bad influence on these boys.'" Shirley had her arms all wrapped around my little brother again.

"On these boys," Red said and her face came close to my cheek and her thick red lips brushed against my face. "These sweet little boys," she whispered and her breath tickled my ear. Still even through all the fascination her touch held over me, I could smell the acrid scent of her last cigarette, and probably all the cigarettes in her life, in that tickle of breath. It didn't really free me from the electric warmth of her touch, but it kept some small part of me aware of the closed motel door and of the big, loose world outside it.

"Mine's cuter than yours," Shirley said, and she let the corner of her robe fall off her shoulder as she held Robbie tightly. One of her breasts was fully exposed, the round brown nipple pointing up at my brother, and he was squirming now to get loose. That was when Red leaned over to me, showing me the freckled cleavage inside her flannel shirt and kissed me on the cheek.

"Oh, I don't think so," Red said, and she took my right hand and guided it up under her shirt.

"Maybe we aren't up to the old lady's standards," Shirley said with a little laugh. But I couldn't see her anymore, and I barely understood her words. I was gone, and a cutely there at the same time.

"You boys wouldn't tell on us, would you?" Red whispered to me, and my hand was on her breast, drawn like a magnet. The nipple was like a hard bead in my palm, and her red hair was brushing all over my face. All I knew was the deep red hair on my cheeks, and the freckled breast in my hand, until suddenly I heard Shirley groan, "Hey," and Robbie came at me like he was stealing home and I was the catcher with the ball in my hand standing between him and the plate. He just rolled straight into me and shoved me out of Red's embrace. The next thing I knew he had pinned me against the motel door with a narrow shoulder, and with both hands he was fumbling at the doorknob. In a moment the metal door sprang open from my weight against it and Robbie and I tumbled out onto the gravel drive.

Robbie was up on his feet immediately, staring down at me. The night was filled with the laughing of Red and Shirley, as they sat back in the yellowed light of the room. Shirley's robe was down now completely around her waist, tangled with the bedclothes, and Red stood a step or two back from the door, with her one freckled breast gazing out at me. She was slowly wiggling one finger at me, gesturing to me to come back inside. Their laughter seemed to come from everywhere but their red, red lips. "Run, Will," Robbie yelled down at me. He grabbed my arm around the elbow and pulled me onto my feet. I couldn't keep from staring back inside at those dancers smiling out at me, their
breasts waiting for me, urging me to come back inside the room, while their soft laughter filled the wide night air. "Will," Robbie started to drag me away, "let's get out of here. C'mon."

I turned to run along with Robbie, but the bent lump in my pants wouldn't let me move anyway except sidewise and crooked, staring back toward that room. So with my little brother out ahead of me, and Red laughing and waving at me in farewell, I limped away past the pea green Kaiser and back into the quiet, small town night.

*   *   *

His tent was pitched at the edge of the school grounds, with the elephant and the white horses staked all around it. The night was quiet except for singing crickets and the occasional snort of a horse, or the elephant flapping its ears. But now and again his deep voice boomed out softly as he sang in some language we didn't understand.

His tall tent glowed a pale yellow in the dark, and we crept closer to it. Someone inside it was walking, and Burton sang a little louder and then stopped. "Ill-a-rose-O!" Robbie mouthed at me so I understood, though he didn't even make a sound. I nodded yes. Then we heard Burton's big laugh.

Bright light leaked out of the seams of the tent, and shadows moved around inside, passing through the light, so large they stretched out to the tent ceilings around the tall posts.

The long red Buick had the top up and closed and it was parked next to the tent. The white trailer of Zambutti Sam was hitched to it now, ready to roll away at any moment it seemed. But for now it sat in the light dimmed by the canvas walls of Jack Burton's tent. And a line ran from one of the tent posts to the antenna of the car. From it hung a few pieces of white clothing, a pair of brown pants, and a cardinal red shirt.

"Ill-a-rose-O!" I whispered this time, letting a tiny sound whisper past my lips. Then with a tilt of my head I gestured a 'Let's go' to Robbie. We walked up to the flap door of the brown canvas tent and, before I could call out, there was a little flurry of movements inside as the shadow's shifted broadly against the door.

"Who's out there?" boomed Mr. Burton. "Announce yourself, stranger."

"Mister Burton?" I said, surprising even myself at how clear and loud my voice was in the night.

"Ill-a-rose-O!" Robbie sang out.

There was silence then for a moment inside the tent. Then we heard Mr. Burton say softly, "Sammy, there."

Suddenly the flap of the tent was pulled back and the warm light from inside flooded out onto Robbie and me, standing in front of the opening. At first all we could see was the dark shape of Mr. Burton in his chair in front of us, dark and featureless as a shadow, with the lantern light behind him.

"Miei ragazzi!!" he boomed, and then he gave forth a great, rumbling laugh.

While he was laughing at us, Burton wheeled himself out of the tent a bit and he gazed this way and that around into the dark schoolyard. One of the horses snorted somewhere. Then, once Jack Burton was satisfied that we were alone, he wheeled himself backwards and off to the side. "Come in, ragazzi," he said, "Come in."

Robbie walked in first, eagerly, that lunk of a backpack over his shoulder, but I followed right behind him. A couple of electric lanterns hung from the peaks at the top of the tent poles and in the center of the room sat a round propane heater, glowing red and warm, even in the summer night. On the other side of it the mountain gorilla rested, unchained, one front paw on his lap and the other on the ground, holding him up as he leaned his bulk on the curled knuckles of other paw. He sat on a low wooden stool, with a piece of Indian carpet draped over part of it. The wooden stool was only about eight inches high, and it's seat was a curved wooden board of dark black wood, so dark it seemed painted though if you looked close you could see the lines of the dark grain in it. Zambutti Sam's stool was worn and old, and the wood was thick and sturdy, so it looked like it would be heavy for a man to lift. Impossible for Robbie or me to do much more than shove it around, and hard to imagine a man in a wheelchair, even one as agile as Burton, would be able to lift it.

As we came inside, Burton spoke to the ape, "Zambutti, indietro." The great ape rose on its haunches, lifted that stool with one hand and moved back further into the tent, making room for the rest of us to sit around that warm heater. He set the stool down softly, with hardly a sound, adjusted the chunk of Indian rug, and then sat again with one paw in his lap, the other on the grassy floor of the tent.

"Sit down, little ragazzi," and Burton gestured to a stretch of rug on the dirt and grass that the gorilla had just left empty.

Robbie and I stood there for a moment, wondering about how close we should get to a loose and free mountain gorilla, bigger than both of us rolled together twice. An ape who could lift that stool with just one hand.

"Sit down, sit down," Burton gestured his hand at that rug. "Come in! Sit down! It's okay!"

Then he looked at us just standing there, and he laughed at us.

"If you boys had come this afternoon, you wouldn't be afraid of old Sammy," he said. Then he rolled his chair over so that he sat next to the great ape, and where he would be between us and Zambutti Sam. "Where were you today? You couldn't come to the circus, my little friends? Even for free?"

The gorilla had a black, flat face and a huge rounded point that rose up from his wrinkled brow, and his small, black eyes kept moving around, looking us up and down. His feet had fingers like his hands, even though they were curled up and tucked lightly under his heavy stool.

"Come in, sit down, ragazzi," Burton said, and waved an open hand at the stretch of rug in front of us. As we came, silently around to that rug, he reached behind himself and pulled out a couple of flat, hard pillows, with tassels at the corners, and tossed them over to us. "Please, my little friends, have a seat. We're sorry, Sammy and I, that you couldn't make it to the big top today. We did look for you, you know."

"Mama wouldn't let us come," Robbie said, as he put his pillow down on the rug and gently set that knapsack of his beside it.

"No circus for her good boys?" said Burton.

I wouldn't have said anything, just let the man in the chair think we had better things to do, important things that kept us away. But Robbie was nearly bursting with outrage and the need to tell it all.

"We got grounded," Robbie said, once he was plopped down on his pillow seat. "'Cause Mrs. Coogan called Mama. She told her we were sneaking around at the motel last night. So we couldn't go. We had to stay in our room and we even had to eat our peas tonight."

"Ah, even your peas, il piccolo?" Burton said, shaking his head back and forth sadly, at the great tragedy of the green peas.

Robbie nodded his head yes, pleased at the shared indignation. Then he explained, "That's why we decided to come with you."

Zambutti Sam made a little snort at that, as if he understood my brother's dream.

"Will and me, Mr. Burton, we've just had it with all that. So we're going with you," Robbie said, and patted his life's belongings in the knapsack beside him. But then he paused and the training of our mother's politeness showed through his earnest eyes. "That is, if you'll take us, sir." He paused impatiently. "You will, won't you, Mr. Burton?"

Jack Burton stroked the white stubble of beard on his chin, and he looked over at Zambutti Sam. The ape shifted a little on his stool, and then shook his head back fiercely, looked up at the center pole of the tent, and snorted one loud, swallowed growl. It seemed like a great affirmation, the beginning of a grand adventure for us all, even to me.

"Ill-a-Rose-O!" Robbie sang out proudly, answering the ape's growl.

This brought a little smile to Burton's lips, but he didn't laugh, and he didn't really answer.

"I've had about enough of that Mrs. Coogan myself," he said, leaning forward in his chair and nodding at Robbie. "With all of her nosing around and complaining at me. That's why you find me here, tonight, ragazzi. I moved out of there, I did, and back into this old tent, me and ol' Butto Sammy. We like it better here anyway, it's more like home, though we do miss the plumbing. So we left her little softheaded inn. Ah, the tent and the road, the only things you can trust in this world. That's where we belong, my boys. We don't need any more 'Missus Coogans' hanging around, do we, my little ragazzi cari?"

I found myself nodding yes, along with Robbie. But the pillow underneath me was hard and the schoolyard dirt was scattered all across the Indian rug at me feet, deadening the warm colors in the lamplight.

Then Robbie piped up, "But them girls told us Mrs. Coogan kicked you out." He looked up from his seat into Burton's face, and then over at the great ape. "And not 'cause of Butto Sammy, they didn't know nothing about him 'cause we never told. Did we, Will? We never told nothing." Robbie sat up straight, and looked back at me for verification. "And them girls, they didn't know nothing about Butto Sammy, no sir, Mr. Burton. They said you got thrown out 'cause of Will and me."

Robbie sank back down on the pillow, like the wind had dropped from his full sail ahead dreams. "You got grounded too, Mr. Burton. Just like Will and me." He stared down at Burton's still feet on the rests of the wheelchair, and it was enough to break anyone's heart to see him, all flat and dejected.

So I spoke up, for the first time really, about our running away. And I did it by saying only that one mysterious word, just a nonsense word to us, a magic incantation. "Ill-a-Rose-O!" I said.

Robbie looked up from the dirt floor at me, and then over at Burton in his chair, with the mountain gorilla beside him.

"Well, mi' piccolo povero," Burton said, "I'd say we've had about as much as we can take of all of that. Am I right? For this day, anyway?"

"Ill-a-rose-O!" Robbie whispered.

Burton grinned at that, maybe because we mispronounced it, maybe because we didn't know what we were saying. "Besides, O ragazzi," he said. "I tell you I'd had enough of the old lady Coogan and her nosing around. I left that half-bit hotel of hers on my own, boys. So now, who are you going to believe, a couple of dancing sirens wearing nothing but dusty sequins they can hardly shake anymore, or your old pal, Il Rosso?"

"Ill-a-Rose-O," we muttered in answer together, still trying to imitate the music of his words. But then, furtively, Robbie glanced over at me and it told me all I needed to know. Like me, the story that Shirley and Red told us, it fit a whole lot closer to what we knew of Mrs. Coogan, than what Mr. Burton was trying to say.

But our doubts didn't really matter, because we wanted to believe in Jack Burton. And somehow, because we knew that whether Mrs. Coogan had thrown him out, without ever knowing about Butto Sam, or whether Jack Burton had packed up and left of his own accord, it amounted to the same thing. And that same thing felt a whole lot more like what had happened to us, two boys who couldn't go to the circus, grounded in their room with nothing but chores and cleaning up to look forward to for all of time ahead, as far to the fore as we could see. And that tent, with its lantern light and its free ranging gorilla, whether Mr. Burton was lying or not, was our one path to whatever of the big world outside we could ever hope to see. And we planned to take it.

And so, together, we said a bit louder and throwing all our voices into the last note, "Ill-a-Rose-O!" The great ape rustled on his stool, and outside the tent one of the white horses shook its mane. And Jack Burton laughed loudly at us.

"Damned dancing girls," he muttered softly under his breath, thinking we wouldn't hear him, or understand. Then he looked down at both of us, and the sparkle of his eyes held us tight, and he said, "It's not ILL-A-ROSE-O, my boys. My name is Il Rosso," and the "r" tripped of his tongue with a whir and the "s" sound burred and buzzed, as he made this name sound like a song.

"Il Rosso," we imitated the roll and the buzz.

"Il Rosso," he repeated, and it took us a few more tries to get it right, or close to right, to make it sing off our lips like it did from his. But sing it out we did. Again and again.

"Il Rosso."

"What does it mean?" I said, and I settled down in the hard pillow, putting my hands out behind me to rest my back, and without realizing it, feeling more comfortable and at home there on the ground, in our little circle by the heater.

Burton sank back in his chair, as if it was some overstuffed Lazy Boy and not a wheelchair, and he seemed as comfortable as if he was sitting in the lap of some luxurious study within a dark and many roomed Victorian manse, beside a roaring, cozy fire, surrounded by leather bound books and not canvas walls. But he was only resting back on a worn wheelchair, made of steel and some sort of artificial leather vinyl, fraying at the edges into dirty white twine.

"It means the Red," Burton said wistfully. "And if I were to tell it to you whole, boys, it'd be Il Rosso Piccolo. The Little Red Lad." He chuckled a little and looked into Robbie's eyes. "Or Little Red, I guess. That'd catch it." He smiled at us and whispered, "Il Rosso Piccolo."

"Did your hair used to be red?" Robbie asked. He was thinking, I know, of this kid a grade between us in school, Red Gleason, with a shock of hair on his head the color of a peony, because I was thinking of Red Gleason too, and trying to fit him to the old man in the chair before us.

Burton brought a hand up and scruffed at the thick grey and white stubble on top of his head, and laughed. "No, no, it wasn't my hair." Then he was quiet, as if he was thinking about what and how much to tell us. He rolled his chair back toward a little wooden chest on the floor behind Butto Sammy. He switched a tiny tin latch back and flipped the carved lid back on its hinges. From where I sat, if I leaned way over to the side, I could see the soft fabric lining, bright red, inside the little chest, but I couldn't see what was inside it. He pulled some things out of that box, tossed some of them in his lap, and kept the other, smaller items, hidden in one hand, before he slapped the lid of the chest shut.

Then with his one free hand, he wound himself back around toward Robbie and me. Once he was settled again, back in the circle around that little propane heater where we all sat, with that same free hand he picked up by its bowl an ivory pipe with a thin, curved stem as long as my forearm. It was all of one piece, smooth and yellowed a little from handling and age.

"No, my boys," he said. "That name has to do with the shirt that's hanging out there to dry." He pointed with the long yellow-white stem of his pipe toward the canvas walls and the ceiling of the tent. But he meant what we had seen hanging outside, in the cool night air of the summer. Then Burton looked over to the ape. "Butto," he said softly, "mi porta la camicia."

The gorilla looked at him, and then at us with his beady black eyes, as if to be sure it was all right, then he rose from the stool and lumbered gently across the tent, walking on his hind feet and on the knuckles of his front paws. With barely a motion of one of his arms, he slipped smoothly through the tent flap and out into the dark outside.

I thought, 'If only Mrs. Coogan and all of her kind out there in our little bitty town could know that the great, beady eyed ape was free and loose, wandering unfettered and unattended, in the dark knight of their summer dreams, it would shake them all to the root of their safe and secure souls.'

"It was the General who gave me that name," Burton said proudly, "back after our first battle in his own countryside. Back after his great defeat." He was looking at the pipe in his lap, and he seemed far away. "I wasn't always in a chair like this, ragazzi. There was a time when I could run faster than you can dream, and I could climb up into the billowing sails of a ship, higher above the world than you can imagine. There was a time, O ragazzi."

Robbie sat beside his knapsack, entranced. "When was that, sir?" he said, gazing up at Burton in his chair.

"Long ago, I guess," he said wistfully. "Long ago, by your time anyway."

I didn't understand then what he meant, speaking of "our time." Many years would pass, and I would have to do a lot of growing up, and even then I would need to learn to give up on the things that I knew, before I could began to understand the mystery that he meant when he spoke of "our time." Because, for one thing, it was really the mystery that was "his time" that was past any rational understanding. But that night, in that moment, was the beginning of my understanding of the mystery of time, of how it bends and stretches and turns back on itself, and how the age of the hairs on your head has little to do, and everything to do, with the way your memory winds and curls around "your time," always seeming to run relentlessly forward, but never until you finally disappear is it able truly to escape the fronds of the past that lap over into the present and make the future repeat itself over and over again. That night, in that sentence, "Long ago, by your time, anyway," was the beginning of all that for me. And in some real way, more real than that relentless press forward, and more real than the difference between my brother's tallow haired fluff and the brisk, steely gray on Burton's head, that moment when Jack Burton whispered about "my time" to me, that moment still lives, right now, and requires all the searches and questions, all the moments that follow it, seemingly without end, but in the end illusory beside that one moment of that one night "long ago" where this all began. In our time.

"All of my people, my father, my mother, my brothers and sisters, they had all died," Burton said. "And I seemed to be only about your age, Will. When I seemed to be about your age, Will, I had already outlived them all. So I was all alone in Montevideo, working on the docks, doing whatever I could to get on.

"I seemed to be young and spry," Burton whispered, "and I was spry. Yet I had outlived them all. I was young enough still, to need to do the hard work to eat, to feed myself. So I was carrying bales and hauling barrels of pickled beef and crates of cheeses. My back was my only asset, you know. That's when Ciccio found me. You see, he thought I was just a lad."

The door flap of the tent parted and into the yellow lantern light Butto Sam slipped soundlessly. His black eyes glanced at me and at Robbie, not trusting us, then he blew a hard, clicking breath through his teeth, just once, and he lumbered back over to his low wooden stool. The knuckles of his right front paw held his shoulders and head up, as he moved across the floor of the tent, walking three legged. His left paw was pressed against his chest. And in it he clutched Burton's red shirt, gently in that big black hand.

"Ciccio found me working on the docks in Montevideo, and he felt sorry for me, I guess. Because he strolled up to me and said, 'Il piccolo,' that's what he called me right at the start. 'Come with me,' he said. And he gave me a job; I was his steward, he called it. But I was really his student, you know.

"We set sail on a Sardinian brig called the Bifronte, and I've never seen Montevideo or the mouth of the River Platte, or the shores of Uruguay again." Burton reached over to Butto Sammy and without a word or a command, the ape handed him the red shirt, still damp from the night air. "Zio Ciccio," he said, "to him I looked like I was about your age, my little friend, Will. How old are you, lad?"

"Twelve," I said, stretching it by a year.

Robbie looked at me with outraged surprise, and that made Mr. Burton laugh out loud.

"Yes," Burton said, "I guess I looked to my Zio Ciccio like I was about ten or eleven." Then the old man grinned at me, and it made me shrink down on the pillow.

"Age is not a matter of numbers, ragazzi. Trust me, young Willie; it's not got to do with counting the years. Not at all. And that was where Ciccio was wrong. But he had a big heart, and I won't fault him for that, boys. I won't."

Burton held his shirt in his lap, and it covered the long ivory pipe, hiding it from our sight. "He said to me, many, many times, 'Ho un cuore che troppo sente,'" Burton whispered those singsong words, "In the short time that I knew him, he would always say, 'Mi' piccolo, ho un cuore che troppo sente.' And I guess he was right, too."

Then Burton looked up from the red shirt and into Robbie's confused gaze. "It means," Burton smiled sweetly at my little brother, and at me too, "'I have a heart that feels too much.'"

*   *   *

Burton folded the crimson shirt in his lap so the double row of buttons down its front was squared up with the collar. Then he smoothed the folds in the fabric evenly, to crease it, and he set it, pressed tightly now in a square, on top of that little wooden chest. He patted the shirt with something like affection once he had placed it safely aside there.

"I didn't know when we set sail on the Bifronte where we were headed, boys. The ship slipped out of Montevideo into the Atlantic without a touch of fanfare. There was no one waving farewell to us from the docks. No teary eyes on the shore left behind. No. Not a one. And I had not the slightest idea, lads, what our great goal was. How lofty our destination was, lads. How it would change my whole life. For me, it was just work, and a journey that would steer me away and out of South America, where I'd been stuck for too, too long. I had no home to yearn for then, no country even to work my way home toward, for I belonged to the world then, lads, to the whole big world, O ragazzi. I was a man without a country, wandering from land to land. But I knew deep in my heart I didn't belong to Montevideo any longer.

"And I could see, right from the start, that my new friend Ciccio was just trying to help me. My dear old Zio Ciccio," Burton said, as he picked the ivory pipe up from his lap again. "Do you know what 'Zio' means, little one?" he said to Robbie.

My brother didn't speak, he just shook his head slowly no.

"You Zio is your uncle, lads. And before long, that's what I called him, you see. And that's how I came to feel about him. He was my Zio Ciccio."

263

Robbie kicked his feet out in front of him, and settled on his side, down with one arm over his knapsack, and he never once looked away from Mr. Burton.

"I didn't know anything about him, then, but Zio Ciccio, he says to me, once the Bifronte had lost sight of land, 'We are on a great voyage, il piccolo. This is the beginning of a great and a true adventure.'

"'Where are we going, my Zio?' I asked him.

"We were standing in the prow of the brig, with the Atlantic casting itself against our keel, and the breeze steady at our backs. 'We are going to a country that doesn't exist,' Zio Ciccio said to me. 'We are going to make a country that needs to exist, to free its many lands from all the priests and all the blue bloods.'

"Now, you must realize, my little friends, I didn't know what in hell he was talking about. He made no sense to me at all. No more than you know what I'm telling you about right now. I was as confused as you little lads are right here, and right now. But already I knew, I would entrust my whole life to my Zio. What cause was his, was mine, lads. For if it was his cause, it had to be true and be grand.

"But it was still a long, slow voyage across the wide Atlantic, more than two months we were at sea, always heading to the north and the east, and on the voyage my Ciccio taught me many, many things. Sometimes with tears welling in his eyes, he told me about the Austrian soldiers who ran roughshod over Lombardia and the Veneto, they drank the wine and sang loudly in German in the cafes right down in Piazza San Marco. And he talked of the Frenchmen too, in cahoots with the Popes, those Frenchmen who ruled in Piedmont and the Romagna and propped up the Papal States, with little Napoleons who weren't worthy of that great name. Sometimes he would bemoan the sweet orchards filled with blood oranges on the sides of Mount Etna, and the sweet lemons of Sorrento, all harvested for some Spanish King who reigned in Napoli. 'We are on a voyage to give birth to a country, il piccolo,' Ciccio would say to me, his chest swelling with his dreams. 'We will be the fathers, all of us together, the fathers we need to bring this struggling infant to life, free of the chains of the old Papal Swiss Guards, at last on her own two feet. Standing up, free and straight. Italia. Our Italia!'

"But I didn't understand any of that back then. I just knew this good man, with the fire of dreams in his eyes, he had picked me up from the dirt and the wage slavery of an endless Uruguayan dock, and shared with me his hopes."

Burton paused there to press a pinch of something into the bowl of his long pipe, and then he packed it down hard with his thumb, until it was deep in the bowl. The long ivory stem trembled a bit at the pressure he used in the bowl resting in his palm.

"The first night out, once the shores of Uruguay and Brazil had sunk behind us on the horizon, and the round Brazilian sun sank down chasing after them into the sea, the word went out around the ship. Tonight, at moonrise, we must all meet on deck. Amidships, the General will speak to us. 'Il Generale,' went out the word, from man to man, 'Stasera. Tonight.'"

Burton lifted the pipe to his lips, held it there unlit for a moment, calmly remembering something about that night long ago. Then he took the pipe out of his mouth and gently sniffed at the bowl, to be sure something was right. With his thumb he tamped down again on the paste he'd placed inside the bowl, making sure it was pressed into the tiny bowl even tighter still.

"Zio Ciccio's eyes glowed when he told me, lads, 'Tonight, il piccolo, you will begin to understand. You are going to hear the General speak. Il Generale! Stasera!' We went up onto the deck, gathering amidships, and my Zio sat at the foot of the stairs that lead down from the compass bridge, and I stood next to him. Before long a thin needle of moon began to rise out of the Atlantic off to our starboard, slowly ascending into the star-filled skies. The wind was low and gentle, and the gaffs drooping low in the mizzenmast flapped loosely as the breeze dropped. Ciccio rested his back against the stair and he scrubbed nervously at his clean-shaven chin. His hair was dark black, and he cut it off himself well above his collar, to keep himself cool. He had a black moustache drooping at the corners of his lips, and it was thicker than mine, ragazzi. Thicker than mine is now, as many, many years as these whiskers here have seen, his were thicker still. But Zio Ciccio always kept his chin smooth and clean. I never saw him needing to shave, not once in all that voyage, all those days. Always clean-shaven. Never, I guess, except . . ."

Burton trailed off there, lost in his memories for a moment. The great ape behind him was still, sitting quietly on his stool, listening to the music of Burton's voice, waiting for it to return in the circus night. Butto Sammy's little eyes darted quickly around the room, every now and then, as if he were a guard on the look out, watching for the slightest movement from anyone foolish enough to intrude.

I thought Robbie might be falling asleep, slung out on the Persian rug as he was, with his head resting on one hand propped up by that knapsack of his. But I leaned forward a little so I could see his face, and though he glanced at me with a bit of annoyance, his eyes were wide and locked on Burton.

"Ciccio rested back against the stair," Burton said, still fiddling with the pipe in his lap. "But he seemed weak then, suddenly. His eyes were darker and shadowed by something deep, and he closed them. My Zio coughed a little then, like he had the old remnants of a cold in his chest. He seemed tired suddenly, and I tell you truly I wasn't sure what I should do." Burton reached a hand over absently to touch that red shirt on the little chest, and the ape's eyes followed it all carefully.

"But then there was a stir among all the men on the deck, the fifty or sixty of us in all, everyone crowding out onto the decks between the two masts of the brig. And Ciccio, at the sound of the men's restlessness, he opened his deep eyes and immediately, without glancing around him at all, he rose gracefully up on his feet, as if he'd never coughed and never been weary in all his life.

"And then, ragazzi, the General came up from below. You know, my boys, I'd seen him before, on the docks as we prepared to depart, ordering the supplies stored safely away, laughing and joking with the sailors and the longshoremen all along the docks, like another seaman with his legs tired of walking on the solid ground. But that night, beneath that slivered Brazilian moon, my boys, he came up from below decks and he was different, lads, he was transformed.

"You see, the General, he was not a big man. He stood much shorter than me, by an inch or two, and I'm shy of six feet by some inches, I am. But he was thick and solid and he could stand his ground and you knew he was there, that his boots were filled with iron, you knew that. But this night, O ragazzi, with that needle of a moon low to the starboard and by the light of a million stars to the larboard, the General strode up onto the deck, with an old brown woolen poncho wrapped over his shoulders, draping down over his back like a short, dark cape, and he seemed a foot taller than everyone on board right then. His step up out of the belly of the ship, where he'd been sleeping and eating with all the men, just another human soul down below with the crew, it was that step alone that made a giant of him. Seemed he was no longer one of us, lads. I tell you. He was now Il Generale!"

Burton stopped then and a smile creased one side of his mouth, filled with a pride of having been there at that moment, of having known him on that night, I suppose. His pause didn't last long.

"At the edge of the stair he came upon my Zio, and he stopped. A broad grin broke across his face, and his teeth shone in that smile. He wore a little brown cap, like the peasants of Uruguay and Argentina wear, and though he had it tilted a little over his right eye, he still looked at that moment like some long lost gaucho finding at last the endless grass of the pampas.

"'Il Colonnello!' he said to Ciccio, and my Zio responded with a straight up stance and a salute.

"'My General,' Ciccio said.

"That made the grin on the General's face turn into a gentle laugh. He clapped my Zio on the shoulder and said, 'Ciccio, tonight we begin our journey home at last, my friend. Our journey, Ciccio, to make our home.'

"A big smile opened on my Zio's face, and his eyes glowed again like they did when he asked me to come along on this voyage. He laughed too, just a bit, but with an irrepressible excitement. 'At last, Peppino,' he said. 'At last.'

"Then he turned his brown eyes on me. 'And who is this young man, Il Colonnello?' The General had fair, but not blonde hair. There was a bit of red to it like the light mane on a chestnut mare. It was growing long and it hung down to touch his collar, and he had a full beard and moustache of the same fair color. His beard was so thick it seemed to grow straight out from his cheeks. His eyes looked me up and down, measuring me, and they were the lightest brown I've ever seen of a pair of eyes, and they were sweet and soft, but piercing too. They gazed right through my soul and read me inside and out like a newspaper headline, in bold print, and all of that in just a moment of time, and yet there was no level of judgment in them. They just looked into my very being, and accepted what was there to be seen. And after a moment of that, I swore to myself I would follow this man anywhere he asked me to go.

"'This is Gianni, my nipote,' Ciccio said, and I hate to admit it, my lads, but I blushed as red as a virgin babe on her wedding night. See, he called me his nephew, lads, his 'nipote.' I had no idea he felt that way about me. You know, I called him Zio, and I sure saw him in so short a time as the only family I had in the world. But I had no idea my caro Ciccio would call me his blood. And to the General, too. But there it was, ragazzi. He says to the General himself, while I'm all tongue tied and dumbfounded, 'Peppino, this is my nipote.'"

Robbie pulled his legs in and sat up straight, Indian style by his knapsack, and I realized that I was leaning forward toward him and Burton too. I think now we were both nodding our heads yes, we knew the feeling, in so short a time. To be family, or maybe something even stronger than that, when kindred souls meet on the wandering roads of the big wide world. Robbie and I, we knew what he meant. We knew that night. And we believed.

"'Peppino,' he said to the General as he reached out a hand and put it on my shoulder. "This young boy has the heart of a free man. He will help us to make our home, Peppino.'

"Then Il Generale stared deep into my eyes, and locked my soul into place with his fair brown stare, and it was a moment of time that seemed to stretch out over the years, ragazzi. I can feel it even now, as I try to tell you this story."

Jack Burton's own gaze fixed on something past the walls of the tent and out into the grassy schoolyard beyond, and he seemed lost in this distant past as he spoke.

"It's hard to describe a moment like that," he said, and his stare hardened as the corners of his eyes creased into loud crow's feet. "It's a moment, my little friends, when there are no calendars or clocks. It is part of the always now, you see. It will never go away from me, not as long as I breathe." He stopped there, and then he gazed at me, and I felt his eyes bore down inside of me with a magnetism I'd never felt before.

"That moment, when the General gazed into my soul," Burton whispered now as if he wasn't even speaking to us, "it is more real to me than this moment right now, and it glows in a hard true light, deep down in my soul, lads, deep down into the cellars of my soul."

Butto Sammy stirred on his stool, and I swear there was some sort of flash of light or something, but I heard Burton say, "That moment. It will never die."

Robbie and I had never heard anyone speak like that, especially an adult as incandescent as Burton was just then. Even at our grandmother's funeral, where there were tears and wailing that we barely understood, and there were lots of fervent prayers in the pews, and sacred words read from the pulpit. We had never heard anyone, child or man, speak with such intensity. Burton looked away, and then he held up that ivory pipe of his, and pressed his thumb down in the bowl again, but it was still unlit, and then he spoke.

"'I think you may be right,' the General said to my Zio. And then Il Generale asked me my name, and I answered him, and it was as if from that moment on I had enlisted in our cause. By just speaking my name out loud, I had signed on, though I didn't even know then what our direction would be."

Burton sat back in his wheelchair, and I realized at that moment that it wasn't just we boys who'd been stretching toward him as he spoke. He had been leaning out of his chair toward us. "Butto," he said. "Fuoco, Butto."

The ape rose from its stool and took out a heavy steel urn, the size of my palm, from inside that strange little box, being careful not to drop or wrinkle the red shirt that sat on top of it. He held the urn over to Mr. Burton, and the old man cradled it in his hand, his two first fingers on one side of the steel urn's stem, his last two fingers on the other side. With his thumb he flicked the lid of the urn back and revealed that the thing was some sort of elaborate lighter. With his thumb then he worked the lighter and the low yellow and blue flame sprang to life.

He put the long-stemmed pipe in his mouth with the bowl tilted sideways and he laid the flame up against the bowl, and drew in a long swallow of breath. Almost no smoke escaped from the pipe, it all went into his lungs, and then he breathed it out. It was strange, like no smoke I'd ever smelled before, as acrid and sweet as church incense, but not so heavy in the air. I found myself breathing deep, trying to absorb the scent of it all around me.

Before he rested back in the wheelchair, he turned the long stem of his pipe over to Butto Sammy. The ape took the ivory stem into his black lips. Burton tilted the flame into the bowl again and the mountain gorilla drew it in without any coaching.

Then Burton handed the pipe and the urn lighter back to Butto Sammy, and he rested down in the chair for a long moment, his eyes staring blankly down into his lamp.

Robbie looked over at me, with a million questions in his eyes, but I just shrugged. So Robbie asked, "What did the General do then?"

It roused the old man from his reverie and made him laugh. He whispered his name, quietly, to himself really. "Il Rosso," he whispered. Then he looked from Robbie to me and back again. "Ah, yes," he said, "my Ciccio, he was telling the General who I was. 'He is a good lad, Peppino,' my Zio said, while the General was staring me in the eyes." At that point,

Burton held first my eyes and then Robbie's in his stare, but without stopping his tale. " And the General, after he's looked me over, he said to Ciccio, 'He will do,' with a little note of approval. He reached out and touched my shoulder, right where Ciccio still had his hand on my shoulder, remember, lads. And then he said again, 'He will do.'"

While Burton spoke, the ape took a little spoon and gently scoured the inside of the bowl of the ivory pipe with it, cleaning out all of the burnt black crust. Butto Sammy was swift and skillful, working with the little spoon in his big paw, completely engrossed in his chore.

"The General walked away from us then, leaving with just a little, casual salute to Ciccio and a muttered, 'Il Colonello.' The he strode out to amidships, among the 50 or so men of the Legion, and stood on his sure sea legs as he slowly strolled around among them, touching a hand here or a shoulder there, greeting others with a grin or a laugh or a quiet, private word you couldn't catch. A name, a title, a rank. We were all waiting for him to speak."

The ape took that little spoon, with its accumulated crust, and put it in his mouth, licking it clean. Then he, almost silently, opened up the little box under the red shirt, and into it the pipe and the urn and the spoon all disappeared. Without noticing a thing, Burton just went on with his story.

"That old Sardinian brig rocked gently in the South Atlantic sea," he said, "and the General paused there. He put his hands behind his back, they were hidden under his poncho, and he strolled slowly across the decks. The men parted around him, though we were all crowded into the same space. And there was whispering and excited muttering all around. Now and then a few agitated laughs would rise from one corner or another, from that little group of friends, or from those two or three men here and there. But the General, he just strolled thoughtfully across the deck, his head lowered a bit as he seemed to ponder how to tell us of the hard dangers that lay ahead. The brown of his poncho flapped a little, as it brushed against the men on deck. When he strode over beneath the mainmast, he turned back, and he lifted his head so his fair beard pointed out high and proud. The evening breeze caught at the fair locks of his hair around his collar, lifted them in a ripple, and then again.

"'We are headed home, mi' amici,' he said. But you know, lads, all his words are gone from me. I can see him, standing in that evening breeze, his voice booming out to us, his hands outstretched to us, and then from time to time he would pound a fist into his palm to make his point clear. I don't think, either, that he spoke for long, lads, though to me now, remembering it all this very night, he seemed to speak forever. But the words, O ragazzi, they are gone. I can remember almost none of them, only these few that I report to you now tonight, and that's it. He began by saying to us all, 'We are headed home, my friends.' And then there was the one word that rang out often, through all of what he said. I remember that, because he seemed to repeat it like it was the refrain to his song. Freedom! He would say. 'Liberta'!' It would ring and ring in all our ears. Liberta'!

"And each time it set loose a great huzzah from all the men. I looked over at my Ciccio, and though the shadows still covered his eyes, he held a fist in the air above his head, and a broad smile filled his cheeks, and he shouted, 'Liberta'! Liberta'!' This was what he loved the most. 'Liberta'!'

Burton's own hand had closed into a fist and he held it up in the air as high as his head, as if he was grasping at something in the air, and he grinned at us. "Liberta'!" he said. "Liberta'!"

And Robbie and I joined in, each time, in an echo. "Liberta'!" we yelled, and while I was grinning, Robbie looked back at me with a fire in his eyes that had nothing to do with just having fun, and everything to do with his freedom. You see, for me it was just a rebel yell, a cowboy shout, and tomorrow I could change sides and be the Indian. But for Robbie, the oppression of being grounded in his room, the grand injustice of being punished just for trying to see a gorilla, it filled him with a real desire to break free. "Liberta'!" he yelled, from deep in his little heart, and with his knapsack cradled under his arm, he was I know ready to follow Jack Burton anywhere.

After a moment, Jack Burton went on quietly, "What a night that was, ragazzi, on the quiet, cool sea, under the sliver of a southern moon, Il Generale pulling us all together, speaking from deep in his soul, until we all became one lone heart, beating strong, beating together. And while he spoke, , a tall black man dressed in a scarlet blouse moved across the deck toward Ciccio and me. He smiled at us and stood very close to my Zio. 'Buona sera, il Colonello,' he said, and then he nodded at me, too, because I was so clearly close at hand.

"'Liberta', Aguiar!' Ciccio answered him softly, grinning."

Burton looked over at me, and suddenly felt the need to explain. "This was the great Aguiar, my little friends. Aguiar, the General's batman, by his side in all the struggles from Gualeguay and Rio Grande do Sul to San Antonio, and in the expedition to Salto, too. Aguiar was there, and he was with us across the lakes and on into the Swiss frontier. Still he rode next to the General, on his midnight black steed, sporting the scarlet of Montevideo, until finally he fell that summer's day, defending the fallen Roman Republic. Aguiar, miei ragazzi. Next to my Zio, I think, he was the closest comrade the General had. In those days."

Burton paused a moment, seeing both these men in his mind's eye I suppose, and then realizing too that Robbie and I were now confused. "But I'm getting ahead of myself, boys," he said. "These are things still to come in the swirling clouds of time."

* * *

Jack Burton sat quietly then for a moment, resting his eyes and he seemed to relax and slowly gather his senses together. When the euphoria of the smoke mixed with memories cleared from his mind, he seemed ready to go on. "It was after the General was done and we all of us knew that we would follow him and defend him and our freedom, right to the Gates of Hell herself, it was then he gave his orders, softly, though his voice grew a little louder and firmer as he went on. 'During this voyage,' he said, 'those of you who know how to read and write will be teaching those of you who are now ready to learn. And that, my compatriots,' the General paused to clip us to attention, 'that would be any of you who can't read.'"

Robbie looked back over at me, confused again, and I was too. I mean, I thought, what's the big holy deal about reading and writing? But then I noticed Robbie's eyes were big with some kind of fear, and not just this confusion of mine.

Burton saw the looks on our confused little faces, and he went on, " I remember the General folded his arms over his chest, and announced, 'So now, who here is ready to learn? Raise your hands.' It was not a question, lads. No, little friends, it was an order.

"And, O ragazzi miei, I was one of them. In all my years, scrounging and scruffing along, I'd never once seen the inside of a schoolroom. Not once. I'd never cracked open a book or read a paper. And I was ashamed, because by God I could scale the rigging like a spider, and I could even take the wheel and steer the whole damn ship, and I could follow a compass and even name the stars in all the Southern skies, and

I knew the planets by name when they rose in the heavens. But I couldn't even read my own name, boys. I signed 'John Burton' only when I had to, and when I did, I had to use an 'X,' lads. Just an X.

"And so, with more fear than if the brig was plunging into heavy seas and taking on water, I raised my hand in front of the General. Aguiar had an arm around my Ciccio's shoulder now, and Ciccio said quietly, 'I will teach you.' And I looked at my Zio and his tall friend, both of them so close to the Generale, standing side by side, then all my fears faded away like so much fog under
the morning sun. That's all he said, ragazzi. No big words or plans, he just said, 'I will teach you.' And over the next few months, he did."

"You mean," Robbie blurted out, "you had to go to school?"

Mr. Burton looked up at my little brother, and I saw the slight haze of the sweet smoke from his pipe behind the color in his eyes. He smiled very gently and then he nodded his head yes.

"Ahhh, Geez," Robbie moaned, but Burton raised an open hand, just the way the General had done in the story he told us, and Robbie sunk down on his knapsack, and didn't make another sound.

"That night, my little friends, the General did one last thing. He strode from beneath that mainmast to amidships, and the men all stood and moved closer around him, as if by instinct. My Zio stood tall as he could and stepped into the circle gathering around the General. I followed behind him, and Aquiar once again slid easily through the crowd until he stood, solid on both feet, right beside my dear Ciccio.

"The General looked all around at us, turning in a circle so he could look each of us in the eye, one by one, slowly. And as he turned, arms now crossed on his chest, he asked us, once by one it almost seemed, 'What is the name of this ship?'

And we answered 'Bifronte,' and some said, 'The brig Bifronte,' or sang out, 'Bifronte, flying the colors of Sardinia.'

"'This is no longer a suitable name for a ship bearing so much of the future in her hold. No, my friends, she is no longer the Bifronte. Not on this voyage, she is not.'

"Then the General reached over to his friend and batman Aguiar, standing close beside my Ciccio. And Aguiar, from inside his red blouse, pulled out a bottle of brandy, taken from the stores below. It had all been carefully planned. Aguiar handed the bottle over and the General held it in both his hands, and then he seemed to speak it, 'Bifronte is not a name for the bark of grand venture. No, my compatriots.'

"Then the General strode out of our circle, past the backstay and the shroud, and around the foremast until he had climbed out into the bow of the ship. He stepped up and put a foot on the bowsprit and raised that bottle up to that Brazilian moon and the southern stars. Everyone crowded into the bow after him.

"'Good brig Bifronte,' the Generale announced to the sea and the stars, 'We, the Italian Legion of Montevideo, the Victors of the Pampas sailing home to our freedom, we christen thee . . . ' and he paused there and took that brandy and crashed the bottle into the bowsprit, 'La Speranza.' And a great yell rose up from all of us. 'La Speranza,' we yelled in one voice. 'La Speranza.'

"From out of nowhere, but certainly from somewhere Aguiar had carefully prepared, two open bottles of brandy appeared. And they went from hand to hand, and that name became a toast, over and over, 'Speranza,' we cried. 'Speranza,' we whispered. The hard wine tasted bitter and strong, always chasing down that name, 'Speranza.'"

Burton leaned forward in his wheelchair, and he took little Robbie's shoulder in his hand, and his other hand reached out across the tent toward me. In his eyes was the fire that lay behind whatever it was he'd been smoking, but it echoed the taste of that brandy from years before. "Speranza," he whispered to us.

Butto Sammy stirred on his stool at the sound of that word, at the urgency in the old man's voice. "Speranza," Burton whispered again.

Robbie and I sat frozen and still, while he sat back in his chair then and tilted his head back and laughed long and hard, with a deep happiness that made you hungry to share in it with him. "' Speranza,' my General cried," Burton nodded.

"Speranza," Robbie whispered, rising a little from the knapsack. And so I joined in too.

"Speranza," we said together, in hushed, little boy tones.

And then everything was silent for a while. Burton seemed content, resting there in his thoughts and the great ape sat quietly on his stool, gazing fondly at the old man. Something of the same soft glow that shone in Burton's look sang behind his grey black eyes. The sweet vanished smoke of contentment.

For a while only the choruses of summer crickets made any sound, and then as if to start us out of some reverie, an owl who-hooted once in the night.

"What does it mean, sir?" Robbie spouted up.

Burton smiled fondly at my little brother. He stayed, resting back in his wheelchair, not sitting up or moving a limb. He just said, "Hope, il piccolo. It means Hope."

"La Speranza," said Robbie again.

Burton took a deep breath and he scrubbed his hand across his chin. It was hard to tell if it was memories or smoke that drifted through his mind just then. But suddenly he went on with his story. "It was the next morning I dug out this

Bible of mine. Some missionary in the backwaters of Argentina had forced it on my father, when my old man was dying of hard, strange fevers in Costa Brava, up the river from Montevideo. This was the book, the only one I had, that I took to Ciccio and said to him, 'Teach me to read, caro Zio.'

"Ciccio took the volume out of my hands and turned it over once or twice, looking at its cheap cardboard binding. 'Where did you get this?' he asked.

"I told him the book's story, and he seemed to look at it differently then. Just when I thought he might throw it overboard, he handed it back to me, and then he reached inside his shirt and pulled out some loose, blank sheets of paper.

"'I'll teach you to read, il piccolo, but not with that,' he said. 'Enough evil has been done in this world with those words. You don't need to start reading with that.'

"Then he wrote out the letters of the alphabet, one at a time. And after them five words. And so we began. We practiced every letter and its sound. And then we did it again.

"Then he pointed at the first word on the paper, with his finger leading me along, pointing back to the rows of alphabet from time to time, prompting me when I need it, he helped me to read my first word. 'Jack,' I read aloud, and then 'Jack Burton.' See, Ciccio showed me how the sounds and the letters worked until I could read my own name. And that was where we started. 'Later on, when you can read on your own, il piccolo, then you can read that Bible of your father's if you want. But you must start first with your own name. That will set you free.' And Ciccio nodded sternly at that thought."

Burton ran a tongue around his teeth and sighed deeply, and sat for a moment. "Cibo, Butto?" he softly asked the ape. Butto Sammy looked up from his own reverie, and stared calmly at the man in the wheelchair. "Cibo?" Burton repeated, even more quietly.

And so, with a soft, clacking snort, Butto Sammy slid forward off his stool and put part of his weight onto his knuckles, and out of the tent he lumbered, into the cricket filled night.

"What were the other three words?" I asked.

"Yeah!" Robbie piped up.

Burton grinned, and he hid his smile under the finger that he brushed at his moustache with. "So you were listening, lads. You were. Even if I was telling you about 'my schooling' on board that ship."

Outside we heard one of the doors to the Buick open with a creak. Butto Sammy was climbing into the car.

"What were the other three words?" I asked again.

"Ah, the next two were tough, my boys. I couldn't get them that first day, and it took me a couple of days to read them easily. And my Zio, he had to break them up into parts, so I could read the words piece by piece. But they were Ciccio's name. That's what they were. 'Francesco Anzani.'"

He let the name roll off his tongue like music, and he seemed to think we would know it, recognize the name of this great "Colonnello." But of course we didn't. "'Francesco Anzani,'" Burton repeated, for sheer love of the sound, and maybe for love of the name too. Then he looked at us, through his hazy eyes, and said, "It's a name the whole world should know by heart. My dear Ciccio. But he's been forgotten, 'lo these many years. We only remember Il Generale, only his name resounds through all the seasons, not 'Aguiar' who stood with him, and not my Zio, 'Francesco Anzani.' They are forgotten."

Suddenly Burton shot up in his chair, leaning out to where he could grab Robbie by the shoulder. There was a crazy fire in his eyes that belied the many things he had done and might do in the world. "But not by me, santo cielo! Not by me. I'll carry those names down through time, forever and ever."

It seemed that he should have added, "until the day I die" to the end of that "forever and ever," but he didn't. Not then and not ever. And this is why I still search for traces of him, everywhere I go.

"What was the last word?" said Robbie, as if the fire inside Jack Burton had spread into him through the grasp of the old man's hand.

Burton held his shoulder in his grasp, and he looked at him, and then at me. "Il piccolo, bring me that desk, mi' figlio. Over there." He pointed to a wooden chest in the far corner of the tent, sitting on a set of wheels.

Robbie hopped up and nearly skipped over to the trunk, he was so full of the energy of discovery. "Inside there," he said. The chest was about half the size of a steamer trunk, made of wood that was grayed with age and worn by handling at the edges of the lid. The hinges were brass and the corners had brass tips. But the wood was old and its finish had worn mostly off. Big straps of black fraying leather stapled with brass tacks to the wood held it latched.

"Open it up and, bring me my desk, my boy," Burton said.

I rose up onto my knees, because I wanted to see what was down inside the chest, even if I hadn't been the one chosen for the chore.

"Yes, sir, Mister," said Robbie, restraining a giggle of delight.

Robbie flipped back the soft latches and opened up the case. Inside it were stacks of paper, filled with handwriting and carefully bundled together with string. Off to one side rested a dark wooden lap desk.

"There, bring me that, my boy," Burton said.

Robbie lifted the lap desk out of the chest and brought it over to Burton, who took it and set it gently on his knees. It was obvious from the way that the desk rested comfortably in his lap that he had held it there for many hours on many a night.

Burton opened the lid of the little desk and extracted from it a plain white piece of paper, a pair of glasses and a large wine-colored pen. Then he carefully closed the lid and, setting the paper securely on the desk, and the wire-rimmed glasses on his nose, he wrote out some words with the deep indigo ink of his fountain pen.

While Burton wrote, Robbie closed the lid of the little trunk and slipped back beside his knapsack, which I think he now saw as his little trunk of valuables, someday to be filled with treasures just like these things in the old wooden chests of Jack Burton.

Outside there was a squeak from the car door, and then we heard it slam closed latched softly. In a moment, that tent flap parted and in waddled Butto Sammy, one of his arms cradling a bottle and a wrinkled brown paper sack, the other arm working as his third leg. "Ah, grazie, Butto, grazie," Burton said quietly, without looking up from his desk. Butto set the bottle and the sack on the rug beside Burton, and then went straight back to his stool, though his attention was locked onto the things he'd carried in.

A moment passed, and Burton was done. He handed us the sheet of paper. Robbie and I held it between us, each with a hand on the paper, like it was some sort of relic. "This is how I learned to read, my boys. From a sheet of paper that looked just like that one."

Burton's handwriting was large and florid with lots of tales and feathers, and over the years as I have pursued him through many times and places, I have come to know that handwriting well, from the traces and fragments he has left behind him, and at least once in an anonymous manuscript. I knew it was his by that very hand, not to mention the abandoned diary found in Siracusa that I still believe was his, though no one else (including Robbie) will agree, and the two or three times he had left me a letter or a note, before he slipped away again to unknown parts. But that night I was looking at his hand for the first time, and I couldn't help but see how ornate and decorated it was, while still always remaining absolutely clear.

Robbie was staring at the sheet of paper, trying not just to read it but to see into its deeper truth. While we read, Burton picked up the bottle and uncorked it. It had been opened before, and the cork had been shoved back into it, so it slipped out into Burton's hand with barely a pop.

The words and letters on the page were odd, not what I expected to see. But it took a few moments to understand what was missing. Robbie noticed the name first, and then, at the moment he spoke, I saw what was missing in the alphabet.

"Hey, Mr. Burton," Robbie said, his nose scrunched up around his glassed, "that's not your name, sir."

Burton had extracted a flat chunk of ham and a ball of hard white cheese from his paper sack. Then Butto Sammy, without any command, drew a little knife out of somewhere, and handed it to Burton.

I counted them over, and saw there was only 21 letters to his alphabet, written carefully across the top of the page in three downward columns.

"Where's your name on here?" Robbie demanded.

Burton took the little palm knife from the ape and he draped a white cloth over the lap desk. He straightened it carefully so it covered all the wood, and then he set the ball of white cheese on it alongside the flat ham.

There were several letters missing from his alphabet, and I quietly began to figure out what was left out. Because the large capital letters were arranged in columns, it took a while to see them, and I noticed the gap at the end first. There was no 'w,' 'x,' or 'y' on this sheet.

"What's this 'Gig Anna'?" Robbie said.

Burton chuckled a little, and silently proceeded to pare slices from the ham. Once he had a little stack of the salted meat, he took up the ball of cheese and curling it around in his palm, he deftly shaved long yellow-white spirals from it. There was a look on his face, as he gazed through the glasses on the end of his nose, of great and simple contentment.

And I saw next, by starting at the beginning, that there was no 'j' or 'k' in his alphabet, either. All the rest of the letters appeared to be on the paper, though. I didn't say anything about the strange, short alphabet, as yet.

"That's my name, il piccolo," Burton said, not looking up, paring out his spirals of cheese, each one a little longer and a little more curled than the last.

"'Gig,'" said Robbie, "''Anny,'" more than a little outraged.

Suddenly it clicked. For some reason there was no 'j' or 'k' in his alphabet, and that made it pretty tough to write out 'Jack' on a piece of paper. Or even the more formal 'John' for that matter.

"That is his name," I said, proud of myself. "See," I pointed at the first set of letters. "This says 'Johnny Burtoni,' doesn't it?"

Mr. Burton looked up from his preparations, over his spectacles, and smiled at me, "Very good, mi' ragazzo. Bravo."

"Gianni Burtoni," I repeated, reading the letters that he'd written in his flashy hand.

"But why is it spelled like that?" Robbie protested.

"Because, il piccolo, it's not written in English," Burton said. "English may be my first language, and when I met my Zio we were speaking Spanish, you know, but, il piccolo, he taught me to read in his language, in Italiano. Because this is where we were headed on the Speranza."

"'Gianni Burtoni,'" Robbie read from the page.

Burton chuckled, and muttered, "Very good, little one."

"And this is Francesco Anzani," I read out, torturing the pronunciation.

"Si," Burton said, "my Zio," and then he let the name roll from his lips with all its music, softening the first 'c' into an Italian 'ch.' "Francesco Anzani." he said. He set the knife down on his little lap table, and rested back in his chair from a moment, gazing again at something in the haze of smoke and memory.

"Francesco Anzani," I repeated.

Then Robbie read out the last word on the page, or at least his version of it. "Liberty!" he exclaimed.

Burton let a little smile drift across his lips, and then he said through the haze behind his eyes, "Liberta'."

"Liberta'," I repeated in my best faux Italian, pointing for my little brother at the last letter on the word.

Then Robbie and I read it out together. "Liberta'."

At that point, Jack Burton surprised me again, as he has always and continually seemed to do everywhere and everytime I have found him, or even any trace of him. He carefully selected a slice of the ham and a curl of the cheese and he handed them over to Butto Sammy. He who brought the food always ate first, in the circle of Jack Burton. "Cibo, Sammy," he said, and the food disappeared into the ape's big paws and then it was gone.

Burton took a long swallow from the wine bottle, relishing its taste, and then he offered us the food by holding out his lap desk, turned now into a serving tray. Butto Sammy watched the tray as it was held out toward us, but never moved for it, and every few moments Burton world handed him another sliver of ham and another curl of the hard cheese.

"So a paper just like that one was how I started to read," Burton continued, as we munched on the food. "Everyday, my Zio would write out more and before long he had me reading sentences and writing them out on my own. Soon, what he wrote out were questions, and I would have to answer them on the paper, with his help."

The meat and cheese were salty and bitter, not really the kind of food that Robbie or I would eat, if we were home and having lunch at the table. It was the kind of stuff that Robbie would complain and whine about, and leave little crumbled up and fingered chunks of on his plate. But we both took it up eagerly now, and we chewed hardily on the provisions. For me, it was curiosity about what this man and his ape lived on, and a deep sense of adventure. Robbie was the really picky eater, at home he was always moving his food around and around the plate, seeming to hope it would either change or go away. But there was none of that here. Robbie had plans to ride off over the horizon with this traveling troupe, and if this is what Jack Burton ate as he rolled merrily along, then even Robbie was going to do his best, and clean his plate without a word.

"After a while, I graduated up to some pages of old newspapers that were left on board the brig," Burton said. "They were mostly old news from Sardinia, about the King and all his doings, and Ciccio would always comment on them, editorializing on what was left out between all the words and the headlines. It usually had to do, my Zio's comments, with peasants doing all the work while the aristocrat lived off the wealth of the countryside and the fruits of the common man's labor.

"'The time has come to turn this over,' Ciccio would say, and his gaze would wander over my head and past the sails into the blue Atlantic heavens, my boys. His gaze would stare at the horizon. 'The time has come,' he'd say." Burton stopped there, and ate a little of his food quietly, but a great sadness seemed to radiate from him then and linger low on the tent.

"It was around that time," he said, after a long while and after another swallow or two of wine, "I began to notice how, late in the day, when Ciccio would be teaching me to read, before the dark of night came on, that his hand would tremble. He would be handing me a piece of old newspaper, and suddenly the whole paper would shake, just a little, and only for a moment, but it was a definite shake.

"'Growing chilly in the night air, non e' vero?' he would say, and laugh, and though it was still warm on the deck, he'd pull a piece of blanket around him, before we'd continue. But then, latter on, he would be pointing with his finger to a word I couldn't make out, and he'd slow me down and make me pronounce every letter until I could get it right. But in the middle of this, his finger would tremble, and quickly he'd withdraw his hand.

"'Ciccio, are you all right?' I would say.

"'It's just the cool air out here,' he'd answer me. But sometimes, as the voyage lingered on, it would happen when we were below decks. And then, I wouldn't say anything, and Ciccio would just ask me a question about another word, or give a little speech about the peasants and the lords, or just plain hurry on to something else."

"Was he sick?" Robbie asked.

Burton looked fondly over at Robbie, and then over at me, and then he said, "In the daylight, Ciccio and Aguiar and I, we would take our shift, and all three of us could hoist sails and run the rigging and move our stores in the hold around, we'd work hard and sweat would pour from us like a spring.

And I seemed to get stronger and more fit as the voyage went on, just the way the General wanted. Aguiar was already a mountain of muscle and strength, and the three of us together, I felt like we could do anything that was asked of us. And I still believe we could.

"See, Francesco, my Zio, was a little man, but not slight. He had arms that were thick with muscle, and they seemed, like his square chest, to be trying to rip out of any shirt he wore. Even out of the crimson blouse of the Italian Legion.

"But I just noticed it, in the evenings, when he would teach me to read, that sometimes he would tremble. He was no youngster, you know, he was a full-grown man, but I began to see the gray strands of hair on his temples and running through the droopy moustache he wore. Every day I thought I could see more and more of them."

Then Burton spoke in a long sigh, gazing somewhere past us into the thin air, "I'd already outlived everyone who loved me, all of them, every one. So I guess that's why I couldn't see it, boys. Because I didn't want to see it coming at me again, and so I tell you I didn't." He paused again and took a long draught from the bottle, and then he gave a healthy handful of slivered meat to Zambutti Sam, while he whispered something softly in Italian to the ape, and one of his hands stroked the ape's head like he was a puppy. "I tell you, I didn't see it," he muttered to no one, and to everyone at once.

Without looking back at us, he went on, "Then came the night of the storm. It had been a peaceful voyage thus far, but that night I was below decks with Ciccio. The seas were a little rough, and so the night's reading lesson was hard. Ciccio turned in, and I noticed that his eyes seemed even darker in the shadows than usual. I sat up in an upper bunk and tried to write in a little journal my Ciccio had given me, but the ship began to rock too much to write and then even to read, so before long I fell asleep too.

"Aguiar was on the first watch that night, and I believe I can say we stayed alive because it was him. Somewhere in the dark of that night, the head of that storm hit us and the seas rose up like open jaws and swept over the decks, and the little brig started to pitch to and fro, and the waves threw us around like a paper boat. But it was the yell of Aguiar that roused me. I heard his big, bass voice call out, 'Fire on board! Fire!'"

Burton lifted his hand up to his tensed shoulders, and his eyes were wide. "I sat up straight in the bunk, 'Fire,' I thought." He leaned back in his chair and his eyes were wild now. "My God, boys. 'Fire on board!' I tell you, ragazzi, there is nothing in the world as frightening as that alarm in the night. To be far out at sea, with nothing but the broad ocean all around you as far as anyone can see, and to be tossing about and fighting to stay afloat in the high waters, in a wooden boat, ragazzi, a ship made of wood from stem to stern, and then to hear those words." Burton jumped forward until I thought he might fall onto the ground, but he clung to his chair and he whispered the words at us, with those eyes of his burning into our frail hearts. "'Fire!'" he whispered. "'Fire on board!'

"I tell you, lads, it rattles the foundations of your mortal soul, and you feel the infinite calling to you with all the fears of all the ages wrapped into one tiny wooden trap all around you, the hell of time flaring and flinging toward her end, with no more repetitions or routines in sight, just a burning wooden bark, sinking down into a saltwater infinity. Time has come at you at last, lads, and you've got to choose, to burn quickly in a fast furious burst, or to drown slowly in your own frigid exhaustion. Fire or water. How will you go out, my boys, how will you choose to go out, when you hear that call rousing you from your sweet, gentle sleep in the night? 'Fire!' It will catch your breath away, lads. 'Fire on board!'"

Then Burton flopped back into his chair and he roared a deep, booming laughter. If he'd jumped up and said "Boo!" right then, I know I'd have fled that tent, with Robbie running right behind me. But he stopped laughing and listened for a moment to the night crickets. Then he said, "I can see it now, as if it was tonight. I looked down in the bunk below me, and even with the running and shouting on the decks above us, my Ciccio was still sound asleep. For a moment, I thought he was dead, lads. But then I saw that his mouth hung open and he was dragging in deep breaths without snoring. Great swallows of air were filling his lungs, and he was somewhere else, dreaming sweetly.

"So I jumped down onto the shifting floor and I shook him awake. 'Fire, Ciccio,' I said with my hands on his shoulders. 'Fire on the ship.' His dark eyes opened and without a pause or a thought he rolled out of his bunk and onto his bare feet, with the blanket still wrapped around his shoulders. His deep calm came from years and years of battle, all around the world. At the sound of alarm, he just awoke and arose and was ready to fight, even when he wasn't sure where he was or who his enemy might be.

"'Where is it?' he asked, standing beside me but coming only up to my shoulders. I had never noticed before how short he was. But mortal danger does that to you, ragazzi, you see things you've never noticed before, right before your eyes. 'I don't know,' I said. But he had already heard the calls of Aguiar over the scrambling feet pounding above us on the decks. He said nothing else, just climbed up the stairs and out onto the main deck, with that blanket still wrapped around his shoulders. As we came up from below, onto the tossing seas amidships, the winds caught his blanket and waved it in the air like a cape. He hung onto it with one hand and with the other he held himself steady by grasping a railing. His knees were bent a little, and his bare feet clung flat to the wooden deck, and he seemed to ride with the pitching brig like she was a galloping horse. I couldn't help but admire his sturdy sea legs, for I was clinging with both my hands to the rim of the stairs, almost down on my all fours, trying to stay aboard her in the storm.

"What we saw out on those decks of the Speranza, my boys, rolling out before us, awash with the retreating waves and buffeted by the winds, it was surely a vision of Hell itself, lads. Surely frigid, wind swept Hell itself.

"The decks were crowded with men, soaked to the bones, grasping at one another in panic, rushing to and fro, screaming like the gates of Old Dante's Hell had opened to swallow us all. Here there were three of them, nearly naked, clinging to some loose shred of the rigging. There a man, flat on his stomach, was washed across the deck until only a railing kept him aboard. Such screaming and open terror I'd never witnessed before. Not in all my years at sea.

"A group of six men clung to a stanchion by the hold, and out of the belly of the ship poured a huge cloud of black smoke, obscuring parts of the brig as she pitched back and forth. A white, frothy wave would crash onto the deck, grasping at the men. The cold water would pull that poor soldier on his stomach back from the railing and then sweep him across the deck again, his arms waving in the air, searching for anything he could hold onto, but reaching nothing. And then the sea would slosh down into the hold, only to be met by a rush of steam, mixed inextricably with the bellows of smoke crowding up out of the bowels of the ship and into the low, black skies."

Burton stopped there, lowered his eyes and looked again at something in his memory. After a moment, he said, "These were the men of the Italian Legion, boys. They'd survived the siege of Montevideo, the battle of the Rio Grande de Sul and Costa Brava, they'd braved the great retreat of the

Salto. They'd stared at death, and worse, at dismemberment and destruction, on battlefields across South America. Hardened veterans they were, lads. The men of the Italian Legion. But I can't describe to you what it means to be far, far out at sea, with your world ablaze on a wooden ship. The men of the Italian Legion, hardy and brave and true, ready to charge into the bayonets of the Oppressor, they were racked with pure terror, I tell you. There was no order, it was pandemonium, and yet, there was nowhere to flee, not for any of us. Staring out there from the top of the stairs, for me there was only a simple decision to be made: to drown or to burn. Perhaps, in even greater agony, to do both, if I didn't have the courage to decide.

"There came a moment then, just a pause, when the water retreated and the deck of the Speranza seemed nearly level. Out of that absurd moment of peace and calm, the sounds of all those men, and all their terror, bellowed up out of the ship like the smoke and steam rising out of her hold, cries from lost souls into the black and indifferent storm.

"That terrible noise was enough to freeze a man into place, my friends, but I saw my Zio suddenly rushing straight across the decks from the hold, and I rose up on my feet and followed him as closely as I could. Over the general rancor and disarray, I heard Aguiar's deep voice, and it dawned on me that Ciccio was headed toward his call, with me in tow, though he knew it not.

"As the brig suddenly pitched to the starboard, Ciccio disappeared down into the hold. I thought for a moment he'd fallen, or even been washed overboard. Yet with an instinct I barely understand, lads, an instinct we all label devotion, I followed him down into the smoke and steam in the belly of the ship. I chose the fire, because my Ciccio did.

"Below, in the hold, everything was surprisingly clear. Once I had pierced blindly through the clouds of smoke, I opened my eyes and found myself in the lowest part of the hold, with a strong course of wind blowing through my hair. I guess the fire had created some funnel of air to channel the smoke up through the lid of the hold, like a sort of smokestack. Down there, Aguiar and the General and three other men were fighting the flames with buckets and wet blankets.

" The fire was smaller than it seemed from above, from the volume of smoke it hurled upward, onto the deck of the brig. Still it burned hot and intensely, and it licked at the stores of our food, the dried meat and fruits and the hard tack stacked in bundles. Alongside the food, it blazed hottest at one point, and in the next instant it was clear to me what the problem was.

"In a corner of the hold there were cases of brandy stacked a couple of crates high. Not many, only six or so it seemed. But the two of them closest to the barrels of foodstuffs were at the center of the fire. Somehow, someone had set this brandy afire.

"My Zio ran in his bare feet over to the General, and some words I couldn't hear above the uproar were exchanged. Then Ciccio took a bucket from Aguiar's hands and doused himself with seawater.

"Oh, my lads, you never saw such a thing as what happened next. Ciccio threw that wet blanket over his head until it draped over his arms too, like he was playing at some gray ghost, he strode barefoot right up to the fire, blind beneath the wet blanket. He picked up the two offending crates of brandy and instantly ran straight up the plank and out of the hold of that brig. Aguiar ran just a step ahead of him, his booming voice calling out, 'Qui! Qui! Qui!' And by that he led Ciccio safely across the rocking deck of the ship.

"There was a moment when the eyes of the General met mine. But then without thinking I simply followed Ciccio's path. I picked up the next two crates of alcohol, and I followed behind Aguiar and my Zio, up the planking and out of the hold. I could see where I was running though, because the crates of brandy I carried were not on fire.

"Ciccio blindly collided into the rails and into the grasp of Aguiar, who held him aboard, and my Zio hurled the two blazing crates of liquor overboard and into the riled sea. It was no sooner overboard, than Aguiar had thrown him down onto the deck, and together they rolled to and fro, to put out the fire and free him from the smoldering blanket. In that same moment I hurled the two other crates of brandy in my arms overboard as well."

Jack Burton paused then and he set the lap desk down on the rug floor of the tent. Then he shook his head at something in his memory, and he laughed at it. "I'll not ever live that down," he whispered softly, speaking only to himself. Then he looked up at us and said, "No, that's not true. I guess, by God, I have. Haven't I? I have lived it down, boys. I have. Like everything else, I've outlived it."

We had not the slightest idea at that moment what he was rambling on about. But that didn't give Robbie a moment's pause. "Did you put the fire out?" Robbie said, out of his own held breath.

"Il Generale did, mi' ragazzo. He and those other three men with him. But not before we lost a lot of our food, and much of it spoiled in the equatorial heat over the next few weeks. It made for a longer voyage for us, ragazzi. We had, after that night, to ration out the stores carefully. And we got pretty hungry, we did, by the time we made the coast of Spain."

"But at least you didn't burn up and sink, sir," Robbie said.

Burton first grinned at him, and then for some reason at me, because I suppose my eyes were as big as my brother's about then. Jack Burton had a good laugh then, though the fondness in his eyes didn't disappear.

"It's true. But it was hard on my Zio Ciccio, boys. I tried to save the best of my share for him, but even that was too little, and going rotten, and not good. It made it worse for him."

"Did he get burnt up?" Robbie said.

"No. It was just really that. See, after I'd pitched my crates of fine, sealed brandy overboard, I hit the deck too, helping Aguiar. At first I thought Zio was burned, boys, because he seemed to be thrashing around in Aguiar's grasp. But as I held him too, and beat the flames around him away I thought, while waves of saltwater washed over us, soaking us down in every thread we wore, I realized that my Ciccio wasn't writhing in pain from the flames, or struggling to put out the heat, he was wracked with coughing. He was coughing himself to death, lads."

Burton reached down beside his wheelchair and picked up that bottle of wine he had set there, but he didn't drink from it right away. He just held it for a while, and he looked over at Zambutto Sammy. "E' stanco, Sammy" he cooed at the animal, and he reached out a hand a stroked the ape's great brow again. The gorilla lowered his head a bit, basking in the man's touch.

"What was wrong with him?" I asked.

" My Ciccio?" Burton asked, glancing over at me. "Mio caro Ciccio," he sang out in a whispered breath.

"Yes," I said.

"It wasn't the fire, lad. Though the fire didn't do him any good. No. And it wasn't the rotting food we had for weeks then aboard our Speranza, and the little of it to go around. But that didn't do him any good either. No." Finally Burton took a long swallow from the wine, and when he finally went on, he gazed down at the bottle in his hands as if it was a last, desperate distraction.

"We all gave him the best part of our rations, you know. And nobody more than the General.   There were days, I think, when the General ate little more than a handful trimmed off the edges of the rot, because he gave everything that was any good to Francesco.

"I know I was hungry, but I gave him the best of what we had. Still his eyes just grew darker and more shaded by his brow, and the little cough was persistent. Always there, lurking just behind every word he said. He kept on with my reading lessons, but at times he'd have to stop and cough and cough and cough, until we had to quit.

" In the evenings, under the stars on the deck, Il Generale would lead us in the singing, and we all got a draught of the brandy that was left. He did this, the General, to keep the fires of freedom burning in our hearts, because now the voyage was months on, and growing long. And we were hungry.

"And dear Ciccio, he would insist on standing amidships and singing right along. But even though he had part of my draught of brandy, and usually all of the General's too, and even Aguiar's, too, sometimes he would start to cough and it wouldn't stop, and we would end up carrying him down to his bunk below, Aguiar and I. His arms around our shoulders, but his whole body thrown and tossed by the coughing, until he curled up in a ball in the bed, trying to hold himself still, but shaking with the hard rhythm of his cough"

"What was it?" Robbie said.

Burton ignored us then. He was somewhere else and the disease of his soul didn't need a name for the disease of his friend. He said, "One night, mi' ragazzi, after Ciccio had fallen asleep, I was standing alone at the stern of the brig, watching the wake diminish and disappear behind us out on the Atlantic, when Aguiar wandered up after his watch, and stood there beside me. He had a cigar in his mouth, and he chewed on the end of it, but he didn't light it. It was one of the General's, and there were only a few left, so Aguiar wouldn't waste it by lighting it except every once in a while. Mostly he just held it in his lips and chewed on it.

"But he stood there beside me, with one long arm cast up in the rigging, holding that cigar to his lips, moving it around with his other hand and tasting the tobacco, and I asked him just that, because I was confused. 'What is it?' I said. I don't know that I believed he could answer me. It was really just a plea.

"But he told me then about my friend Anzani, and how he had traveled the world, lads, fighting wherever he could in behalf of Liberty. Wherever in the world some small band was standing up against the lords for their freedom and their equality, no matter how slim their odds were, that was where my Zio stood. Francesco Anzani." Burton nodded his head with a confident air at that.

"'He's not been home to Italy in over twenty seven years' Aguiar said. That tall man, as black as the moonless sky, eyed me then, measuring me as if I was a boy. But there was no way he could know my history, understand how old I was. It was impossible. Because it is impossible.

"'Ciccio was a student,' Aguiar said to me. 'He was studying the course in mathematics at the University in Pavia, and he was a smart young man, il piccolo. He'd have gone far if he'd stayed, he'd have become a professor or a scientist. But Anzani has a heart that is too big for that, il piccolo.' That's what Aguiar called me, il piccolo, if he had only known.

"But that was the year when the Greeks rose up to fight for their independence. And my Ciccio, he left the university and the easy, learned life and he went to fight for their liberty. For the independence of Greece. This is what Aguiar told me about my Ciccio, while we stood in the stern of the Speranza."

Robbie floated up onto his knees and clapped his hands together. And I couldn't help it, because I was sitting straight up too. At that moment, filled with the drama the lurked in

Burton's eyes and spurred on his speech, filled with our own little excitement, we startled the ape out of his drugged lethargy over on his little stool. He lifted his head and snorted once or twice in confusion.

Burton just laughed at the two of us, and I guess at old Zambutti Sam too. He reached out and patted the ape's broad brow again, and then laughed a bit more at my brother and me.

"Woe, miei ragazzi, woe! Don't get too excited! Let me tell you the whole of his story, before you get too ready to run off from your school days. See, Aguiar says to me that night, 'He could never go home to Italia. After he fought with the Greeks, he was an exile. He was a man with no home, a man with no country.' You boys, you are too young to know what that means, to wander through time across the face of this dark earth with no place to call a home. Hunted by the names and the families and the things you've done in your past, with nowhere but inside your own shoes to live, it is a terrifying thing, O ragazzi, no matter how old you grow. How can I tell you poor lads how this is?" Burton said more to himself than to us, mournfully. "You boys can never know this. You have a home in this world, you do."

I was still up on my knees, but Robbie in front of me seemed to sink down a little as Burton spoke. And suddenly I felt the weariness of the night pressing on me.

"My Ciccio, he spoke to me once of this, boys, 'Whenever peace comes, that place is no longer my home. I will always search in every other part of this world for the battles that will devour me.' This is what he told me, boys. For the battles that will devour us. It was his passion, and it was his curse."

At that Burton fell silent and, gazing blankly at the tent walls around us, his hand touched the big animal beside him. Zambutti Sam snorted again and moved over from his low stool onto the rug that lay on the ground beside Burton. Then like a loyal old dog, the ape leaned quietly against the strange man in his wheelchair.

As I watched, I sank down onto the floor too. I was too young then to know the destitution and the loneliness he must have felt, or even to recognize what it was. But I felt it, even if I didn't understand it, and Robbie did too. After the fires of leaving school to fight for liberty, this heavy cost, whatever it was, it weighed down hard upon us, weighed us to the ground.

"He went from Greece on to Spain, Aguiar told me, and then from there he fought for the liberali in Portugal. From one struggle on to the next, he went, without a home. With no home but the battlefield in all the world's guerilla wars. That's what we call them now, lads, guerilla wars. Back then, it was just the only way to resist. 'It was there, in Iberia, that he was wounded the first time,' Aguiar said to me, and as he spoke on the deck of the Speranza, he pointed with the long finger of his hand to his own side, under his left arm. 'He keeps the wound hidden, you know, and he won't show it to you. He'll even deny it if you ask him, but somewhere there in Spain or Portugal, a bayonet got him, and it had to be deep in the lung. And that, il piccolo, that was the start of all this.'

"What Aguiar meant was the coughing and the weakness and that dark shadow that drifted over his eyes at night sometimes, most times by then. You see, the wounds from his fighting in Iberia had led to the consumption that was slowly eating up his lungs.

"Aguiar told me, in the days when they'd first fought in Uruguay, for the Republic of Rio Grande, that my Ciccio could hide his illness. 'He was young, and strong as a wild pony, and he could run and ride and fight with the best of us. The General never knew, not for the longest time, not for years,' Aguiar told me. 'But slowly it caught up with Francesco, and we began to see him change. He was turning in earlier at night, drinking too much wine to deaden the pain, and then, finally, running out of breath. I was there, il piccolo, the night il Generale cornered him and asked him what was wrong. That was when he showed the General his old wound. It is still the only time I've seen it,' said Aguiar. 'And so now, my friend,' Aguiar, who would die defending Rome, said to me, 'now we have come to this.'"

Burton grew quiet again, and seemed to go somewhere that my little brother and I couldn't follow. Then suddenly, he breathed in deep once and said to the ape, "Butto, mia pipa." The gorilla moved aside and then lifted and handed over the little chest to Burton. The red shirt lay folded carefully on top of it, and when Burton put a hand on it he paused. "I haven't spoken about my dear Ciccio in a long, long while," he said, as if he was talking to himself, as if he was trying to explain away something that he dared not try to understand, not even from a great distance.

Then he began the ritual with the pipe again, in silence this time, until he had warmed the bowl and lit it and swallowed hard and whole the sweet white smoke, and again passed it over to the ape who smoked the last of it and then carefully scraped the bowl clean, eating every crumb of the resins.

"I don't do this every night," Burton muttered, staring down into his lap, "almost never twice." He sat back in the wheeled chair and closed his eyes. His chin was lifted a bit in the air, and he appeared to sleep for a while, though once in that time he muttered the name "Anzani." Zambutti Sam tucked away the cleaned pipe and all of its accoutrements in the little chest, and smoothed the folded red shirt over its top. And through it all, even in the dreamy quiet, Robbie and I were riveted to the scene before us. The whole tent seemed to us to be part of some wild other world, and our little house in our small hometown and all the Mrs. Coogan's of the world seemed to drop away like so much sweat in a darkened steam bath. I think now, as I look back on that night, it may have been the traces of that sweet white sunset smoke that lingered in the air like incense at a holy mass, it may have been that which took us all so far away. The journey, the real one we still wander on, had begun. Yet it may just have been the traces of that crazy smoke.

I don't know how long we were like that. Time had become an illusion to me then. But after a while had passed, Burton began to speak to us again, as if we were emerging from an old dream and his story had become our common reality. The tent lay in total darkness, with only the soft glow of the heater lighting our faces and the glimmering of our eyes.

"One night, as my reading lesson was ending, and dear Ciccio seemed so tired, he began to cough. And his coughing went on. And it wouldn't stop. Eventually he curled over on his side in his bunk, and blood began to leak from the corner of his mouth, and hard black clots of it came up from his lungs. I was wiping up the stained sheets with a rag, my hand resting on Ciccio's trembling shoulder. Aguiar got up and ran off to the mess, and he came back with the General behind him and the last of the brandy. The General took my place beside Anzani at his bunk, and fed him the brandy slowly until he settled down and the coughing stopped. The General wiped at the sweat on Ciccio's brow, and that care alone seemed to quiet him, though I know it was the brandy slowly sinking in, letting him rest.

"'That's the end of it,' Aguiar said plaintively. 'The last of the brandy we've got left on board.'

"'We're only a day or two out of Spagna,' the General said, as he was ever the optimist. Then my Ciccio laughed out loud.

"'What is it, Francesco?' the General said, smiling down at Caro Ciccio and gently mopping the sweat from his brow. There was a deep, old fondness between those two men, for they had so long been brothers, comrades in the same long struggle.

"Ciccio chuckled a little, and then he said, 'You mean to tell me, mi' Generale, that we would have had all the brandy we could drink, all the way across the wide, wide Atlantic, if only my little Burtoni here wouldn't have thrown the half of it away?'

"The General and Aguiar laughed together, and I confessed, 'But Ciccio,' I pleaded, 'I was only following your lead!'

"'Ah, il piccolo,' said my Zio. 'But what I threw away was on fire!' He coughed a few times, but ever so gently now, and a bit controlled. 'You tossed the good stuff overboard!'

"Aguiar clapped me on the shoulder from behind, and I heard his big laugh rumble out, and then the General's too. 'If I hadn't needed to catch you, Francesco, and keep you from going right on overboard, I might have tackled the little one and saved at least a bottle, maybe even two,' Aguiar said.

"It was good for all of us, for Zio Ciccio especially, to laugh. And not to think about his deep, hoarse cough and his blood staining the sheets.

"'Soon,' said the General, 'soon, we'll all be sipping sweet Spanish wine, and soaking up the sun on the shores of our dear, old Mediterranean Sea.'

"And as the General said it would be, so it was."

A broad smile spread across Burton's lips, and he gazed up over our heads at some Mediterranean place in his long memory. "That was a day, O ragazzi. Oh, that was a day. We sailed on an easy wind right through the straits of Gibraltar and we put in, on a shining, sunny afternoon to the port of Santa Pola, on the south coast of Spain.

"He orderd us not to go ashore, to stay on board, for we needed to press on toward Italia. But the men argued with him, after months at sea. 'Let us go put our feet on the ground,' we cried out. Still he held to a higher plan, our Generale. He sent Gazzolo, the ship's captain, ashore alone to see about supplies, and then he went below to see how Ciccio was doing. 'Do you need to go ashore?' the General asked only Francesco. 'Do you need a rest?'

"'Mi' Generale, are we not headed for Italia?' was Ciccio's reply, and I thought an argument between these two old friends might rightly ensue. But right then we all heard the shouts of the men above us, 'Liberta'! Liberta'!' they cried. And over that came the voice of Captain Gazzolo, 'Generale! Generale!' he cried.

"As the General rose from my Ciccio's bedside, Gazzolo came barreling down the stairs, with Aguiar right behind him, both of them breathing hard, and the both of them came up short at the sight of the General, and they stood at attention.

"'What is it?' he said.

"O! Miei ragazzi, what a day that was," Burton said, and he laughed and laughed. He shook his head to and fro and his eyes winced shut in pure joy.

"What was it?" Robbie said, after we grew tired of listening to Burton's laughter.

"What was it?" I said.

Burton stopped and he looked over at us, and his hand reached over and touched the red cloth resting on little chest filled with his smoking implements. His smile now wrinkled into a twist of amusement. "Ah, my boys, may you have many days in your lives like that fine day in mine. Days you remember with great joy for all of your time.

"You see, the Captain held in his hands a dozen or so pages of some Spanish newspaper, pages that someone had carefully clipped out and saved. Some patriot stranded on the shores of far off Spain, like the General and my Ciccio had been stranded in Montevideo, some exile, hiding in Spain from the aristocrats and the church, waiting for il Generale's return. Someone had saved this pressing news, hoping against hope itself for our return.

"'Oh, mi' Generale, it has started! Look!' Captain Gazzolo cried. 'Read, mi' Generale, read!' And he shoved the sheaf of papers in his hands at him.

"Ciccio lifted himself up on one arm from his bunk, and suddenly his darkened eyes seemed brighter. 'It has started, Francesco,' Gazzolo said to him.

"'The revolution,' Aguiar said from behind the Captain, 'It's the revolution, Anzani.'

"Gazzolo nodded his head in agreement. 'We have come home at just the right moment,' he said. Meanwhile the General was reading through the papers with a furious glare, shuffling them like he was holding a hand of cards dealt from history's deck, lads. He was eager to see what was on the page that followed, then shuffling back to be sure he had read the news on the first page right.

"'What is it?' said my Zio to him, as he sat up in his bunk. Above us I heard the furious pounding of feet on the decks, and the chants of 'Liberta'!' The men were dancing with some old, wild frenzy on the decks amidships.

"The General lifted his eyes from the newspaper and gazed over at his old comrade-in-arms, Francesco Anzani. He wore no smile, and his eyes were fierce. 'We have risen in Milano, Francesco. We have taken the city back from the Austrians.' And he handed the papers over to my Ciccio, with the pounding feet on the decks above him like the rattling of drums, and the voices of the men faint above that, singing old hymns in Italian.

"'And in Napoli, and in Venice,' said Aguiar, grinning, his arms akimbo.

"Captain Gazzolo stamped a foot on the wooden floor, and said to the General, 'Emperor Louis-Phillippe is gone from Paris, and the Metternich is gone from Vienna. And the Croat soldiers of Austria have fled from the streets of Milano.' Then he raised a tight fist in the air before him.

"Ciccio just stared down at the newspapers and his feet touched the floor beneath his bunk. He looked over at me, as I tried to follow what all this talk meant, and my Zio said, "It has begun, il piccolo. The renaissance of our people has started at last.' Then he paused before he and the General said, quietly and instinctively, and almost at the same moment, 'Viva Italia!'

"That was the moment, O ragazzi. In all of our joy, that was the moment when their great misunderstanding began. It would mark Il Generale for the rest of his many long days, still it was nothing but a mistake. And yet, I will never forget that wonderful moment, filled with such verve and spirit, yet eternally darkened by a simple mistake between these two old friends."

Burton stopped there, he looked down and seemed to see the ground under us, beneath the carpet, the simple dirt. Then he spoke to himself, I think. We could barely hear him, it was so soft. "Neither of those two great men knew how much they loved one another." He shook his head back and forth, just tiny millimeters, and just for a brief instant. "They never knew," he whispered. "They died without really knowing what it all meant."

"What happened?" I asked, and both Burton and the ape behind him looked up at me, as if they were surprised to see me sitting there, so deep were they both in the fog of their smoke, and for Burton so deep in his memories. Robbie glanced back at me, he was up on his knees now, and he looked worried.

"What happened, sir?" he repeated.

Burton rested back in his wheelchair and seemed tired and old for the first time that night. You could see the doubts in his eyes, did he want to go on, to tell us the hard part, the part about the failures and the death. What happened when the glorious voyage was over, with all its hopes and dreams, until only defeat and despair lurked ahead of them.

"My Ciccio," was all he said, and his eyes closed on the world.

I guess we let him sit there in his wheelchair, looking older than the giant elms scattered around the schoolyard, trees that were soon to grow streaked with death and ill and then to be cut down and burned in order to desperately and vainly try to defeat the disease that was spreading through the land. We left him alone for a time, and Zambutti Sam stirred in his little stool, and gazed on Burton with warm, steadfast eyes that told even me, with my few years, that this was not the first night Jack Burton had taken to his pipe in order to ease himself off into his sleep.

"Sir?" Robbie said to him softly, and Burton's eyes opened slowly. He looked at us, uncomprehending for a moment. But I knew then he wasn't sleeping, or absent. He was just deep and deeper in his memories.

"Carlo Alberto," he said.

"Who was that?" I said, and Robbie sat back on his heels, and then as Burton began again to tell us the story, Robbie tilted back over to this side and rested his weight on an arm.

I realized that I was lying back now with my head cradled in my hands, my legs stretched out in front of me toward the glowing propane heater. Singing behind old Burton's yarn was the music of crickets and the now and then snort or the shake of a mane from the circus horses staked outside in the playground.

"That night, resting off the coast of Spain," Burton went on, "in the safe harbor of Santa Pola, the men were dancing on the decks of the Speranza. And my Ciccio, he was sitting up in the bed, his feet were again touching the boards of the floor, his coughing had died down and the blood at the corners of his mouth had been wiped away, gone from his lips. And then the General said to him, 'Carlo Alberto has declared war on the Austrians, Francesco, and his army has marched into Lombardy, to come to the aid of the Milanese.'

"'Viva Italia!' shouted Captain Gazzolo."

"Who was he?' said Robbie, because like me, he was suddenly lost. And we had never seen an adult behave this way, not in all our lives. Adults were supposed to be clear headed and certain and in charge, telling us what to do, whether we liked it or not. Adults were not supposed to be filled with dreams and yearning for lost lands and distant wars. That was for kids and people in the movies, not for adults.

Burton stared blankly past us, speaking as if to ghosts, as he explained, "Carlo Alberto was the King of Sardinia, my boys, with an army of 60,000 men. And he led these men into Lombardia, and declared war on the Austrian oppressors. He came to help the rebels who were rising in Milano and Venezia. So the war for Italy had begun for real, ragazzi, and Carlo Alberto meant to unify it all under the House of Savoy. It would all become the Kingdom of Sardinia, and the Frenchmen and the Austrian hussars would all be gone. That is who Carlo Alberto was: King Carlo Alberto of Sardinia.

"So, you see, lads, Aguiar and the Captain gave out a great shout then. 'Viva Italia!' they cried, and this brought a big grin to the General's lips, an old warrior's grin, filled with hail fellow-feeling and grand victory dreams.

"Il Generale stood straighter then it seemed to me, and he said to Gazzolo, 'No time to go ashore, Captain. Do we have the supplies to make for Nizza?'

"'We will, my General. There is a boat on its way at this moment, bearing us the water and food we need. Given to us by the patriots of Santa Pola.'

"I saw the General glance over at my Ciccio, and he seemed surprised. You see, my boys, my Zio's head had once again sunk down into his shoulders a little, though he stared hard at the General. And this again made the General, and the rest of us, worry.

"'We must sail straight on for Nizza, Captain,' the General said. 'We need to make shore and join with the armies of the King.' But the General kept his eyes cautiously on my Ciccio as he spoke, and never looked over at Captain Gazzolo. 'Is there brandy for my friend Francesco on that boat that is coming so soon, Captain?' he asked, his gaze never leaving my Ciccio for a moment.

"'Yes, sir,' said the Captain.

"'Good,' the General replied, and then finally he squared his shoulders and turned toward my dear Zio and asked him, 'Are you sure you are well enough to go on, Francesco? Do you need now to go ashore here?'

"My Zio shook his head no, violently shook it, lads. 'To Italia,' he said, but still he kept staring at the General, and his head hung weakly from his shoulders.

"'What is it, my friend?' the General said, seeing my Ciccio's agitation. 'What's wrong, Francesco? Is it something the brandy won't kill?'

"'Yes, Peppino,' Ciccio said, and he looked away from the General. 'It is something that your brandy can't kill.'

308

"'Then,' the General said, 'what is it?'

"'It is this King,' he said, 'this Carlo Alberto.'

"I looked over toward Aguiar and at the Captain, because you see, lads, I didn't understand. But this was a new tone in my Zio's voice. There was a heavy moment of silence, and then it was broken by the General's laughter. And that broad laughter of his sealed the freight of their misunderstanding. It would lie in the hold of both their ears as long as they lived, though it was just the laughter of a moment, it was like a weighted cargo filled with the lead of disappointment."

Burton stopped there, and with his face cast downward onto the dim light, his eyes gazed up from beneath his gray brow, and stared hard and still at something just above our heads and in the distant past. But nothing was there.

"Ciccio was fierce as he spoke out then, and his voice cut through the General's laughter, and silenced it at once. 'There are no more Kings,' Francesco Anzani spat out. He sounded as he spoke as if he would never need to cough again.

"The General paused for a moment, and then he tried to explain to his friend, 'Francesco, first we will make a country, first we must create Italia. Then, when we have won our unity and Italia is clear and on every map in all the world, then we will see about our King. Don't you see, Francesco? We will use Carlo Alberto and his armies and his treasure and his Kingdom of Sardinia to make ourselves into a country, a real country, that reaches from Sicilia to Nizza, a country of our own.'

"As the General spoke, his head reared high and his voice rose, the way only his voice could, and it stirred around in my soul, and I knew then, lads, I knew I would follow him anywhere he needed me to go, and I could see in the light behind the eyes of Aguiar and Captain Gazzolo that it was true for them too. He would lead us on toward victory, and to the glory we could only dream of, and we knew it was so. Our hearts sang and told us it was so.

"But it was not so for my Ciccio.

"Short, little Ciccio Anzani got up on his feet and stood chest to chest with the General, though he seemed tiny and helpless when he did it. But the anger in his face made all the veins in his neck tight. 'Peppino,' he said, 'My friend Peppino.' And that word 'friend' was buried under the irony of his hard tone. 'There are no kings, Peppino.' His head nodded to emphasize his every word. 'You are dancing with a demon, my General. And this demon, he will take away . . . '

"But that was as far as my Ciccio could go. I had never seen him so angry before, and the fire in his heart broke then, lads, and he collapsed back down onto his bunk, and suddenly he began to cough and cough and the spasms of mucus in his chest rattled and shook, and he leaned over sideways and again the blood began to leak from his lips. I took hold of his shoulder and tried to hold him still, but he rocked and shook with the slow rupture in his lungs.

"But the General did not move to his bedside. He glared down at him, with a fury unbroken in his eyes, and he did something then, I know it, boys, I know he would regret it for the rest of his days. He turned, with a rolling horseman's turn on his heel, and he strode right past Aguiar and Gazzolo and climbed back up to the deck, where his men were dancing for joy and for freedom.

"And when he reached the top of the stair, he stopped looked back down at us, at Aguiar and at me holding my Ciccio's trembling shoulders. 'Captain,' he snapped, not addressing us but Gazzolo. 'Those supplies.' he said. 'On board yet?'

"Then he turned on his heel again and disappeared above us. Aguiar helped me as we eased my Zio back down into his bunk, and the Captain, with a clipped nod to Aguiar, followed the General onto the deck.

310

"My Zio was so weak then, and too angry to do much of anything but lie there and try to find stillness, try to ease his lungs into not a peace but a quiet. Aguiar must have seen the confusion and the fear in my eyes, because he laid one hand on my shoulder. And I felt the warmth of it like a comfort.

"'King,' my Ciccio spat out with his blood on the dank sheets.

"'Rest,' said Aguiar, his hand still on my shoulder, and speaking not just to the sick man, but to us all. 'Rest now.'"

Burton didn't really pause so much as he shifted back in his chair then. He scruffed at the short gray hair on his head, and a smile returned to his face. "In just a few days the Speranza arrived in Nice. Now, back then, ragazzi, a ship coming in from a voyage across the sea, it should have been quarantined for days, but not the Speranza. As we sailed into the harbor in Nice, we were met by hundreds at the fort proclaiming 'Long Live il Generale! 'Long Live il Generale!' Oh, they sang out all around us.

"And on the first boat plowing toward us, among the dozen headed to the ship, stood the General's wife. She was tall and slim, and her hair was thick and deep nut brown almost black, and so thick it had a life of its own. Where he was all blonde and burnt rose by the weather, Anita was olive and brown, with just a hint of the Amazon in the cast of her dark eyes.

"And, oh, my boys, there would be no quarantining of the Speranza. Not with bold Anita leading the hundreds on the shore into the little boats to greet us, surrounded by the cheers of the volunteers on the land and on board the ship. It seemed in no time, surrounded by the whirl of the volunteers, that we were carried ashore."

"What about Ciccio?" Robbie said. "Was he cheering too? Was he carried too?"

"Yes, my boy," Burton smiled at him with a paternal glow, "Anita had my Ciccio carried off to the house where she was staying, the house of the General's mother. And so the mother and the wife took to caring for him. I slept in the summer warmth out in a little piazza, before their house, but I spent my time there beside my Ciccio. His eyes, over those days, grew clearer and he sat up and drank soups and ate bread that the General's mother made for him. And there was red, red wine, filled with breath and life, to be had. And, maybe it was just that this soldier, this cavalryman from all the world's armies, maybe he grew better because his feet were back on solid ground, and he could dream again of being astride a horse. Whatever it was, we all began to feel better, watching my Ciccio recover."

"Where was the General?" I said.

"Did they make friends again?" said Robbie.

"Oh, there was no time to wait, not for the General, much as he would have loved to sit up of an evening, with his children around him, with his dearest Anita, in his mother's house where he'd spent his own baby days, and drink that dark red wine 'till late in the night with his friends Francesco and Aguiar. But for him there was a country to be won, a revolution to stir to life, and liberty to be had for his land, like the liberty in America and in France.

"No, he and his legion of men, which over those first few nights I believed included me and my Zio, they were headed for Genova. In just a few days, the Speranza was readied and the men were waiting to charge forward, as they listened every night around the hearth fires of Nice to the news and the stories coming back from Milano and Venezia of revolution and rebellion. In two or three days, the General was set to return to Genova, to the heartland, to find King Carlo Alberto and offer him the services of this General and his Italian Legion, veterans all from the wars of South America.

"In the evening of the next day, he found me outside, sitting in the shade of his mother's house, tossing marbles in the dust of the piazza with some of his children. 'Burtoni,' he said to me, and led me aside, away from the children and from that child's play. It was the first time he'd spoken directly to me, and used my name, too. 'Burtoni,' he said. So I knew it meant he had orders for me."

Jack Burton grinned again at that memory, and then he told us, "Il Generale was more clever than I realized then." And Burton laughed to himself. "He said to me, 'Francesco seems to be feeling better, no?'

"'I think so, sir,' I answered him.

"'I have seen the way he watches after you, Burtoni,' the General nodded his head and gazed straight into my eyes. 'And the way you look out for him.'

"I muttered 'Yes, sir,' though it wasn't all that clear to me.

"'But, I have to tell you, though this is hard, he's not well enough to come with us, Burtoni,' Il Generale frowned. 'It would be the end of him, I'm afraid, if he tried to come' He stopped, and then he looked even deeper into my eyes and I knew again that I would follow him into whatever battle he led me, however lost or hopeless, wherever he led me, I would go. But then, lads, he said the impossible thing.

"'I need you to stay here with him, Burtoni. It would be good for you to come with the Legion, to join us in the revolution, but what I need is for you to stay here with our dear Anzani. It will be the only way that I can convince him to stay in Nice, with my mother and Anita. So that he can get well.'

"'But!' I said.

But it was an order. And I knew it.

"So the General clapped me hard on the shoulder, and then he promised me, 'We will meet again, Burtoni, in a new land. In a new country. Reborn from its ancient ruins. We will be together. And our dear friend Francesco Anzani, he will be standing beside us.'

"And so they all left, long before the earliest light, the Speranza carrying the Italian Legion of Montevideo off to the peninsula, in search of the revolution. And I was the one who woke my Zio in the morning with the news."

"Was he mad?" said Robbie.

Burton seemed more sad than amused, but a crooked, little whisper of a smile graced his lips. "Mad is not the word, ragazzi. He was not angry. That was not my Ciccio's way. He was not even disappointed, or even surprised. It was almost as if he expected as much from Il Generale, and from me. So no, he wasn't angry. But he stood up out of his bed, and he dressed himself and he was filled with determination. He took some bread and a little milk mixed with coffee, and then he headed down the hill toward the port.

"I followed behind him, telling him repeatedly that we were under orders from the General to wait with his wife and mother, until the time was ripe for us all to return to Italia. We've been ordered to look after Anita and the family,' I pleaded with Ciccio as we stepped together out into the piazza.

"Clouds had rolled in over the morning sky, growing ever blacker in the west. 'Where are you going?' I said to him, just as big round drops of rain began to splat on the yellow stones around us.

"Ciccio laughed loud and turned to me, 'You've been ordered to look after me, Il Piccolo,' he said. "That's what you've been ordered. And I've been ordered—indirectly ordered, I must add—but ordered, still, to stay behind.' Then he rounded on his heel and strode down across the piazza toward the waterfront. His black hair, streaked now with gray, it blew back from his brow as he headed into the summer wind blowing up out of the morning sea.

"'Where are you going, Zio?' I said.

"'To see when the next ship can take me to Genova,' he shouted over his shoulder, with nary the sound of a cough. 'You stay here and take care of Mama.' I ran after him and as I caught up, he said, with his shoulders squared, 'Peppino doesn't think I can keep up with him. He's got a start on me, but he's forgotten what a heart I have.'

"As we made our way down to the docks, the wind rose and the rain broke hard and the storm that had been bearing toward us across the mountains of Spain came blowing full on. But the hard weather didn't even give Anzani a pause. My Zio strode right on, and we got ourselves drenched in the process, but we wound up standing, so wet Ciccio's hair dripped down his back and the drops just rolled off him because his red shirt was already completely soaked, and there was nothing for the water to do but roll off him, but yet we stood in the rain and he bought us tickets on a mail boat. He bought his passage to Genova. And when he was done, he looked at me and laughed and then handed me the coins to buy my own passage too.

"And that was how well we followed the General's orders."

Burton rubbed at his chin, and shook his head at something in his memory, then he went on, "As luck would have it, that same summer storm that drenched us drove the Speranza south, carrying the General and his Legion with it. But Ciccio and I hopped that old mail sloop in the afternoon and we made straight from Genova. We landed ahead of the Speranza, and so we met the crowds waiting at the docks. You see, lads, the word had run out ahead of us. The Italian Legion was coming, with the General at its head. And just as it was in Nice, a crowd was waiting for him in Genova.

"We came ashore, still damp and cold from the morning's rain. And me, looking like a kid, I tried to tell them all that we were with the Legion. That this was Francesco Anzani beside me, who had ridden and fought beside the General in Rio del Sol and defended the walls of Montevideo as a soldier in the General's Legion.

"But the Genovese, what they saw was a sick, weakened man, old before his years, and a cheeky young loudmouth. I tried to tell them different, but Anzani only smiled and kept his mouth shut, and he held his head high.

"'So why are you coming on this old mail tub, little soldier,' the Genovese laughed at my barking pride.

"My Ciccio only grinned at me and shook his head at my spouting off. He didn't say a word. He didn't need to say a word, because he had nothing to prove."

Burton laughed at himself, and then said, "I wasn't as young as I acted, or as young as I looked, ragazzi. But here is a lesson for you boys: Want to look like a youngster? Want to be treated like a green kid? Shoot your mouth off a lot, with no way to back up your word.

"I learned after that to keep still, like Francesco Anzani did, because what you do speaks for the ages, not what you say you did. And with what has happened to me," he stopped to laugh again. "With all that I've seen and done, nobody would believe me anyway. Not if I dared to tell all that I've seen and all that I've done."

He leaned slowly forward in his wheelchair, and his chest and shoulders seemed to press out of his shirt toward Robbie and me, and he said, "Do you, little ragazzi? Do you believe me?"

I saw Robbie's head nodding yes in front of me, and then Burton's gray eyes slipped over and held mine, and I said, "Yes," and I nodded like my little brother.

"I do, sir," said Robbie.

Burton laughed an evil laugh that made me wonder why I did believe him. But I can tell you, after all these years, I'm still hunting for traces of Jack Burton, wherever I go in the world. And I've never yet found any trace of Il Rosso that wasn't as hard to believe as this was, or even harder, and that wasn't also as true as life itself, as far as I could see.

Jack Burton reached back and took up the wine bottle and swallowed another draught. Then he set the bottle down, and he grew serious again.

"Night fell on the port of Genova then, and the salty breeze blowing in was cool, even in July, but Ciccio and I were still waiting with the restless crowd for the arrival of the Speranza. We'd eaten a little and shared a bottle of red wine, and our clothes were now mostly dry. Ciccio seemed tired, after the long day, but I guess the wine buoyed him up, because he never complained, and only rarely did he sit or rest. Mostly he wandered about the dock, always gazing at the horizon.

"There were lanterns lit on the waterfront, and it was a night like this one, summertime but cool and damp by the seaside. And then the first shout went up, 'Thar she be!' they sung out. 'The Speranza!' And men were suddenly straining to see around one another.

"I suppose it took an hour for the brig to come into port, and during that time the crowd around us grew and grew, and now and again a shout would roll up out of the men, 'Viva

Italia!' or "Viva Milano!' And there developed a low and constant murmuring of men's voices, filled with anticipation and wonder. Around the edges of the crowd, the carabinieri had gathered, looking nervous but knowing all the time that this was a crowd beyond their control. Children, up past their bed times, they hid around the edges of the noisy crowd, hoping their mothers wouldn't notice." Burton stopped, grinned at the two of us, but said nothing.

"So it was, the Speranza sailed into port and she was tied down speedily, amidst the shouts and the cheers of the men, men on the docks and men on the streets of Genova, and men on the decks of the brig. One shout would bring on another, and then the answering call of another. But Ciccio and I, we stood quietly and watched our old ship settle into her moorings.

"After a while, with the men on board scurrying about, and the rounds of cheers rolling through the crowd and across the decks, the General strode up and stood in the prow of the Speranza, where he could look down on the assembled men, his countrymen, he would make them his countrymen, he would, and he stood where they all could see him, as well.

"The crowd knew him in a moment, because they recognized the red blouse and the long blond locks falling onto his shoulders, already the stuff of legend, it was. 'Viva!' the men on the docks yelled, 'Viva!'" Jack Burton yelled out those words in the schoolyard night, but we were so enchanted within his world, we did not jump or stir. We just listened, as we'd never listened before.

"The General stood there, his head high, with dark Aguiar dressed in the red blouse too and right at this shoulder, and then Il Generale raised his arms above his head with his palms out toward us, and at just that simple gesture the crowd fell completely silent.

"He spoke then, and he went on for a quarter of an hour or more, and whenever he paused to breathe, the shouts of the crowd rose up. But I didn't hear much of it, or I heard it, but I don't now remember much of what he said. I remember the shouts of the men on the decks behind him, and the men on the docks around Ciccio and me. But mostly I remember this.

"'Viva Italia!' the General said to start, and it caused an uproar. The Carabinieri behind us shuffled from foot to foot nervously, their hands touching their sidearms gently, checking they were ready, but some of them I think even joined in the cheers. My Zio held a fist in the air. I don't think he had the strength in his lung to shout, so that gesture was his cry. But his heart still felt strong, too strong. And then it happened.

"Il Generale, in the next moment he cried out in a shout over the noise of the crowd. 'Long Live Carlo Alberto,' he called to us, with fire in his eyes that I could see across the rows and rows of men's waving arms ahead of me. 'Viva Carlo Alberto,' he cried, and some men began to toss their caps in the air. Then the General held his left hand out, open and welcoming, as if to bring an old friend in close to his side. But there was no friend. And he would learn there would be no friend. There was only this operatic, flowing gesture, filling an emptiness beside him he couldn't see, lads, and yet there was his shout, 'Viva Carlo Alberto!'

"I saw my Ciccio grow rigid, and the fist he had in the air dropped to his side. The veins in his neck tightened again and, in a moment, his face turned feverishly red. And then, as the men shouted 'Viva Re!' all around us, Ciccio collapsed onto the ground. He landed on his side and instantly curled up into a fetal ball, and he didn't really cough so much as just vomited blood from out of his open mouth. But his body was wracked with spasms, so I think now, my boys, that he was not really coughing anymore, no, truly he was gasping just to breathe. But I couldn't hear him over the cries and shouts for the King and the General. The fever of the crowd itself, it buried the sound of his lurching cough."

"Was he all right?" Robbie blurted out.

Burton looked at him, with an arched eyebrow, measuring I guess how much to say to one so little. Then he just said, "No, caro piccolo, he was not." Then Jack Burton looked over at me, to see how I was taking it all in. The arch in his eyebrow disappeared, and his face went strangely blank then. "He was not," he repeated. Not really speaking to me.

"It was dark, even under the lanterns, and from somewhere two or three men and this old woman gathered around us. I discovered I was kneeling bedside my Zio, with both my hands on his shoulders." Burton held his hands out from his lap, and I could almost see that he was holding something gently in his grasp. "I tried to stop the lurching and the trembling in him. But I couldn't. None of us could hear anything over the chanting of the crowd. So with simple gestures that took command of the moment, the old woman had my Ciccio lifted up and carried away, and someone put his arm around me and led me too, along behind.

"I don't remember how, but somehow from the midst of that cheering crowd, the old lady took us to a little stone house, a few narrow streets up from the docks, and they laid my Zio in a bed. And again, I suppose, there was soup and strong, fortified wine. But now, too, there were blankets. Heavy, woolen blankets. For my Ciccio, when he stopped coughing and gasping from exhaustion, and he would collapse into some form of fevered sleep, before long he would be awakened by his own cold shivering. The fever had him freezing and quaking in the warm July night. And then the trembling would start all over again, until he was exhausted, and he collapsed again into brief sleep. If indeed it was sleep.

"You see, it was a sleepless night for me too, as I held my Zio by the shoulders, or I cradled his head in my hands and mopped the sweat from his brow, or I soaked up the blood and spittle and sputum that come from his lungs. His eyes were lost and distant all of that night, and he didn't not know who I was or where he was. I don't think he did, at any rate, but there was no way to tell. He had not the strength to speak, even in his rare calm moments of rest.

"And so it went through that night, now and again interrupted by the old woman, bearing wine or broth or a clean, cool towel. When daylight came, I'd fallen asleep in the morning light, because my Zio had so exhausted himself that he had, I supposed, just passed out.

"I was awakened from my short rest by the old woman leading the General into the room. I know what day it was, too, my boys. I'll always remember the date. It was the Fourth of July."

"The Fourth of July," I said, startled. Jack Burton had taken me far, far away from Independence Day celebrations, so just the sound of that holiday seemed to come at us from a foreign world.

"You knew it, because there were hot dogs and rides and fireworks, didn't you, sir?" said Robbie, and his legs squirmed up under his butt, and Robbie bounced up to attention. It made even me, as green as I was to the world, aware of just how young and foolish my little brother was.

Burton only chuckled a little. He reached back and stroked the black fur tufted on Butto Sammy's crown, and the great ape snorted a little recognition at the touch, and then settled back sleepily on his stool, his black eyelids heavy and drooping. "No," said Jack Burton, and his heart seemed to lighten for a moment. "No, ragazzi, This was not in America. There were no fireworks or carnival rides that day.

"And I wasn't thinking of it that morning, because I didn't know then what that day meant. But now, because of that day, and what happened on the next, I will always remember. See, when you Americans shoot off your fireworks and march your brass bands around, and wave the stars and stripes, I always remember those few days in Genova.

"It was the last time il Generale and Anzani met, and I found out later, it was the birthday of the General. But more than that, when you Americans play your anthems and shoot the skies full of fire, I always remember it as the day they spoke their last to one another. And oh," he paused to take a sharp breath, even after all the years, "the things they said to one another."

He stopped there, and he swallowed hard, and then his head fell forward into his hands, and Jack Burton looked at no one for a long while.

Butto Sammy awakened from his napping, grunted and moved toward Burton. The mountain gorilla bumped him then, gently but surely, with a thick, long forearm. But even that didn't initially rouse the old man in the wheel chair. Butto Sammy looked all around the tent, and he shifted his weight from one front paw to the other, slowly back and forth. And his quiet snorts grew a little sharper, and then a little louder. Finally, after a moment or two of this, he stood up from his stool, and now the ape gave Jack Burton another bump roughly with his shoulder against the old man's shoulder.

Burton jerked up in his wheel chair, his eyes were hard and steely, and with his fists now clenched in his lap, he shouted loudly at the gorilla. "Sit, Butto,' he fairly yelled at the animal. "Down."

I know I sunk a little lower to the ground, to keep out of the way of whatever was coming, and Robbie jumped and shifted back and away from the wheelchair.

"Down!" Burton said, loudly, but not in a shout now. Butto Sammy snorted in defiance, but he did sit back on his little stool. His eyes drooped again and the mountain gorilla seemed calm and content once more. He had achieved what he had set out to do.

Burton cast his head down in his hands again, for a moment, and muttered something in Italian I couldn't make out. Then he sat up and stared at us, at Robbie and me, with the fire gone in his eyes replaced by an old and lingering hurt. He said quietly, "I haven't talked about this, not to anyone, in seventy or eighty years." It wasn't really meant as an apology, he was just thinking out loud.

But it set me to wondering again just how old this man was. It is a wondering that goes on in me to this very day.

"At the sight of il Generale, my Ciccio sat up in his bed. It was the strongest I'd seen him look since he collapsed at the dock the day before. 'Francesco,' the General said. Ciccio smiled at him. He seemed better than he had in the hours and hours of the night.

"Then the General looked over at me, and said, 'Comrade Burtoni, I thought we had an understanding. I believe I gave you some orders.'

Before I could answer, my Zio said, 'But you didn't give me any orders, Peppino. You were rying to leave me behind, you were.' My Zio winked at me. 'So don't blame the boy, Peppino. He's a good lad. But not good enough to keep Francesco Anzani out of the action.' Then Ciccio laughed, but it turned into a burst of coughing that went out of control. And both the General and I had our hands on him then, trying to hold him still, as he shook and shook and shook, trying to get hold of his breath.

"As Ciccio slowly settled back into the bed, the General cut me a look over his shoulder. He didn't have to say anything, because I understood in a moment that I had failed him. This is what I was trying to prevent, is what the General's eyes said. This is who you have failed when you chose not to follow my orders.

"Lying on his side. Ciccio said, once he could get his breath, 'We beat you here to Genova anyway, Peppino. What happened to you?'

"This brought to the General a great laugh. 'Ahh, Francesco,' he said through his great rolling laughter, 'what am I going to do with you?' He ran a hand through his long fair locks, pushing the reddish blonde hair back from his brow. It was the only sign of how worried he was, as he laughed boisterously all the while.

"Then he looked up from under his brow, and he spoke very seriously. 'I want you to stay here, Francesco.' Then his gaze shot over at me, and he said, 'And I want you to stay here with him, Burtoni, until Francesco is strong enough to join us.' His eyes told me this last part was a lie that we both understood. Francesco Anzani was going nowhere. But I nodded yes anyway.

"'Sir,' I snapped back, to affirm his clear orders. Then I added, trying to lie as well as the General, but maybe too I was still young enough to believe in what I said. 'We'll join you in a week or two.'

"Ciccio sat listening to us, seeing straight through it all. 'Where are you headed, Peppino?' he asked, with a steady gaze at the General. It was the only thing Ciccio had left that was steady.

"'I'm taking the Legion,' he answered.

"'The Italian Legion,' Ciccio interrupted him.

"The General cracked a little smile, ' I'm taking the Italian Legion to Roverbella, to the front line, to join in the rebellion.'

"Ciccio nodded, and whispered 'Viva Italia!' in a tortured breath, trying to fight off another spasm. In a moment, when he had regained control of himself, he asked, "Who is there, my General?"

"At first il Generale just ignored his question. 'We now have 169 men in the Legion, Francesco. A hundred more have joined us here in Genova.'

"'But who is in Roverbella?' Ciccio pressed his point, his suspicions were high.

"'An army of 96,000 men, Francesco, arrayed against the Austrians. Ready to throw them out of Italia, our Italia, to unite behind the rebels of Milano and Venezia and to free the north of the Austrian tyranny.'

"Ciccio frowned, he stopped and rubbed agitatedly at his forehead as if a headache had struck him suddenly. 'And who is at the head, Peppino, of this army of thousands that the Italian Legion will join? Who will they give their allegiance and their very lives over to, Giuseppe?'

"The General didn't answer. His feet shuffled on the floor, but then he planted them firmly.

"'Who, Giuseppe?' Ciccio said. I had never heard him call the General by that, but the sound of that full first name in the air changed the whole tone of the moment. 'Will it be you, Giuseppe, my General, at the head of that mighty liberating army?'

"'The King of Sardinia is in command," The General said, clearly, if not proudly.

"'Carlo Alberto?' my Ciccio spat out like it was a curse. The General stood still, and did not respond. There was no need to respond.

"'Our Italian Legion, Giuseppe, the heroes of Montevideo, joining the army of the King of Sardinia? Joining the King!'

"'Francesco, you know the old saying, my comrade. You must first catch the hare, before you worry about what sauce to cook it in.'

"'But this hare, Giuseppe . . . No. This King of yours, my General, he may just have the sauce ready for you.'

"'It will not be like that, Francesco.'

"'He will cook you and our whole Italian Legion. Little Peppino, served up on a pretty Sardinian platter for the Austrian's pleasure. And when they are done with you, Giuseppe, I ask you, what will you have? Even if you survive this little feast between these Kings. What will you have left?'

"'We will have an Italia free of the Austrian hussars,' the General said, and he seemed even more planted and square than before.

"'No, Giuseppe, you will have a string of graves scattered for miles and miles around the . . .' Ciccio paused there, and then he spat out again the next few words, "the Kingdom of Sardinia.'

"'No, Francesco, you are wrong.'

"My Zio rose up in the bed, and held himself steady. It was amazing to see, for he truly had not the strength to do it. 'He will use you, my General, and use the whole Legion too, and then he'll make fools of you all. He knows your little proverb about your rabbit stew, Peppino. Kings are always Kings. They don't change because we strolled in wearing our red shirts and toting along a sack of words and dreams.' Ciccio had to stop then, because he did not have the wind to say more, and he would suddenly collapse weakly into coughing if he tried to go further.

"The General took the chance to speak, 'You're wrong, Francesco. It is the first step to our Liberty. You'll see.'

"'No, Peppino,' my Zio said. 'You're just another fool for some other king.' He fell back onto his bed then, and all the glow and the hope from just moments before was gone. 'Leave me alone,' he wheezed.

"'Francesco,' the General said.

"'Get out of my sight,' Ciccio whispered between racked breaths, and he turned away from us.

"The General brought his shoulders up even straighter, and then he barked out, "Captain Francesco Anzani.'

"'Out, fool,' was all Ciccio could say, his head still turned away. 'Fool of Kings. And General of Fools.'

Il Generale drew in a great breath, and his chin pulled in toward his swelled chest. 'You will see, Captain Anzani,' he said.

"'The fool of Kings,' my Ciccio said again, curled on his side and facing away from the General and me. Then he rolled over, and used his last bit of strength to say, 'Get out. Both of you.'

"The General glanced over at me, and his mouth opened to speak an answer, but then his eyes hardened, and with a sharp click of his heels, he just turned and left the room.

"I looked at my Ciccio, and I said, 'Zio?' but he just kept his back toward me, and didn't speak.

"So I honored his wishes, and I left him alone and I followed the General outside. I found him stopped, standing in the cobbled street, his hands behind his back, his head lowered and his back to the door of the little house where my Ciccio lay. That great chest of his was no longer swelled, and he was so lost in thought he didn't notice me behind him, in the doorway to the old lady's house. But I was there, and I heard his whisper. 'Addio, Francesco,' he said. And then more softly, 'Caro Francesco.' And then his head rose straight. And without even a glance backward, he strode away toward the docks, and his ship the Speranza, and to the men of his growing Legion."

*   *   *

"That night, my Zio spent in delirium. He slept little, but he tossed and turned, and in his shouts and cries he seemed to fight every war over again, from Greece to Spain to Uruguay, the battles raged all inside of him again. When the dawn came, I found I'd been up most of the night without any sleep. My eyes burned and I ached in my neck and shoulders, but I had gotten beyond weariness. I felt, ragazzi, like I would never sleep again. Never, never, no never again. No rest. Ever.

"With the daylight, my Ciccio came around, and suddenly his eyes were bright and calm and filled with a new and peaceful clarity. He wasn't able to get up out of his bed, but old Angelina brought us some soft yellow polenta, cooked in chicken broth, and we ate it together. That warm corn meal slipped into me, as I gobbled it down, and I felt life flowing back. And my Zio too, he seemed to grow stronger and his eyes came out of the deep shadows of his brow.

"'Bring me my bag,' Ciccio said, and from the foot of the bed I got the canvas sack that he'd hauled all the way from South America. Sitting up, he dug around in the bag, and out of it, quickly, as he knew just where it was, he pulled out his red blouse. He shook it loose and looked at it, and the he folded it carefully in his lap. Then, very simply, he handed it over to me.

"'Take this to him, Jack Burton,' he said, and the sound of my whole name seemed ominous on his lips.

"'But, I should stay here, 'till you are well,' I protested.

"'No, Peppino is wrong, Gianni. He is making a terrible mistake. And when he discovers this, when he realizes I was right to warn him against this King of his, he will need to know that we are comrades still.' Ciccio shoved the blouse over into my arms. 'Whatever happens to me,' he said. Then he gave me orders again, and again he used my full name. 'Take this to him, Jack Burton. It is the most important thing that you can do now.'

"'But my orders are to stay here with you, my Zio,' I said.

"Ciccio grinned at me, seemed almost fatherly, and then he said, with no little pride, 'I'm giving you your orders now, il piccolo, not our poor mistaken Generale. Not now.' And that lighter tone, and that il piccolo told me all arguments were over.

"Still, I could see a way, I thought, to follow both sets of orders, to follow both my General and my dear Zio, at once.

"'Go. Get some rest, before you leave,' my Zio said, and I had no idea then what he was up to.

"I stood, and turned to head out of the little room, through the same door the General had strode the night before. But I knew I was not leaving. With the red blouse tucked under my arm, I would be back after a few hours of sleep, and I would wait my Ciccio out.

"When I reached the door, and opened it, I heard my Zio speak to me. I turned back, and found he had slumped back down low in the bed. He was breathing shallowly, and he said it again to me. 'Ho un cuore che troppo sente,' he said, though I could barely hear him.

"How could I know those quiet, soft words would be the last words I heard him speak? How could I know?"

Burton sat still in his wheelchair, and the red shirt rested on his little chest behind him, like a lamp now in the darkening tent.

"How could I know?" he muttered again.

"What does it mean?" I said, and I chanted out a few of the sounds, "'Oh quarry . . . what does it mean?"

Burton didn't seem startled by the question, even if he'd seemed distracted moments before. A soft little smile graced his lips.

"I have a heart that feels too much," he said. And then he repeated, "How could I know?"

"Is that the red shirt, right there?" Robbie piped up. "Is that Ciccio's shirt?" He pointed at it, and it seemed to us to glow with legendary fire.

Burton smiled at us, but only for a moment. He reached over again and he put a hand on that red blouse, and he laughed a strange, interrupted laugh. "No," he said. "I gave that shirt to the General, just the way Francesco wanted. This one is my shirt," he said, filled with proud determination.

Jack Burton quietly lifted up the bottle at his feet then, and he took a long draught. But before he drank, he held the bottle up to the heavens, and he said, "Cuore mio" out loud. Then he wiped his mouth on his sleeve, and looked at us, at Robbie and me sitting up straight on the floor.

"It's getting late, lads. Shouldn't you be heading for home?"

"Home!" Robbie cried, and pulled that leaden knapsack over to him. "We left there," he announced, in no uncertain tones.

Burton shook his head, and he was about to tell us that we were not going anywhere with him. But he paused, and seemed to think better of it.

"What happened to Francesco?" Robbie demanded, but I was just quiet, hoping to keep the night going on a little further.

Burton nodded his gray head, and he corked the bottle up and then set it on the ground beside him. "All right then, my little wayfarers," he said, and laughed broadly, but not at us.

He leaned forward out of the wheelchair again, and now he told us the rest of his tale, or as much of it as he was going to tell us, straight away and without a break. From that point, his arms waved in the air, and his voice rose and fell, and he practiced all his charms on us. The lethargy of the smoke was gone. The rest of the story rolled out of him in one great gust, storming over us like a high tide in the wind, relentless and enchanting, until its end. There was no looking back and no longing for voices, for past arms. It was all of a piece. And now it was ours, shared at a run.

"I thought I could follow them both, boys, I would stall and wait for my Ciccio to get stronger, and then I would ride off on some stolen horse to find the General and deliver the red shirt to him. I would tell him Ciccio was well now and waiting, as he rode at the front of the 96,000, raising a country up out of the oppressed lands before them. Everyone's orders would be followed, and everyone was well.

"What did I know? I was younger then. Dreams seemed easy and reachable, and the world in that moment seemed just and fair.

"But what did I know?

"I slept hard for several hours, just blanked out with no memory, dead to all and every sensation, dreamless. It was as if I blinked, as if I just closed my eyes and opened them. But in that flash, hours and hours passed away. I cannot say how long.

"But it was old Angelina's hand that roused me. 'Burtoni,' she said, using the name the General had called me. 'Presto, Burtoni,' she said, 'Presto.' Then she led me down a hallway, so dark I could barely see her black draped form, and then into my Ciccio's candlelit room. I followed her shadow across the darkness, slowly piecing together my sense of who I was and where we were.

"His bed clothes were soaked, and his color was simultaneously burning red and a bloodless white. 'Ciccio,' I said, and took his hand. He looked over at me, but he didn't see me. "Blanco' he muttered. And then he shouted 'Gomez.' His head
lolled back and forth, and in his eyes he saw, I know now, the great retreat from Salto. 'Water,' he called for, 'Giuseppe, water. Acqua.'

"Angelina brought him a cup, and the both of us tried to get him to drink, but he wouldn't take it. He'd just turn his burning head aside, and call out again for 'Water!'

"When I told the General about these last minutes, and about the strange words Ciccio cried out, the General just nodded his head and explained it to me.

"'He was living again our great defeat at San Antonio, il piccolo,' the General told me. 'We retreated under fire to Salto, but for a day and a half, under the burning Uruguayan sun, little Burtoni, we were penned down by the forces of Gomez's Blancos. Pinned down, in full dress and arms, under that huge hot sun, without a drop of water to be had. Gomez thought he had us then, with the sun and the heat at his side, but we fought so bravely, and how we suffered, until we won our retreat back to the safety of Salto, and the waters of the Rio Uruguay. To that sweet water. Never has there been any sweeter, il piccolo. Never. But Francesco, my dear Anzani, he was living it all over again. Those long hours under that torrid sun.'

"But it was only a little while that my Ciccio called out for his General, and he never really came around. His head tossed back and forth weakly for a while, and then it came to its rest, turned away from us. Old Angelina crossed herself, and she leaned past me to close his eyes, and turn his head back to rest gently. And he was gone. Gone to that great rest that waits for all of us. Some of us too soon, like my dear Zio. Francesco Anzani, gone before he'd seen forty years. And for some of us, it seems never to come. We just go on and on, growing older and feebler, suffering more and more, and all the more and more alone.

"Angelina took me away from him, then. There was no more for us to do, and life needed to go on. She fed me in silence at a table in her tiny kitchen, a thick and grainy soup, filled with beets and parsnips and other roots from down in the earth.

"It was there, eating silently, waiting for the undertaker to come and remove my dear Zio, that I understood. Ciccio had known exactly what he was doing. I was free now to follow all my orders, to follow both the General, and my Zio.

"You see, Ciccio was sending me away. He was setting me free, and at the same time charging me to find Il Generale, to deliver the red shirt, and to save him. This was what he had ordered me to do. Not to linger around, worrying over his remains. That was of no importance to him.

"What was of import to my Ciccio was the General, that is, to save the General from his own mistakes. This was the most important thing I could do now. And at last I understood it.

"And so, my boys, I left my dear Anzani in the care of old Angelina, and right that moment I set out on the trail of il Generale. I took only my few things, and my Ciccio's red shirt, and with his last real words echoing in my ears all the way, I set out on foot for Roverbella, where the General and his legion had gone a day ahead of me.

"I walked across the short plain and then up into the mountains, the Apennines that hung down to the coast there in Liguria. But as I strode along, I realized how far I had to go. The Legion was ahead of me, but they were rested from their days in Nice, and from the long wandering voyage to Genova. They were marching east across the mountains toward Mantova and the Romagna at double pace, with the General and Aguiar at their head, the heroes of Italia. The General on his white charger, and Aguiar the batman right at his side.

"But I was trudging along, alone, armed with only Ciccio's pack on my back, and with days and days of spotty food and sleepless nights caring for my Zio behind me. My Ciccio, now dead and gone. It was not long, only a mile or two into my march to the Apennines, before I realized how worn and tired I truly was, and how rugged the way ahead lay over the mountains. And so I fell far behind the Legion, and I stopped to sleep in the summer woodlands, and along the way the good Ligurian liberals would feed me, and point me the way that our Legion had gone on ahead.

" You see, I was following in the wake of the good will of Il Generale and his march, and I benefited time and again from the Manzinians along the way, who fed me and put me up, and told me which towns were filled with the priests and the sympathizers of the Austrians and their Croat mercenaries, the Ligurian patriots told me which places to avoid or to pass through quietly, and at night. And where I could not go safely. Still my pace was too slow and circuitous, for I was one and not a Legion of hundreds marching through.

"And along the way, as I climbed up over the Apennines and the down into the wide valley of the Po, into Emilia Romagna and the Veneto, the news of the General and his men kept filtering back to me, traveling from tongue to tongue, the tales of his fate at Roverbella and beyond. And with every piece of news, it became clear how far my Zio Ciccio had seen into the future. Francesco Anzani had understood something about kings and their ilk that the General, great as he was, could not see. He was too trusting a nature, il Generale. So my Ciccio was right, after all, and he'd sent me off not on some wild hunt, but for a reason. I was to save the General from himself. This was my charge, from the deathbed of my Ciccio.

"You see, little ragazzi, when the General and his Legion arrived, ready to lead the charge against the Austrians, King Carlo Alberto already had other ideas. This King was a sharp one, lads, sharp enough to realize that a revolutionary like il Generale was more dangerous to him than the Austrians were. With an army of 96,000 at his beck and call, what did he need from a rebel and a couple hundred of his veteran followers? Noting at all. Nothing, lads, that's what.

"So by the time I crossed the pass and reached Bobbio, the word had already traveled back to Liguria, and to me. The king had turned the Italian Legion away. He'd sent the General and his men away to the War Office, back in Torino. Far, far away from the front lines. Hundreds of miles from the front line, from the ensuing battle.

"And so from Bobbio I turned to head off to the north, toward Milano, thinking I might cut the triangle and catch up with the Legion on their march to the west. This hope lifted my spirits, and I picked up my pace, but I only arrived in Milano to hear the news. The General had stopped there, and appealed to the provisional government of the new Lombardia. 'Give me a post, so that we, the Italian Legion, can fight the Austrians. We will fight for Lombardia, if the Sardinians have no use for us.'

"But, before I was even half way to the outskirts of Milano, the General and his men had pressed on for Torino. He'd gone on to report to the War Office, as ordered by the King. And the word on the streets of Alessandria was that

Mazzini had spoken for him, but the Lombards too were afraid of this wild, fair-haired South American General from Nizza.

"So I headed after them west toward Torino, across the valleys and the plain of the Po again. But Francesco Anzani had been right. When the General arrived at the Sardinian War Office, they'd already heard from their King. They too had no use for the Legion, even 200 miles behind the front lines. They told the General to go and try to help in the Veneto, to go to Venice and become a privateer in the Adriatic and defend the Venetian Republic. In other words, ragazzi, they all told the General to go and get lost.

"So the General and the Legion turned back for Milano, where Mazzini had been pleading his case. When I arrived in Torino I learned that the Legion had been sent further north, to Bergamo, where the General and his men were put safely to work training the army's reinforcements.

"But I was exhausted by my journey then, and at times I despaired of ever catching up with the men of the Legion, as they were bounced around the foot of the Alps like a child's ball. But in time, I found a friend of my Ciccio's, one Danielle who had fought with him in Greece, though now an old man of 80. I stayed with him there, sleeping in a bed at night and eating hardy during the day, thanks to Danielle's love for our dear departed Anzani. It crossed my mind to find some work there in Torino, and maybe make this fine town my home at last, because I had grown weary in heart and body of chasing after the General. He was being run and run around the countryside, with every leader of every stretch of a little land afraid of him.

"Yet I knew, O lads, once I'd rested that Francesco Anzani's scarlet shirt was still in my pack. And I knew, more than ever, that my Ciccio was right, and he'd sent me on a mission to save his old comrade, and in saving him, to save our mutual cause. To be true, it was Danielle who stirred me to go on. For he understood in his old age, the importance of the wishes of a dying man. And the importance, too, of true friends.

"And so one morning, with the summer sun already rising high, and with the Alps ahead of me. I waved goodbye to Danielle and I set off again to the north. This time I would catch up with them in Bergamo."

"But a strange thing happened then, lads. As I pressed on, walking the dirt roads on foot, to Bergamo, the news of what was happening in the fields of that summer began to filter back to me, piecemeal, at my every stop along the way. You see, the damned Austrians under Radetzky defeated the great army of the 96,000. He whipped them like they were scared children, in a big empty field near Custozza. Radetsky routed them, he did, and sent them off at a run in every direction. And then he marched on toward Milano, to seize back that rebellious city.

"Suddenly, the grand Republic of Milano was lost in pure terror, sure that the city and its revolution would be ransacked by the angry Austrian forces and their lean and hungry Croat mercenaries. The new Republic of Milano just folded up and died, and in their panic they began to evacuate the city.

"It was in a little hollow, a day or two's walk from Bergamo, that I came upon a fire burning under an old oak tree, and I met two of the fleeing soldiers of Carlo Alberto, escapees from the battle of Custozza. One was named Paolo and the other Umberto, and they were so young they seemed only a little older than me. Of course, it wasn't true. Lads, it only seemed that way. I had decades of age on them, even if they couldn't see it.

"I joined their fireside, and they shared with me some of the two rabbits they were roasting there on a spit made of sticks. And they told me, as only young men still charged with the excitement of battle can talk, about their frightful defeat at Custozza. Of the way the fearsome Croats in stark white uniforms marched out in such tight formation they seemed like blades of ice, and they mowed across the campo slicing through the Sardinian lines despite the superior numbers on our side. And oh, how every single one of the 96,000 was turned and then fled before that white, bayoneted precision, flashing across the grass.

"And then, with my hands greasy from the hare I was eating, it was Paolo who said the words that nearly made me choke. 'But those damned Croats have yet to meet the Anzani Brigade,' he said. I nearly dropped the hare's leg in my lap.

"'The who?' I said.

"Umberto nodded his black hair, all mussed and standing up in the air, and said, 'From Milano, they've sent out a small band of soldiers, all dressed in Red tunics, to harass the goddamned Austrians on their push toward the city. And they will do it, by God.'

"'The Anzani Brigade,' Paolo said, his mouth full of rabbit.

"'Who leads this brigade?' I asked. 'How many are there?'

"'It's only a few hundred men,' Paolo said, and then he wiped his mouth on his jacket sleeve. 'Every one of them in bright red.'

"'And who leads them?' I repeated.

"The two lads shrugged, but I was sure this was my General. I wiped the grease from my hands on my pants, and then on the grass, and got them as clean as I could, and then I carefully pulled out my Zio's shirt, folded in the bottom of the pack. 'This is Anzani's shirt,' I said, holding up the red blouse for them both to see.

"Their eyes grew big and I told them who Francesco was, and how he died, and who I was searching for. 'It's him,' I said. 'It must be him.'

"'It must be him,' repeated Umberto.

"And so that was it, ragazzi. In the morning we rose at first light, and the three of us together set out to find the Anzani Brigade."

Robbie popped up unto his knees and shouted out, "Anzani!" It made Jack Burton laugh, and then we all laughed together.

Robbie looked over his shoulder at me, and with burning eyes, he whispered to me, 'The Anzani Brigade! That will be our name, Will." Then his round head shot back around to Burton. "Did you find them, sir?"

Burton sat up a little straighter in his chair now, and he licked his lips once or twice, as if he was tasting that old spit roasted hare from long ago, but it may have been just the long, long tale he was telling. "We did not find il Generale at first. He was moving faster than we were, and the country was changing right under our feet.

"But Paolo, Umberto and I, we were moving more quickly now, lads. We had just two smooth bore muskets with us, and they were still wearing their sky blue uniforms. So along the way back toward Milano, we met many, many folk ready to feed us or to offer us a ride. But as we grew closer to the city, the crowds began to change. Suddenly people were fleeing, and when we asked them if they'd heard where the

Anzani Brigade was last seen, they all just pointed to the north, to the north and then they hurried on to the south.

"Then one day, as we reached the outskirts of the city, a gray bearded man with a donkey cart full of wine casks waved us over to him on the road. 'You boys,' he warned us, 'Ragazzi miei, take off those jackets and lose them. And hide those muskets somewhere too.' His eyes were staring wide, and he shot glances all around us at the bustling roadway, filled with people pressing their way out of the city, carrying whatever they could on their backs and in hand carts or dog carts or anything that would move.

"It was he that told us the news. Carlo Alberto had surrendered."

"No," Robbie and I said in the same breath.

Burton just nodded his head, sagely it seemed to us. "The war was over, lads. The dream of Italia was dead and gone again. And my General, he was now an outlaw. So much for the brave hearts of Kings, O ragazzi."

"Ciccio was right," snarled Robbie, and he seemed truly crestfallen. His little hand lay limp and still on his lunken pack.

"Still, all was not lost to the treachery and cowardice of the King, lads. No, you see, the General had turned the Brigade northward again, and his plan was to head up into the lake country there, and the Brigade would fight a guerilla war, just as he had done in Montevideo and in Rio Del Sol. The Anzani Brigade would fight, harassing the enemy from the mountains around the lakes, and then slipping off into the safety of Switzerland when they needed to rest.

"Radetzky and his Hessians pushed after the Brigade, passing through fallen Milano without a fight. Paolo, Umberto and I, trying as we were to catch up with the Brigade, we wound up in the countryside around Varese, between the slow advancing Austrian horde and the swiftly moving General and his cohorts. He and his men were moving so quickly about, it seemed for a long while hopeless that we could ever catch up with them.

"Then one night, by a little pond in the Varesotto, the three of us were resting by our fire, eating a duck we had taken from the pond, when someone approached us out of the dark. Umberto seized his gun, and rose up onto his feet. 'Show yourself,' he commanded into the dark around us.

"Then I heard my name. 'Bur-Burtoni?' the voice said, but I didn't recognize it.

"'Who are you?' I said, and a man emerged out of the dark with his hands up. 'How do you know me?' I said to him, for I swear I had never seen him before.

"Paolo too now had his musket unshouldered and pointed at the stranger. 'I don't know you,' I said to the scruffy man who emerged into the firelight.

"'I wa-was with the Ge-General,' the stranger stuttered, out of fear I thought, but I was wrong.

"'I don't remember you, signore,' I said. 'You were not on the Speranza.'

"'N-No,' he shook his head, and started to lower his arms.

"'Keep them up,' snarled Umberto.

"'No,' he jerked his hands back up in the air, his stutter disappearing for a moment in fear, and he stepped forward until I could see him more clearly in the firelight. He was unkempt and ragged, in just his shirtsleeves, though the summer night at the foot of the Alps was cool. 'I wa-was in Ni-Ni-Nizza,' he said, his Italian accent florid with French, even through his ragged stutter. "I ja-joined the Bri-Bri-Brigade there. And it was the-there I saw-saw you, with Fran-Fran-Francesco Anzani, and the-the General's mother, Bur-Bur-Bur-Burtoni. You don-don't know me, but I know-know you.'

"I realized there were not many who would recognize me as the lad who'd stayed with Ciccio there at the house of the General's mother. So he had to be someone who was with us, at least from the landing at Genova. 'Sit down,' I said, and nodded him toward the fire. Paolo and Umberto slowly lowered their arms, still not quite sure of the stuttering stranger. We gave him some of the duck we had taken from the pond, and he sat and ate hungrily.

"And then he told us, in his broken way, where the brigade was and how it was fairing. When the news of the King's surrender came to the Brigade, the stuttering soldier said, there was great dissension in the ranks. You see, more than half of them understood that to fight on was fruitless. The Austrians with their ruthless Croatian mercenaries had won, taking everything at Custozza, and then Milano and most of the Veneto had fallen, with Venice herself surely soon to follow. Still, despite the armistice Carlo Alberto had signed, our General decided to continue his fight as long as he could.

"After that, some of the Brigadiers began to slip away every night, and before long fighting broke out amongst the men. Those who were loyal to the dreams of the General tried to hold the deserters, to call out the traitors and threaten them. But this led only to a real danger of mutiny, and the General understood that.

"So it went, until one night at Castelleto, the General brought everyone together. 'Almost a th-thousand men,' said the stuttering Brigadier. And there the General announced his plans. He had written a document. It was a manifesto, and he read from it for those of us who couldn't read. So our little stuttering Brigadier then he pulled out three or four sheets of a broadside, they were folded up and tucked inside his pocket. He handed one of them over to us.

"This is the drift of what it said, boys.

"Il Generale, with his great heart, lads, he announced to the assembled men that those who wanted to go, who wanted to give in to the foreigners' domination of our country, they were free to go. He would not have Legionnaires spilling the

342

blood of other Legionnaires. So there would be no fighting amongst the men, and no one would stop those who chose to leave. But only on one condition could they desert so freely. And at that, he set a stack of handbills on the ground and said, 'If you desert us now, at least take these and post them in every town and village, wherever you go. Abandon your red shirt, but take instead all you dare to carry of these, and let the word get out that not everyone is so weak as our so-called King.'

"Umberto and I snatched the 'Castellato Manifesto' up as greedily as that little Brigadier had eaten his duck just moments before. And as we read the General's proclamation that the war of independence was not yet over for him, the stuttering soldier told us more.

"Over half of the Anzani Brigade deserted peacefully that night. And maybe only half of those fleeing the Brigade had the courage to take copies of the Manifesto with them. By daylight the Anzani Brigade was only a hundred men or so again, and the General marched them along the River Ticino toward Lago Maggiore. We were down, now, to the true and great men of the Speranza. And we were a Legion again. We were the core of the Anzani Brigade now, we were the Anzani Legion. And we would stand by him always.

"The other thing the stuttering soldier told us was what the General planned to do. With what was left of the Brigade, with his Anzani Legion, he seized the town of Arona on the shores of Lago Maggiore, and from there he commandeered two little steamships, the Verbano and the San Carlo, built to haul rich Swiss tourists around the lake. So the General was on the water again, a sailor once more, where he always felt most at home.

"At dawn we left the stuttering soldier asleep by the ashes of our dead fire, and we headed to the north and the west, pressing toward the General's base, Arona. But in my heart I knew that the Anzani Legion with its two ships on that great lake would be hard for us to catch. They would be moving quickly, from the western shore to the eastern shore, raiding the Austrian forces quickly, and then disappearing just as they had appeared.   And they would be almost impossible, without a touch of dumb luck, for three young lads on foot to find. Not to mention that there were dangers, lads, for us in asking after the two ships. We couldn't just question anyone. Many, many along the way favored the Austrians, or feared them. And it would do me no good to find myself locked up with Paolo and Umberto under some Croat guard, with the red shirt of Francesco Anzani certainly seized and destroyed. That would be no way to fulfill my Zio's last wish.

"So, it was with high hopes, lads, but little in the way of a plan that we marched off deeper into the lake country. We moved, naturally, toward Arona, though the chances that the Verbano and the San Carlo would put in there were slim. The Legion could not as yet defend a home, so it could indeed not have one. Still, Arona seemed the place to start searching for Il Generale and his men.

"That sunny afternoon, on a dirt road headed west, Paolo spilled out of his bag a little three button bandoneon. As we walked along, our bellies full, with Umberto's and Paolo's young hopes high, Paolo shouldered his rifle and started to play a dancing tune on his little squeezebox. 'This is my home country,' he said happily.

"Umberto laughed at him. 'We're walking away from there, Paolo,' he said.

"'Well, back there in the Val d'Arno,' he said anyway. 'We're close to my home.'

"'To our home, but were still walking away from it,' Umberto said. Then suddenly, he started to sing to the melody of the bandoneon. They were nonsense syllables, just musical noise, but he followed along with the tune on the little instrument, and surely it was an old country tune from deep in those boys' homeland. It wasn't very long before I joined in, for the melody was sweet and simple, and easy to follow, and so the three of us strutted down the road toward the great lake, singing as we went."

Robbie laughed and rolled back and forth on his knees in some rhythm he heard in his head. "We can do that too," he shouted. "We can sing as we march along."

Jack Burton grinned at my little brother, but he didn't answer. He looked over at the sleepy-headed ape sitting on the stool behind him, and he whispered to him. "Zambutto," he whispered. "La musica."

That was all Burton needed to say, for then Zambutti Sam rose up on his thick haunches and moved almost soundlessly across the floor, walking on all fours, the knuckles of his curled forepaws carrying him gracefully to the door of the tent, where he slipped out through the canvas and into the dark night outside.

Meanwhile, Jack Burton leaned forward in the wheelchair, and went on with his story as if there'd been no interruption. "One morning, as we were approaching the outskirts of Arona on a dusty and rutted road, Paolo was whistling happily, when suddenly Umberto put a hand on both our shoulders and said, 'Listen!' Once we stood still, and Paolo stopped his little tune, we heard clearly the sound of horses and the clatter of arms. Paolo's eyes grew big, and he whispered, 'Austrians.'

"'Or mercenaries,' hissed Umberto, who with the wave of his hand, led us over into the trees, off the side of the road.

"As we moved deeper into the pines, the sounds of the army marching grew louder. We crept up to a high ledge and peeked over it, down into the vale below us. There lay a wide, sandy carriage road heading toward the lake and Arona, and it was filled with soldiers and cavalry and mules pulling ten or twelve pieces of artillery.

"'The Austrians?' I said. 'Ahead of us.'

"Paolo and Umberto didn't respond. We just laid low on the ground and watched the troops march by, and I realized slowly that these troops were wearing the same sky blue uniforms that my two friends had abandoned back in Milano. Then a little fat man on a black charger sporting a lot of silver brocade rode back from the front of the line and shouted some orders to the men with the artillery mules.

"'The Duke,' whispered Paolo, and glanced over at Umberto. He gave just a short nod, and then Paolo whistled his wide-eyed surprise. Umberto silenced him with a glance.

"So we watched as this army marched on into Arona ahead of us. When they'd passed by our brushy ledge, and were out of earshot, I asked my friends, 'Who are they?'"

At that moment, Zambutto Sammy lifted the tent door and lumbered awkwardly back inside, on three legs. Cradled in his left arm like an infant was a bright red octagonal box, closed with straps of red leather and brass buckles. The ape rose up onto his hind legs and waddled like an old woman across the rug laid out on the ground, and then sat down carefully on his stool, before he leaned forward and handed the red and brass box in his paw over to Jack Burton. It was all done so easily, even if it was done awkwardly, and with only the slightest gestures from Burton to direct the mountain gorilla, who gave out an occasional small snuff and grunt as he clambered over to his place on the stool. I knew that this was not the first time Zambutti Sam had been sent out for the magic red box.

Burton stopped his story then, and laid the box quietly on the rug at his feet. Zambutti Sam settled onto his stool, and the cloud of smoke drew back over his eyes, and he seemed even more content than before. Skillfully, Burton unlatched the brass buckles and unfolded the box, and before our eyes it turned into a little red bandoneon, with worn brass buttons to match the buckles.

Burton slipped his hands through the leather straps and then gently pulled the instrument open. From it streamed a wheezing high chord, not loud but intense. In the next moment we heard the clicking of the buttons and saw Burton's fingers fly, and an old melody ushered out in to the circus night, and filled the tent with the sounds of far away and distant lands beyond broad seas filled with uncertain wayfarers and warriors for long lost causes. The music poured easily into our open ears and then filled our two hearts beating with longing and wanderlust. It was magic, even though it was simple.

Somewhere, in the midst of this forlorn little song, Burton began to speak again, and now he was accompanying his story with the strains of the bandoneon. "This, my boys, this is the little squeeze box that belonged to Paolo, indeed. Whenever I remember he and Umberto and those days, I need to pull this out and play the old tunes he taught me around the fires at night. And the song that he and Umberto sang that day at Arona, it was like this one, as best as I can remember, lads. As best as I can remember." Zambutti Sam sighed loudly, contentedly, and the ape settled over on his side, resting on one of those great long forearms of his, and I saw the beast close his eyes. I think he went to sleep, happy at the sound of Jack Burton's voice, and at the familiar strains of the red and brass bandoneon.

"Who were they?" I asked, still in my mind's eye somewhere on a ledge in the brush above a dirt road that led into Arona, near the shores of Lago Maggiore.

"It was the Duke of Genova, leading an army of that vile surrendered King, Carlo Alberto of Sardinia. This is what Umberto told me, after they had marched on past us and entered Arona.

"But I was confused, lads. 'Why don't we go join them,' I said happy as a fool. We had found our way to the fight at last, I thought. 'They are with us!' I nearly shouted, 'and maybe they know where we can catch up with the General, and the Anzani Legion.'

"Paolo and Umberto looked at one another, and I said to them, "What is it?'

"'Burtoni,' Paolo said, eyes wide. 'We are deserters. You forget.'

"'Oh,' I muttered, and then I was about to object, because after all everyone had deserted from the fields of Custozza.

"But Umberto didn't let me go on. He led us quietly into town, after the troops, and he reminded us that the King had signed an armistice. And he was right, lads, because that night we drank wine at an inn and with the vino came the truth from the soldiers of the Duke. You see, O ragazzi, the Duke had been sent by old Carlo Alberto, who was his brother, to arrest our General, and to bring in the renegades of Anzani, all of them under their new treaty with the Austrians. They were not only cowards, ragazzi, they were traitors. The bunch of them. Traitors. They'd run from the Austrian Hussars, and now they had turned and were marching on their own heroes."

"Did they get him?" said Robbie, sounding a bit breathless.

"Oh, hell no, lads," shouted Burton. "Hell no. The Anzani Legion was long gone ahead of us, and in fact we learned that night of their victory across the Lago to the north. At Luino, just two days before, the Legion had been attacked by a detachment of 700 Croats, and the General and his men had sent them fleeing away, and then they sailed off across the lake with 33 Croat prisoners, besides.

"The word had already traveled back to Arona, and the Duke's soldiers were worried. They were angry at this forced march, and they were angry at the Anzani Legion, roaming wild through the lands around Lago Maggiore. And now, with the word of the Croats' hard defeat, they were afraid of the General and his renegades, too. Traitors, filled with fears.

"So we understood, quickly, that Arona was no place for three young soldiers trying to join up with the Anzani Legion. It was no longer safe to be secreting a red shirt around in your pack, especially one that had belonged to old Francesco Anzani himself, and one that was meant to be given to our General.

"'What do we do now?' said Paolo as we were settling in to sleep on a hillside outside of town, still warmed by the red wine we'd shared with the soldiers of the Duke.

"'We head north, around the lake and then up along the west shores,' I said.

"'Until, somewhere, we can catch up to the Legion,' Paolo said, his teeth shining in the dark from his grin.

"Umberto, sleeping between us, began to snore open mouthed. Umberto was one of those lads who sleeps hard on a bellyful of wine, boys. Paolo gave him a poke in the ribs and it startled him. 'Heah!' he grunted, and then flopped over on his side. 'Get some sleep,' he muttered crankily.

"Paolo's white grin shone on a little longer. 'Buona Notte,' he said, and lay down flat, the wine making him want to talk. 'We'll catch up with them to the north. And then we'll be part of the Anzani Legion.' And he talked some more, but it was to the summer stars, ragazzi, because the wine and the sound of his warm voice chattering on and on, punctuated with the fat snores of Umberto, they carried me sweetly off to sleep."

I let loose with a big yawn, brought on by Burton's story of the sleeping lads, and by the soft wheezing music of Paolo's bandoneon. At the sound of my yawn, Robbie jerked around and stared at me, furiously. He whispered my name, and I nodded my head and sat up straighter. Burton grinned at the two of us, but he never paused in his story. He was back there again himself, enchanted by his own bandoneon playing.

"In the bright dawn we hiked off to the south around the foot of the lake, keeping the waters of Lago Maggiore off to our left almost always in our sight, and with high hopes of at last finding the Legion.

"But they were moving quickly, boys, always a day or so ahead of us, it seemed. It took us two days walking around the lake, before we reached the little town of Algera, and that was where we heard the news. You see, the General had split the Legion in two, because he knew the Duke of Genova was coming at them from the south, and from the northwest the Austrians were marching, a huge army under d'Aspre, to cut off his retreat into Switzerland. He understood that he was caught between their pinchers. So he sent most of the men away, on board their two ships, carrying their prisoners east and south along the lake, and he told them to escape. And when the time was ripe, to be ready to fight.

"And then Il Generale took just 60 of his men and they marched south across the mountains toward Varese. His plan was to be small, to move quickly, and to fight his war in the mountains between Maggiore and Como. I knew these were the men from the Speranza, Aguiar and Captain Gazollo and the others. They were the ones who had the heart of Anzani, beating still in their chests, feeling too much, lads. Feeling too much.

"Umberto looked at Paolo, and he said, 'My friend, we are headed home.' But I didn't understand what they meant.

"'We will catch them there,' Umberto said, with a sharp mod of his head. 'If there is anywhere we can catch up with il Generale, it is there.'

"'We'll take you right to him now,' Paolo said, and skipped a step in the grass as he walked.

"'How can you be so sure?' I said, tired of trudging and feeling the heavy weight of that red shirt stuffed in my pack.

"'Because, Burtoni, we're headed home,' Umberto said, and then Paolo laughed a merry cackle.

"'Home,' he sang, and unpacked this little red bandoneon."

"My two friends hailed from an old medieval town a few miles south of Varese by the Val d'Arno, a village called Morazzone. We reached there in the late afternoon. It was at the end of August. We had spent more than 6 weeks tramping around the countryside between Milano and Torino and Lago Maggiore, living off the good will of strangers and patriots, sleeping under the stars and borrowing a chicken or a rabbit along the way when we needed it, and always with our eyes searching the horizons, gazing off ahead of us into the valleys and behind us on the hillsides, always watching for the foreigner. To put it simply, lads, we were tired. And the sight of the old stone walls and the cobbled streets of Morazzone felt like home to me, so I can only imagine how Paolo and Umberto felt to be home, for true and for real."

Robbie frowned, and he glanced back at me, and over at the napping gorilla. And then he said, protesting quietly, but with a real worry in his voice. "You didn't find them?" he cried incredulously. "You never gave him your Ciccio's shirt?" His outrage overwhelmed his disappointment.

Burton threw his head back and cocked it over to one side, and for a moment he let loose with some wild, dissonant

351

riffs on Paolo's bandoneon, and Zambutto Sammy stirred from his sleep, and then Burton let the instrument wheeze down to a whisper, and without a smile or a laugh, with nary a wink, he said, "As luck would have it, boys, that is where, at long last, we caught up with them." And his cloudy eyes sparkled as he spoke.

Then he settled back in his wheelchair, and he looked at me, straight into my eyes, before he began again to tell his tale to Robbie, and then the gorilla nestled back into his nap.

"As we climbed up toward little Morazzone, nestled on top of a little hill above the valley, we saw some movements in the evening light on the hillside just below the village. So we slowed down, and it was Umberto who, crouching next to us by an old wall, identified them. 'Croats,' he whispered to Paolo and me.

"'Are you sure?' Paolo protested. 'What would they be doing here?' You could tell, Paolo wanted only to go home, at long last.

"'I don't know,' Umberto muttered. 'I can't be sure.'

"And that was when, up in the village, I saw them, clustered here and there in the narrow streets just above us. The Red Shirts. 'It's the General,' I said, searching frantically with my eyes for the long blond locks of his hair stuffed under that scruffy brown hat of his. 'The Legion,' I said, before I was really sure, but pointing anyway, for I could not see the General.

"'It must be their sentries over there, on the lower slope of the hill' said Umberto.

"'It's not the Croats,' said Paolo. 'It is the lookouts of the Anzani Legion, Umberto.' And at that Paolo rose up on his feet and danced up the wooded hillside toward the little village on the crest of the hill.

"Umberto glanced at me, and then shrugged in agreement, and so we followed Paolo up the hill into Morazzone, though I was too tired to do any dancing, and I think, lads, Umberto still sensed that something was not right." Burton let the bandoneon fall suddenly silent. "We should have known we were walking into the opened jaws of a trap."

"Croats," I muttered, involuntarily.

Burton glanced up at me, his eyes wired with sadness. "The Austrian dogs of d'Aspre," he hissed, and the bandoneon snapped closed with a sigh in his lap.

"We should have known. We should have trusted Umberto's instincts. We could have saved many lives that day, including some of our own," Burton said. "But those boys were young, and they were home. Paolo was dreaming of the warm lights of his village, and Umberto loved his friend too well to stop him. Umberto was too young to know how quickly and how hard and unfairly the end can come. And I was so tired of traveling along, in pursuit of some last wish for my dead Zio. I wanted too badly to find the General, and to fulfill Anzani's last wish, that I let the caution of my years slip away. I acted like a boy as young as I looked. So up the hillside we went, sometimes trudging, sometimes dancing, up into the narrow cobbled streets of Morazzone." Burton gazed up then, first at Robbie, and then over at me. "Remember that name, lads," he said

"Morazzone," Robbie replied.

"Morazzone," I said.

"There were old, medieval houses, all stone and many of them three stories tall. And the narrow streets that wound between them were cobbled, most of them mere passages where two men could not pass one another without both of them turning to the side. For long periods of the day, they were so narrow they lay in shadows and so they were mossy and damp from the spray and the fog that rose from the valley of the Arnetto, the little Arno. Paolo, who was lanky and tall, he wandered along the streets, touching the damp walls on either side of him, whistling another tune.

"I followed him and Umberto up through that maze of streets, and wherever we came upon a cart or a donkey or even a friendly dog, we had to press to the side, to one wall or the other to get past. Still Paolo scurried along, skipping like the boy he still was at heart," and here Burton opened the bandoneon and played that lilting tune again. "And in just moments he led us out into a sunny little piazza, with the wooded hills across the valley rising high all around us, and with a little stream trickling down from the center of the village. There was a well there, with a spring fed trickle curling down through an old stone channel into the valley, with stone pools of fresh water along the way. Around the well spring, that little piazza was filled with people, women and children, the villagers, and standing scattered about among them were the men in their Red Shirts, mixing into the old yellow stone of the piazza. And that is where I saw him.

"He was giving out orders to the Legionnaires around him, trying to keep everything together and quiet, but without much luck. And he was arguing, too, with a tall black haired man in boots and a fine leather vest. 'If you don't give it to us,' he said to the scowling man in the vest, 'you will force us to take it, Signore. And we don't want to take it. We don't want to do things that way.'

"'Threats!' shouted out the man in the vest, and he spat on the stones of the piazza, though carefully not messing up his boots. 'And what do we do when the foreigner comes? Huh? Do we feed them too?'

"'Signore, they won't ask first,' said the General, looking past the man and eyeing the rows of hillsides across the valley. 'They'll just take what they need. And then, Signor Podesta, they'll take what they like. And when they are done with that, they'll take some more.'

"Paolo fairly waltzed his way across the square, slipping past the villagers and the Legionnaires like a child in a crowd, and then he strode directly up to the General. 'Signor Antonio, what is the problem?' Paolo said, loudly enough so we could hear it across the piazza.

"This man called Antonio was shocked at first, and then a big grin brightened his scowling face. 'Paolo,' he said, and then seeing us following him across the stones, 'Umberto! You boys are alive!' he cried out.

"That was when the General saw me. 'Burtoni,' he said quietly, and then more loudly, 'Il piccolo.' And while there was no smile, I felt the warm welcome in his eyes. But he and the Legion were hungry, and he was still negotiating.

"It took only moments for the homecoming of Paolo and Umberto to change everything. And soon we were all eating, sitting on the stones of the piazza, jugs of wine, rounds of bread and pieces of roasted chicken appearing as if from nowhere into the hands of the women and children of Morazzone, as they spread it out amongst us, and as Paolo flitted around the piazza with a bucket of spring water from the well and a dipper, from which we all drank happily.'

"Did you give him the red shirt then?" Robbie squirmed on his knees.

Burton smiled sweetly, and said, "Not yet, piccolo mio. Not yet." The old man paused and his eyes rolled up to the ceiling of the tent then, while he gazed at something deep inside himself. Then he took in a deep breath, and it made me wonder again about the smoke, which had filled his head and made Zambutti Sam so sleepy.

"Umberto, good Umberto, he stood there beside the General, his eyes filled with ardor and courage. Oh if you could have seen him, with his great fire. But I heard a deep voice sing out my name just then, and there was Aguiar, sitting on the little bench beside the well, with his hand dangling down near the cool earthy waters. He waved me over, with a chunk of bread and half a chicken grasped in one big hand.

"And so we shared the chicken and a beaker of red wine, and as the food soaked into me, I realized how truly tired I was, how all the wandering and roaming over these hills on foot or sometimes with a borrowed ride on a cart or a wagon, it had all worn me down. How good it felt to sit still in that little piazza centro of Morazzone on those old stones, and to eat with my old comrades from the Speranza. The comrades I thought I might never see again. But it wasn't long before that mood changed, once we were rested and eating, and all the halloos were over, when Aguiar, with his big hand on my shoulder, asked 'You were there when Francesco died, Burtoni?'

"I nodded yes.

"'Tell me,' Aguiar said, 'was it easy? Did our friend die well?'

"I nodded again. 'He died knowing he would be remembered,' I said. 'He died knowing we would carry his struggle onward.'

"'So Francesco died a happy death,' Aguiar said to the clear waters of the well beneath his dusty boots. I didn't need to say anymore, though I felt the weight of my Ciccio's shirt, like the weight of his soul and his dreams, beside me. The time was coming soon to relieve myself of all that weight. But at that moment, sitting beside my good friend with a pitcher of wine between us, and a full clay beaker in my hand, I was in no hurry to stop watching the gentle waters sparkle under our feet.

"'How many of us are left?' I asked the General's batman, as I gazed lazily around at the scattered red shirts in the piazza. Paolo, over with some young women in the afternoon sun, had pulled out his bandoneon, and his lilting melodies were wafting across the stones like laughter.

"'Just these few men you see here,' Aguiar answered. 'Maybe fifty of us. When we left the lake, il Generale dispersed most of the Legion. He sent them away, to find their homes, and wait until the rising begins again. All of them, except these few men.

"'Most of us,' I said, glancing around at the familiar faces, 'were with him in Montevideo.'

"'All of us, il piccolo,' he said, 'We were all but one or maybe two of us on the Speranza.'

"I took a sip of the strong wine, and gazed around the square at faces I knew from that voyage, wondering as I drank about who was missing, who besides Francesco Anzani was absent, as Paolo's dance drifted across the old stones in the failing light of summer's dusk. But I had a warm, full belly for once, and a good friend in Aguiar at my side, and the General was near at hand. So all was well with the world, just then, it was.

"Until I remembered the men on guard, the men below in the darkening valley. And though I was tired and filled with wine and bread, I remembered them. When Umberto and Paolo and I had arrived, no one was eating. And that meant the guards out there had yet to enjoy the good food and the warm hospitality of Morazzone.

"'I must get Umberto,' I said, as I got up on my tired feet again. 'Come with me, Aguiar.'

"'Where are we going?' he said, but I was already several steps out ahead of him, so I don't think he heard me when I answered.

"'We must feed the guard.'

"In a moment I was beside Umberto, and I put my arm around his shoulders. Aguiar strode up from behind us to stand beside the General.

"'Il Generale mio,' I announced, grinning broadly, and then I looked at Umberto. The late summer light in the piazza had taken on that rare golden shade that only comes for a few moments at dusk. The General looked over at me, and I went on, 'Umberto, we must collect some food for the guard, don't you think? Can we get a few baskets, and a bucket of water? And you and I and Aguiar here, we can take it down to them. Non e' vero?'

"'Down to them?' Aguiar said, frowning.

"'Yes, down in the valley below us,' I pointed to where we'd seen the men moving about in the forest above.

"'Il piccolo,' the General said, a dark and weary shadow crossing his blue eyes. With just a nod of his head, he pointed out to us his guards, in their red blouses, standing in pairs eating and drinking at the mouths of the many narrow entrances to the piazza, and then to where the outer guard should be, deeper in the streets. But those men we'd seen on way up the hillside, there were no red shirts among them

"'What did you see?' Aguiar whispered, his eyes staring out of the piazza then toward the edge of town.

"The General was already scanning the forested hilltops across the valley, the tight wrinkles around his eyes cutting deep as he squinted to see into the distance, searching where I had pointed. 'Get everyone out of this piazza. Now,' he barked, and it sent the three of us running.

"So it was, lads, at that very moment, when those Austrian hounds saw the alarm in our movements, they must have seen too Umberto and I pointing down into the vale, and then they saw the scurry of warning in our steps. For at that very instant, I turned and saw Paolo, the singing bandoneon still in his hands and the pretty dark haired neighbor girls gathered around him, at that very moment I saw him fall to the stones like he'd been struck by lightening. Suddenly, there were bugles blaring, and the pretty hum of that little accordion had vanished, silenced under the shouts and cries of the townspeople all around.

"In just one beat of my heart, I swear, I reached Paolo across that stone piazza as everyone around me ran in every direction at once, but, lads, I reached him only in time to see his blood pouring out all over his face. He was gone, O ragazzi, before I could even touch him. An Austrian bullet had taken him straight in the face, breaking his jaw, and knocked off the back of his skull too. He was screaming, amongst all the other screams, but only for an instant. Because he was gone, that quickly, before I reached him across that little piazza."

Burton snapped the bandoneon in his hands shut then with a sharp slap. It was just a little red octagonal box again. The instrument was gone, and so was all the music. "For some reason, I still don't know why, lads, not even now. I guess I loved him, O ragazzi, I guess I loved him. But I took this little bandoneon out of his still warm, his still too soft hands, and then like everyone else in that piazza, I turned and ran back into the narrow streets."

Burton set the little red instrument down in his lap, and carefully, gently, snapped the leather straps down that held it closed. The sound of the leather sliding into place felt like the rattle of stones on a new grave.

"Once I reached the shadows of Morazzone's narrow streets, I stopped and looked back. The piazza was nearly empty of everything but a few overturned carts, a spilled bucket or two next to bread crusts and wine bottles, and the bodies of the dead. Three of them, and among them lying on his back with his head turned and gazing up at the sky, was Paolo. A few short blocks from me, I saw Umberto with his arm around the shoulders of Signor Antonio, who'd taken a bullet in the thigh, and found it hard to walk. Umberto was helping him into the shadows when the hard silence that followed that first volley of Austrian fire fell across the piazza.

"Out in the center, with his fair locks spread on his shoulders and in his red blouse, the General stood with an arm straight out, pointing down into the forest below at the edge of the village. He was shouting out orders in the silence, standing tall and alone on the stones, as if he could not be touched. But his orders told us to retreat our way back into the forest, into the west, from which we'd all come, his orders disappeared then in the blare of Austrian bugles on the hill, sounding the charge.

"Aguiar was nowhere to be seen, but the General stepped toward me. 'Run,' I cried at him, knowing the Austrians were reloading as I called out. But he strode slowly toward me, stepping unevenly on the old stones, as if he had lost his balance, and I realized something was wrong. I thought he'd been hit, somewhere, because it was clearly not the stones, but a limp that halted his labored steps.

"Still, he kept his head high, and he tried to make it seem that he was just walking on without fear. I crouched down and stuffed this bandoneon in my sack, next to the red shirt of Francesco Anzani."

"The red shirt!" cried Robbie, bouncing up onto his knees. "The red shirt!"

But Burton went on as if he hadn't heard my brother's cries. "I tossed the bag over my shoulder, and ran back out to help the General across the square. He put just one hand on my shoulder, said, 'Il Piccolo,' but refused more help than that. Somehow, we stepped up our pace, and when the next volley of Austrian fire roared up at us, we were nearly into the dark and out of the bright piazza.

"My eyes searched him up and down, looking for blood or at least a tear in his clothing that would show me where the wound was that could hobble him so. But I could find nothing, not a trace, the only sign of his pain was in the hard set of his teeth, bared in a frown under his mustache. It was, still, a miracle that when that second volley of shot blazed through the piazza, we were both untouched. And somehow, through the grace of a power bigger than all of us, we made it into the shadows of Morazzone's alleys.

"'To the forest! To the west!' the General commanded us, over the calls of the enemy bugles. We knew that their charge was rushing up into the village from the east, and like the General, I saw that our only chance was to get through the valley and then fight them off from the safety of the western hills.

"But the General and I were making poor time, limping on the stones of a winding street, just heading toward where the sun had sunk in the high hills, and an early darkness was falling. It was slow, and it was confusing. I began to fear that the Austrians advance would charge up behind us, and the General and I would be captured long before we could reach the safety of the distant hillside. In my heart I decided that it would be better to die there, on the stones of Morazzone, than to let myself be captured.

"But then from out of a side alley, I heard the shouts of Aguiar's deep voice. 'Generale!' he cried, 'Generale!'

"And I shouted, 'Here, Aguiar! Here!' at the top of my voice. There was a loud clopping echoing around the walls and then out of the shadowy streets emerged black Aguiar leading a saddled black horse.

"'Generale,' he cried, and in moments the batsman had his General mounted. And it was true, the General seemed powerful again on his horse, though it took some help from Aguiar to get him up and mounted. The General's arms were strong, but he had trouble now with his legs, and he needed the batsman's help to lift them to the stirrups. I could see there was no sign of a word or a gesture between them, but I noticed Aguiar acted without orders. Clearly he had seen Il Generale hobbled this way before.

"But like I say, lads, once that old sailor was up on horseback, Il Generale seemed transformed. No longer the old salt stumbling on stones. No. He stood the horse with elegance, and with a shake of his head he tossed his blonde locks back like they were some sort of mane. 'To the forest!' he cried, and then he was off at a dash through the narrow streets of the village."

*　　　　*　　　　*

361

I asked, "Where were the foreigners?" remembering the bugles Burton told us had already sounded the charge.

"I think they were afraid of us, lad," Burton said, a quizzical grin on his face. "For at that moment, they could have risen upon us and seized us all, every one of us, trapped us right in that square. It should have been a massacre, lads, I tell you, a slaughter. It should have been the end of the Anzani Legion."

"How could he lead you into such a trap?" I asked, and that brought Burton up short. Even now, years and ages later, Jack Burton didn't like doubting the leadership of his General.

"It was indeed, lad, a great mistake," the old man said, his eyes glaring at me now. "Perhaps one of his greatest mistakes, to lead these men into such narrow and confusing straights. But, you know, O ragazzi, I think he too was tired, and hungry, just like Paolo and Umberto and me. And remember, something was wrong; he was not well.

"But even when we were tired and hungry and sick, and even when they had the superior numbers too, and the moment of surprise, even with all of that, my boys, they still feared us. No, lads, I'm wrong. They feared him. They were waiting for dark, and maybe even then they weren't coming at us at all. If it had not been for Umberto and me, pointing down toward them on the hillside, they may never have charged.

"This is the difference, lads, between mercenaries fighting in foreign lands, for money and spoils, and men who fight for their own freedom.

"But on they did come, and Aguiar and I followed the General at a run through the streets and out into the protection of the trees. With the Austrians invading the square behind us, slowly and too cautiously for their own good. Meanwhile, the General tried to gather his Legion in the forests to the west. But everything around us was a great confusion, lads. The General pointed straight at me and Aguiar, and he ordered us, 'Pull them together on that high ground.' He pointed to the foothills across the valley. Then he slid a saber from the scabbard at his side and sliced the air with it. 'You, and you,' he ordered a pair of men, pointing with the tip of the blade. 'Follow me.'

"And with that he turned the horse and dashed back into the streets of Morazzone, with two men in red blouses, bayonets at the ready, right behind him. With just those two men, and a horse, he moved about those alleys and kept the too cautious mercenaries at bay, while darkness fell. I think, perhaps, some of the residents fired a random shot or two, from one window or another, at the invading dogs. But for better than an hour the Austrians were stopped on the other side of the piazza, halted by three men and a horse, moving about in the dark.

"And all the while, Aguiar and I did as we were ordered. We gathered all the Legion up on the top of a tall wooded hill, across the little vale of Morazzone, and we waited in the dark for the Austrian charge."

Burton paused there a moment, and he turned and set the closed bandoneon on the ground, beside the little chest that held his long pipe and that strange tobacco he smoked, with the red shirt folded carefully and laid on top of it. When his hands were free then, he reached over and stroked the great ape on its brow. Zambutti Sam almost cooed at the touch, and his tiny black eyes took Robbie and me in, before they rested again, devotedly, on his master.

"Aguiar and I split up and moved around in the forest, searching for the men of the Legion who'd been scattered or lost, and sending them as we found them up to the high ground the General had chosen. Almost every member of the Anzani

Legion knew me from our voyage across the Atlantic, and they all knew, of course, the General's batsman, Aguiar. So it was easy to move through the trees, call them out of hiding, and then send them up to the higher ground where we would make our stand, to await the General's orders.

"It all went smoothly, except for one moment. I was pressing my way along a steep cuff covered in underbrush, when out of the darkness I heard a strange voice call out, 'Il Piccolo.'

"'Who are you?' I answered, wondering whom but the General would call me by that name.

"'Here!' the stranger's voice answered.

"'But who are you?' I called out, and slunk lower to the hillside.

"'It is Antonio,' the voice cried. And then he said, 'I have our friend Umberto,' before his voice broke abruptly.

"I crawled over toward the voice through the brush and found them, in a little clearing beneath the low shadows of a great old hemlock tree. It was Signor Antonio, who knew me only by the name he'd heard the General call me. He was on his knees with blood staining all down one of his legs, and his head was bent, and he was weeping. Beneath him, on the soft brown hemlock bows, many seasons old, Umberto was sprawled. But his legs were splayed awry in a twisted position that told me immediately something was wrong.

"'He's gone, the dear child,' said Signor Antonio, through his tears, once he saw me approaching.

"'What happened?' I asked, as I took those twisted legs of the dead boy and turned them back to a more comfortable position.

"'He was hit in the back,' Signor Antonio said, 'just as we came out of via San Angelo. He was helping me, because of my wound.'

"I nodded my head remembering the two of them leaving the piazza.

"'The Austrians shot him in the back,' Signor Antonio said. 'He fell forward on his face, and from that moment his legs were dead. I dragged him down here, il Piccolo, but this was as far as we got. He died here, with me holding his head, just moments ago. He died right here. Just now.'

"And then old Signor Antonio broke down and wept, as I held Umberto's hand, still warm and still relaxed, just as I'd held poor Paolo's hand not an hour before. In that little stretch of time, just sunset of an August evening in the village of Morazzone, they were both gone, like the day's light. They just came home, and then their lives drained suddenly away, and that was all. Once again, I'd grown close to dear friends, and then, as I always do, I outlived them."

Burton stopped, and I watched as he looked from me to my even younger brother, and a deep sadness I could not understand at my young age flashed across his eyes while he watched my brother Robbie squirming on the rug, beside his little backpack, like the restless child he was. "It is my curse, to out live them all,' Burton whispered, and for once he was not speaking to anyone at all. "And I don't understand why," he whispered. He was silent for just a moment longer, before he went on.

"'So Antonio and I, we carried Umberto back up to the hilltop, where the General had ordered us to gather. There didn't seem anything else to do. And it took us a while, because old Antonio was wounded in the leg from an Austrian bullet. But we climbed the steep hillside with Umberto between us, and then we waited with the others for the Austrian charge, and I guess Umberto became, and Paolo too, true members of those last days of the Anzani Legion.

"We buried him, all of us, quickly, and we laid a big stone over his grave, so he could be found again when all this war was done.

"It wasn't long after that, the General and his pair of legionnaires joined us on the hilltop, and then it was approaching midnight before the foreigners came on, charging down out of Morazzone and then up the dark and wooded hillside at us, and all through that night we repulsed them. Over and over again, from different angles and directions, their white coats came up the hill to no avail. And I'm afraid, O ragazzi, in the tumult of that fight, as they came at us and we retreated or we held our ground or we advanced, back and forth across that steep hillside, somewhere in that tumult, Umberto's plain stone was rolled aside or knocked asunder. Because years later, when I returned to old Morazzone, I found Paolo's grave in the churchyard, not far from signor Antonio's. But though I searched that hillside up and down, and I asked everyone I could find who was of an age to know. No one, none of us, ever found the remains of Umberto Trovesi again. He's gone, lads, every trace of him but what is in my heart has disappeared. All, but what is in my heart."

"We will remember him!" Robbie said, earnestly. And it made Burton grin.

"I suppose you will, ragazzo mio," he said. "Perhaps you will."

But the grin on his face quickly disappeared. "When the dawn of that August morning began to break," he went on, "it was obvious to us all that they still held the little village, and now they were setting fire to the buildings on the outskirts of the town. It became clear we could not hold our forest line against them in the broad daylight, when they could bring their artillery to bear.

"And so, quickly the General gathered the men again, and told us to bear north, using the wooded foothills of the rugged landscape as cover, and using the footpaths in the mountains where the foreign army could not follow. So Aguiar helped the General back onto his horse, and we all retreated quietly and quickly away from Morazzone, heading northward around Varese and into the winding trails above the Valganna.

"I rode with Aguiar on his brown mare, clinging to his shirt as the mare's butt bounced me around. And we followed as close as we could to the General. Again, the foolish Austrians, when they saw us retreating, they did not press after us in a concerted charge that would surely have broken our ranks. No, out of fear, and perhaps out of some rebel respect for the Legion itself, they let us slip out of their grasp.

"But the traveling across that difficult ground, avoiding the roads and easy pathways of the Valganna, was hard. And moving as quickly as we could, with some on foot and some on horseback, even as hard as the General tried, we could not keep the Legion together. There were feints and attacks from the Austrians along the way, and our stragglers fell behind us and into the pursuers' hands. But most of all it was the narrow trails and footpaths we used. The landscape made it impossible for the Austrians to come at us as a whole, for an army of their size could not move through that country in any organized way. But it also meant that we could not keep the Anzani Legion together, moving as we did. Our advance guard became separated from our rear, and some of those in the middle were lost, and stragglers fell behind everywhere along the way.

"We traveled all that day and all of the following night, and in the dawn light the General and Aguiar and I rode out into a clearing in the high hills. Below us, over a short plain we could see Ponte Tresa and the waters of Lago Lugano. It was the Swiss border, and the sight of safety. But as the General looked around him, there were barely twenty of us left. The Anzani Legion was straggled all across the mountains above the Valganna, from here all the way back to Morazzone.

"He turned his horse so he could face the few of us left, and he gave us his last orders. 'Men, you have been true to the dream of Francesco. The dream we all of us shared. But the Anzani Legion is no more.'

"There were shouts of 'No' and 'Never' and 'Viva Anzani,' but the General raised a palm and shook it back and forth. He drew in a deep breath and said, 'In a few moments we will cross that border into safety,' and he pointed out at blue waters of the Lake. 'From there, my friends, we must all go our separate ways, and the Legion must vanish into Switzerland. Vanish from this earth, vanish everywhere but in your hearts.

"'Some of you may stay in Switzerland, and some of you may return quietly into Lombardia, or head back to Genova. Some of you may hide with the French.' He said this because, as all of us knew who'd sailed on the Speranza, he was thinking of his Anita and his children in Nice.

"'But wherever you go, you must keep your ear to the ground. Keep your bayonet at hand, and listen for the hoof beats to rise again, and rise again we will, my comrades. For we are beaten now, but we are not vanquished. In our hearts we keep the spirit of Francesco Anzani alive.'

"And so it was, we rode down onto Ponte Tresa and crossed quietly over into Switzerland, and we each went our many ways, to escape, and to await the General's call."

"But what about the red shirt?" Robbie protested.

"Yeah," I added my two bits worth, feeling cheated to have come so far without an end.

Jack Burton smiled, and he gazed over at his shirt on that chest. I thought then he was admiring it, remembering its story. But as the years have passed, I think now that Burton was pondering whether he needed another long draught from that strange pipe inside the chest in order to complete his tale. But the end was close at hand now, and so he charged ahead.

"Once we'd crossed the border and we were safe, Aguiar pulled his horse up, and he whispered quietly to me, 'Stay with him, Burtoni, and I'll go on ahead.' And at that he slipped me down from the back of his brown mare, and looked over at our General.

"'I'll ride ahead, sir, and find us a place,' he announced.

"The General, who seemed distracted, just nodded his head. Aguiar, with a kick of his heels, was off galloping to the north along the lakeshore toward Lugano. I walked alongside the General's horse for a while, as we wandered along behind Aguiar, and then the General seemed to come around, as if he'd been roused from a dream.

"'Il Piccolo,' he said to me, stretching out an arm, 'Com up here, behind me.' And he took his boot out of the stirrup so I could use it to mount the horse.

"With a hoist and a lift I was up and seated behind him on the black horse, and as I settled in, I noticed for the first time the streams of sweat that had run down from under his hat brim and dampened his beard. He was flushed red too and his eyes, now that I was close to him I saw, they were dark and shaded.

"'Let's go,' he said. 'Andiamo, mi' piccolo.'

"And with the horse at a leisurely canter, we followed northward after Aguiar. It was as if now that we had crossed into Switzerland, now that we had left the dream, his dream and Anzani's dream, left it all behind, in the burning alleys of Morazzone, now all of his weariness could come to rest upon him at once.

"And rest it did, lads, because it was not long, a half an hour or so, before the General nearly collapsed and fell from the horse. Now I understood what his batsman was up to, for he knew the General had come to the end of his tether. Aguiar had left me to get his General to the city, but I knew without

369

asking where we were headed. Where ever we could find him a bed, a place to recuperate. This was where Aguiar had gone. To find a hospice for his leader.

"At that moment, as I held him in the saddle and we cantered along, I thought it would be my fate to watch him die too. Anzani, Paolo and Umberto, and all their dreams, and now Il Generale, too.

"But I stiffened my arms and grasped the saddle horn, and I held him up and kicked that horse into a lope. It was the best that I could do, without losing my hold on him and letting him fall to the ground,

"Aguiar was waiting for us, on the road at the outskirts of Lugano, and he led us to an inn by the lake and we took him down from the horse and carried him inside. He was barely conscious, but as he came down from the back of that horse into our arms, he grumbled and moaned at the bending of his knees and anytime we moved his legs. This man who had run and fought and ridden across Lombardia and the Piedmonte, who'd spent hours and hours, if not days, on his feet marching forward, without ever a complaint, with always a grin or a snarl on his face, and a strong word to urge the rest of us on, here he whimpered and moaned at being lifted from his horse, and just bending a knee.

"When we had him down, he looked up at me out of his fever and exhaustion, and he said, 'Il Piccolo,' in recognition. Then he was gone into pain and delirium again.

"The inn Aguiar had found was run by Swiss who had their eyes on the border, and knew who Il Generale was. So they gave him a little room at the rear of the inn with a bed and a chair, and out the window a view of the ice blue lake and the alpine peaks around it.

"And through that first night, as Aguiar and I took turns sitting up with him, I did not believe the General would survive. I was certain he would die before the light of another day. And so I resolved that, somehow, I needed to give him

Ciccio's shirt, before he was gone. He needed to know of Francesco's undying faith in him, even though they had disagreed so fiercely before my Ciccio was gone.

"So I went to my pack and pulled out caro Ciccio's red shirt from where I'd tucked it under Paolo's too silent bandoneon. And as I took it out, I promised myself that for the memory of Umberto and Paolo, I would learn to play that little instrument. I would learn to make it sing, as Paolo had. That would keep something of them alive, as long as I was around." Burton paused, and again his eyes seemed dazed. "As long as I'm around," he repeated.

Then he went straight on with his story. "I held Ciccio's shirt in my lap, waiting and hoping against hope for a moment of clarity in the General's long night. Just one chance, before he too departed from these earthly shores, and sailed off to that other, further foreign land.

"It was in the blackest part of that August night, turning toward the autumn of September, that the General moved his legs in his sleep, and the very pain of them roused him from his deep sleep. With a grimace and a moan, he looked up at me from the pillows, and his dark, shaded eyes seemed confused and lost. I feared he would just plunge back into his delusion, not knowing where he was. But as his eyes lingered on me, he began to smile with recognition. 'Il Piccolo,' he said, as if seeing me there reminded him of where he was, and what causes and struggles we were about. 'Piccolo,' he said again, and he was ready to fall back to his rest.

"'Il Generale,' I said, lest he slip away, 'Il Generale, I have something for you.' And as I said it, I realized how much this scene was like that night when my Zio Francesco had given me this very shirt, and with it the task to deliver it. 'I have something for you,' I repeated. 'It's from Francesco.'

"'Francesco,' he said, confused again for a moment in his illness.

"'Zio Ciccio nostro,' I said.

"His eyes brightened and a little smile grew faintly across his lips. He nodded his head and said, in a whisper, 'Anzani.'

"'My General, on the night my Zio died, he gave this to me,' and I held out the red shirt toward him in the bed. 'He told me that this was my most important task. Ciccio said there would come a time when you would feel betrayed, and all would seem lost. And that I must, above all, give this to you when those defeats rained down upon you.'

"And then I laid the folded red blouse on the General's chest, feeling a deep pride at having at long last fulfilled those final orders from my dying Zio.

"The General seemed confused at first, and he put his hands on the red blouse. His eyes, so dark and dim, gazed at it and he asked, without looking away from the shirt, 'This is not mine?'

"'No, my General,' I said. 'That is our Ciccio's shirt. He ordered me to bring it to you.'

"The General lay there, with both hands resting on that red shirt, and I suppose, lads, he felt in that plain red cloth all the battles across South America it had seen, and all the dangers it had shared with him, at his side, and survived. I don't really know what he felt, my little ragazzi, but I can tell you that his eyes filled with tears, and they ran down his cheeks like the sweat I'd seen on him the day before. 'Francesco,' he said. His old and loyal friend, lads.

"Just then a bird sang in the night, and he raised a hand from the red blouse on his chest, and he said, 'Listen!' I turned and looked out the open window toward the lake, and saw the soft moonlight on its waters.

"'A nightingale?' I said to him, not sure of what I heard.

"But he didn't answer, and in just that moment, I looked back at him, and he was asleep again, or passed down under the fever and exhaustion he suffered."

"Did he die?" Robbie asked, interrupting again.

"No, lad," Burton whispered with a warm smile. "Not that night anyway."

Jack Burton drew in a deep breath, and then he gazed for a moment at me and then at Robbie, and finally he said, "Every three or four hours the Swiss brought soup to him. That first night it was just broth, and then as the days went by, the soups grew thicker and hardier and after a while they came with a crust of bread. And never once, unless it was Aguiar who took care of it on the sly, though I don't know how, never once did I see any money change hands. Those innkeepers never asked for a cent, only for the chance to help bring our General back to life. And slowly, with our care and their good food, he did come back to life."

"What was wrong with him?" I asked.

"Oh, lad, he had in his legs and hips a hard rheumatism, and all the rest of his life, when he tired himself beyond some great extreme, and even when the weather turned, it could cripple him like this.

"Aguiar knew it, and he told me so himself. I think, though the General would never admit to this on his own, I think he suffered that pain all the time, sempre, lads, sempre. But only when he was exhausted or sick did he ever let it show. The rest of the time, in front of us, his men, you would never know he was anything but fit and strong.

"It was a few days later, when he was much stronger, that I came in to relieve Aguiar and take my turn sitting with the General, and Aguiar stood up and walked to the doorway, but he didn't leave the room. The General was now sitting up in bed, and he reached over and patted the seat of a chair next to the bed. 'Il piccolo,' he said, 'sit down here, my young friend.'

"Aguiar stopped and leaned on the doorknob as if he was waiting for something. A grin spread across his face, and the General went on, 'My good batsman here, he has told me all about your journey, trying to catch up with the Legion.

Walking all that way, and finding along the way those two good lads who saved us in Morazzone, and then we left their bones to rest there. He told me all about it, il piccolo. Quite an adventure you've had, little one.'

"I looked over at Aguiar, and he was still grinning like he'd swallowed the last drop of brandy in the last bottle on board. It was true, I'd told him over these last few days in Lugano, waiting for the General to come around, my whole story of starting out alone and then finding Umberto and Paolo. But I wasn't ever planning for him to pass my story on. It was just talk to pass the long nights of watching over il Generale.

"With a nod of his head toward his batsman, the General said, 'Aguiar.' His voice carried that natural authority of an order again, returning to him with his strength hour by hour. The black man needed no more than that to know what was demanded of him. From out of somewhere in the General's gear he retrieved the red shirt and handed it over to il Generale. I thought Aguiar might start to laugh out loud, his grin was so broad. And then came one of the very greatest moments in all my days, ragazzi, maybe even the greatest moment of all.

"'Il piccolo,' the General said, 'you have served us well on this campaign. By delivering this to me, in that my darkest hour, you have fulfilled our dear Ciccio's command, and it has given to me the memory of Francesco's undying heart and eternal faith. As he knew it would, it has restored in me the dream to press on, until my dying breath if need be, to reach our dream.'

"'But now,' the General didn't pause. 'This red shirt has done its task. I do not need it anymore, mio piccolo, for what it means remains in my heart. And so, my young friend, I give it now to you. I am as sure as I can be that Francesco would want you to have it, for you have earned it, il piccolo.' And then he passed on to me that red shirt of Francesco

374

Anzani, folded into my hands.   As I took it from him, he said, 'il piccolo rosso.'

"It was good soldier Aguiar, across the room, who laughed out loud finally, and then he gave me my name, lads. 'Il Rosso,' Aguiar said with a shout.

"'Il Rosso,' the General repeated with a curt nod of his head. The 'piccolo' was gone."

"Il Rosso," Robbie said.

"Il Rosso," I said.

And then we all laughed together.

"So that, little ragazzi, is how I came by my name. "

"Il Rosso," Robbie repeated, with a hush of reverence in his tone.   My little brother's eyes were glowing with excitement. I suppose when Jack Burton had looked at mine, he thought the same thing.

"So where did you go then?" I asked Jack Burton. "When the General got better? The three of you? Where did you go next?"

"Yeah," Robbie said, his head snapping back and forth from me to Burton.   "The General and you and Aguiar. You three!" He didn't need to add, 'just like us!'

"No, no, lads," Burton said.   "It's getting late and it's time to turn in."   Then the old man drew in a monstrous big breath and yawned like an old lion in the afternoon son. "It's time for you lads to head home."

That drew us both up short. "But," I said.

"We're coming with you," Robbie protested. "Just like Aguiar and the General."

"Like Paolo and Umberto," I said.

"O ragazzi," Burton said, giving us both a stern look. "Stop your dreaming, and think, my little ragazzi."

There was a moment's pause, and then Robbie stood up. "We're coming with you," he announced. "I've thought about it."

I guess the remarkable thing is that Jack Burton didn't laugh at us then. His face stayed as stern and serious as the dawn before a battle.

"But, laddies," he said, "think about the plan. I've got a show to do tomorrow night, and the feeding of Jessie the elephant tomorrow afternoon."

"The what?" I said.

"You boys come here tomorrow afternoon, and you'll see. But if you try to hide from your parents for a whole day, why," he shook his head back and forth, worried, "why they'll have the police all over us and, then . . . "

"We'll get caught!" Robbie said, but he pitched his little shoulders back anyway.

"That's right, mi' ragazzo. So you go on home tonight, and you boys sleep in your beds, and never let on to anyone that we talked at all. That you were even here tonight.

"And then tomorrow, at highest noon, meet me here by the big tent, and we'll make our final plans." He leaned forward in his chair, and slowly he glared at Robbie and then at me. His blazing eyes bored through us, and I have to admit, he frightened me. I suppose that was his intention. "Tomorrow. High noon. The Big Top." He pointed a finger at Robbie. "We'll make our plans." Then he pointed it at me. "Now, go." He sank back in his chair. "Go on home, miei ragazzi."

And so Robbie and I trudged back to our house, and crept through that window and crawled back into our beds. But it was a long time that night before we fell asleep. And Robbie kept that knapsack of his packed, and stuffed under his bed, even though it raised one leg off the floor and made the bed wobble when he moved in it.   Still, he fell asleep before I did, and in his sleep I heard him say, "Il Rosso."

At a quarter to noon we were at the door to the Big Top, but so was half our little town. Every kid we knew was there, and a goodly number of adults from town, too. The crowd milled around, kicking at the sand and chatting, and a game of rough and tumble tag had started up around behind the tent.

Jack Burton was nowhere to be seen, so Robbie and I went round to his red Buick, but he wasn't there either. As we poked around at his tent, hoping to find him away from the crowd, we heard a loud snort from the white cart.

"Sammy is in there," I said, and at that Robbie and I went over to the little window where this whole adventure started. But this time there was no need for me to boost my brother up in the air to look in.

"Zambutti Sam!" Robbie called out, his little arms akimbo and his sneakers spread out solid and set in the grass.

We heard a little cough of recognition, and then the gorilla's black face rose up into the barred window.

"Sammy," we shouted.

His small, black eyes were soft and watery, and he gave us a gentle little moan for a hello. It seemed a shame that he was locked up inside there, but I think we both understood that Burton had to keep up the appearance of the wild gorilla for his show, and that an ape like that, strolling around loose in our little town was surely not safe. At worst, someone was likely to take a shot at Sammy out of fear.   At best, some policeman or warden would haul Zambutti Sam away to a zoo, and he'd be lost to Jack Burton forever, and to us too. So we understood why Sammy sat inside his cage during the days. It was all an illusion, just like the way we'd crept back to out beds the night before.

Still I wandered around to the door at the back, and found a little padlock hanging from the latch. But with just a turn of the wrist it fell open, not even locked, just set to look like it was. Robbie and I creaked open the wooden door, framed in steel, and then Sammy came forward to us.

Inside he had his short, curved stool, and the rug that had been the floor to the tent last night, the rug Robbie and I had stretched out on to listen to Burton. It was spread out now over part of the ape's small cage. Part of it was rolled up against the wall. And the little chest was there, tucked carefully beside the stool.

The little room inside the trailer was dark and warm, but it was comfortable. And I noticed for the first time how Burton had pulled the Buick around so Sammy's cart was tucked under one of the big low oaks, so it would be all through the afternoon under a cool heavy shade.

Sammy sat at the edge of the door on his haunches, so that Robbie and then I could stroke his hairy graying brow, just the way we'd seen Burton do the night before. And I noticed then how old the ape seemed, with streaks of gray and white across his head and over his shoulders.

That was when we heard a cheer rise up, and in the midst of it Burton's deep voice calling out, "Avanti!"

It took us only a moment to say goodbye to Zambutti Sam for now, and softly close the door to his cart. I know we didn't think to latch it again, and I'm sure we left that little open padlock lying on the ground. But we heard again Burton calling out, "Andiamo, Jessica, andiamo!" and another cheer went up from the children's voices. And with a dash across the schoolyard, we were back beside the Big Top.

It was quite a sight to see, at least in our little town. Here came the Indian elephant, stepping gingerly and slowly across our schoolyard. And beside her Burton rolled himself along across the grass, one hand on his wheelchair, and in the other he carried a short thick stick with a blunt iron hook on its hand. And ranging around behind the animal all the kids in town, curious enough to get close, but with every step of the elephant, like a nervous swarm of bees, they were slipping and shifting and scurrying off to the side and away.

"Avanti," Burton shouted, "avanti!" And the elephant moved ponderously down the gradual slope of the schoolyard and out onto the paved street. From there, it was easier for Burton to maneuver his chair alongside the animal.

There was another carnie, a young guy in a denim shirt and an open leather vest, who moved along behind the elephant, helping Burton lead her down the street. He carried a short stick too. But he never said a word, and he tried to seem invisible, just part of the swarms of kids. It was clear to me that Jack Burton was part of the show. The spectacle of watching an old man in a wheelchair lead an elephant down the street was clearly part of this display.

The whole deal was advertising for the evening show, of course. A little taste for free of the wonders to be seen beneath the Big Top that very evening, to all who'd pay the fare. And so down the street through our town went Jessica the Indian elephant, with Jack Burton in his wheelchair leading her along.

They came to my father's gas station, and there stood my father beside a big steel washtub, with the gray-green garden hose in his hand. And as we approached, in the lieu of the elephant, Burton rolled himself up, and shook our father's hand. And they both grinned and, I suppose they knew it was good for everybody's business, because they spoke to one another happily, and Robbie and I lay low, off to the side. We were afraid, you see, that if Jack Burton knew that his new chum here was our Pop, that would be the end of our great escape with the circus. So we hung back and hid around the corner of the gas station where the empty pop bottles were stacked in wooden cases. But we couldn't go away entirely.

See, our father was about to water Jessica the elephant. He stood there, in his gas station uniform with its shirt all oil-stained, but with a straw fedora cocked on his head because he knew the photographer from the weekly paper would be there. And he wanted to look good. That straw fedora sported a silk band that was striped cream and dark burgundy. He was not wearing his gas company cap, not this day.

And then, as Jack Burton maneuvered the animal up toward the steel tank, my Pop looked up and his eyes wandered across the swarm of kids, his eyes squinting under the August sun. We knew, instantly, that he was looking for us. He wanted his two boys in that shot on the front page of the weekly, beside the great gray elephant. I grabbed Robbie and dragged him back behind the station, out of sight.

"Hey, I want to see it," Robbie whined.

"We can't let Mr. Burton find out that's our Dad," I said.

Robbie understood the problem immediately. His face settled into a worried scowl, and he looked back up the hill toward the motel where Burton had been thrown out by ol' Mrs. Coogan and where the hoochie-coochie girls were probably still resting on their beds, waiting for some little boy to come by, and then he looked the other way toward Main Street. His nose scrunched up like he smelled something.

"Follow me," he said then, and ran around to the back of the garage, far from the pumps and the watering elephant.

In a moment, I was following him as we climbed up a pair of used tractor tires tilted against the wall, onto a fuel oil tank and then with a shimmy and a leap we pulled ourselves up onto the flat tarred roof of the station. It was warm enough under that August sun that the tar was soft, but not hot enough to be sticky. We ran across it and in a moment we were looking out over the brick ledge at the front of the gas station. Though the roof stank a little of the softened tar, we didn't care, because we were staring down from the big 's' in 'Standard Oil' onto the amazing show below.

There my father had the hose in hand, and Jessica the elephant had her trunk in the tank. She was sucking up a trunk full of water, and then shooting it happily into her mouth. Pop thought he'd be funny, I guess, because he lifted the stream of water from his hose up onto the elephant's back. She let loose a trumpet of delight at that cool water, and all the kids down below us moved back two steps in unison, it seemed. Father was laughing, and he had a big grin on his face, and he used his thumb to jet the water up onto the elephant's dusty, leathery back.

Burton and his carnie friend were looking around, a little nervously at all the kids, I guess because they knew Jessica the elephant better than the rest of us. But our Pop was having himself a time, and I think we were pretty proud of him, right then. It made me wonder why Robbie was so full of running away. This was pretty exciting, and we could still go home at night, you see.

It was getting pretty warm on top of that tar roof, so Robbie laid down on his stomach on the brick ledge, and he lifted his feet up off the black tar. It looked pretty damn cool, and I was thinking about doing the same thing myself, because my feet were getting warm, too.

But right then Jessica the elephant leaned forward and pulled her trunk out of the steel watering tank. Her trunk was, by God, all full and loaded. And she pointed it straight out at my father's chest, as he was laughing and spraying her with water, and with the blast of a bass trombone, she let loose with a whole trunk full of water that hit our Pop on the chest and sat him down onto the seat of his pants right on the concrete driveway. He was drenching wet with water and elephant snot, sitting on his duff in the driveway, that hose still in his hand piping water up in the air like a fountain. And that snazzy straw fedora of his was floating along across the concrete toward Main Street, riding on the run off of oil and elephant snot.

And everyone was laughing. The kids all around, Burton and his carnie pal, and our Pop too, sitting in the puddle under his own fountain. And of course, Robbie and I were laughing too.

Then what happened next, because it all happened at once, happened fast. Robbie was bouncing on his stomach from his laughter, and suddenly he started to slip off the roof. He was going head first, so I grabbed his belt to hang onto him. His arms were flailing out in the air, and he dragged a shower of gravel off the roof ledge, it rattled loudly off the 'S' and then a piece of the bright red letter broke loose and tumbled down toward the concrete driveway below. My feet rose up off the tar roof, and Robbie's weight started to pull me over too, but instinctively, I set my sneakers against that inside wall of the ledge and I fell backwards, back toward the roof. Meanwhile, that heavy red glass from the 's' hit the concrete and shattered with a loud crystalline jangle, and I think I screamed. But somehow, I had gotten Robbie righted and back up balanced on the ledge.

That was when our mother stepped out of the doorway of the station, onto the shattered red letter on the concrete. She looked up and Robbie's eyes met hers. Then her mouth dropped open. I know she yelled out our names, though I don't remember hearing it. I stood up beside my brother and looked down at half of the town looking up at us. But I don't recall the look on Mother's face, or on Pop's. What I saw was Jack Burton, a crooked grin spread all across his lips, and I swear, he winked at me. Or at us. Because then Robbie shoved himself back onto his feet on the tar roof, and he said plainly, calmly to me, "We better get down from here."

He turned crisply and crossed the roof at a run. It took just a leap and a bounce on those old tractor tires, and we were back on solid ground. And on the run again.

At supper that night Robbie and I were expecting the third degree. After nearly falling off the station roof, and breaking that big red sign, we were both sure it meant going to bed early, being grounded for many long, boring summer days, with no deserts for the foreseeable future, if ever again. It was enough to cement our resolve to run away. But what was worst of all, we both knew it was now going to be harder than ever to break out and get to the circus to meet up with Jack Burton. And we feared our dreams of that fine escape were dying fast and sure.

But at the table, though my Mother frowned a lot, Pops was having none of it. He was still full of his adventure with

Jessica the Indian elephant, and so he laughed a lot, and talked about it, telling the story over and over of how it felt to have an elephant hit him with a jet of water. Patting his chest and retailing again with joy how that powerful stream of water and elephant juice had sat him on his tail, he even included Robbie's close call, and the crashing letter 's' in his yarn, as it all grew bigger and funnier the longer and more often he told it. The more he laughed about it all, the more my Mother frowned.

And to top it all off, he leaned forward at one point and pulled out of his pocket a handful of tickets. Fanned out in his hand were four tickets to the circus that very night. "That fellow in the chair," Pops said, 'That circus fellow. Burton. He gave me a pair of these."

"And where did the other two come from?" Mother said, showing no emotion. Which of course, meant the worst.

Pops just smiled, and tried not to look too guilty.

"I'm not going," said Mother.

I glanced furtively over at Robbie, and saw that both our flagging hopes were rising again.

"Oh, come on, Melody," pleaded my Father

It went back and forth like that a couple more times, and then my Mother simply stood up from the table, and without so much as a word, left the room. I was carefully quiet. Robbie wasn't as good.

"Can we go, Dad?" he begged.

My father handed us a couple of the tickets and said, "You boys run ahead. Your Mother," he looked out the doorway of the kitchen where we ate, "and I will catch up with you."

Then he stood, still gazing out the door my Mother had stepped through. And he said. "But be good kids, and clear the table first, do the dishes, before you go. Right?"

I nodded yes, clutching my ticket tightly in my hand.

"You bet," Robbie sang out, way too loudly.

Father left as I was poking Robbie, and telling him to hold it down.

Robbie had his knapsack stuck under the bench seat beneath him, when Jack Burton, dressed in his intense red blouse and with a flat black beret cocked on his head, rolled himself into the single ring of the Big Top. "Maestro Il Rosso," his grandest voice boomed out to the house, "presents to you now, this very evening, the horrifying man-beast from deep in the jungles of highest Zambutti."

And then Shirley and Red, the two hoochie-coochie girls, came striding out into the ring, each of them pulling a red velvet rope, and they were dressed in these green and white sequined swimsuits, I'd call them. The men in the crowd let loose with a wave of whistles and hoots that died very quickly, on the pointed elbows of their wives. Shirley's and Red's faces were all painted up too, and on their heads, braided into the big buns of hair, stood little sequined princess crowns that each sported a tall frilly feather. Shirley's was white, and Red's was green. And of course, they were wearing spiked high heels, sparkling with the same sequins.

Attached to the other end of their red velvet ropes was a stall steel cage, maybe ten feet square and six foot tall. It was draped with a red curtain. This cage, while it was imposing and black, still looked like it was wired together with bailing twine, and it shivered as it rolled across the dirt in the ring.

"Thank you, my lovelies, thank you," boomed Jack Burton, as Shirley and Red laid their ropes on the ground and then retreated to stand just outside the rear corners of the cage. Burton rolled himself around beside the cage, and began to sing out the dangers of "Darkest Africa" and its "deep impenetrable jungles" covering the "long forbidden islands" where he had been lost for years, and where finally he himself had captured "Zambutti Sam, the wild man-beast."

At that, the cage shivered again, and hearing the sound of his name, the mountain gorilla let loose a low, sinister growl. Then as Shirley and Red tugged at something, the red curtain dropped to the ground to reveal Sammy. He bolted from one end of the cage to the other, on all fours, charging toward the crowd and making the people jump in their seats. When he charged toward where Robbie and I sat, I noticed he was wearing make-up, streaks of bright, blood red underneath his eyes and at the corners of his mouth. Whenever he charged toward Shirley or Red, at the corners of the cage, they would scream loud and shrill, and jump away from the bars as if their lives were at risk. After he'd frightened every section of the bleachers, Zambutti Sam retreated back to the rear of the cage, and sat glaring around at us all for a while, as if he was choosing his victim. Once the crowd was quiet and everyone thought Zambutti Sam had settled down, the gorilla rose up on his hind legs for the first time, and then bellowed out some kind of awful rebel yell that he had to have been taught, for it sounded like no human utterance and surely no ape had ever screamed so. And then he beat his chest like a drum. His head lolled back and forth on his neck, and the horrible yell sank down into a vicious snarl, and then the sound of it frightened even me, though only a few hours ago Robbie and I had been stroking Sammy's gray, weathered brow.

Burton rolled himself over to the cage then, and in his hand he unfurled on the ground now a long leather whip. He gave it a snap, and at that sound, Sammy landed again on all fours and charged around and around the cage. Shirley and Red stepped back, as if in fear that this King Kong might drag then into his imprisoned grasp. But Burton cracked the whip on the ground again, and called out, "Zambutti," and now the ape fled back to a far corner of his cage. Then Shirley and Red together opened a door into the pen, and in rolled Burton, the whip coiled in his hand.

It was quite a show from there, as Jack Burton cracked and snapped the whip, and seemed to force the wild beast through a series of puppy dog tricks. Sammy rolled over, he stood on one leg on top of a barrel, he walked on his hands. And of course, there were somersaults and leaps. And at the end, for the finale, Burton was sitting in his chair, both arms in the air, at the front of the cage, begging for applause from the crowd. But Sammy behind him was creeping forward, his ivory fangs bared with some sort of red greasy drool dripping from his mouth, until at precisely the moment when the ape's paws were nearly on him, and the crowd had fallen into a fearsome silence, Red and Shirley together let loose with a timed and terrified pair of screams. At that moment, Burton twisted, and turned his wheelchair to the side, twirling it up onto just one wheel for a moment. And the ape went somersaulting across the dirt floor right where the old man's wheelchair had been, while Burton rolled himself agilely out of the ape's grasp and then out of the cage, as the two hoochie-coochie beauties opened the gate for him and slammed it behind his chair, amidst peals of delighted laughter from the crowd.

And so, as Sammy charged around the cage in melodramatic anger, Burton took his bows, almost rising out of his chair, and the two girls raised the red curtain up again. Strutting like TV bathing beauties on the runway, they picked up the red velvet ropes and pulled the snarling Sammy away, hidden behind the curtain, locked in his cage.

In a moment, Burton was gone, and a sad hobo clown was sweeping up the dirt floor where Sammy's cage had been. The clown chased a brown clog of dirt the size of a hotdog around the ring. He'd step near it, and then wrinkle his nose up into an amazing prune face for the crowd. It had to be a stinking chunk that poor Zambutti Sam had left behind. Or so they would have us believe.

How Robbie and I laughed and laughed at the clown, and his little stinking mess. Wherever he swept it, it hopped like a bug away from him. A couple of times, it popped up in the air. Once it seemed to be headed flying straight into the crowd, and everyone was laughing, pushing and shoving to get out of its way. Finally the silent clown tossed a bucket of water at the clever little heap of dung, and that seemed to dampen its wings.

So he pulled out a giant purple dustpan out of his baggy pants, and held just a tiny little paint brush in his other hand. With a proud nod to the crowd, and a fresh cock of his broken hat, he turned and stooped as he strode toward the mess, at last to do his job and clean it up. But then, at the very last minute, his poor feet in those oversize shoes slipped one way, and though for a moment he caught his balance, the wet mud flew, and still his feet when out from under him in a crazy ballet. So he danced this way and that until, at last, he belly-flopped down onto the ground and right on top of Zambutti Sam's little mess. Robbie and I laughed so hard that little brother nearly slipped off the bench and fell down though the bleachers.

When the clown stood up, a huge red frown on his white face, the whole front of him was muddy brown, or worse. His nose wrinkled up in that big brown prune face again, and as he looked forlornly up at us, the lights went down and we were all plunged into the blackest darkness.

It was only a moment before the lights came back up, but our clown was gone. The ring was empty, and a blare of trumpets announced the entrance of Jessica the elephant. The carnie in the leather vest was there, leading her into the ring, but he was in a royal blue tuxedo now. "Ladies and

Gentlemen, Signori e Signore, enter the massive pachyderm," he announced over the sounding horns. And up on Jessica's back rode Shirley and Red, still in their little red and green swimsuits, except now their midriffs were bare, and in their naked navels sparkled something I was sure were diamonds. Jessica stepped slowly into the ring, and the two girls leapt from its back onto the ground on either side of the elephant. And Shirley and Red, with their tops jiggling as if they might come loose, my eyes couldn't decide which one of those diamond navels to watch.

But at that instant, Robbie poked me in the ribs. "What?" I complained, but I said no more.

Robbie pointed down to the main entrance of the tent, and there were Father and Mother. He was sporting his straw fedora again, though it was a bit stained and dusty from the afternoon, and she was wearing a black frown. Pop was looking this way and that in the crowd, searching for us.

"Let's go find Mr. Burton," Robbie whispered, as he slouched down and put his two hands on his little pack.

I wasn't so sure I wanted to miss more of the show, what with Shirley and Red losing clothing with each succeeding act, but I was still game for the fun. So Robbie and I slipped down through the risers, and crawled beneath them and out under the canvas wall of the big tent. I knew then, as I remember it now, I wasn't so determined to run away as Robbie was, but I did come along with him. Maybe it was to keep him safe. Maybe just to see what would happen. All I had was a spare pair of Connies and a summer jacket in my bag, and I hadn't loaded up any of my valuables the way Robbie had. In that khaki green pack of his, he had his four favorite toy soldiers, and a red toy motorcycle, and his little telescope for peering at the stars. But I hadn't even brought my Bob Gibson baseball card, so I guess I have to admit I wasn't really planning on going anywhere. I was just along for the ride.

So, with one last glance back through the bleachers at the diamond navels of Shirley and Red, I crawled out under the canvas. Robbie was already up and gone by the time I stood up outside the Big Top. I looked both ways, but there was no sign of my little brother. So at a walk, rather than a run, I headed for where I knew he had gone.

He was standing under that oak tree, the backpack strapped tight on his back, his feet planted square on the ground, but his head was cast down in dejection. The great red Buick, with the white convertible top, was gone. And so was the white cart, the cage of Zambutti Sam, with its exotic legend on the side: 'Far from the Cape of Lost Hope.' There was nothing but tire tracks and disappointments waiting for us under that oak tree. Jack Burton was gone.

And so, that night Robbie began his search for Jack Burton, Il Rosso, the search that would come to preoccupy both of us from that day to this. That night we wandered all through the town, asking everyone we knew. But most of our little hometown was under the Big Top, ogling at Shirley and Red, amazed at the big circus elephant. They only remembered the way Burton turned his chair on one wheel and escaped the grasp of the wild beast. They knew nothing of his other escape.

"Just another carnie," everyone said when we asked. "They are always here and gone." They said, "Just like a carnie." And the more often than not, they would ask, "Did he steal something from you?"

Perhaps he did. Perhaps he stole our dreams. I know he stole our hearts.

One night about a week later my Father came home from the station for his supper with a story to tell.. He said he was talking with a highway patrolman who'd stopped for a Coke and some peanuts at the station. "This patrolman told me he saw a red Buick, just like that Burton fellow's, speeding along in the night a week or so ago."

Robbie and I held our breath, I'm afraid, trying not to let on. Father had a little glint in his eye as he went on with his yarn. "This patrolman, he swears as that car rolled past him, he saw the monkey driving it. So he flipped on his lights and gave chase, but that big Buick eight just stepped on out, and it was long gone across the state line."

There was a moment of dead quiet, and then my Mother started to laugh. "Artie," she said, "don't be teasing the boys."

It wasn't until a few years had passed, and I'd studied some history in high school, that I realized we'd truly been had.   I went to my little brother, who was still down in the middle grades, and told him it was all a pack of lies.

"It has to be, Robbie," I said. "Add it up. If he was really on the Speranza, then that means he was better than a hundred and twenty years old. Right when we were talking to him."

Robbie nodded yes, but I could tell in some deep part of his heart, it didn't matter. He still believed in Il Rosso. "I know," Robbie said. "It can't be."

"He was lying to us," I said.

But it was a good lie. Because even now, wherever Robbie lands in this big wide world, my brother always lingers awhile. He always looks around for signs of that strange man, and he asks after Jack Burton. Everywhere he goes. He's still in search of the last slight trace of Il Rosso.

And I know now, of course, as does my little brother who searches for Jack Burton still, there is no such thing in the world as an Island Gorilla. Nor is there any place in all the continent of Africa and all her surrounding islands that is called Zambutti. But there was a Zambutti Sam, I swear. I saw the beast with my own eyes and I believed in him, just as my brother did.

There was Zambutti Sam. We saw him.

And so to this day whenever my brother finds something, a scrap of paper, an old circus poster, an old timer's story about an amazing ape, word of it comes straight away to me, always directly to me. Because Robbie knows only I will understand, only I will never laugh at him, only I will respond as quickly as I can, when the word reaches me of some lost trace on the trail of Burton of the Red Shirt.

Beyond Aspromonte
or,
How Burton Survived the Night of the Thirteen Daggers

PROLOGUE

Two weeks ago I received a small packet in the mail from Italy addressed to me, Robert _____. Inside the brown padded envelope were a key, and a blank deposit slip from the central post office in Jesi. There was nothing else within the package. Not a note, not a word, not even an initial. But I recognized the hand which had addressed the outside. It was my brother's writing.

I tried for a few days to find him, calling everyone I knew, and got nowhere. No one had seen or heard from him for weeks, it turns out. But I learned one disturbing piece of news. His research fellowship at M_____ University had been continued, and they were expecting him in the fall, but he had failed to sign up for any classes during the registration period that opened the month before, and his Department Head a certain Dr. John McCabe mentioned that this was "just not like him," when I spoke with him on the phone. I knew that too. If anything, my brother has always been the overly organized one of the two of us. I'm the free agent, which has driven him crazy for years.

So after a long distance call to the Postal Inspector in Jesi, who told me only that "Yes, that is the number to a deposit box in our office," I took a plane to Rome. On the six or seven hour train ride from Termini to Jesi, jet lagged and nearly broke, I realized how angry I was with him. More than once I thought, 'You better be in some trouble, Big Brother. If

this is some prank, you will be in trouble when I find you.'
But then, of course, I felt guilty about those thoughts
immediately. I'd rather be angry with him, and spend a few
days wandering around in Le Marche again, than be as worried
as I am now, having found what I have found.

In Jesi, in the late afternoon, the inspector I spoke with
on the phone, whose name is Umberto Tasso, took me into the
safe. "You must be very worried," he said, as I described my
situation again to him. He took the key and matched it with
his and opened the safe deposit box. Inside was a long grey
drawer, which Inspector Tasso extracted and then he led me to
a little room where I could open the box in privacy. "Signor
Roberto," he said, "let me know if I can be of any further
assistance. My office is there, on the right. I will wait for you,
and then we can lock up."

"Thank you, Inspector," I said as he closed the door to
the little room with dusty gray shades discretely covering all
the windows.

As I opened the lid on the box, there was a dry lump in
my throat. After all we'd been through together, my brother
and I, suddenly I was afraid to see what waited for me inside
that box.

But it was just a red folder, and nothing else. Carefully
tucked inside that red folder was a thick sheaf of plain white
papers. There was a clasp on the upper right hand corner that
held the pages all together, and I remembered that this was
always my left-handed brother's way, to clip pages together
like that. On the paper was his precise neat handwriting,
covering both the front and back of every page. As always, he
was being frugal. But before I began to read, I noticed
something truly disturbing. On the first page, the backside of
the document, his handwriting had dramatically changed. It
was slanted drastically to the left, and the words were
sometimes blended together. In fact, the very last paragraph
was written as if it was one long word, without a break except

at the end of a line, all the letters connected as if his pen never left the page. But he'd gone back then, after the fact, and put the punctuation marks in below the solidly handwritten lines. And then, printing so fiercely they often creased the paper, like he was scratching them on stone, he had made all the appropriate letters capitol. Perhaps what was most disturbing was that all of this, the punctuation, the fervently etched capitols, they were all of them perfectly correct. Even though the story he told was leading him into some intensely complex and convoluted sentence structures, all the punctuation was scrupulously correct.

Here then is what my brother wrote:

"He is on the run," Naguine told me. "As long as I've known him, he has always been on the run."

"But why?" I asked her. "He should be a hero in this country, I would think."

Naguine just stared at me for a long, quiet moment, and then she said, "Signore, do you know this country?"

I found her here outside of Jesi, living alone in an aluminum trailer parked by the train tracks. And her car, Rob, her car, I swear it is an old red Buick with a white soft top just like the one Burton drove back home with the circus. It can't be the same car, not here, not fifteen years later and halfway around the world. But it is his taste, isn't it? It's one of the ways I'm sure that he was here, that this is him again. That bright red Buick convertible pulling a shiny aluminum trailer. It had to be him. Rob, we're on his trail again. And we're getting close this time. I think.

It was easy to find her, even when I didn't know her name. You know, Jesi is not a big town, and it's a little out of the way. So you understand how it goes: I asked around for Burtoni in a few trattorias and coffee bars. He's easy to describe, what with the wheel chair and the red shirt, and the way he can get around. Before long, in a day or two, I had her name and I was looking for a traveler, a woman called Naguine, living completely alone.

In fact, it was all too easy, Rob. Too easy. And that tells me that when you were here, two years ago, Burton was here too. I think this is true, Rob. When you came straight up here from Siracusa, with Sister Teresa's letter in your back pocket, ignoring that job they wanted you to do in Texas, you found him. By God, Rob, you did it. But Jack Burton didn't want to be found then, Rob. He was here, he may even have seen you, but he didn't want to be found. And so he wasn't.

But he's long gone from Jesi now, I'll tell you, and that is why it was so damn easy for me to find Naguine. She's ready and waiting. She wants to tell his story.

I think it is because, like you and me, she misses him.

She says her name is Naguine, and everyone here calls her that. But this evening before I took her out to dinner (this is one way to get her to talk) I stole a glance into the glove box of the Buick. I was hoping to find Burton's name on the papers, Rob. But instead, I found hers. Her real name, I suppose. She is Sophia Ziegler, and there is a Bologna address under her name.

Naguine says that isn't her name, it is someone else who Burton knows and that this Buick is his car. I don't believe her. For some reason I don't understand yet, Sophia wants to remain invisible to the authorities. She wants to remain unknown, to be Naguine. Perhaps one night, when there has been enough wine at dinner, she'll tell me why.

*   *   *

This old trailer she lives in is tiny, but it is immaculate. Just one spotless room with a bed that folds into the wall and a table that is attached to an opposite wall, and two loose wooden chairs. Naguine survives now by taking in mending, and she does alterations. I think she drives around to all the little markets, from town to town, collecting the piecework and then returning it repaired and altered to her customers on her next round. So the back wall of her little trailer has a steel rod across it, and there hangs her work, all in a row.

Funny thing is, never once in all the time I've spent talking with her, never once has she had a piece of clothing in her hands. It all just hangs there waiting at the rear of the trailer.

I think it is because I came here asking about Burton. It's obvious she misses him, and talking about him brings Burtoni back to us for a while. That's what everyone here calls him, of course, Burtoni.

I think Naguine loves him.

But I don't think that love is returned.

It would be easy to see Burtoni's attraction to her, though. Naguine is a beautiful woman, still, wearing her fifty or so years very well. But we know about Rafaella Sciascia, about Burtoni's great love, lost forever as his heart was, in Sicilia. So I don't think, beautiful though Naguine is, Burton's interest lay in her.

How to describe her? You must come soon to see Naguine for yourself. I'm afraid, my brother, she is irresistible. But perhaps I say too much.

He face is shaped like a heart, with a tiny pointed chin under the wide expanse of her deep brown eyes. He skin is the rich color of an overripe peach, rosy but burnished, and she has a little black mole, just off center of that sweetly pointed chin, and it draws our eyes away from the perfect symmetry of her face. It is all framed by her wild brown hair, highlighted with the deep auburn dye she puts in it, lifting the rosiness of her skin until it seems to glow with its own light.

When she laughs, her eyes begin to spark like struck flint, and she laughs easily and with honest delight. The tears come to her eyes just as quickly, and she is comfortable enough with them to let them slip down her cheeks without wiping them away or trying to hide them. Her voice, when she speaks, has a music all its own, and her Italian is accented with the sounds of other languages I can't identify, so her words draw you in like her eyes.

It is hard to imagine a man who would be invulnerable to her charms. I don't think Burton was, not entirely. Yet there is something else, perhaps a greater attraction than Naguine's own earthly beauty here, something else would draw Burton here, I'm sure.

But I'm getting ahead of myself.

You see, after dark in the late evenings, long after we'd finished eating and we'd drunk away all the wine, and once we are deeply involved in telling our stories about Il Rosso, the great Burtoni, Naguine always does something I know you'll recognize, Rob. From a drawer hidden in the floorboards of the Buick, she extracts a small, carved wooden box. Inside it is her pipe in two pieces, long and thin and ivory, with a tiny bowl like a thimble. When the memories of Burtoni are present enough, and her eyes well up with tears, she fills it with that black brown paste in the box and smokes it, just one pipeful or maybe two. After a while, her damp eyes grow blank and the memories continue.

Though she feels comfortable enough to smoke in front of me, Naguine never offers any of it. Never once. In fact, the way she handles it, she seems to say it is too precious for me to even dare to taste.

But I know you remember the sweet, pungent smoke in the tent by the circus, and Jack Burton and his trained ape imbibing as he spun his stories at us, as we two children looked on and listened.

I believe this is Naguine's true attraction for Jack Burton, the dulcet world of the pipe. This is why Burton with his broken heart, wanders here into the byways of Le Marche. It is not love, but the relief the pipe grants him from living so long with his old soul and all his endless losses.

I suspect, somewhere deep down, Naguine realizes this too. Her Burtoni is a lost and wandering soul, with no real love left in his heart, no room for love, except of course for his love of Rafaella. Forever. And with only the pipe to grant him peace.

Naguine must know, as you and I know, as Sister Teresa knows, how old a soul he is.

"I believe it goes back to Aspromonte, and what happened there," Naguine told me. She was lounging on the bed in the dark one night or another, after she'd smoked a pipeful of her sweet brown tar. She said to me, "But Burtoni doesn't think that. He always says that it was what happened in Castellnotte. Not at Aspromonte."

With a thin waft of smoke drifting before her eyes, she tried to explain to me what Jack Burton believed, and why he was wandering and wandering so. It was what happened at Castellnotte, this is what he believed. "The people down there in Sicily, they have long, long memories," Naguine said to me. "Burtoni believes the picciotti down there are hunting for him, still hunting for him after all these years. And he still fears their black hands."

Naguine exhaled slowly the last of the white smoke she held in her lungs. "But I would say to him, 'Burtoni, how can you be so sure?'" With all the stories he told about what happened in the mountains of Calabria, all his talk about the foolish battle at Aspromonte. "How can you be sure, I would say to him, it's not all about Aspromonte?"

Naguine let her hand rest back on the pillow that night, her rich dark hair surrounding the diamond of her face in the dim light, with the smoke raising clouds behind her eyes, and she told me all about Jack Burton's fears.

"'How can you be sure?' I would ask him. He would only mutter his answer. "Castellnotte, my dear, Castellnotte. This is where it all starts.'" And so, on one night or another, Naguine told me his story.

They were in bed, arguing, because he was haunted by all his memories, until she objected and said to him, "So tell me, Gianni Burtoni, why did the stabbing occur when it did?"

It made him angry that she brought it up, because clearly he didn't want to consider what he knew to be true. 'The third of August,' he muttered, though it bothered him to speak of it.

"One year to the day," Naguine said. All she really wanted to do was embrace him, to hold him until his demons went away. But instead she pressed the point. 'It happened on the first anniversary, exactly to the day, one year after the attack at Aspromonte," she said.

He was silent. He wanted to object, he wanted her to be wrong and he wanted to be angry with her, with the whole world. But what he was, was silent.

"Gianni Burtoni, my dearest," she said to him, and ran her hand along his soft bearded cheek. "You know these people, Gianni. You know how they think, you know how it works. They did not pick that day for nothing. It was no accident."

He didn't answer for the longest time, he just maneuvered himself with those strong arms of his so he was turned away from her. After a while, he just said, "It wasn't only that."

I didn't interrupt Naguine that evening, I only listened and let her journey through the smoke, doing all the talking, though I didn't follow much of what she told me. Still I asked not one question, because I didn't want to stop the flow of words and memories. Before long, in the daylight, I let her tell me what happened at Aspromonte. She spoke easily, and in the afternoon, with no wine or narcotic to help, because she liked this story, because it made a sense to her, a sense that kept Burton safe in the world. It was an explanation, and explanations, whatever else they are, they are a comfort.

The beginning of this story always made Burtoni smile.

"They sent us all home," he would say, with that little, proud grin of his. "After the handshake at Teano, after the General handed over the whole of Southern Italy, from Naples clear to Marsala, after he gave his whole new and free empire to the King from Piedmonte, Vittorio Emmanuele, then they were afraid of us, little Naguine. The Thousand. We were just a ragtag bunch of lads in red shirts carrying the old worn out muskets they gave us, and still they were afraid of us."

Burtoni would stop there and laugh out loud about that. "We'd marched from Marsala to Naples, through Calatafimi and Milazzo and we'd sailed across the straits of Messina, riding on a streak of luck and a lot of little tested courage. But mainly we counted on the cowardice of the Bourbons, and they rarely let us down, girl, rarely.

"So after Teano, Cavour and his boys up north, they were afraid of us. 'On to Roma, and the Pope,' we'd be shouting. We were ready to press forward, and I think, Naguine, they believed that if we took Rome, we might have made the General into our King. That's what Cavour and his clever diplomats were really afraid of, Naguine, they were all afraid of the Generalissimo.

"So after Teano, after the handshake that gave it all over to the King, Vittorio Emanuele and Cavour sent us up north somewhere, to keep us quiet.

"But Corrao and I didn't go. Giovanni said to me, 'They're trying to bury us up there in the snows. I'm a southern lad, Burtoni. I'm not going.'

"So we went back to Palermo, Giovanni Corrao and I, because he knew a place in the Albergheria where we could stay."

Naguine winked at me, then, and said, "That means old Corrado kept a lady back down there." She chuckled at that, but I knew too that Burton must have gone back there hoping to find Rafaella Crisiana again. From reading those old journals of his we were given in Siracusa, I know, he must have been hoping to find his Rafaella, and to make it all right with her. And either Naguine didn't know this, or she didn't want to know it.

They lived in the Albergheria for a year, that time. He worked now and then on fishing boats, and sometimes he sold fish in the Vucciria. Burton did just enough to get by. And old Corrao, he became Dottore Calogero again, and people came to him all the time for his cures and his powders.

I suppose, Rob, that the main part of his 'cures and powders' had a lot to do with that little brown paste both Naguine and Burton kept hidden around them. Don't you think this must have been when Jack Burton discovered the pipe? It was probably his friend Dottore Calogero, a.k.a.

Signor Corrado, or, as history knows him now, General Giovanni Corrao, it was he who introduced Burton to the sweet smoke of that pipe. That was when he started, Rob, to quell the pain already in his heart, to kill the hard memories of all he'd lost.

Naguine told me more, Rob. Burton and Dottore Calogero were waiting down there in Palermo, I think. And the General didn't let them wait for long. Burton claimed that nearly a year passed like that, working and taking life gently in Palermo. But when the heat of the summer came back again, they began to hear rumors of the General's return. There was no Rosalino Pilo now to spread the gossip, so the word wandered out on its own, arriving with every ship that sailed into the port of Palermo, and it came wandering down from the mountains above the Conca d'Oro, where the contadini and the picciotti were waiting too. Il Generale will come, soon, they all kept hearing it on the northern winds. But they didn't know who or what to believe. How could they know?

But then real news came. The General had made a speech, the newspapers said, in Locarno, calling for Rome and Venice to be free. That was the first we heard of it. But even Corrao and Burton believed it then. After all, there was no Pilo out there in the world to make it all up. So they began to wait and to watch and to listen differently to the rumors on the wind.

In Palermo, then, some of the people, the old aristocrats mainly, spoke of separation. Sicilia must be free, she is her own land. In the trattorias at night in the Albergheria, back then, daggers would flash and there were fights in the alley and streets. "Rome and Venice," one side would say. "Free Sicilia," another would yell. And then the blood of brothers would spill on the stones again.

It was the old aristocrats, still sitting on all their land, with all their old estates, and the churchmen too, with all their old influence and their favorites. They used this strife, playing brother against brother, while they sat on all the property, on all their heaps of wealth.

But then, almost like a dream, the General finally did arrive. Burton would always pull himself up taller in his chair to tell Naguine about those days. "O sweet Naguine," he would mutter, "I remember the day well. The 27th of June, it was. He arrived as if from nowhere, Little One, without any warning, like a god descending from the heavens above. Like a mystery from deep in the flowered earth, Naguine. There in the Piazza beside La Martorana he stood, O Naguine, his blonde hair flowing in the breeze, one of this boots up on a stair as if he were ready to rush on the palazzi of the rich, his arm flung out to the growing and cheering crowd. And he was wearing the red shirt again, by god, Naguine, the Red Shirt again."

When Burton told her this the first of many times, he wasn't wearing any shirt at all. He was sitting up in bed, his bare back all hard and brown from the sun, the muscles in his arms tensed with his excitement. But he touched his chest as if he were wearing that red shirt, and it was almost as if Naguine could see it. "Il Generale didn't really need to speak, Naguine. That Red Shirt blazoned again on his back, and his stance on the stairs, poised to leap forward into the future. It didn't matter what he said, Naguine. That Red Shirt said everything that could be said."

To Rome and Venice, was his cry. That was all they heard, and all they needed to hear.

When Corrao and Burton appeared, they were among the first lieutenants at his side. But it was to Burton the General spoke first. Though Corrao was standing right beside him, with an old musket in his hand, the General shouted, "Il Rosso!" and laughing he clasped Burton's hand. The two of them embraced then, and holding him reminded Burton of how small and frail the General truly was, how the years were wearing on him since they'd first sailed the Atlantic together.

410

He was growing old, Burton thought. It was hard to feel it in the frailty of his bones, because when he stood there on the stairs of La Martorana, he seemed so strong and tough, he seemed invincible again and it seemed they would have him forever. But Burton remembered the rheumatism in the General's bones, and the way he'd limped into Lugano and how Burton had nursed him to health again in Switzerland back in '48.

As Naguine spoke of this, she paused and looked away from me then. She said, "The strength in my dear Burtoni seemed to fail and weaken, right at that moment, as he went on talking to me about the General growing old. He said, 'Soon enough we would all see how frail Il Generale was at Aspromonte.'" Then Burton fell silent, and would tell her no more, not until later, when she asked him again on another day, and they argued again, about everything and nothing, and again in the dark of night.

On a different night, when his spirits were higher, when the fire in his eyes returned, Burton told Naguine more. "At first, it was like our ride with Rosalino," he said. There they were, riding across the mountains and the plains of Sicily, gathering men to the General's side as they went. "But, Rosalino is gone now, Naguine, gone like so many others."

"It was different that time, Naguine," Burton would say. This was in the height of the Sicilian summer, and it was hot as hell itself when they rode down out of the Peloritani

Mountains. But in some ways it was easier too, for now the men seemed to sprout up as if out of the earth itself, joining them as they marched along like the harvest from seeds planted the season before.

By the time they reached Catania, they had grown to thousands strong. It was not just the Thousand, no. They were thousands upon thousands, and more were joining them with every day. "To Rome and Venice," was all the cry. "To Rome and Venice." So many of them together, that suddenly the General had a new problem.

"'Once again, as they did two years before, they had the sea to cross. How was he to get an Army of five thousand and more Red Shirts across the Straits of Messina? This was the problem. When they marched into Catania, more than 5,000 strong, the city rejoiced and the crazed celebrations began, the lights of the city burned all night, with bonfires in the streets, and the dancing and singing didn't die down until almost dawn. And all of it because the General had arrived. But there was other news, too. You see, old King Vittorio Emanuele had declared them all outlaws and rebels. And from Genova, General Cialdini was sailing south with sixty battalions of the new Royal Italian Army to stop them. The Army of Italia had launched her ships against them, against the General who had given birth to their country.

It was Giovanni Corrao who told Burton that news, for he had been with the General when that message from the north was delivered. And it was hard news that meant civil war, Italian against Italian, on the battlefield, brother against brother. Suddenly their cries of Roma! and Venezia! seemed shallow indeed, and touched with an evil bitterness.

So there was hesitation, Burton said. It followed hard upon all the rejoicing of their arrival, and that long night of revels behind them. But after a few hours sleep alone in his room the General emerged, his eyes tired and his walk still arthritically stiff. Yet he held his head high. He said to them all, "We must act quickly, my friends! It must be now!" What he meant, Burton told Naguine, was that with General Cialdini bearing down on them, they could not wait and be caught on this side of the Straits. They needed to cross immediately to Calabria, with as many of their 5,000 as they could muster, and as soon as they could. You see, the General never really believed that it would come to civil war. When the confrontation came, when they in their Red Shirts met the battalions of Cialdini on the field, brother would not shoot brother down. The General believed that in their hearts, whatever uniform they wore, they all knew that Rome was their Capitol, and Venice was the home of their hearts.

"Roma o Morte!" the General said to them, to just a few of them in the room. But it became their battle cry. And it drove them on.

"Roma o Morte!" Burton shouted. He cried out that night so many years later, at the memories of Catania, and the crossing to come. But it was into the moonlit shadows of Naguine's bedroom in Le Marche that he cried. "Roma o Morte!"

So in the morning they commandeered two ships lying in the Port of Catania, an Italian frigate who joined them without resistance, and a French merchant marine they took at gunpoint. The old sailor who lay lurking in the General's heart, he showed his salty hand, and he took control of this new, pirated navy. They were a little piecemeal, and yet they were bold. They were the Navy of the Red Shirts of the Italian Republic, they were, by God. Pirates in red shirts, they were.

They filled the two barques with as many men as they would hold, and set sail across the Straits. And they landed at Melito, Burton said, at the same sure place where they had come ashore two years before. "So you see, my dear Little One," Burton whispered to Naguine across the rumpled bed sheets, "almost exactly two years later, we landed at Melito to complete our unfinished task."

Roma o Morte! was on all their lips, as they disembarked and, just as the Thousand had done in '60, they marched straight up into the mountains of Calabria. I suppose there were, then, only two or three thousand of them, for not all of them could make that first crossing in just two ships. But they couldn't wait for the whole force to gather. And they believed that like it had been back in '60, the people would rise up with them and march on with them to Rome, where the people of Rome would hand over the city, while the Pope with his French protectors would flee. But I'm afraid, brother Rob, I'm afraid they were wrong. The General, too. All of them, they were all so wrong. It was the first sign they had that the world was different. It was only a few years later, but everything had changed.

My guess, Rob, it was the priests who got to them. Because you see, they were marching on the Pope this time, and not the Bourbon King of Spain. When they cried out as they marched along, "Roma o Morte!" they meant to take the eternal city right out of the Pope's hands. Burton always believed it was the priests who worked against them then, who hardened the people's hearts into papal stones.

But whoever or whatever it was, they marched up into the mountains with precious few Calabrians joining them. They were moving quickly, because they knew Cialdini was coming for them. For two days and a night, they marched in the summer heat, and with not even a bite to eat. And still no one joined them in any numbers. Almost no one. And only a straggler or two along the way met them, and not even one child ever offered them a tiny taste of food. Not even one.

And so, after that long hungry march across the mountains, the General pulled them up on the broad, high plain at Aspromonte, and there they rested. Some of the Red Shirts roamed out and returned with a few head of sheep. Without wasting a precious shot, they slaughtered and roasted them. And so they ate and rested, but it was food they took, not food given to them, just food needed to feed a tired army before it could ready itself for the march on to the capitol.

And when the marauding soldiers came back with the sheep, they returned with news, too. You see, they all believed in their hearts that the Pope would abandon Rome when they marched within sight of Lazio. But Cialdini had landed his battalions at Napoli, in order to cut them off as they maneuvered to the North. The Italian forces were waiting for them there: Cialdini's sixty battalions.

And yet, there was worse news too. The Royal Army of Calabria was now advancing ahead of Cialdini's men, marching toward them under some colonel named Pallavicino. He led just six or seven battalions toward them now, but he would intercept the Red Shirts in days, if not in hours. He was coming, and he was closing in.

"We will have to meet this Colonel here," the General announced to his assembled officers. And so Corrao and Burton marshaled their positions, and they waited for this man Pallavicino and his little Calabrian battalions. Still they were all sure in the depths of their hearts that the regulars would fail to attack. Certainly these common soldiers would come to, they would awaken, once they faced one another on the field of battle, with the General between them. "Fire not one shot," the General ordered them all in the assembly. "Not one shot!" Then he strolled from one corps to the next corps, shouting out to them all the same simple order.

"Stand your ground. But fire not one shot," he shouted his orders to the men. "Not one shot!"

"Why does Burtoni always call you his 'Little One'?" I asked Naguine.

We were sitting at an open fire outside the silver trailer late on a warm and sultry night. I was pouring some fine verdicchio that we had set beside us in a tub of cool river water, and it's dry sweetness went down well and easy, and I suppose we were deep into the second bottle then. There was nothing but stars and the low firelight, and sometimes in the dark night, Naguine would sing in her deep, warm voice, in a language I couldn't quite place in the world. It seemed to come from everywhere, but always somewhere far away.

She smiled when I asked her that question, and a length of her black hair fell loose across her face, hiding that smile for a moment. When she pushed her hair back the firelight caught her face again, and I could see that her teeth were parted just a little, so the pearl of her smile was nearly a laugh, it was so joyful.

With her head tilted forward toward me, and that pretty mole on her pointed chin, and that nearly laughing grin on her lips, she reached a hand out and touched my wrist. Her touch was warm too, and she seemed—maybe this is just the verdicchio talking—she seemed just a girl. "His little one."

But she didn't really ever laugh. She just held that strange parted smile as she spoke. "My husband was a guitar player," she whispered. Her dark brown eyes caught the firelight and seemed to shine like water in the moonlight. "No," she said. Then her brown gaze looked away from me to somewhere, and I felt the loss. "He was the greatest guitar player of our time," she said, out loud now. "People came from far and wide, from all over the world to hear him. We lived then, our whole family, and three other families, in a camp like this just outside of Paris. And every night he would walk into the city to play in the cafes. When he returned in a taxi in the morning, there was money, oh money galore, in his pockets. And all of us, his family and all the others, I suppose there were thirty or forty of us then, we ate and lived well. We had everything we wanted, anything we desired, and more, all because of his guitar."

Naguine moved over to sit next to me then, as if she was cold, though the night was warm. She put one arm around me, and I nestled into her side, my face burning where her hair touched it. "I know," she said to the fire, "you're wondering why, if we had so much, why we lived in a camp outside of town. But this is how we lived, this is what we loved. My husband's guitar bought us all the freedom to live together, in our own way. This was our dream.

"It all happened back between the wars, in the 20's and 30's, when there were still so many of us around, and we could move around the way we loved to move around, freely. You see, when the leaves started to fall in Paris and the winter winds would begin to blow through Paris, we just packed up our things and wandered down here into Italy. My husband and his guitar were so famous then, we would all stop at Nizza, and he would play there in the casinos and cafes, and when the cold worked its way down and arrived there on the coast of

Provence, we would just pack up our things and drift down to Bari or Capri, or sometimes into Spain, down to Barcelona and then all the way to Valencia, or even Cadiz if the winter was hard. We jut followed the warmth of the sun, and lived on the six strings of his guitar. It was a beautiful life. So easy and so beautiful, it was all a dream."

"But when does Burtoni come into this?" I said, more to keep her soft body close to me than to find out about Jack Burton, even though I wanted to know.

"He came the first time when we were staying in Paris. I think he heard my husband playing in the Can-Can or the Bal Tabarde, I really can't remember which. But dear Burtoni was so intoxicated with the music, Will, he followed my husband all the way home to our camp one morning, after a very long night in the cafes. And we all loved Burtoni in an instant, well, you know how he is. Big and bellowing and full of stories and full to the brim with love. He was gadjo, you know, but he was more like one of us. He was a traveler, too, in his heart if not his blood.

"I think it was partly the way he loved the music. But it was also partly because he didn't have a home. You know, Will, he belongs to the world, not to any place in the world. He moved where he wanted to, or where ever the world sent him.

"It was only later, after my husband died, that I found out he wasn't really like us. No, he was running away, he was moving around to stay invisible. He is different than I am, he just seemed the same to me back then. The life of the road is not the same for everyone.

"What is he running from?" I asked her, forgetting for that moment that the old Nun had sent us here to kill him. But now Naguine was holding my hand in one of hers, and I forgot everything else.

"This is why I'm telling you these stories. Only because you seem to love him too," Naguine said, then she took a sip

418

from the glass of verdicchio in her other hand. "You fool," she added, just a little too late.

"But . . . " I wanted to object to something about this, though I'm not sure now what it was.

Then she rested her hand on my shoulder, and though she is twice my age, I just wanted her to stay there beside me for as long as possible. "Burtoni was younger then, you know. He did not look so old as he does now. But he was new to his wheelchair back then. He didn't get around in it like he can move around now."

"New to the chair?" I said. "But how?" I said.

Naguine ignored me, saying only, "I can't tell you every story at once." She laughed a little then, through those parted teeth and that lovely smile.

I should have objected, I know. I want to know how he wound up in that wheel chair, what happened to him. But you must understand, Naguine was there beside me, and her hair was draped gently over my shoulder, and the firelight and the stars were bright, and the verdicchio was so sweet and dry at once.

She just went on. "So that first morning when he came home to our camp with my husband, when the light rose and it was time to sleep, Burtoni needed help. He was having trouble getting into his chair, from out of the cab they came in. Now he didn't want any help, though my husband and the driver tried to offer him a hand. He pushed them away.

"But his chair rolled a little, and he was going to fall, I thought. So I just ran toward him and braced the chair with all my strength, and Burtoni smiled over at me, lifting himself into it, and said, 'Thank you, my little one.'

"I think he let me help him because I was just a little girl then. I was still a little child, so he looked at me, with my grimaced up face and my shoulders all pressed tight against the back of that chair to hold it steady, with all my slight weight behind it, and Burtoni chuckled as he hoisted himself over into the seat.

"His arms were strong, you know, but not as strong as they are now. He was, like I told you, new to this chair then, and the strength in his arms was not what it has become.

"'Thank you, my little one,' he said, and then he touched my face on the chin. He brushed his big rough thumb gently right here," Naguine touched that pretty dark mole on her chin, the one that draws your eyes to her face and to the dark angles of her eyes.

"Later in the morning, when the music and talk died down and everyone was falling asleep, I held his chair steady again so he could lie down and stretch out on a blanket to sleep under the noonday sun alongside us. You see, our life then was like a dream. 'Good night, my little one,' Burtoni said to me, though it was the middle of his day.

"So ever since I was just a little girl, he has called me his 'little one.' As long as I have known him, no matter how old and drear I grow, I'm always his 'Little One.'"

That was when I made my mistake, Rob. I said, "But you were married."

Naguine stared over at me from under her lifted brows, as if to ask, 'So?'

"How old were you?" I demanded.

"I was ten, maybe eleven then. I'm not really sure, just now."

"What was your husband the guitar player called?" I asked, though she knew I meant to ask her how she could be married and a child at the same time.

Naguine answered my real question, and ignored the one I asked. "Among us, the marriages are always arranged. And they are arranged and set when we are very young. So, yes, I was married when I was nine or so, partly because I was growing up so fast. And mostly because, well, look who was

420

my husband. Any family would like to marry a daughter to a great man like he was. "

I tell you now, Rob, in all of these conversations, over a month's time, never once did she use her husband's name. I think I asked again that night who he was, but that was the last time. I sensed, before long, Rob, that Naguine would not use his name. She would not speak it out loud. Instead she would go around and around awkwardly in her sentences to always just say 'him' or 'he' or at most 'my husband.' I think it is some sort of superstition, Rob, some belief that to say his name aloud would disturb his soul., so I just stopped asking, and let it rest at that.

Naguine laid her head on my shoulder then, and she whispered softly, "We were not married that way you think, you little American fool. No, I was just a little girl, still pure of heart and soul. We were not married, not the way you are thinking, not for several more years. It was not like that." She put all the stress on her last word, and I understood it was the first of her invitations to me. It wouldn't, Rob, be the last.

On another night, sitting together under the Le Marche stars, Naguine went on with Jack Burton's story. Or maybe it all was the same evening, I can't be sure anymore. My brief time with her is all blended and mired in the detritus of my mind. She said to me, "One night, when Burtoni and I were both awake in bed, when he couldn't sleep because of all his memories, and I was stroking his forehead like this and comforting him," Naguine let her gentle fingers flutter through the hair brushing my forehead like a soft breeze. "He told me the rest of what happened at Aspromonte. I suppose because he was still troubled by it.

Burton said to Naguine, "Remember, the General had commanded us, 'Not one shot!' So we waited on the broad plain in the low mountains, as Pallavicino and his six battalions of Royal Troops approached us from the west."

There were so many youngsters with them on that battlefield, on both sides of the field. They were just boys really, who had not seen the fierce action at Milazzo or made the bold charge at Calatafimi, so many who had never even seen a battle before. They were jumpy, and excited, and more than a little afraid, on Pallavicino's side, as on that of the Red Shirts.

You see, after the great triumph of the Thousand, after they'd marched clear from Marsala to Capova, all across the South, after that there were many, many more than a thousand men in Sicily and Calabria who strutted around and claimed to have been with the Thousand. If everyone who ever claimed to march with the Generalissimo back in '59 had really been there at his side, the Red Shirts would have been 100,000 strong.

But what all that really meant is when the General returned to Palermo crying out, "Roma o Morte!" suddenly all the talk stopped. Every braggart and every boy who'd claimed to be among the Thousand, and even the ones who'd only claimed they dreamed of marching with the General, but responsibilities, mothers and sisters and families had held them back, now suddenly they all had to show what they were truly made of. "So you see, dear little Naguine," Burton said to her, "we had thousands of lads on our side of that long plateau at Aspromonte who were both scared to death, and didn't know themselves what they would do when the real fighting, and not the bragging, began."

For Colonel Pallavicino it was probably even worse. More than likely even his veterans in the Royal Army of

Calabria had never seen a moment of action, they'd only seen the parade grounds in Caserta and Benevento. They'd never, most of them, faced oncoming fire, or the charge of anything even a little like a thousand Red Shirts.

Burton stopped there, and his eyes suddenly filled with tears at what he was about to tell her. "I don't think I can go on," he muttered, his head hanging down, his eyes shielded from her gaze. He was in such pain, just within his memories alone, and he whispered their names to himself, "Francesco. Rosalino." Naguine tried to comfort him with an embrace, and with kisses. "All gone," he whispered. "Antonio. Matteo. Gone." She showered him with kisses, and she offered him more than that. Naguine thought that surely she could distract him, but it was no use. He was in real pain, all these many years later. "My lost Rafaella,' he whispered over and over again, his face twisted with regrets. "My lost Rafaella." He kept repeating her name, and then Naguine was afraid for him. She was afraid, and she could tell me no more of his story.

She got up and left my side by the fire then. She stood up without saying another word, and I suspected it was all over for that night. But I sat there anyway, gazing at the dwindling flames alone, drinking the last of the verdicchio. It had grown dark and late, and Jack Burton seemed far, far away and strangely unimportant in the world.

But in a little while Naguine emerged from her silver trailer, and walked silently across the darkness toward me. She wore a scarf now, royal blue with some kind of pattern of deep red and dark green running through it, but I couldn't understand the patterns in the low firelight, and in the way she wore it wrapped around her head like a veil. When she came close, she looked at me blankly, and her eyes were glassy and deep, catching the flames from the ground. She seemed relaxed, and her face in the dim light was a pure olive, without a wrinkle or a crease. In her calm, she seemed younger, nearly a girl again, I suppose, all the worry and care of the years gone now.

She nestled next to me and I put my arm around her, as if to make a refuge she didn't need. But she rested against me anyway.

"I gave him some of this that night," she said, and from out of the folds of that deep blue scarf, she pulled her little wooden box. "And then he was able to tell me the rest of what happened." She set the intricately carved box in her lap, with both her hands around it, safely tucked away from even my touch. She never offered to even open it for me, but I know that she had gone away from me to smoke from it, alone and out of my sight. And this was how she seemed so young that night, how beautiful it made her, that sweet smoke of youth and gentleness.

I knew, even then, that if I asked to share it, to have a try at it, the smallest taste, she would say no and never. "You are young, and you are just playing with it." I knew this is what she would tell me. "It is too powerful for you. It would swallow up a young fool like you. When you are a hundred years old, and you've seen children dying in battle, over causes that don't exist, over lies told about the moon by leaders with wide sincere moonfaced eyes, then you come find me. But now," she would laugh at me, "now you have no use for this. It has only a use for you."

So I didn't say a word that night, I just sat with my arm wrapped around her, and she with her hands folded around the little box, and she seemed young and ageless, and the night could last forever, I dreamed.

"The boy's name was Matteo, if I remember it right. Burtoni told me his story that night, after we smoked and it had cleared and rested his mind.

This Matteo was just a lad, Burton told her. He had a mop of curly brown hair that sprang around his head like a halo. And his hazel green eyes were as bright as his laughter. And his smile, it was broad and flashed easily across his face, and it was filled with his white, crooked teeth, big and sparkling. Burton sighed then as he said, "He was just a lad, my dear Naguine. Only a boy."

Matteo was born up north, around Vignola, where they grow the sweet cherries that made his cheeks so red. He'd joined the Royal Italian Army, as soon as he could lie about his age and get away with it, because he was filled with talk about the General, il Generalissimo, he'd say. But the King and his counselors sent Matteo off to Palermo, to be like a policeman in restless Sicilia. So ironically, though the King had tried to bury his kind, Matteo was in Palermo when the General arrived. Matteo was there to hear him singing out, "Roma o morte!"

Once he heard the General speak that day in the piazza, Matteo deserted. He hung onto just his rifle and his pants, but that was about it, you see. He showed up in Corrao's face, tearing his shirt from off his own back, and demanding of Burton, "Give me the Red Shirt!"

Well, the lad was so sweet and sincere, it was impossible to turn him down. So they got him a shirt and a belt, and soon he was shouting "Roma o Morte!" with the best of them. He was one of the first recruits.

Matteo marched with them all the way across that island. And then on through the three days of hunger to

425

Aspromonte. And so there he stood, on the plateau of Aspromonte, he and a few thousand like him on either side, as Pallavicino's battalions came toward them, and then they began to fire at them.

But the General stood before all of them on that plain, his arms outstretched, and he cried out, "Not a Shot!" And still the Royal battalions came marching forward, and the scattering of fire on the other side began to grow. The General stood in his simple Red Shirt, with his blonde hair tossed back in the breeze, and he kept crying out to them all, to both sides of the lines, "Hold fast!" In his heart, he believed that when the King's battalions charged, they would just be swallowed by an embrace.

"Fraternize," Corrao muttered under his breath, in disbelief. They weren't going to fight. He stood beside Burton, and the General with his arms spread out was just before them, with his back to the enemy, proclaiming with his stance that they were not our enemies, they were all countrymen, they were brothers in arms.

It seemed crazy as Pallavicino's men moved toward them, and I think in some places their line collapsed and the Red Shirts began to fire back. But it was all, for a moment, still scattered and strange, unlike any battle Burton had ever seen. And there they stood, so near to the General, none of them would dare to even raise their arms. "But still, my Little One, Pallavicino and his men kept marching toward us" Burton said. At some point, I think, those young lads in the Royal lines must have been emboldened by the way the Red Shirts stood there so still, bright shining targets not responding, as if they weren't even human.

Burton could see the buttons on their blue uniforms glinting in the sun, and the sweat streaming off the Generalissimo's brow under the August sun, and he thought even then, at that moment, that maybe there were tears welling in his eyes, and not the tears of a General.

426

Matteo, youngster that he was, he could stand it no more. As if in a fit, he broke ranks, with all his heart and his courage overwhelming him, he charged forward a few steps, lifting the fine rifle the King's armorer had given him. But he was pointing it now at the King's men.

Our General moved toward him, his arms out, ordering, "No! Halt!" But at the lifting of his rifle, Matteo began to take on fire. "No!" my General called out. There was a crackle of a dozen guns from the Royal lines, and Matteo went down on his knees. "As the General was reaching for him, I saw what I could not then believe, my Naguine, my sweet Little One," said Burton. "I find it hard to believe this, even now, even a whole lifetime later."

Burton had stood bedside him in the streets of Palermo, he'd ridden with him out of Morazzone and led him to Lugano when he was ill, and he'd charged behind him across the bridges at the fortress of Milazzo. He'd seen him standing tall and fearless, under heavy fire, with bullets and shrapnel hurtling past where the rest of the rebels hid. Though Burton had never thought of it so clearly, not until that moment, I guess he believed the General was free in some powerful way, the General couldn't be touched. The rest of them, all just mortal lads belabored by fear, they could fall and die at his side, or be wounded permanently and vitally, but he, their General, he seemed impervious to it all. He was as untouchable as he was fearless. But Burton was wrong. This belief of his, though nebulous and unclear, was just foolishness. They all were wrong. Aspromonte taught us all that.

Old Jack Burton fell silent for a moment then. He looked up at the heavens above them, though he was lying beside Naguine in her bed. It was as if he was seeing it all happen again in his memory, in ways he couldn't ever escape. Then, just as suddenly as he had ceased speaking, he began again.

"O Naguine, as the General stepped toward the fallen Matteo, trying to lift him, a bullet ripped through the thigh of his pants. I saw it bite, like a pitch of light, and in a blink, the blood was streaming down his pant leg. He never winced, or paused, he just strode forward, hoping I think to pull Matteo back up onto the lad's feet."

It was too late. The General had been hit. His blood, his impossible blood, was staining the ground. And sunny, young Matteo was on his knees in the short grass. And so, the hot burn of anger rose up from Burton's gut, and under the Royal fire, he lifted his Musket, ready to return their fire and to charge at the bastards who threatened to down him, his Generalissimo.

But Giovanni Corrao stood beside him. The same Corrao who had moaned at the order to hold their fire, who had scoffed at the thought of fraternizing with enemy brothers. It was he. Giovanni Corrao saw Burton lifting the musket to his shoulder, and whatever Corrao believed, he followed the General's orders. "Jack!" he said, calling him by his English name. "No, Jack!" he said. It was strange to hear that English word come from him.

Then Corrao reached up with both his hands, and snatched the barrel of Burton's cool musket, pulled it away from him. Burton clung to the musket stock at first, but Giovanni Corrao was stronger than him, by far, and he just pulled the gun away, right out of Burton's grip. But in desperation, in that brief struggle, the gun went off. The force of Corrao's hands jerking it away from the twisted grip of Burton was enough, that he pulled the trigger. "Remember that, Little One," Burton said to Naguine. "It was I who pulled that trigger, Naguine. Not Giovanni. It was not Giovanni Corrao. It was I."

For a moment, then he stood, with his hands in front of himself, empty. Corrao smoothly slipped Burton's musket into his ready grip. And then, like it was a spell, like it was all imagined, a dream, the scattering of fire died away in front of them. Pallavicino's men, at least the men just before them, in the front of the lines, they held their fire. The battlefield all around them fell silent.

Burton confessed to her, "I don't know that it was my shot. It could easily have come from the Royal lines, or some say now it was just a ricochet, from a rock or a tree. I will never know if it was my shot, but I can tell you this, Naguine, it was at that very moment, the exact moment of my shot, that he went down."

The General had leaned over to reach for Matteo on the ground, when the bullet, no, that's not right. When Burton's bullet tore into the General's ankle. This time it was no flesh wound in the thigh, drawing sacred blood. No this time the bullet ripped through all those delicate bones, shattering the ankle like so much thistle and grass, and down the Generalissimo fell.

At first, no one was sure what had happened, in all the excited fray. But the lines of the Red Shirts, and the Royal lines facing them, they all saw one thing. They saw the great, impervious General crumble to the ground, and lay bleeding now in the grass. And they saw Giovanni Corrao standing above him, rifle in hand. The barrel of his gun, they thought, still warm.

This is where all the stories come from. There are some, even now, who will say it was Corrao who brought him down. The tongues, the wagging tongues of Palermo, they whispered and whispered for years, about Corrao and his jealous heart. Corrao, the man who would be general, as if there was need for a general.

And these same nasty, lying tongues are the same who say it was Corrao who shot Rosalino Pilo, up in the hills above Monreale. The same jealous heart, from the street urchin of Alberghia who passed himself off as Doctor Calogero, that lying heart wanted to beat in the chest of a high and powerful General. Corrao was such a one as could not be trusted, because his desire and hunger was so deep in him it was murderous, when he was given a chance. Both times, in the heat of battle, given the opportunity, Corrao could not resist his own murderous envy. It was in his soul, deep in his soul.

"This is what they say, Naguine," Burton told her. "But it is only their disappointment talking, my Little One. It was only their own murderous envy talking."

You see, Rob, Jack Burton was there. He was at both places, he knows what happened at the Monastero, and at Aspromonte. Burton was there, and he can still tell the tale, to set things right, Rob.

Jack Burton was quiet then, sitting and staring at the rumpled sheets on Naguine's bed. She told him, this is why you are running, because of this lie. But he shook his head no.

"Surely some would prefer that I was dead and gone," Burton said, "and then they could tell their tales the way they want them told. But it is not these people who want my head."

430

Burton laughed at the end of his story then, but he would say little more to Naguine that night. Nothing more than a repeated, "I was there." And once, out of nowhere, on the verge of his sleep, he whispered, "It was my shot.

I went searching in a record store in downtown Jesi, and when that was a dead end, I drove into Ancona and went there to the University library. With everything in Italian it was tough, but it was a day by the sea away from the long shadow of Jack Burton's overflowing stories. It was, though, not a day away from Naguine.

You see, my dear brother, her liquid brown eyes have begun to burn their way into my heart, and I'm not sure now, Rob, if I'm still searching for Burton. When Naguine sits besides me, and I long to kiss her pointed, pretty chin, I realize that it is not me she is interested in. With a pain as sharp as a stab wound, I know this is true. She tells me her stories about Jack Burton in order to hold her dear Burtoni close. He has taken over her soul in the same way she has taken in mine. And I listen to her, no longer in search of Burton, Rob, but in order to listen to her voice and too look into her eyes. Burton's crazy stories are gone for me, brother, though I know that is almost sacrilege to say this to you. But it is Naguine I need to know more about, and I search for her now in all the little comments and memories tossed in among the yarns and adventures of Burton.

I keep her talking about Burtoni so that I don't have a reason to go away.

So it was I went to Ancona to find out about Naguine. I went to find out who this husband of hers was, for maybe, when we've exhausted Jack Burton in her life, maybe this musician in her past will give me some reason to stay behind, a reason to sit beside her longer, perhaps for nights on end.

Still Naguine speaks of him only with extreme care, never with a name, always beside some other topic, just faint hints of him on the periphery of her life. She is protecting him, I know, because of some belief in his spirit and its need to rest.

So in Jesi and then in Ancona, I try to search him out, this guitarist with an illustrious past, yet without a name. And in the library I collect a list of famous guitarists. Especially the obscure guitarists. But the greatest players on the continent in the time between the wars, some of them with names that will live forever, like Django and his brother Nin-nin, but there are many of them who never recorded, or left few recordings, like Baro Ferret and Auguste Malha and Oscar Aleman. And others, already forgotten and left to footnotes of arcane reference books and odd inaccurate histories of lost music: The Brothers Garcia, Coco and Matteo and Serrani, or perhaps Poulette Castro. All of them just names left behind in books, listed in silent indexes, with no sound left to be heard.

One of these men, perhaps, is the unnamed husband of Naguine, or Sophia, if that is her true name. Perhaps she is the widow of the great Django, or of Oscar Aleman. But perhaps it was someone else, someone whose name and music is forever lost to the world, gone like the breath of a flower, vanished in the spring breezes left only to the dying memory of

432

a few, only fleeting briefly across a scattering of old and lost minds.

I generated the longest list I could, in that afternoon in the library, and heard in my mind only the strains of all those guitars, like the ashes left behind in their dead fire. It became a reverie, sitting alone in a library carrel, listening in my mind to this music that I hoped had filled the memories of Naguine. Naguine.

"Serrani," she said, looking past me at the dark evening sky. Her brown eyes saw what couldn't be seen. "Serrani. I'd forgotten him," and this brought a smile to her lips, and it wrinkled the sweet point of her chin. "Yes, he could play," she said, then she looked at me, with one eyebrow raised archly. "He was beautiful, too. Serrani. Matteo and Coco were good, but we girls we liked to gaze at Serrani while he played. His little black mustache, and his black, black eyes. And always that Galousies dangling from his lips. Oh, yes, we liked to watch him play."

The names, I thought. So these men were off the list. She spoke their names, and so they were not him, not the musician without a name.

"Problem was," she laughed at her memory, "Serrani knew we all liked to look at him. And that made him dangerous."

Naguine laughed again and hugged me then, delighting in the memory of old nights when she was a girl, and Serrani was a danger, more than she could handle. He would not be a problem now, I thought. The smile on her lips as she held me, the way she cocked her head back when she laughed, I think they could fill me for days on end. I did hug her back, and she lingered a little too long in my embrace for it to be accidental. She was becoming the dangerous one now. At least for me.

When she let go of me, and eased away, I tried to remember the names on my list, but they were all gone. All of them. I could only recall the most famous one of all, the unforgettable one, the maestro. So I said, "Did you hear Django play?"

Naguine looked at me, and her pretty eyes wrinkled almost closed. She pulled away and gazed distantly at me, and then she reached over and touched my cheek with her warm fingertips.

"Why do you want to know all these things?" she said. "All these things about me?" She laughed a bit at that and her fingertips moved down along my cheek until she touched my neck, and played with the collar of my shirt. "I thought you were here to find Signor Burtoni."

I admit it, Rob, I was struck. The warmth of her touch had confused me, and I had nothing more to say. Nothing. And so she went on then, with Jack Burton's story. But it was not because I was pursuing him, not because I had asked her to tell me more. It was because she wanted to continue his story, wanted to conjure him back between us. So we know the rest of this story, Rob, despite me, not because I pursued it in any way. Not past this point.

"'They hauled him down to the port at Scilla,' Burtoni told me." Naguine kept an arm around my waist as she spoke. I felt her warmth. We were inside her wagon, sitting side by side, on the edge of her bed.

"They carried Burton?" I asked, thinking we knew at last something of how he was injured.

"No, the General," Naguine said. "Il Generale's ankle had been shattered by that shot from Burtoni's gun, or from some stray shot, I guess."

He was, as the General always was, fearless and strong. He could no longer stand, and he told the doctors to amputate immediately if they needed to cut at all. But they refused, and after the surrender at Aspromonte, Pallavicino had him carried down in a litter to a ship in the harbor at Scilla.

"I remember it clearly," Burton said to Naguine, and then he pulled himself up straight in his chair as he spoke about it for a long while.

They carried him on board the Duca Di Genova, and from on her decks the Generale pulled himself up onto his feet again and saluted to Cialdini, that bastard. One soldier to another. One the conqueror and creator of Italia, now a prisoner of the country he'd made. The other a little lap dog of the King, a marcher in the courtyard and never on a battlefield. And then Cialdini, the little son of a bitch, he refused to return the General's salute.

"'When Corrao and Burton saw that they realized the royalist generals could not be trusted. They recognized it right away. Right from that moment on the shore at Scilla, they understood it all.

You see, Pallavicino had made promises, when the General surrendered. There were many, many promises made at that surrender. But the General wanted only one thing: amnesty, complete and total for all his army. Amnesty for the Thousand, and especially for those like Matteo who had deserted from the King's army to join the Thousand in their

435

crusade for Rome. Burton and Corrao held him up between them, and his son Menotti rushed to his side, before the General fell onto the litter that carried him down to Scilla and to the prison ships. But before he fell into the King's hands, he addressed us all, leaning then on Menotti's shoulder.

"Lay down your arms, my heroes," the Generale said. "You will not be forgotten by me, O my men, nor punished by your new country for trying to free our capitol, the capitol of our destiny." And so, as they always did, the Red Shirts trusted in his words and followed him as best they could. They all surrendered, and marched in loose order down through the foothills into Scilla. Corrao and Burton, with Matteo along, they followed the General's litter down.

But Giovanni Corrao always kept about him the wits of Dottore Calogero. So at Corrao's lead, they began to fall back to the rear, he and Matteo and Burton. The rest of the Red Shirts, the Thousand and more, they pressed forward to stay close to their wounded General, to follow his litter toward the ships. And ringed around them all were the soldiers of Vittorio Emanuele, the battalions of Pallavicino.

But like a cat with an instinct to stay wild, Corrao held the three of them back to the rear. And then they saw the salute. They saw that pompous ass in a uniform, they saw him turn away and refuse to salute their General.

"See," Corrao said to Burton, "I told you." And so off came his red shirt, and with just a nod of the head from him, Matteo and Burton did the same. At that moment, there was a great "Huzzah!" that rose up from the Thousand and more. The General had saluted his men from the decks of the Duca di Genova, and the whole crowd pressed forward.

And Corrao used the pandemonium of that moment, when the Red Shirts pressed forward toward the ship and Cialdini's army reacted at once with fear. Would that unarmed mass of fiery red swarm onto the Duca di Genova? Swarm over the guns of the King? Their bayonets flashed, and little Pallavicino shouted orders no one could hear.

With just a glance at us, Corrao led Matteo and Burton away. They were bareback now and sweating in the August sun of the Mezzogiorno, and no one seemed to notice as the three quietly slipped away and joined the crowd of onlookers. They became peasants, fieldworkers from the hills, anyone but a soldier of the Thousand.

Burton dropped his red shirt on the ground alongside Corrao's, and later they pilfered a little laundry from a window on their way out of Scilla on foot. But even before that, bareback and sweaty, they looked only like poor Calabrian laborers.

So they stole a little fishing boat, sky blue and lined with strong red edge, and they rowed again across the Strait to Messina. "Where are we going?" Matteo asked once they were out of sight of the lights of Messina. It was only then that Burton noticed what Matteo had done.'

"Palermo," shouted Corrao, "We can hide in Palermo as long as we want."

"Or as long as we need to," Burton answered him.

But that little Matteo, he had with him still, stuck under his arm now, the red shirt the General had given him. He was still carrying it.

"Get rid of it," Corrao told him.

"Never. Not as long as I live."

"Lad, that shirt will be the death of you," ordered Corrao. "I'll get you another one when we reach the Albergheria."

"Never," said Matteo again.

And so there was no point in arguing anymore. In Messina they put their trust in no one, not even their old comrades from their days with Pilo. Not any of them. And Burton fell silent in telling his story, refusing to name any names, as if he was all these years later still protecting some rebels or insurgents. "It was only later," Naguine said to me, and now she glanced away. "I realized it was her. He didn't want to mention her name to me."

"Rafaella Crisiana," I said.

Naguine looked back at me, and her brown black eyes were watery and filled with sadness. She didn't say the name either, but I could see the hurt. All this time, all these years passing, and Burton's love for that woman in Sicily would neither die, nor even grow cold. Not even with her grave between them. And I could see then the pain in Naguine's eyes. Her Burtoni, her last love, perhaps her only love, could never truly love her, he could never give his heart entirely away, for the main part of it always and forever belonged only to "her," to Rafaella in her dusty grave.

It was then, Rob, without a pause, that I reached over and pulled Naguine to me. Her waist was soft and easy, and she came gently into my arms. I meant at first, I think, only to console her, for I felt for her pain, and I felt the long, old pain of Jack Burton too. My gesture was meant to be only an embrace, a consolation. But then, somehow, in some totally unplanned way, our lips met and we kissed.

I think that Naguine, in her heart, was still giving herself over to Burton. It was not me, truly, that she kissed. But at that moment, to me it did not matter.

Because that night everything changed, Rob. I could never go back to where I was, to what I had become. In that long and sudden kiss, my life changed course. The days of grad schools and academic careers, of safety in the groves of the academy melted away, and a different future emerged for me, little brother. I have become a wanderer, Rob. My home, as it is for Naguine, as it is for the great Burtoni himself, it is nowhere. Like a chain of causation, except that of course there is no cause or effect involved, the kiss of Rafaella Crisiana unmoored forever the ancient soul of Jack Burton. And for Naguine, it was Burton's kiss that led her away from the caravan's of her people, and made her a solitary. I know that to her tribe, to her family, his touch, his kiss, his embrace made her unclean, as he was unclean. It made her, at once, powerlessly alone and filled her with the endless power of independence. And when she kissed me, that night, it freed my gypsy soul too. The soul I didn't even know I had.

I know, you are saying to yourself in the midst of this long letter that is supposed to be about Jack Burton, that she is at least twenty years older than I am. Probably more. But I think I'm trying to tell you, Rob, that in searching for that great wanderer Jack Burton of the Red Shirt, Il Rosso of the Thousand, I'm trying to tell you, Rob, I think I have become Jack Burton.

In the morning, we awoke in her trailer, with the covers over us to keep out the morning cold, warm in the warmth of our two bodies. There was no remorse, there was no bashfulness, but instead there was a new closeness, as we shared our nearness to one another, and to the spirit of Burtoni that lingered over us both.

Later in the day, after we had eaten, Naguine sighed distractedly and she muttered, "Poor Matteo. He was as young as you are."

"What do you mean?" I said.

"That boy was executed, you know," Naguine said. Her eyes rested on me, and I believe she might be seeing that young Matteo in me. "They took the Generale and his son and half a dozen more of them off to prison in the North, in Liguria. And Burtoni and Corrao worked their way cautiously across Sicily to Palermo. After a few months, the General was released and allowed to go home to Caprera. But Matteo, he didn't make it to home, or Palermo. He didn't make it anywhere."

"Why?" I said.

"Because he was young, he was still a dreamer," Naguine reached across the table where we sat over black coffee and a few blood red oranges, and she took my hand in hers gently. "He was still an idealist, like you are." She ran her index finger, with its bright red nail, softly across the heel of my palm.

"But what happened to him?"

"Burtoni told it, he said that Matteo just didn't believe anything he'd done was a crime. He was a patriot, he thought. Mostly he was young."

"He was a patriot," I said.

"Yes, he was," Naguine stroked the back of my hand softly then. "But he was also a deserter from the Royal Army, and the leader he followed was in prison for treason. It was then he decided to turn himself in. The young boy turned himself in."

"He did what?"

"That's right. Burtoni and Corrao tried to stop him. They were, the three of them, working their way on foot to Palermo. And they were 'borrowing' a few boats along the northern coast, too. When they were near Spadafora, Matteo up and announced to Burtoni that he was going to turn himself in. He would report in at Milazzo, just ahead. He was not a deserter, he was a hero, Matteo insisted. 'But don't let Giovanni know,' Matteo said.

"So, of course, that's just what Burtoni did. He went straight to Giovanni Corrao and told him what Matteo planned.

"'Stupid kid,' Corrao shouted. 'They'll toss him in jail on some island and throw the keys into the ocean.' If only that was the case. But there was no stopping Matteo, Burtoni told me. He was already gone, in truth.

"'I'm not guilty of anything,' the kid had said. He put on his red shirt again and walked off then, headed back alone for Messina instead of Milazzo, and no one ever saw him again."

"He just disappeared?" I said.

Naguine wrapped her hands around mine as if we were praying together, and pressed them to her chest as if I was a lost child found. "You could say that," she whispered in my ear.

"What happened to him?" I demanded, but I didn't pull my head away from her embrace.

"No one knows for sure," Naguine went on, and gradually her embrace of my hands went slack. "You see, my dreamer, there was around Messina then, in those days right after Aspromonte, when the Generale was locked up in a prison ship still, headed North, there was Major in the Royal Army. His name was Dell'Utri. Silvio Dell'Utri. This Major Dell'Utri in those days before the amnesty came and the Thousand were all freed, before that he rounded up a handful, maybe a dozen or so, of the soldiers who had deserted from the Royal Army to follow Il Generale. Dell'Utri put them up against a church wall, and shot them all dead before a firing squad. Then Major Dell'Utri and his men stripped the bodies clean, and burned their clothing in a red, tall bonfire, while he buried every one of them naked in one mass grave."

"And Matteo?" I said.

Naguine paused, and though neither of us knew this poor boy from the past, it was a long silence. "Burtoni believes Matteo wound up in that unmarked grave, with a dozen others. But he was never seen again. Never."

Naguine took a long sip from her coffee then. I split open a rosy orange with my thumb and peeled it away some, and the dark red juice spilled onto my fingers.

"You know what is even worse? Burtoni said it was the worst that could happen, after that." Naguine looked at the red juice on my hands, watched as I tasted its bitterness with my tongue. "That Major, that man Silvio Dell'Utri, he got away with it. The government in Torino didn't want any more trouble, and people from all over Europe were calling for the General to be freed. So Il Generale was released and went home to recover on his island. And everyone just wanted it all to be over. So the grave was never found, and Major Dell'Utri slipped away to the North. And the whole world just looked the other way."

She took my hand again, and kissed away the sticky juice. I fed her an orange pip red as my blood, and we stopped talking, of Matteo, of Major Dell'Utri, of Burtoni, for a while.

So I know from what Naguine told me, and I think too from things Old Sister Teresa said in Siracusa, and maybe, Rob, from things Burton said that night years and years ago when we were just boys, enchanted in his firelight, I know that he went to live in Palermo. He and Giovanni Corrao lived in the Albergheria quietly for a year. I suppose they took on assumed names. I'm sure they did. Corrao became Dottore Calogero again, I imagine, and he treated the mad and the sick with his hands and his potions, and probably most of all with the smoke from that blackened sweet powder of his. I don't know what Burton called himself, but I suppose there may have been many names. It doesn't matter. It was a dark year of silence and mystery, when Jack Burton labored on fishing boats and on the docks to earn a few lire to live. He and Corrao, or Calogero, tucked themselves away in an alley somewhere, and they just pretended not to exist.

Tonight we are sitting outside, by a blazing fire, under the shadowy hills lined with row upon row of vines filled with verdicchio grapes. I have an arm around Naguine, around her

443

soft, full waist, and I hold her to me. Her body keeps me warmer than the fire. Still she is distant, though I hold her tight. She is in the arms of her Burtoni, I suppose. For earlier, after the sun had long set, when I rose to stack wood on the fire against the damp and cold of the oncoming night, Naguine drew her little box and her pipe from somewhere in the multi-colored blouse she wore, and she lit up two tiny bowls of it, but not for me. Perhaps one of them was for the Burtoni who sat with her in her mind. In just a few, deep swallowed breaths, the black paste was gone, with little or no trace of its scent even in the air. She took them both, without even a glance at me. There was not even a gesture toward sharing it.

We'd had wine, and perhaps I had breathed in a little of her smoke in the air, but before long she lay against me, and her eyes, her wonderful black eyes deep as the Adriatic, were just slits of sleepy shadows, and her head then rested on my shoulder, and all that magical black hair of hers fell around my shoulders and surrounded me.

In that strange, helpless stillness, she began to talk. "He only mentioned her to me once," Naguine said. I didn't say a word, under her spell where I stayed, but I knew she meant Rafaella, the one great love of Jack Burton's long life. "Only once did he talk about her," Naguine said, and I answered with my silence in the faint diminishing night. Naguine filled that night with her voice, telling the story Burton told.

"'That was how they knew,' Burton had said to Naguine and then he hung his head low as he spoke, too. He was filled with deep sadness again. 'I was the one who gave us up to the knives, and those short, bitter blades were meant for me, my Little One. They were meant for me. Not for Giovanni.'

For some foolish reason, Burton got the idea in his head-
-it was just vain, stupid hope—but he thought if he could just
find Rafaella, he could tell her what had happened, and she
would understand, then. She would know how her father died
that day, and most of all, Burton believed she would forgive
him. So he went up to Monreale, where they had made their
vows to one another that night long before. He went up there
on the same night, only two years later. On their anniversary, I
guess I should call it. It made no sense, but he believed he
would find her there, because it was the anniversary, the night,
they pledged their eternal love to one another, the night they
were married in their hearts. So he went back to where they
had promised to love and trust one another forever, believing
somehow she would be there, and believing that promises
would hold true.

Burton went to mass there, under those glorious
mosaics, and in the evening candlelight the hand of the Lord
reached out and engulfed everything and everyone, and he was
filled with his desperate hopes. Afterwards, he walked back in
the moonlight into the cloister, and she was there.

Burton said to her, "Rafaella," and he walked toward
her. He was about to say more, to begin to try to explain how
everything between them had come apart, to explain the death
of her father, and what had happened that day at Castellnotte.
But before he could approach she glanced up, and it was
immediately clear that she had not come there expecting to
find him. "You," was all she said. She didn't say his name,
just that one word of shock and surprise. "You."

And then Burton saw that she wasn't alone. Beside her,
wrapped in the flowing folds of her skirt to keep the child
warm, was a little girl.

Jack Burton bent down on his knees, to be closer to the child, but Rafaella drew the little girl away from him, deeper into her skirts, and the girl, who was fair and rosy white as her mother, was sleepy and bashful, reading instinctively her mother's fears, the little girl hid her face shyly in her two tiny hands.

"Where are you?" Rafaella said. She didn't ask what he was doing there, near the Cloister of Monreale. It was obvious to them both why he was there, but Rafaella didn't want to talk about that.

So Burton told her then about Corrao, and how they were living in the Albergheria., about their jobs and their shifting names, and then he started to try to explain again how her father had died. He managed to say only the first word of it. He said, "Castellnotte.'"

But that was all. Rafaella held up her hand as if toward off a demon, and it stopped him. She didn't want to hear it, not one word of it. For her there was no explaining. It was all too painfully clear. She picked up the little girl and held her away from him, shielding the child with her body, and then she said goodbye.

As she started to walk away, he stopped her by asking, "What's her name?" At first Rafaella didn't respond, and just continued to walk away with her back to him. "What is our daughter's name?" Burton shouted in that vast space beneath the mosaics, with the Creator looking down on us. For he knew, from the moment he saw the child, she was theirs.

Rafaella turned around once, and now she had her hand over the back of the child's head, pressing his daughter's face deep into the fold of her blouse. "She's not yours," Rafaella said flatly.

"What's her name?" he repeated stubbornly.

"Rosalina," she answered, softly, as if not to wake the child. But the girl was wide-awake, squirming to get free, maybe wanting just too look up at Burton, this stranger who

446

upset her mother. Then Rafaella turned again and walked away, out of the church, out of Monreale. Out of the rest of Burton's life. He never saw Rafaella again. Never again.

But he knew only one thing for sure. Rafaella wanted him to believe that this child was the daughter of Rosalina Pilo. She wanted Burton to believe that she and Pilo were lovers. But she had forgotten one thing herself. Burton knew Rosalino Pilo, and loved him like an older brother. Burton was there when Pilo died at San Martino; Burton saw the shot that killed him in his prime, before Rosalino could see the march of the Thousand into his old Palermo. He knew him. And he knew Rafaella, too. It was her father Lombardo who had worn many faces, not Rafaella. And not Pilo.

Naguine said to me, "That child, Rosalina Crisiana, she was his daughter.'

That was when I reached up, Rob, and touched Naguine's cheek with the tips of my fingers. I swept the long black hair back away from her face, and I kissed her on the forehead. I didn't say anything, because I didn't know anything to say. But I could no more comfort her than she could comfort Jack Burton. There was no comfort to be had. Not for any of us, Rob. Not then. And not now.

After a while, Naguine spoke without lifting her head from my shoulder. "Burtoni kept saying to me all that night, 'They wanted me, and I gave him up.' All through that night, he said not a word more about that woman or about his child. Not one more word. I gave him everything I had to give that night. And he took it, my darling Burtoni took it all. But it didn't matter, because still he said, over and over, whenever the night was silent and calm, aloud he spoke and in a whisper too, 'They wanted me, and I gave him up.'"

"He gave up Corrao," I said. Naguine didn't answer at all, but that only meant I understood completely.

Now comes the craziest part, or at least that is what you will think, Rob. I guess even to me, it seems mad. But it didn't seem that way that night, not in any of those days I spent with her. And if things were different, even now, I would do it all again. And maybe the end result would be different. Maybe.

I think, Rob, I'm writing all this to you now to try again to explain it myself. I started out, you know, to report to you what I found here. But now, now it is all different. And I need to know how, even if I can't know why.

It was just a few days later, Naguine and I were strolling along the Esino, enjoying the spring sun blazing on the stream and on the vineyards lining the brown hills above us. The sky was almost a silver blue, and the rows of verdicchio vines were just beginning to show off their budding leaves, while the Esino was running high, full of snow melt and all the signs of life reborn. I was holding her hand, and we were lazy as children without a care or worry, and I proposed to her then.

"This has become my home," I said to her. She smiled but didn't respond. I suppose she thought I meant this valley outside of Jesi, so I tried again. "I don't mean here, in Jesi, Naguine. I meant you."

She stopped walking, but didn't let go of my hand. Her dark eyes were smiling, and she lowered her head a bit, and cocked it to the side, so her long black hair fell over the tip of her shoulder.

"You have become my home," I said, finally.

The silence of her response was unnerving. Though her eyes were filled with fondness, she said nothing. After a few minutes of, for me, endless and nervous quiet, I began to walk along the riverbank again. I was still holding her hand, but it was more like clinging now. So I wove my yarn out into the springtime air, like a fine fabric of dreams spread under that silver blue sky, the way I understood it all. It was intoxicating, as if the vines of verdicchio had filled the air with their sweet, dry liquor. I would become a traveler I said, just like she was, along with her. We would be our own band of gypsies, following the summer sun north into Europe, and letting it lead us with its warmth south in the winter. Free, attached only to one another, we would live easily, wandering from market to bazaar, plying our little trade to get along. But always and everyday, we would be together.

I'm afraid I went on for a long while, sounding more desperate the longer I talked. And realizing as I talked that, unlike her, I had no trade to ply. Still her silence was the answer I didn't want to hear, and so I talked and talked and talked, because if I paused she would have time to tell me that

I belonged somewhere else, back with my schools and colleges, back in my dry and barren studies. Oh, it seemed so frigid then, in the warming light of Le Marche along the banks of the slow, full Esino. But eventually, I ran out of words to say. And still, she had not answered the question I was afraid to ask.

Instead of answering, Naguine told me her story. She stopped walking and sat us both down on a large stone by the water, warmed by the easy afternoon sun.

"My husband was only ill for a little while," she said, holding my hand in her two hands in her lap. "I was still very young, younger even than you, and so I didn't see any signs of it coming at us. We were up above the Padna, near the foot of the Alps, just enjoying the early spring coming on, like it is today here. He even spoke about how we needed to move over to Nizza soon, where he could play and make some money before we traveled back up to Paris for the summer season.

"That afternoon, he just went for a stroll alone, like he often did, to have a smoke beside a creek there, under a tree somewhere. But he came back to the wagon too soon, not having been gone for even an hour. He said he was feeling dizzy, and his forehead was warm from a fever. So he went to bed inside the trailer, at the height of day. It only seemed like a cold coming on. That was all. How could I know?

"In the morning, he didn't get out of bed. He just lay there, not sleeping, but just lying around. In the afternoon, I got him to sit up and eat, and he said he felt better, that maybe

450

he wouldn't catch the cold after all. He asked for his guitar and all the rest of the daylight he played, fast, dancing runs on the strings, he played boleros and czardas, and 'Nuage' and 'Honeysuckle Rose' and 'Blue Drag.' He played alone like that until darkness fell, and then he set his guitar aside. He told me how he'd learned on a six-string banjo when he was a kid, because a guitar was too quiet to be heard in a band, it was only good for rhythm. No one could hear your melodies over the violins and the accordion and the horns. He patted his guitar, it was big as a cello and made of smooth blonde wood, and he told me what I already new, that he'd had this guitar specially made, that is why it was so big, so it was loud enough to be heard, but still sang with the warmth of the wood, and not the bright slap of the skin on a banjo.

"I believe he knew what was happening, and he was saying goodbye to me, and to his music. I began worry him then, about getting him to a doctor, to see what was wrong. He never, never believed in doctors, and he always fought about even going near them. So I should have been suspicious then, about how bad he was feeling, because he agreed with me. Right away, without any arguing. He said in the morning, if he didn't feel any better, we would go to find a doctor in Verona. I should have known right then what he was about. But I was still so young and trusting. What did I know?

"The next morning, of course, he never woke up. By the time the sun rose, he was gone, warm still to my kisses, but gone. We took him in the afternoon to a church near there, and the priest gave him a mass, and there were just all of us in the family then, Gyorgy and Aziz and Giuseppe and their wives, Elena, Emilia and Sofia. And me. That evening we buried him there in the churchyard at Asolo, and then we all went back out to our camp in the countryside. Everyone, the priest especially, was happy to see us go. They wanted it all over fast, and that was fine. It was our way.

"But the next day, that was the time that was truly amazing, Will. That was when I realized how special he was. For us he was dead and buried, and it was time for his spirit to move on, and be free of attachments to us. We never again spoke his name. Never once have I spoken it. But even despite that, among the musicians the word of his death spread with the winds and the breezes. Some of the musicians began to turn up late on the day we buried him, and by noon the next day there was a crowd in our camp. They came from all over, from other camps of the people, you know. But mostly they were gadje. A lot of them came on trains, and some in their motorcars. The famous one's like the violinists Stephane and Stuff who loved him, they came in the long, black motorcars with drivers.

"The Garcia brothers pulled up together in a big Packard, Coco and Matteo with Serrani too in the back seat, with a little gray in his moustache but still turning all the girls' heads. Baro Ferret was there, and August Malha, way up in his eighties then and not long for the world himself, but he came. Poulette Castro and Oscar Aleman came driving down from Paris, together in a swift little Bugati two-seater. The Bugati belonged to Poulette, Oscar told me, a little touch of sad envy in his voice. Not long after them on a little Gilera motorbike, Nin-nin rode in, bringing his apologies. His brother was away in the studios back in Paris, making records with some of the men who played with the Duke, and so he couldn't get away. He couldn't come."

Naguine pressed my hand a little tighter, and looked over my head at the hillsides, and said, "After dark, once we'd started the fire, Burtoni arrived. I don't know from where. He embraced me, and his eyes were red from the tears. How he knew, how they all knew so quickly, it was like magic. As if something was in their bloodstream, they all knew that part of the music had died."

Naguine let go of my hand and she folded her hands together at her waist, and she was about to stand up. But I covered her folded hands with mine, and she stayed sitting beside me. "The music they played that day. It was something. Because you know, it was simple. They were all, every one of them, masters. Virtuosi. But that day, and probably that day alone, there was no showing off. There was no competition. At least, they didn't compete with flourishes and speed. No, it was all simple. And if they competed, it was to see who could put the deepest feeling into every note.

"So they played the afternoon sun away, with hardly a pause, and precious few words, just strains and strains of endless melody, running toward the dark. As the evening came on, we began to build the fire, and the family helped me as we hauled out all of his things, and put them on the pyre. We needed to free his soul from us, from his brothers and sisters and friends, and from me. And even from the musicians, too. So everything he owned, everything that was his, it all went into the flames.

"The last thing of all was the most precious. When the fire was burning at its highest, I brought out his great blonde guitar, and I hurled it into the flames."

Naguine shook her head and laughed then, and hugged herself. There was a fretful frown on her lips that wrinkled up her pretty chin. "It was Burtoni who couldn't take it," she said through her laugh. "But then he wasn't one of us, so he didn't understand. He may be an old soul and a wise one too, but he is still gadjo, so he didn't understand." She paused a moment, and then looked straight into my eyes as if to warn me of these truths. "It's why I am alone. Why I travel by myself now," she said. And those words pierced my heart.

I couldn't ask her more then, for fear of what I'd learn. I realize now I didn't want to understand what she meant. Though I did understand, right at that moment, I didn't want to. So instead I asked about Jack Burton, and not about Naguine.

"What did Burton do?" I said.

"He pulled the guitar from the fire, and held it in his lap. 'We must save this,' he called out to everyone and to no one, and he held that great instrument up before us. 'It was his,' Burtoni said. 'So we can remember him.'"

I knew that Burton must have spoken his name at that point, though Naguine even now carefully left it out.

"It was Nin-nin who took it away from Burtoni," Naguine went on proudly, that wrinkled frown turning to a wistful smile. "Nin-nin took the guitar in his hands, and announced to us all, 'Django could not be here, but instead he told me to bring you this.' And then Nin-nin began to play Django's old tune 'Nocturne' for him, and slowly everyone else joined in."

"Django's 'Nocturne' was composed for your husband?" I said.

"On that day, as everyone played it, it was," Naguine nodded her head as she spoke, as if in the slow rhythm of the song.

"When they were finished, Nin-nin took the guitar and he handed it to me, knowing what I would do. He explained to Burtoni, 'We must let his spirit go, my friend. It is our way," he said, as I put the great blonde guitar back onto the pyre, and slowly it went up in flames. For a long while, as that instrument burned, we were all silent. But when the neck cracked in two from the force of the steel strings on the steel struts, Matteo and Serrani began to play again, and before long everyone joined in. And then the music flowed and flowed all night, until the dawn sent us, one at a time, away to sleep it off by the cooling ashes of the fire."

That was how she said no to me, Rob. I never asked her again. I never tried to object, or to plead my love. Though I wanted, no, that's not right. I still want to ask why, to plead yes, to whisper why not to her. But it has never once come up again between us. Never.

"I kept saying to Burtoni," Naguine told me, a few days later, "it was Aspromonte. It was all revenge for what happened at Aspromonte. That was why Giovanni Corrao died. You know, many people still blame him for that gunshot that felled the General. Many, many of them did."

A week or two had gone by, and I knew now that I would have to leave eventually. But I was searching for ways to stall it off, and Jack Burton's story, Rob, has become my only reason not to say farewell to Naguine. So now, I pursue it like a last thread of hope.

Naguine and I spent days and days as the summer came on, and the iris began to bloom in the gardens of Jesi, and I lingered. I was living with her then, and I know that the time had come and gone for her to move on, to the next market, to deliver the clothes she had mended, to take in more work to be done. I know that Naguine missed several of her appointed rounds then, and I took that in my stupidity as a faint ray of hope. There would be grumbling from her customers later.

But still she lingered with me, and my silly dreams allowed me to fool myself.

But for her it was all about Jack Burton. Talking to me, telling his story, kept Burton alive for her. And so my presence gave her a reason to talk about him. And for me, Burton's story gave me a reason to linger in Naguine's embrace, and to bask in her deflected attentions.

I was sitting on the floor of the trailer, leaning against the bed where Naguine sat, sewing by hand as she altered someone's shirt. She wore a long, brown skirt that reached nearly to the floor, and her feet were bare. Her toenails were painted a red that was nearly as dark and brown as her eyes. My hand was wrapped around her ankle, holding her in that way in the warmth of late afternoon.

"'No,' Burtoni would say to me," Naguine's dark eyes were lowered, as she concentrated on the needle moving deftly in her hands. "'It was me they were after,' he would say, and I couldn't change his mind. He was sure of it. And sure they were still hunting him, too.

"Often he would say, 'Thirteen men died that night in Palermo, including my old comrade, Giovanni Corrao. But it was all for me. All of it. They were searching for me,' he would say. 'They thought they'd found me.'"

"Thirteen men?" I said to Naguine.

She nodded her head, without even glancing up from her needle and thread. "It's still called the Night of Thirteen Daggers, down in Sicily, in Palermo." The point of her chin made the moon shape of her face against her black hair a swift, smooth blade piercing into my heart, as I looked up at her. I embraced her ankle gently in my hand. "You don't know about the Thirteen Daggers?" she never even glanced up from her work, but she kept her foot exposed to my touch.

I said that I hadn't.

With wrinkled concentration furrowing her brow, she worked the fabric around in her hand for a moment, and then she said, still without ever looking at me, "Let me tell it to you the way Burtoni tells it." Though it took her a day or two to tell it all, in the end I pieced it together like this:

The first time that he saw them, he was working as a porter at the train station, at Centrale, Burton told Naguine. He was toting luggage around on a big wooden cart. They were short and dark, and wearing suits that looked like they'd been fitted on them over their peasant clothes, just so they could go to town, and there were three of them. Round heads and black hair oiled back tight, and all of them well short of five feet. With their size and the dark sunburn of their skin, Burton knew they came from the interior, from up in the Madonie. Palermo was no more their home than it was his.

He noticed first the way they were hanging around the station, out in Piazza Cesare, always the three of them together. And no matter who or what Burton carted around, the three of them would turn up somewhere, watching him, but never approaching. Once he nodded to them, but they only glanced away nervously, and acted as if they hadn't seen his gesture.

He'd been around Palermo long enough then to be suspicious of what it meant. So he left work early that day, and he didn't tell anyone where he was going. Burton just abandoned the job, right then and there. He walked slowly up Via Maqueda to the Quattro Canti, without any hurry, and sure enough, those three little men followed him. They tried to hang back, and then they even walked on the other side of Maqueda. But they were following along behind him.

So he turned and went straight into Martorana and strolled up to the front pews right under the lectern, and knelt down there to pray. The church was empty in the late afternoon, except for two old women in black veils whispering to their rosary beads. Burton heard the doors to the church open and close twice behind him, but he didn't turn around to see if it was them.

After enough time had passed so he seemed to have said all his prayers, and was done, he stepped back out of Martorana into the Piazza Pretoria and as he strolled along, there they were, the three of them. They were just sitting around the big fountain in the piazza. So he strolled right past them and nodded again in their direction, to let them know he'd seen them. They still didn't respond, other than to watch Burton saunter by. He headed up toward the Corso. They, of course, followed along at a distance.

It wasn't hard to lose them, though. He just hurried across the bustling Corso, stopping to wave at them from the other side. It was clear they were not from Palermo the way they struggled along the busy street. But he turned off into the Vucciria, disappeared into an alley or two, found his way to the back of a fishmonger's stall where he'd worked a few days now and then in the past. It didn't take even a glance for them in the stall to understand he was trying to disappear. They sent him directly out through a back door.

Burton didn't see anymore of those three little backcountry friends that day. But he knew enough not to head back home toward the Albergheria until nightfall. When he told Corrao about them, later that night, Corrao laughed at him.

"They look like they're from back up in the Madonie," Burton said.

Corrao was stretched out on his bed, with his hands tucked behind his head for a pillow. "Burtoni," he said, "the streets of Palermo are full of little men from the countryside."

"I think they're from Castellnotte," Burton said.

That just made Corrao laugh at him a good, loud guffaw. "When did you become such a coward, my old comrade in arms? You, who stood under the guns at San Martino! Time was, you'd have laughed at them, even if they came from Castellnotte." Corrao had a big, deep laugh, you know, and he rolled it out grandly then, and seemed to enjoy himself at Burton's expense. "Even if they looked like the little cousins of old Lombardo the snake."

He reminded Corrao that no one in that country ever forgets anything, and what they did back there in Castellnotte, even if they were the orders of the General himself, it was all remembered. Every bit of it. Everything that was done. All of it.

"There were no orders from the General,'" Corrao said, and now his laugh had disappeared. "Not for what you did."

"I know," Burton said.

"Time was, Gianni Burtoni, you'd still laugh at them, and not be running scared, not even if they all, every little one of them, looked like our sweet, little Rafaella.'

But Corrao shut up then, and there was no more laughing. And Burton had nothing more to say to him. Corrao knew at once he'd gone too far, mentioning her. He knew how they had been. And Burton had told Giovanni Corrao about how he'd gone back to Monreale that night, and about the child. So Corrao shut up then, and there was no more of his big laughter. He'd gone too far, and he knew it.

They didn't talk about any of it for a week or more, not about Lombardo or Castellnotte and what went on there, and not anymore about the three little men following Jack Burton around downtown Palermo. But a week or so later, Corrao realized that not only had Burton abandoned his porter's job at the Stazione Centrale, he had not even gone back for his pay. That, for Giovanni Corrao, was too much.

"They owe you for a whole week," he said in amazement. "You're so scared, you're just going to let them keep your money?"

Burton told him it wasn't worth that little bit of money, not to let those toughs from the Castellnotte hills find them. And they didn't need the money. He was lying low, just like Corrao should be. That's what Burton told him.

But this was just not the way Giovanni Corrao worked. So he put on his best Dottore Calogero suit and he strutted on up to the office at Centrale, and he demanded all the money. He told them that Burton had gotten sick so he wasn't coming back for a while, but that Burton owed him money for the medicine he'd given him.   Even in Stazione Centrale, in the office, they'd heard of Dottore Calogero. So they gave up the pay, or the better part of it, since the manager kept his 'fee' for holding the money. Giovanni didn't get it all, but he got all he was going to get, so Giovanni was satisfied.

Yet as he was leaving the station, Corrao saw their three friends, or probably three more of them, knowing what we all know now. But Corrao, being Giovanni Corrao, he walked across the Piazza Cesare to where they were leaning against a wall at the corner of Via Maqueda. He agreed with Burton, he told him later. There wasn't any doubt in his mind these men came from back up in the Madonie. They had the faces of Castellnotte.

"'Waiting for somebody?' he asked them, using Sicilian and not Italian.

"'Who wants to know?'" the tallest of the three short men answered back in Sicilian. One of the other two pulled out a dagger and calmly started cleaning his nails with its long thin blade, far too long for how he was using it.

Corrao used Burton's name then. He told those men that he was Gianni Burtoni.   At the sound of that name, the little man with the long awkward dagger stopped what he was doing, and then examined Corrao's face. I'm sure, I tell you, he was matching Corrao's face to a description in his head.

"We're not looking for anybody,'" the first man said. But this time he spoke in Italian, and Corrao said he wasn't sure the other two men even knew what was being said.

So Corrao stuck with Sicilian, because he wanted to be sure they all understood. 'If you men need anything else, or if you want to find me, ask around for Calogero. Dottore Calogero. He'll know where to find me.' None of them responded. They just looked him over with silent disdain and acted as if they would never care to see him again.

Corrao repeated in Sicilian, 'In case you need to find me, someday.' Then he turned and strode away down Maqueda. One of the three hung back at a distance, and tried to follow Corrao for a while. But Giovanni knew his way through the alleys of the Albergheria as if they were all perfectly square and straight, and not a twisting labyrinth. He lost his follower when he chose to lose him, and he disappeared down into Palermo's backsides.

About three weeks later, or maybe it was a month, but it was in the hottest part of the high summer, Corrao and Burton were sitting under the awning at Café Rosi, looking out at the Grand Teatro across Piazza Maqueda. They were sipping coffee and trying to stay out of the sun, just waiting lazily for the cool of the evening to return. Burton was slouched low in low chair, still stirring sugar into his cup. Corrao had drained his in a gulp.

The waiter came back with our change, and though he wore a neat suit with a crisp clean collar, he was short and dark like the men from Castellnotte. Burton didn't really notice it at first, because unlike the others, his clothes fit him so well. He didn't seem a stranger to his suit, nor to the busy streets of Palermo either. So it startled him, when he spoke Burton's name.

"Signor Burtoni?" he said. But when Burton looked up, he found the waiter was facing not Burton, but Giovanni Corrao.

Without even batting an eye, Corrao smoothly answered him. "How do you know me?"

"The waiter just shook his head no, as if that didn't matter. He set the few coins down on the white tablecloth in front of Corrao. Burton saw the waiter's sidelong glance examine him, to be sure it was safe to speak. Then he straightened up and his eyes searched the Piazza in front of the Teatro, bustling with carriages and people strolling in the shade and vendors of fruit and ice. The waiter never turned his head, or lifted his body. He just stood at attention, and let his eyes search all around him. He stood as if he were waiting for some orders.

But then quietly and quickly, he said, "You should leave here, Signore."

Corrao glanced over at Burton, but still never let on about the confusion of names. "But we've paid up," Corrao protested ingenuously.

"You should leave Palermo, Signore," the waiter said, whispering through his teeth, though he was still standing at attention. "Soon," he said. Then he turned and was gone, disappearing quickly back inside the café.

Corrao, in the way only he can, he laughed boisterously at him. "What do make of that?" he said.

"He looks like he's from the Madonie, too," Burton said, and he wasn't laughing. "But he's clearly not new to Palermo, is he."

"It's true, my friend," Corrao carefully left out his name, Burton noticed. It hadn't occurred to him until that moment that someone else might be listening and watching. "He's a cousin to our old friends in Castellnotte, but he's been here in the city for a long while."

"Maybe we should pay attention," Burton said, then lifted his cup to his lips.

"This is my home," Corrao said, flatly. Without emotion, he was just stating plain facts. "Nobody is chasing me out of my home." But Jack Burton noticed, he still did not use any part of Burton's name.

"Let's get out of here," Burton said, as he set his empty cup down and stood up. But instead Giovanni headed right back inside the café when he got up, so Burton followed behind him. There he found the waiter, standing with his back to them behind the bar. Corrao strode directly over and said, "Thank you, my brother," to him in loud Sicilian. The waiter turned slowly around, saw Corrao standing there, and then glanced franticly around the room for a moment. Without another word, he stepped back into the darkness of a back room behind the bar, out of our sight and everyone else's. And then, just that quickly, he was gone.

"So you see, my Little One," Jack Burton had said to Naguine, "it was not Aspromonte. It was me they were after. And it was because of what we'd done up in Castellnotte. But the fools, they had our names confused. They couldn't tell me from Giovanni," he paused momentarily, then whispered to Naguine, "But they know now, they do."

"Burtoni would not say any more," Naguine said. "He just hung his head low in deep silence. He muttered a few times, with his head down, 'It was me they were after.'" But he was not speaking to Naguine, or to anyone. She almost couldn't make out what he said; perhaps he was speaking only to his own conscience.

Naguine told me then that she tried to distract him with her kisses and embraces, but on that night he was absent from everywhere except from his memories. He was unapproachable. Lost in his anger and his grief, she realized he was still afraid. "It is why he moves around so much, even now," she said to me. "He won't stay in any one place for long, and he won't put down roots anywhere, no matter how old and frail he gets. But I know, he hungers for a place he can't find. A place that I could give him," Naguine said. I held her in my arms as she told me all of this, but she too was absent, alive only to her memories of Jack Burton. "After what he saw, that one night in Palermo, it is why he will not put down roots with anyone, anywhere," she said more to herself than to me. "Even with me, even though I wander around as much as he does."

I admit it, brother, it made me feel angry and lost, too. I held her in my arms, but she was far, far away and yearning after the embrace of Burton, and not for mine. So I said to her, because I couldn't just be angry, because I was desperate for her attention. "He would put down roots, if it could be with his Rafaella," I said. "Or with his daughter Rosalina."

It was meant to be mean hearted. I said it to make her angry, so that her attention would return to me again. And it worked. With an abrupt shrug of her shoulders, she broke free of my embrace. It was a warm summer night then, and we had been sitting by a low fire outside her trailer. But now she wandered away and off into the dark, in the cottonwoods along the riverbank.

"Naguine, wait, my love," I said, as she walked away into the darkness. "I'm sorry," I said. Then she was gone into the trees and brush. I sat alone for a while, and then I followed her down to the riverside.

There was no moon, so the Milky Way that shone above the Esino was the only light. Naguine sat, her long skirts splayed out over some tall, shaggy grass by the stream. "I'm sorry," I said as I approached her. But she didn't respond, she just stared off into the black waters under the starry night sky. I wanted to repeat it a million times, until it surrounded her. Instead I slipped forward and sat next to her on the ground, listening to the rattle of the low water over the rocks.

In her hands she held that little pipe, and next to her I saw the carved box on the ground. She'd already filled the tiny bowl with the sweet black paste, and for the first and the only time she held the pipe out to me, and then lit the bowl. "Draw in gently," she whispered. "Just let it enter you on its own."

It was easy, I swallowed the white smoke and then let it breathe out of me, and it was so sweet and smooth that I never even coughed. Then I watched as she filled the bowl for herself, and smoked from it twice. Afterwards, she spoke, at least partly to herself. "This is the only thing that gives him any peace," she said.

Suddenly she embraced me then, without another word. Though she was small and lean, her arms around my waist seemed to envelope all of me, and her hair in my face was filled with the scent of dry grass and cinnamon.

Naguine made love to me that night, with our clothes spread out all around us on the grass. It was not the first time, but it was the only time when she was fully in control. I lay tangled in her arms, and in the clothing torn off all around us, and I felt the great and complete unity of her being. All the world vanished into her black eyes, and I lived in the universe of her long arms, and swelled with my whole being in the smooth arch of the low of her back. I murmured my love over and over again into her ears, and into the night sky above us. But Naguine said nary a word in return. She simply and almost silently took total possession of my soul that night. I don't know, still, if she has given it back.

When morning began to break faintly, greening in the East, we lay huddled together under our tangled clothes, exhausted and euphoric. Naguine, in whispered tones, told me the rest of Jack Burton's story then, all in one long whirl. I listened, only half aware, dozing in and out, because my senses were still filled with the taste and scent of her body, and I clung to her, as she did to me, for warmth in the cool of the summer dawn, far from the dying ashes of our fire.

Burton told her:

"I saw them everywhere, after that. Everywhere. Corrao, he laughed at me, he made fun of my worries. He scoffed at the way I looked over my shoulder, whenever anyone came toward us from behind. He laughed and laughed at me. But it didn't matter, for everywhere I went in Palermo, there seemed to be a small dark man hanging around, Naguine. Everywhere I went, one of them was lurking around a corner, or leaning against a wall, or perched in a second floor window, watching me.

"Once to try to escape them, I went into an old, ruined church on Via dei Benedettini, San Giovanni degli Eremeti it was called. I wandered up through its broken old walls into the little cloister up on the side of the hill next to it. In the center of that little cloister, under the shade of an ancient cumquat tree, I sat and rested out of the September heat. The place was empty, except for a workman tending to part of the crumbling walls around the garden, and a brother who strolled in, his hood up over his head so I couldn't see his face, his hands around an open prayer book. The brother walked slowly back and forth, in apparent meditation, and both I and the workman ignored him.

"It was peaceful and quiet there, a refuge from the bustling Palermo streets outside the church grounds, and the bent and twisted limbs of the old tree seemed odd and safe. Time passed, and I was so at peace there, I seemed at long last to rest from all my troubles and all my fears. The old grey bark of the tree and its lime green leaves, they spoke to me of persistence and of hope."

Naguine whispered to me then, as I was still tangled up in her arms, and only half aware of the tale I was being told. The drowsiness of peace and contentment kept threatening to wash over me and carry me off. "You see, it is still on his conscience," she said. "He suffers so, for what happened up at Castellnotte. For the way he was forced to destroy the one thing he loved."

I may have lost awareness, then, for the next thing I remember was Naguine again telling me the story of Burton, and again in Jack Burton's words:

"Just when I felt the peace of true solitude," Burton told her, "I noticed the face of the little brother doing his walking prayers. Our eyes met, and then he quickly glanced away, and I knew he was not praying, no, he was watching me. His face had the dark shadowed hue of the men from the Madonie. You see, even there, even in the cool silent cloister, they were watching me. Always watching me. It seemed to me, Naguine, they were everywhere I turned.

"So I got up in a rush, and did the best I could to disappear into the alleyways north in the Capo, and slowly worked my way around again into the markets of the Vucciria. I did not go back to the Albergheria until nightfall, and until I was relatively sure no one was following me, only then did I finally did turn toward home.

"Oh poor Corrao, he just laughed and laughed and laughed some more at me. He especially liked that I was afraid of an old brother praying in a cloister. 'Gianni,' he laughed at me. 'Half of Palermo looks like they came from the hills around her.'

"'I think half of Palermo is watching us,' I answered him.

"But dear Corrao, he just laughed again, and shook his head as if to say I was impossible, hopeless, far beyond all and any repair. But it was late for him to laugh, late though he didn't know it.

"On the afternoon of October first, Corrao came to our apartment in his suit of clothes dressed as a doctor. He said, 'I had a couple of patients today. Burtoni. They were very nice.' He lowered his head and gazed at me from under his raised eyebrows. "They want to see me tonight. But there are two of them. Trust me, my friend. You will like them, Burtoni. And they owe old Dottore Calogero a big, big debt.'

"He described them both to me, and told me their names, but I don't remember now any of that. He took off his jacket and dusted it off, and he polished his shoes with his spit until they shone, and he whistled a tune from Rigoletto, and I remember he made me put on a suit and a clean collar and he even made me oil my hair. I do remember this, he said, 'She could be the one Burtoni to make you forget that girl of yours in the past.' I remember that he carefully didn't use Rafaella's name, but I don't remember what this girl's name was supposed to be.

"Before we left, he said, 'Let me see.' Then he made me turn around in front of him, and he checked my hands to be sure they were clean. He frowned at them, but I said, 'That's as clean as they come.' Corrao chuckled at me, then he put on a feathered cap and looked in the mirror to be sure it was cocked to the side just so. Then he clapped an arm around my shoulder and said, 'Let's go.'

"At the last moment, just as we stepped out of the door, I remembered that I'd forgotten my watch. Back then it was the prettiest thing I owned, and I thought I should wear it. So maybe Corrao was right, maybe this girl whose name I will never remember, maybe she was the one to let me forget. At any rate, I turned back inside to get it, and Giovanni, glancing back at me over his shoulder, he stepped through the doorway and out into the October night. I heard a quick scuffle of feet on stones, and then I heard him fall, and as I turned back I thought at first that he'd tripped on the stairs."

"You know, he didn't utter a sound, there was not a grunt or a groan. And neither did his attackers. No one said a word. It was dead silence. But when I turned around, this is what I found on the dark street outside. Two short men, dressed in black, dark clothes—it was hard to see then in the poor light—they stood outside past the doorstep. Their faces were masked with black scarves, wrapped around their heads like turbans, so all I saw was the black glint of their eyes. And in their hands I saw the dripping glint of their long thin daggers.

"Between them in the street, face down on the stones, lay Giovanni Corrao. I shouted something at the two daggers, I don't remember what. But their black eyes glared at me, and then they were gone, on the run into the dark alleys of the Albergheria.

"I stumbled out to Giovanni, and kneeling beside him on the stones, as I turned him over I heard the life go out of him like an easy breeze, gently sliding away into a quiet grove beside a cool, spring fed stream. I heard it go out of him. Though I knew he was already gone, after all we'd seen together, after the way we'd stood under fire at San Martino and Milazzo, after we'd marched together through the traitorous streets of Napoli, and stood the charge at Capova. After the way he'd steered me across the dead waters of the Tyrrhenian Sea and through the Straits and into the arms of Rafaella and her father. After all of that, he was gone. Just gone.

"I held him in my lap, and I caressed his hair, while his blood poured out onto the dusty stones. I cried and cried out for help. They'd stabbed him twice: once in the back near his spine, and once into his heart, then slashing down into his bowels with one long smooth stroke.   This was the work of butchers, not city men who sell meat, but men of the country, contadini who know how to kill and butcher a pig quickly and efficiently and without struggle.   I cried out again for help, though it was all too late.   My voice echoed up the empty stone alleyways, and then shortly it was followed by the clicking and turning of latches, clicking and turning, clicking and turning, as the doors and shutters all across the Albergheria silently locked away this trouble, kept it away and outside, and they left me alone kneeling in the narrow street, without a soul who'd even seen the murder on their doorsteps."

"In the morning I learned there were twelve more murders that night, thirteen in all, Naguine. All of them happened at almost the same time, every one of the victims died in the same way, with a dagger plunged into his heart, and with a bloody slash opening the bowels. There were no signs or letters or messages left behind to explain it all. There was no threat to this as retribution, as anything but random death in the streets of Palermo. The victims seemed, in all their variety, to be unconnected. They came from different walks of life, they did not know one another. They were unconnected, and seemed to be chosen to die randomly. None of it made, at first, any sense.

"But the Carabinieri found something they couldn't explain. When the murders were plotted out on a map, their pattern made a strange figure on the streets of the city, like a twelve-pointed star radiating out of one central point. The center, Naguine, the heart of this bloody 12 pointed star, was our doorstep, where Giovanni Corrao, one of the Thousand, the hero of Milazzo, a warrior at the barricades of freed Palermo, the mysterious Doctor Calogero who eased the troubles of the sick, where Giovanni Corrao died.

"Dear old Corrao was the center, my Little One. He was the reason for all the others, I tell you. Twelve other men died that night, all of them in order to hide this one death among the many: the murder of Giovanni Corrao.

"But remember, it was not Corrao they wanted, Naguine. It was a mistake, all of it a simple case of mistaken identity. The murderers came from the mountains around Castellnotte, I'm sure. It was family, Naguine. It was blood. These men were all daggers in the employ of the Crisiani. And it was me they wanted, Naguine, it was me. All thirteen of them died because it was me they wanted dead. It was my blood on the stones they sought.

"The fools. They were confused, these hired men, and it was Corrao himself who confused them. Corrao who laughed at them, and then died in my place on those stones, where his laughter all died away to the sound of doors snapping locked. It was me, Gianni Burtoni, they wanted dead. Not Giovanni Corrao, but me. They all died for me.

"In the papers the next day I read the list of names, the list of the thirteen dead men. And the names, too, of some of the daggers, for the Carabinieri had rounded up two or three of them, the little daggers of Castellnotte, that cursed place, caught fleeing in the strange streets of Palermo. I knew none of them, none except Corrao, of course. They all were strangers, the victims and the daggers, too. Strangers, every one.

"But I knew, too, that somewhere, someone from Castellnotte was reading that list of names, just as I was. And that person, that padrone, he saw just as I did, the names of strangers in a list. But what he didn't find on that list was my name. Gianni Burtoni, the cause of it all, my name was not listed there. And I know, quietly, someone would be checking. Someone would be sent to find out if Gianni Burtoni was among those dead, under a false name. It would take them some time to do it in silence, from the inside perhaps, but someone would check those names. And then they would know that Gianni Burtoni was not there, not on the list, not among the dead.

"I did not need any more lessons, my Little One. As quietly as I could, talking to no one, not even to friends, I took the abandoned money Corrao had gotten from the train station for my work, and I left everything else behind: I needed no more persuasion. I took the first train out of Palermo, and it carried me on a long ride across the island to Gela, and then to Ragusa. In time, I made my way on foot to Noto and then to Siracusa. From there I got work on a boat that carried me over to Taranto, and I began finally to feel I'd escaped them, and so I slowed down.

"In the papers, I watched it all from a distance. A lawyer was sent down to investigate, a man named Giacosa from Lombardy. He and the carabinieri arrested, eventually, about two dozen men, for that night that became known in the papers all across Europe as the Night of the Thirteen Daggers. Giacosa, over that bitter Sicilian winter, interrogated and investigated dozens and dozens of men, and three times men died in his custody. But no one ever talked. No one ever admitted anything, or if they came close to it, they died before they could speak. The lawyer Giacosa never even heard the name of Castellnotte, or if he did, he kept it out of the news reports.

"In the end, this Giacosa was found dead in his office. There was not a mark on him, and no cause of death could be discovered. He was slumped in his chair alone in his office, dead as the stones in the streets of the Alberghia. His desk was clean but for an unsigned form requesting his return to the North, dated on the day before he died.

"And after all of this, Giovanni Corrao was murdered with his guts spilled out on our doorstep, taking my place, murdered ignominiously and nearly alone, without an explanation, without a cause.

"Or so they say, Naguine. For I know why he died, and his death has made me homeless and alone. I am hunted still, my little Naguine, across all this time; the daggers unsheathed by Lombardo, the father of my one true love in all this world, my Rafaella, who cannot forgive my soul, they search for my heart. O Naguine, the stories I could tell you. Believe me when I say this, for I know it is true. She is the one who searches still for my blood. It is she. My one heart. She and her descendants, the heirs of the blood of Lombardo spilled on the stones of a ruined cloister, filled with the remains of a ruined and beautiful garden of oranges, it is they who want to see me dead. It is she. And it is her blood."

I was alone when I awoke, Rob. The morning sun was high and warm in the sky, reaching toward noon, and its glare finally burned into my eyes. The grand sense of benevolence and unity of the whole universe from the night before was gone, and in its place I felt the painful emptiness of solitude.

For a long, long while, I lay there naked in the grass under the hot sun, sweaty and thirsty, but too lethargic to rise.

It may be that I knew already what had happened, and so I didn't want to get up. But simple thirst did me in. I crawled into my pants and down to the riverbank, and drank handfuls of the cool Esino water. Some of Naguine's clothes remained, but she was gone, as I knew she would be, from the moment I awoke.

I was almost afraid to speak her name, but I called out, "Naguine?" It was really just a whisper. There was no answer. I knew there would be no answer.

With my clothes back on, and with a deep lethargy built of fear that is incipit depression, I walked back toward the camp. Of course, it was all gone. The circle of our fire, just black ashes now, was all that remained, other than a few tire tracks in the dry sand that will vanish at the first hint of breeze.

I stood there for a while, wondering blindly what to do. All I had were the clothes on my back, Rob. Naguine had left with everything else. After about an hour, when I felt a little clearer, I started to walk along the highway back into Jesi. I'd only walked for about a mile or so, when a boy on a little Japanese motorcycle pulled over, and gave me a lift into town. In Jesi, I asked after her, but to no avail. The Marchegiani of Jesi were silent, friendly, but without any news. "She'll be back," one after another of them said, sympathetic to the loss and pain in my questions. "She always comes back," they said, often enough.

But I knew better.

I wandered on into Ancona, and then Fano and Pesaro and Urbino, and even over the mountains to Gubbio. But she was gone. Many, many people knew her, remembered her well, showed me jackets and shirts she'd repaired for them. But no one knew where she had gone.

So I have rented a safe deposit box at the post office in Jesi, and I will put this history into safety, and mail you the key. And I will join the long search, Rob. I realize it now. The long search. I search for my love, Naguine of my heart. And she? She wanders I know somewhere just out of my reach, searching for her dream, for Jack Burton, the man who fascinated us as boys. Who fascinates her now. And Burton? He runs out ahead of us all, one step ahead of the daggers of the Sciascias, past the reach of the blood lust of the Crisiani, moving restlessly, always far beyond the pale, always far from Naguine, from my Naguine. He remains alone, searching for the one who long ago ordered that his ancient life be ended. He searches endlessly through time for the lost soul of love. For his Rafaella.

AFTERWORD

So ends the text that I found carefully tucked into the red folder and placed in a safe deposit box at the Postal Service in Jesi. As you can see, I have standardized the print of the last run-on pages according to the punctuation my brother added beneath his scrawled handwriting. It was nearly perfect and correct, I believe. After I finished reading, I was sitting quietly in the little room under the florescent light, when Inspector Tasso knocked once and entered.

"Is everything all right in here, Signor Roberto?" he said. "It's been quite a while."

I didn't answer right away. Then I said, "I think so." But Tasso didn't believe me, any more than I believe myself.

Over the next ten days, with a photo of my brother in my pocket and a rented Fiat Panda, I drove along the list of towns he had mentioned, and well as others on the way. In Ancona they recognized his photo at the Library, but were no help beyond that. It was the last trace of him I could find for a long while. I drove on to Fano and Pesaro, and up to Urbino, and over to Gubbio on the old Roman road, and then even on to Perugia. Everywhere they knew of Naguine the seamstress, but no one recognized my brother from his photo. What began to haunt me was that probably his appearance had changed. This clean-cut college boy in the photo most likely bore little or no resemblance to the man I was now searching for. So he's vanished, as has this Naguine. The same way Burton has vanished, leaving legends and stories scattered all around him, but always remaining just at the periphery of my vision, and now my brother's vision, too.

Meanwhile, Postal Inspector Tasso had reported it all to the authorities. They showed my brother entering the country on his passport 90 days before. He'd stayed in a few hotels, and then vanished. They had no record of anyone named Naguine, but there was a Sofia Ziegler Pantone who carried a Bologna driver's license, married to Luigi Promoteo Pantone who had taught Eastern European languages and literature at the University. Professor Pantone claims he hadn't seen Sofia in seven years, though he remained married to her. It is probably just another dead end, but then again, perhaps not.

I called every day or so and checked in with Umberto. It's been long enough now, the inspector insists I call him Umberto. Most of the time, there is nothing more substantial for him to report than the ephemeral Signor Pantone. But two days ago, when I called from my room in Todi, Umberto had found something.

"Roberto," he said excitedly, "I've been waiting for your call. We found him."

I braced myself for bad news, and asked "Where is he?"

"Well, at least we have a trail on him, Roberto" Tasso said. "Last Friday, someone carrying his passport took Alitalia from Naples to Palermo."

"Palermo," I said. I have to admit, it was the next step for me. If my brother was following this Naguine, and she was following Burton, then Palermo was surely on their way, sooner or later.

I reached there in a few hours on a flight out of Rome. But unfortunately, after searching for all the last week, I'm afraid every trace of him has vanished here. For a solid week, I have asked around and searched through the streets on my own, and the Palermitano Polizia have had notices out. But there is no sign. Nothing on my brother, nor Naguine, nor Jack Burton. All of it now just a strange and silent dead end.

After a week of this searching, and finding nothing but a Sicilian silence followed by a shrug, I tried to think like my brother. What would he be looking for here in Palermo? It finally occurred to me, he remains an historian at heart. So it was obvious, suddenly. Of course.

I went back to his notes, the long history he left for me, and scoured it for hints. I wandered around in the Vucciria and in the Albergheria, looking for traces of Giovanni Corrao. It was all nearly a hundred and fifty years ago, but in the Vucciria the name of Dottore Calogero still roused a smile on these staid Sicilian faces. And nearly everyone knew of the great Giovanni Corrao.

In the alleys of the Albergheria, I swear everyone I met who was older than 50 would without a moment's thought point down some narrow street and say that Corrao had lived over there. Everyone of a certain age knew where Corrao had died on the Night of the Daggers. Of course, every set of directions was different, every story I heard led to a different spot. And everyone knew for sure that this was the spot where he had died. One old woman, hanging yellowed laundry from a second floor balcony, even answered, "Right here. Signore, Dottore Calogero was murdered right here, right where you are standing. And this was his house too."

It seems that Burton and Corrao lived in nearly every other building in the whole of the Albergheria.

But still, I knew I was getting close. I could sense my brother's presence now every time I asked a question about Corrao. Yet no one recognized his photograph or his name.

Then once again the obvious occurred to me, it was my brother's training. He would not just wander around the alleys like this, asking strangers and collecting tall tales and lies. He would want to know where to look. Sure enough, I was once again right about him.

The clerk at the Palazzo di Giustizia still didn't recognize my brother's picture, but he did recognize his name. He sent me straight downstairs to the office of the tribunal archives.

They hid at the bottom of a long row of marble stairs, worn by years of use, down into the basement. The woman behind the desk was sympathetic, and she remembered him well. "It was only a week or so ago," she said. "You have the same eyes as he does, so I can see you are his family, even though you don't look much like him. Although with that long hair, and that shaggy beard, it is hard to tell."

I am clean-shaven and I still have my head razored short like in my army days. She meant to tell me, without saying as much, that my brother is no longer keeping his appearance neat.

"What did he want?" I asked her.

"Oh, that I can remember very well," she said, frowning. "I'm afraid we weren't much help to the signore. He wanted the files from an old investigation, from 1862. From a night in 1862 when thirteen men were murdered at once, in the same way, at almost the same time."

"The Night of the Daggers," I said, though in Italian it has a prettier ring when you say it. It forces you to sing, in a way. "La Notte di Pugnali," I said.

Her eyes widened, but the frown on her lips only deepened. "I see you, too, know about that night."

She was silent for a moment, gazed down at her hands and then shook her head no ever so slightly to herself, thinking I didn't notice. She muttered something in Sicilian of which I could only make out the words "blood" and "family," I think. That part I was meant to hear.

"What is it?"

"I'm afraid, Signore, we made your brother very unhappy. But it is just the way that it is here. Things get lost in all these files, do you understand? They get misplaced, filed away in the wrong place. And there is so much to keep track of here. Sometimes I'm sure it is malicious, because you know, someone wants some information to disappear. But sometimes, you know, it is just the way we are down here." Her hand reached out and dusted off the top of her desk, though it was pristinely clean and polished as it was. "I got away from here, you know, Signore. I went to library school at Sapienza, and I worked in the police archives in Rome for ten years. But then, my father passed away, and my mother was alone here in Palermo. And this job came up and, well, I had to take it, for my mother." She stopped and looked sadly in my eyes. "Things are very different down here. It can't be helped. Do you understand?"

"What are you trying to tell me?" I said.

"Signore, we searched for two days. Your brother, he came back on the second afternoon. We know from the records that there was a great investigation, it went on for months and months, Signore. There were dozens and dozens of interrogations. There must have been at least a drawer, or maybe two, filled with the files of just the main investigator. We can tell that with what our records show."

"Must have been?" I said.

She nodded, and then said, "Gone, Signore. All of it. Not one sheet of paper left. All of it, misplaced or misfiled."

"Or stolen."

"Gone," she said. "It would be harder to take it out of here, Signore, than it would be to simply bury it in all this paper."

I nodded yes. "If someone stole them, and took them out of here, they could be stolen again, perhaps easily, or just sold and then put to a different use."

She smiled that I understood. "It is easier and safer to just move the papers, change a few labels, and they disappear safely for years." We were both looking back at the rows and rows of dusty boxes stacked on shelves in the archive. "Even centuries, perhaps," she said.

"And my brother?"

"He seemed very upset, and didn't believe this was true at first. I had to take him back and show him where they were all supposed to be filed. But you can see, there are crates and crates of files stored down here, and I told him, 'Maybe they are here somewhere.' I thought he was going to get angry at

482

first when he saw what it was. But you know, Signor Roberto, he just started to laugh. And he said something I don't understand. Perhaps you can explain it to me. He said, 'Burton's escaped again,' while he was laughing. What does it mean? 'Burton has escaped again,'"

I admit, I found myself laughing at it all too, which didn't made the archivist happy. "It's just an old friend of ours, Signora," I said. "We just can't seem to keep up with him."

I hung around in Palermo for another week or so, and I even took the picture I had and scribbled in a beard on my brother's face. It didn't do any good. Still nobody knew who he was. And still everybody claimed the house of Dottore Calogero was right over there, right next door, right downstairs. But when that archivist told me about Will's laughter, it was a comfort. Do you understand? I knew then that my brother was okay, and in fact, I knew he was better off. He was finally out of those silly universities where he'd been hiding, and he was off into the world itself. He was searching for Jack Burton, just like me.

Before long, the call came from a drilling company. They need a 'copter pilot off the coast of Venezuela. I went back to work, knowing someday soon I would hear more.

ALSO BY SANDRO DARIOSTO

THE LAST GOOD RUN

HANDS OF THE BIRD AND OTHER STORIES

THE WISDOM RUN

www.ingramcontent.com/pod-product-compliance
Lightning Source LLC
Chambersburg PA
CBHW071630260626
47170CB00001B/43